Dear Reader:

Welcome to *The Wyndham Legacy*, the first novel of the Legacy Trilogy, set in England in my favorite era, the Regency period. There are actually two legacies: one from the distant past; the other a very current one that touches our main man very directly—indeed, one that smacks him in the chops.

Marcus Wyndham never asked to become the Earl of Chase. The Duchess never asked to be illegitimate. And neither asked that their fates become so entwined.

Marcus is passionate, quick to rage, and just as quick to laughter. He's tough, opinionated, domineering, known as the devil's own son. The Duchess is serene and aloof—she has silence down to a fine art. She is always in control, her smiles as rare as bawdy jests in the pulpit. She is self-reliant once she realizes that a very special talent can make her so, a talent that no one suspects she has.

Surrounding this unlikely pair are three servants cast in the Shakespearean mold: Spears, Badger, and Maggie—all cocky, smart, good plotters and better friends who don't know the meaning of subservient.

Add to this the American Wyndhams—and who can trust an American Wyndham?—bucketfuls of intrigue, laughter, and a love story that will wring your withers. I hope you'll enjoy yourself thoroughly with *The Wyndham Legacy*.

Catherine Coulter

Titles by Catherine Coulter

The Sherbrooke Series
THE SHERBROOKE BRIDE
THE HELLION BRIDE
THE HEIRESS BRIDE
MAD JACK
THE COURTSHIP
THE SCOTTISH BRIDE
PENDRAGON
THE SHERBROOKE TWINS
LYON'S GATE
WIZARD'S DAUGHTER
PRINCE OF RAVENSCAR

The Legacy Trilogy
THE WYNDHAM LEGACY
THE NIGHTINGALE LEGACY
THE VALENTINE LEGACY

The Baron Novels
THE WILD BARON
THE OFFER
THE DECEPTION

The Viking Novels
LORD OF HAWKFELL ISLAND
LORD OF RAVEN'S PEAK
LORD OF FALCON RIDGE
SEASON OF THE SUN

The Song Novels
WARRIOR'S SONG
FIRE SONG
EARTH SONG
SECRET SONG
ROSEHAVEN
THE PENWYTH CURSE
THE VALCOURT HEIRESS

The Magic Trilogy
MIDSUMMER MAGIC
CALYPSO MAGIC
MOONSPUN MAGIC

The Star Series
EVENING STAR
MIDNIGHT STAR
WILD STAR
JADE STAR

Other Regency Historical Romances
THE COUNTESS
THE REBEL BRIDE
THE HEIR
THE DUKE
LORD HARRY

Devil's Duology
DEVIL'S EMBRACE
DEVIL'S DAUGHTER

Contemporary Romantic Thrillers
FALSE PRETENSES
IMPULSE
BEYOND EDEN
BORN TO BE WILD

FBI Suspense Thrillers
THE COVE
THE MAZE
THE TARGET
THE EDGE
RIPTIDE
HEMLOCK BAY
ELEVENTH HOUR
BLINDSIDE
BLOWOUT
POINT BLANK
DOUBLE TAKE
TAILSPIN
KNOCK OUT
WHIPLASH
SPLIT SECOND
BACKFIRE
BOMBSHELL
POWER PLAY
NEMESIS

A Brit in the FBI
THE FINAL CUT
THE LOST KEY
THE END GAME

THE
WYNDHAM LEGACY

CATHERINE COULTER

BERKLEY ROMANCE
New York

BERKLEY ROMANCE
Published by Berkley
An imprint of Penguin Random House LLC
penguinrandomhouse.com

Copyright © 1994 by Catherine Coulter
Penguin Random House supports copyright. Copyright fuels creativity, encourages
diverse voices, promotes free speech, and creates a vibrant culture. Thank you for buying
an authorized edition of this book and for complying with copyright laws by not
reproducing, scanning, or distributing any part of it in any form without permission.
You are supporting writers and allowing Penguin Random House to continue to
publish books for every reader.

BERKLEY is a registered trademark and Berkley Romance with
B colophon is a trademark of Penguin Random House LLC.

ISBN: 9780593441152

G. P. Putnam's Sons hardcover / January 1994
Jove mass-market edition / September 1994
Berkley Romance trade paperback edition / December 2022

Printed in the United States of America
1st Printing

This is a work of fiction. Names, characters, places, and incidents either are the product
of the author's imagination or are used fictitiously, and any resemblance to actual persons,
living or dead, business establishments, events, or locales is entirely coincidental.

To Karen Evans,

A sweetheart of a person and a wonderful friend, who's endowed with inexhaustible supplies of compulsive brain power. You're bright and funny and you deserve all the very best. You've got it all over Len D.

Thanks for always being there for me.

CC

Prologue

IN JUNE OF 1804 on the second day of her first visit to Chase Park at the age of nine, she overheard one of the upper-floor maids tell the Tweenie that she was a "bastid."

"A bastid? Go on wit' ye. Ye're not bamming me, Annie? The little nit's a bastid? But everyone said she were a cousin, meybe from 'olland, meybe from Italy."

"Cousin from 'olland or Italy, me elbow! 'Er mum lives down near Dover—that's as close to them strange places as she gets. 'Is lordship visits 'er ever so often, at least that's wot I 'eard Mrs. Emory tell Cook. Aye, she's 'is lordship's bastid daughter, all right. Jest look at those eyes of 'ers, bluer than the speckles off a robin's egg."

"The nerve of 'is lordship bringing 'is brat 'ere, right under 'er ladyship's nose."

"Aye, but that's the way of the Quality. 'Is lordship probably 'as a quiverful of bastids hid about, so wot's one more? But this one's 'ere, so that means she's special. Aye, she's all smiles and sweetness and laughter, jest like she belongs 'ere too. 'Er ladyship will ignore the little twit, ye'll see. I 'eard she'd only be 'ere a fortnight."

Annie snorted, shifting the now-empty chamber pot from one hip to the other. " 'Tis more than enough fer the likes of 'er. Jest imagine, bringing yer bastid to Chase."

"But she's awful pretty the little one be."

"Aye, but 'is lordship is as beautiful as 'is grandda was— me grandma said 'e were as lovely a gentleman wot ever breathed—so it makes sense that she wouldn't be a prune pit. I'll bet 'er mum ain't no scrub mouse either. Twelve

1

years I 'eard Mrs. Emory say they were together—just like they was married, only they b'aint, so it's jest awful."

The upper-floor maid and the Tweenie moved away, still gossiping and twittering behind their hands. She stood there in the shadow of one of the many deep-set niches along the first-floor corridor and wondered what a bastid was. It wasn't good, she knew that much.

The earl of Chase was her father? She shook her head vehemently even as she thought it. No, he was her Uncle James, her real father's elder brother who visited her and her mother every few months to see that they were all right. No, her real father had been killed by the French in February 1797 when French troops landed on British soil. She never tired of hearing her mother tell her how there were nearly two thousand Frenchmen, not really soldiers, but French criminals, all released from gaols and pardoned if they would sail up the Avon and burn Bristol. Then they would go to Liverpool and burn it as well. Ah, her mother would say, but those French criminals landed at Pencaern and there they fought and surrendered to the Pembrokeshire Yeomanry. And her father had led those brave Englishmen who had defeated those wretched French who'd dared come onto British soil. No, her real father was Captain Geoffrey Cochrane and he'd died a hero for England.

Her mother's eyes would always grow soft then, the deep blue glazing just a bit as she would say, "Your Uncle James is a nobleman, my dear, a very powerful man, a man with many responsibilities, but he will take care of us forever. He has his own family so he can't come to us all that often, but it's the way things are and the way they will always be. But don't forget, he loves us both and he won't ever desert us."

And when she was nine years old, her mother sent her to spend a fortnight with her Uncle James at his magnificent mansion called Chase Park near Darlington in northern Yorkshire. She'd begged her mother to accompany her, but her mother had simply shaken her head, making her incredible golden curls tremble about her beautiful face, saying, "No, dear, your Uncle James's wife isn't fond of me. You keep away from her, promise me you will. You have cousins there and you will become friends with them. But stay away from Uncle James's wife. Do remember, love, never to speak about yourself. It is a boring thing, don't you think? Much better to keep secrets and be mysterious."

She had avoided the countess of Chase with little difficulty, for the lady, once she'd seen her, had frozen her with a look of utter contempt, turned, and left the room. Neither she nor any of her cousins joined the earl and his countess in the grand dining room each evening, so avoiding the countess in the evenings never came into it.

Uncle James was different here in this mansion, with all its servants in their immaculate blue and green livery and shining buttons, than he'd been the other times she'd met him. There seemed to be servants everywhere—behind every door and just around every corner, always there, always looking but never speaking. Except for Annie and the Tweenie.

Uncle James was quite attentive at Rosebud Cottage when he came to see her and her mother, but not here at this huge sprawling edifice they called Chase Park. She frowned, wondering why he hadn't even hugged her. But he hadn't. He had called her into his library, a chamber that was nearly as large as her home. Three of its very high walls were covered with bookcases, and there were ladders that stretched upward forever and they moved on rollers around the room. Everything seemed heavy and dark, even the luxurious carpet beneath her feet. When she came in, she had seen nothing but deep shadows, for it was late afternoon and the curtains were nearly drawn. Then she'd seen her uncle and smiled.

"Hello, Uncle James. Thank you for inviting me to stay with you."

"Hello, my dear child. Come in and I will tell you how you are to go along here."

She was to call all his children cousin, but, of course, she knew that already, for she was a smart puss, wasn't she? She would take lessons with her cousins, she would watch them and copy their manners and their behavior, all except for her cousin Marcus, her uncle's nephew, who was currently visiting Chase Park. He was the devil's own son, Uncle James told her, and then he'd smiled, an odd smile that seemed at once resentful and proud.

"Yes," he said again slowly, "the devil's own son, that's what my brother spawned. He's all of fourteen, nearly grown, and thus very dangerous. Don't follow him or your male cousins into mischief. Of course, it is likely that the boys will ignore you for you're just a little girl."

"I have another uncle?" she'd asked, eyes shining with excitement.

He frowned and waved away her question. "Yes, but you are not to say anything to your cousin Marcus. Just be aware of how people conduct themselves. If they behave well, then you will emulate their behavior. If they don't, close your eyes and turn away. Do you understand?"

She nodded. He came around from behind the huge desk and patted her on her head. "You will be a good girl and I will allow you to visit me here once a year. Never speak of your mother or of me or of yourself. You are to say nothing about anything personal. But your mother told you this, didn't she?"

"Yes, Uncle, she said I was to keep secrets and the better I kept them, the more fun I should have, and you and she would be very proud of me."

His mouth curved into a smile. "Trust Bess to make it into a game. Heed her and heed me. Go now and get to know your female cousins." He paused, then added, "They have been told to call you cousin as well."

"But that is what I am, Uncle James."

"Well, yes, there is that."

She understood none of it. But she wasn't stupid and she loved her mother very much. She knew it was important that she be obedient and agreeable and pleasing. She would keep mum about herself. She didn't wish to bore anyone.

That first day, the boys had been civil, then ignored her, but her female cousins, the Twins, as everyone called them, were delighted to meet her.

Everything had seemed beyond glorious until now.

What was a bastid?

She didn't ask her Uncle James. She went directly to the person who disliked her—Uncle James's wife.

She knocked on the door to the morning room and heard a crisp, "Come in, come in!"

She stood in the doorway just looking toward the very pregnant lady who was seated on a settee, sewing something white and long and narrow. The countess was not only very pregnant, she was also heavy. She didn't understand how the countess could sew what she was sewing, for her fingers were very fat. Her face wasn't pretty, but perhaps it had been once when she'd been young. She looked nothing like her mama, who was slender and tall and so graceful. No, the countess looked old and tired and now that the countess saw her, she looked mean, and she didn't bother to hide it.

"What do you want?"

At the countess's very cold inquiry, she licked her lips, suddenly dry with foreboding. But she took a step into the room and blurted out, "I heard one of the maids tell another that I was a bastid. I don't know what that is but I could tell from hearing them that it was bad. You don't like me so I thought you would tell me the truth."

The lady laughed. "Well, it's already out and it's only your second day here. I say, if one wants to know something—anything—just ask the servants, they never fail. Well, child, a bastid is properly called a bastard, and indeed, that's just what you are."

"A bastard," she repeated slowly.

"Yes. That means your mother is a whore and is paid by my husband—your so-called Uncle James—to be at his beck and call and you were the result of one of those becks." And she laughed again, throwing her head back laughing and laughing, and she looked even nastier because her laughter was mean.

"I don't understand, ma'am. What's a whore?"

"It's a female who has no morals. Uncle James is your father, not your damned uncle. But I am his wife and your precious mother is nothing more than a rich man's mistress, a woman he keeps to provide him with . . . well, you won't understand that either, but given your budding looks, I imagine that one day you will quite surpass even your mother. Haven't you wondered why your dear Uncle James is a Wyndham and you are a Cochrane? No, well, it appears you aren't any smarter than your slut of a mother. Now, get out of here. I don't wish to see your face again unless I must."

She fled, her heart pounding, her belly roiling with fear and nausea.

From that day on, she was very quiet, never speaking unless spoken to, never volunteering a word or a giggle or even a snort when she was with others so that she wouldn't draw attention to herself. It was toward the end of that visit that her cousin Marcus began calling her the Duchess.

Her cousin Antonia, only six years old, frowned up at Marcus and said, "Why, Marcus? She's a little girl just like me and Fanny. We're not anything but Wyndhams and ladies. Why is she a duchess when we aren't?"

Marcus, the devil's own son, looked down at her from his vast height, his expression very serious as he said to Antonia, "Because she doesn't smile and she doesn't laugh and she is aloof and more reserved than she should be for a child her age. Already she dispenses smiles and approving nods as if they were guineas and she only has three of them to last forever. Haven't you noticed how the servants rush to do small services for her? How they melt if she but nods pleasantly to them? Also," he added slowly, "someday she will be bloody beautiful."

She said nothing, merely looked up at him and wanted to cry, but she didn't. She merely pushed her chin up and looked beyond him.

"The Duchess," he said, tossed her a laugh, and went riding with her two male cousins.

She bore her title of the Duchess well, for she had no choice. When she heard someone say she was perhaps too proud, another would say, not at all, she was merely becomingly reserved, allowing for no forwardness, her manners a joy to all those in her company.

When she was at Chase Park in June of 1808 at age thirteen, Marcus was also there. He was down from Oxford, visiting his cousins. When he saw her, he laughed, shook his head, and said, "Hello, Duchess. I hear it is your name now. Has anyone told you that it fits you perfectly?"

He was smiling at her, but she saw it only as a disinterested smile, a smile he gave because he had nothing better to do at the moment than speak to her.

She looked up at him coolly, her chin going up a trifle, and said nothing at all.

He raised a black eyebrow at her, waiting, but she held silent, hating his mocking look as well as his mocking, disinterested voice, until he said at last, "Ah, how very aloof you've become, Duchess, how very haughty. Is it because of my prediction when you were a little girl? Perhaps not. And to go with that, you are well on your way to becoming as beautiful as I knew you would. You are thirteen, I hear. Imagine when you are sixteen or so." He paused, adding under his breath, "Jesus, I don't believe I want to see you after you've grown up." He laughed again, patted her shoulder, and strode out of the entrance hall to join Charlie and Mark.

She stood there with her two valises beside her, Mr. Sampson now coming toward her, smiling at her as he always did, Mrs. Emory at his heels, Mrs. Emory smiling as well, calling out, "Welcome, Miss, welcome!"

And everyone now called her Duchess, even her father, Uncle James, even the Tweenie, who had first unintentionally informed her of her illegitimacy four years before. But everyone also knew she was a bastard. Why were they so nice to her? She would never understand it. She was James Wyndham's bastard and there was no way around it.

Had anyone ever asked her, she would have said without hesitation that she had lost her innocence at the age of nine. When her Uncle James visited Rosebud Cottage she came to realize that he slept in her mother's bedchamber. She became aware that they touched each other and laughed, their heads close together, like the devil and an angel, his dark head and her golden one so distinct but blending nonetheless, two such beautiful people, fascinating and gay. Once she even saw them kissing in the narrow corridor of the second floor, her mother's back pressed against the wall, Uncle James hard against her, his fingers clutched in her glorious hair, his mouth heavy on hers.

Just three months before her yearly visit to Chase Park, it was Uncle James and not her mother who told her she was his daughter. She said nothing, merely looked at him. She was seated opposite him on a small pale blue brocade settee in the cozy drawing room of her mother's home. He said without preamble, "You are my daughter and we will no longer pretend that you are not, at least not here. You are old enough to understand, aren't you, Duchess? Yes, I see from your eyes and the set of your mouth that you already know. Well, no surprise there. I told your mother that you did, that you weren't stupid or blind." He shrugged, then said, "Unfortunately at Chase Park the pretense must continue. My wife wants the pretense and I have agreed to it." He said other things too, things she no longer remembered, for she'd thought at the time that they were just words spoken to a child by a man who felt guilty. Did he care about her? She didn't know. She doubted if she would ever know. She had her mother. She didn't need him.

She merely nodded and said, "Yes, Uncle James. I am a bastard. I have known that for many years now. Please do not let it worry you, for I am well used to it now."

He'd started at her calm words sounding so disinterested and flat, but he said nothing more. He was relieved. What more was there for him to say? He looked into his own very dark blue eyes, at his own ink-black hair, the shining braids thick and smooth on her small head. But her mother hadn't been forgotten in the daughter. There were errant curls loose from the braids that curled around her small ears, and he loved to wind his fingers around the mother's curls, so very soft and sweet-smelling. Ah, and she had Bess's mouth, full and beautifully shaped, and her elegant nose, thin and straight. He shook his head and regarded his daughter sitting quietly across from him. He thought fancifully that she was so still, so utterly self-contained, like a statue. She was disconcerting, this daughter of his, not filled with laughter and mischief, not teasing and bounding about as the Twins always were.

It was hard to remember now that he'd not wanted her at first, that he'd ordered Bess to get rid of the brat. But Bess had told him plain out that she would birth the child and he could do what he pleased. What he'd pleased was to keep both of them, for he wanted Bess more than he'd ever wanted any other woman in his life. And now here was his daughter, staring back at him with his eyes, and she looked indeed serene and aloof as a duchess, this once unwanted child of his loins.

The Duchess remembered the two weeks of 1808 very clearly. Her cousin Marcus had made her withdraw even more with his mocking words that had, really, been born of mischief only, nothing more, but the pain of them had made her tremble. Then, on that second Wednesday, her only other two male cousins, Charlie and Mark, were both drowned in a boat race when two sailboats collided on the River Derwent with more than two hundred horrified people looking on from shore and at least a dozen other boys leaping into the river from their own sailboats to help. But no one had come to their rescue in time. When Charlie was struck in the head by the wildly slamming boom, he was killed instantly and hurled overboard. His younger brother, Mark, had tried to find him beneath the wreckage of the other sailboat along with several other boys. He'd drowned as well when the jib halyard had twisted about him, holding him under the water.

The boys were buried in the Wyndham family cemetery. Chase Park was in despair. The Duchess's father locked himself in the library. The countess could be heard crying throughout the night. Marcus was white and drawn, speaking to no one, for he'd survived and his cousins hadn't. He'd not even been on the sailboat with them. He'd been buying a hunter at the Rothermere stud. The Duchess went back to Winchelsea to her mother.

Over the next five years, the countess of Chase was pregnant every year in an attempt to produce another male heir for the earldom of Chase, but alas, none of the babes born to the countess survived their first year. All of them were boy children. The earl of Chase brooded, becoming more solitary as time passed, and bedded his wife endlessly, no pleasure in it for either of them, just grim duty, made more grim by the year, and he began to look upon his nephew Marcus differently, of his blood, certainly, but not his own son, not the blood of his own blood, and he wanted his line to go through his own flesh, not through his brother's.

He came more often to Rosebud Cottage. He was quiet, his laughter becoming as rare as his daughter's. It was as if he clung to her mother, and she kept him close, loving and gentle and undemanding.

But when the earl returned to Chase Park, as he ultimately had to, there was nothing he could do except watch his wife produce one child after another and watch each of them die.

Marcus Wyndham was the heir to Chase.

1

"I'M VERY SORRY to tell you this, Miss Cochrane, but there is more and it isn't good."

Mr. Jollis, her mother's solicitor, didn't sound sorry at all. He sounded unaccountably pleased, which was strange, surely, but she held silent, not only because of her grief over her mother's death but because she was used to holding herself silent. It was a habit of many years. Over time, she'd learned a lot about people, simply listening and watching them as they spoke. She realized in that moment, in Mr. Jollis's meaningful pause, that her father didn't yet know of her mother's death. She'd forgotten him in the suddenness of it, in the numbness it had instilled in her. Now, there was no one else to tell him. She had to write to him herself. She could see him reading her words, see his disbelief, his bowing pain when he finally realized it was true. She closed her eyes a moment against the pain she knew he would feel. He would feel endless pain, for he loved her mother more than he loved any other human being. But her mother, alive and laughing one moment, was dead the next. Her death was so needless, so stupid really: a wretched carriage accident, the shaft snapping for no apparent reason, sending the carriage hurtling off the winding road that ran too close above on the chalk South Downs cliffs, near Ditchling Beacon. Those cliffs rose eight hundred and thirteen feet into the air, then plunged to the deserted beach below. Her mother was killed

12

instantly, but her body was washed out with the tide and never recovered. At least it hadn't been recovered yet, and it had already been a day and a half. She looked up when Mr. Jollis cleared his throat, evidently prepared to finish his thought.

"As I said, Miss Cochrane," Mr. Jollis continued, that smug tone coming more to the surface now, "I am very sorry about this but Rosebud Cottage is leased and the lessor is your, er, father, Lord Chase."

"I didn't know that." Indeed, she'd always assumed that her mother owned the cottage. But then again, perhaps that was the way of it when a man supported and kept a woman. All remained his, thus he retained his power and all his prerogatives. It was merely another unexpected blow that she didn't feel at the moment. She waited, silent, her body utterly still. His face changed then, and he was looking at her differently, not as a man feigning sympathy for a bereaved daughter, but as a man assessing a woman for his own uses.

She'd seen the look before, but not that many times on that many male faces. She'd been protected, but now, she realized, she was unprotected. Her father was in Yorkshire and she was here, quite alone, except for dear Badger.

"I must write my father," she said then, her voice curt, colder than it would normally be, but she wanted him to go away. "I imagine that since the lease will run out soon that I will have to go to Chase Park."

"There is another option, perhaps," Mr. Jollis said, and he leaned toward her, like a hound on a scent, she thought, eyeing him with more hostility than she'd eyed anyone in her entire life.

"No, there isn't," she said, her voice as cold as the ice shards hanging from the cottage eaves outside.

"Perhaps," he said, still sitting forward, his right hand outstretched toward her now, "just perhaps his lordship won't want you to live at Chase Park."

"His wife died seven months ago, just before my yearly

visit. I cannot imagine that he wouldn't want me there. She was the only one who didn't care for my presence, and that, I suppose, is very understandable. She held him as her husband, but she didn't have his regard. I have long understood her bitterness. However, now she is dead."

"Ah, but now his lordship must be very careful, you understand, Miss Cochrane. His lordship is in mourning, very deep mourning. All his neighbors will be watching him closely, indeed, all society, all those whose opinions are important to him, will be watching him closely."

"Why? Surely he won't wed again, at least not anytime soon. I am merely his bastard daughter. Who would care if I lived at Chase Park or not?"

"People would care and they would find out very quickly. It shows the ultimate disrespect for his dead wife, Miss Cochrane. You must believe me, for I know the ways of society and you do not."

She didn't believe him, but she didn't wish to argue with him anymore. "I do not believe men are watched all that closely, only women," she said, her voice remote. "Nor do I believe that men mourn anything all that deeply for all that long a time." Her body became even more still, even though she could feel herself shrinking back from his still outstretched hand.

She remembered when her father's wife had died. His reaction, she'd thought during her visit, when the countess had finally died birthing another babe, had been one of profound relief. When tears had wet his eyes, she knew it was from the death of the small infant boy, dead two hours after its birth, not from his wife's expiration.

"That is possible," he said. "But you have no one to look after you now, Miss Cochrane. Perhaps you should consider looking for someone well circumstanced who would protect you and keep you in this lovely little cottage."

She smiled at him. Mr. Jollis, like everyone else who knew her for a long time, was startled at the smile. It was beautiful and it made him feel warm all the way to the bunions on his toes. She had two dimples and her teeth were small and white and as perfect as her smile. He could not recall ever seeing her smile before. "If I choose to remain here at the cottage, will you tell me who owns it?"

"It is Squire Archibald, but surely since you have so little money, you cannot consider keeping the lease. Why it's absurd, it's—"

She rose, her hands by her sides. "I should like you to leave now, Mr. Jollis. If there is more I need to know, please write me a letter."

He rose then as well, for he had no choice, at least not at the moment, and stared down at her, her beautiful smile forgotten. "You think to be above yourself, Miss Cochrane. No matter, you're a bastard, nothing more, and that's what you will always be. You cannot remain here. The lease on the cottage ends on the fifteenth of next month, and you will have no money to renew it. Squire Archibald is all of seventy and certainly not a candidate for your wiles. No, it is money he would require, not you warming his ancient bed. You will leave then. If your esteemed father wants you, then, he will give you a home, but for how long? Don't forget, your beautiful mother is dead. Do you truly believe he ever wanted you? No, it was your mother he wanted, no other, certainly not you. I would consider becoming your protector, Miss Cochrane—"

Her face was very pale now, her eyes dulling in her rage, but he saw only the dullness, not the fury, for she just stared at him, then turned on her heel and left the small drawing room without a word.

Mr. Jollis didn't know what to do. Would she consider his well-phrased proposal? He thought her uppity, arrogant, but that would change. He wondered if she was a virgin. He wasn't left to wonder anything then, for Badger, the servant who had stood as protector to both Mrs. Cochrane and the Duchess, appeared in the doorway. He was a large man, well muscled, ugly as a fence post, his hair white and thick as a prophet's, and at this moment, there was blood in his eye.

Mr. Jollis backed up a step.

"Sir," Badger said gently, too gently, "it is time to remove your carcass from the premises. If your carcass isn't absent within a very few number of seconds, I will have to see that his lordship learns of your most regrettable behavior. He won't be pleased."

"Ha," Mr. Jollis said, for he knew that this man didn't know what he was talking about. "His lordship would be glad to get the little bastard off his hands and no mistake about that. Soon, Badger, you will be without money yourself, for she has none to pay you. Then, I daresay, you won't speak to your betters like this. It doesn't matter that you have more wits than you should, that you have excellent speech—who taught you to speak like a gentleman?—no matter, you're still here and you're nothing but a servant, of no account at all."

Badger just smiled at him, shook his head, was on him in an instant, lifting him bodily, and tucked him under his mighty arm. He carried him to the front door, and dumped him out onto the frozen ground, that would, in five months, bloom wildly with the Duchess's red, yellow, and white roses. He turned back into the cottage, saw the Duchess, and grinned, showing a goodly-sized space between his front teeth. "He'll rest a bit in the snow, but he's all right, don't you worry." He picked up her hand and made it into a fist. "Now, Duchess, I've told you how to swing and strike and keep your thumb tucked under. Why didn't you knock him over the flower box?"

She tried to smile, she truly did, but her face seemed as frozen as the earth outside. "I just didn't want to see him anymore, Badger."

"No wonder," he said and gave her back her hand. "But don't forget now, if a fellow goes beyond the line, you shove his choppers down his throat, that or you slam your knee upward as hard as you can."

"I will. I promise. Thank you, Badger."

He grunted and took himself off to the kitchen to prepare the curry sauce for the chicken, currently roasting
gently over the open grate. The cook and maid—Miss
Priss, Badger had always called her—had left for Welford-
on-Avon to see her ailing auntie some two years before.
Badger had taken over her duties. He was an excellent
cook. He just wished the Duchess ate more of his wonderful
concoctions.

Mrs. Cochrane had told him many years before that when
the Duchess visited Chase Park, everyone pretended—at
least outwardly—that she was some distant cousin from
Holland or from Italy, though her Dutch was nonexistent
and her Italian was singularly bad. But no one ever said
anything because she was, after all, the Duchess, and she
was so very beautiful and so glorious in her pride and
arrogance that all simply stood in awe of her, striving to
please her, to make her give them one of her rare smiles.
Mrs. Cochrane had smiled her beautiful smile at that, saying
that she'd been positively terrified to let her go to Chase
Park, and just look what had happened. She'd come back
the Duchess and that was what she'd remained.

Badger heard the door to the drawing room close. He
could see her going to the small writing desk, seating herself
gracefully, her movements slow and elegant, and writing his
lordship of their mutual loss.

The earl of Chase read of her mother's death before she
could write to him of it, and he informed her through his
secretary, Mr. Crittaker, that she was to pack her things and
be ready for the carriage that would bring her to Chase Park.
She was to bring Badger along for protection. He gave her
two weeks to comply with his wishes.

The two weeks came and passed. No one came to fetch
her. She didn't know what to do. She stood by the window
of the small parlor and waited. She wondered if she should
write to her father and remind him of his instruction to

her, but no, she couldn't bring herself to do that. It was too humiliating. She would wait. Four more days passed. And she thought: *He grieves for my mother and he no longer wants me. He has forgotten me. I'm alone now. What will I do?*

Then she realized that she'd always dreaded going to Chase Park on her yearly jaunts. Just stepping into that impossibly grand Italianate entrance hall with all its half-millennium-old dark wainscoting and equally old paintings with their heavy gold-encrusted frames, and that huge, utterly overpowering central staircase with still more ancestral paintings climbing the wall along it made her freeze inside and gave her stomach cramps. She had walked through the great oak doors every year and immediately begun to count down the fourteen days she had to remain there, to pretend as though all these noble people and all the children of these noble people and all these servants of the noble people liked her and truly welcomed her, when they all wished she had never been conceived.

At least this year the countess of Chase hadn't been there to shrivel her into herself with her cold looks and the bitter disdain that radiated from her like a living thing. The countess had died just the week before, and the mansion was draped with black crepe and every female wore black gowns, and all the males wore black arm bands. She'd heard the servants whisper that the countess had been too old for childbearing and look what had come of it—the poor dear had died, cursing her husband, for he had forced her this final and last time, forced himself upon her until she conceived—at least that's what all the servants believed—forced her and forced her and look what had come of it. And, after all, she had managed to provide the earl with two healthy boys and twin girls, and it wasn't her fault that both boys had drowned in that boat race and left only the Twins. All waited for the earl to take a new wife, a very young new wife who would breed a child every year until the earl was satisfied that no matter how many accidents occurred there would still be a boy left to succeed to the title and all the Wyndham lands. A man need only wait six months and it was past that time now. That's what she'd heard and then she'd repeated to Mr. Jollis, the miserable creature.

She frowned. Perhaps that's why he didn't want her now at Chase Park. He'd found his next countess and he didn't want to have his bastard there with his new wife. Yes, that was it. He naturally wanted to please a new wife and bringing a bastard into her new home and parading the bastard under her nose wouldn't accomplish pleasure, much less bring any harmony to the new union. But why didn't he simply write and tell her? She believed her father to be many things, but never a coward. It made no sense.

It began to rain, now just a drizzle, but the Duchess knew the signs. Before long, the drizzle would become sheets of slamming slate-gray water, driven against the windows by a fierce wind blowing off the Channel.

Even though he had deserted her now, she had to admit that her father had supported her mother and her for eighteen years, and her mother two years before she'd been born even. She had been like his wife, only, of course, she wasn't, she was just his mistress, with no legal rights, no recourse, nothing. But now that her mother was dead, she supposed she might as well be dead too, for he no longer felt any responsibility toward her, no longer had to pretend liking toward her. He'd probably decided that since she was eighteen, it was now her responsibility to see to herself. But why had he bothered to lie to her? Why had he told her that she was coming to Chase Park? It had been a lie, but why, she couldn't begin to imagine. All she knew was that she was utterly alone. Mama had no one, as far as she knew, at least there were never any letters, never any presents at Christmas from relatives of her mother's. She assumed they were Cochranes, surely that was her mother's name after all and not some tawdry made-up name. No, there couldn't be any brothers or sisters or aunts. It had always been just the two of them and the frequent visits from the earl.

The rain cascaded against the window. She wondered what she would do. Her mother's solicitor had told her in that sniggering way of his, for he knew well that her mother wasn't the widow she always pretended she was, but a nobleman's mistress, kept in this little love nest of a cottage, that the love nest was leased, the bills paid by the earl's man of business in London, and that the lease was ended by the fifteenth of the next month. The way he'd treated her made her feel dirty, but more than dirty, she'd felt incredible anger. He all but told her that she was no better than her mother, and pray, what was wrong with her loving, beautiful mother? But she knew the answer to that, she simply shied away from it as she always did. At least she hadn't allowed him to make his insulting offer of another love nest, this one paid for by him.

She rose slowly, shivering in the sudden damp chill of the late afternoon. The fire was dying down. It was growing colder by the minute. She rose, carefully placed more logs on the fire, then began to pace the small room, lightly slapping her hands against her arms for warmth. She knew she had to do something, but what? She had no skills at governessing or being an old lady's companion or even creating a stylish bonnet. She'd been raised as a gentlewoman, thus her only talents lay in her ability to please a man, all with the goal of finding a husband who would overlook her unfortunate antecedents.

She paced and paced, feeling infinitely bitter, then wanting to cry, for her mother was dead, her beautiful mother who had loved the earl probably more than she had loved her daughter, loved him even more than she'd hated the position in which he'd placed her.

Mr. Jollis had bragged how he knew society better than she. Her eyes narrowed now at that impertinence. She'd poured over the *London Times* and the *Gazette* since the age of ten, devouring all the goings-on of society, laughing at their seemingly endless foibles and acts of idiocy, their disregard of the most minimal restraints. Yes, she knew society and their ways, and as she thought about it, she realized that she did have one talent, but she'd never really considered it as a way to earn a living—she'd never had to.

She stopped in her tracks, staring unseeing at the thick slabs of rain pounding against the drawing room window. Yes, she had a talent, an unusual talent, certainly a talent never recognized as being possible in a female. Was it possible? She would have to discuss it with Badger. If there was a way to make money at it, why then, he would know how it would be done.

As she walked up the charming but narrow stairway upstairs to her bedchamber, she smiled for the first time since her mother's death.

2

MR. CRITTAKER DIDN'T like what he was about to do, but he had no choice, none at all. He was markedly pale, his breathing shallow. He raised his hand, paused a moment as he thought of possible disastrous consequences, got a grip on himself, and finally knocked on the library door. It was late, very late, and Mr. Crittaker knew that this was a gross imposition on his lordship, but he had to tell him what he'd done, or more to the point, what he'd forgotten to do.

There was no answer. Mr. Crittaker knocked again, louder this time.

Finally, an irritated voice called out, "All right, come in before you bruise your damned knuckles."

The earl of Chase was standing in front of the pink-veined Carrara marble fireplace that was the showpiece of the Wyndham library, despite the three walls of bookcases that went up some twenty-two feet and held more than ten thousand tomes. It was a beautiful room, not overly large so that one's voice echoed, but still overwhelming in its dark magnificence. Mr. Crittaker looked toward the desk that backed against the one wall that held a huge set of glass doors. There was a lit candle on the desk, but the chair was empty. He saw the earl standing in front of the fireplace. He appeared to be doing naught of anything, save standing there warming himself. Still, it was near to midnight.

"What is it, Crittaker? Didn't you work me enough all day? I had to scrub to get all the damned ink off my fingers from signing those interminable papers. Well, man, speak up. What new crisis besets me now?"

"My lord," Mr. Crittaker began, not really knowing how to confess his sin, not really knowing if the earl would merely chastise him verbally or boot him out into the March snowstorm. He cleared his throat and began again. This time, he simply blurted it out. "My lord, by all that's holy, I forgot Miss Cochrane!"

The earl just stared at him, obviously at a loss. He said finally, slowly, "Miss Cochrane?"

"Yes, my lord. Miss Cochrane."

"Who is Miss Cochrane?"

"The Duchess, my lord. I forgot her, sir. Her mother died and, well, then your uncle died, and I, well, in all the preparation for your arrival, I, ah, forgot her."

The VIII earl of Chase continued to stare at his now-dead uncle's secretary, now his. "You forgot the Duchess? Her mother died? When, man? My God, how long ago was this?" Then he waved Mr. Crittaker to a seat. "Come here and tell me the entire story and don't leave out any details."

Mr. Crittaker, heartened that he mightn't be cast out into the frigid night by the easiness of the earl's deep voice, came forward and said, "Your uncle's, er—"

"His mistress," the earl said sharply. "His twenty-year mistress. Yes, what about his mistress?"

"Yes, his mistress, Mrs. Cochrane, she was killed in a carriage accident. Your uncle immediately told me to write to Miss Cochrane to tell her to be packed to come live at Chase Park. I wrote to tell her she would be fetched in two weeks."

"I see," the earl said. "How many weeks have passed beyond the two weeks, Crittaker?"

"Eight of them, my lord."

The earl once again simply stared at his secretary. "You

mean that an eighteen-year-old girl has been left alone for two months?"

Mr. Crittaker nodded, so miserable that he wanted to sink into the elegant Aubusson carpet beneath his shoes. "There must be a servant, my lord, surely."

The earl waved that information away, saying slowly, "I wonder why she didn't write my uncle to ask him why he hadn't sent a carriage for her?"

Mr. Crittaker didn't have to pause at all, just said, more miserable now than he had been just the moment before, "She must have believed that your uncle no longer wanted her since her mother had died. He never treated her with any affection when she was here, my lord, on her yearly visits. How he treated her when he visited her mother at Rosebud Cottage, I don't know. No, she wouldn't have said a word to your uncle. She's very proud, my lord. You know that. She's the Duchess."

"Or perhaps her letter never arrived, or it did arrive and you simply misplaced it, Crittaker."

Mr. Crittaker could hear the howling wind outside. He thought again of standing in the blowing snow with naught but his greatcoat for protection. He was forced to admit, "It is possible, my lord, but I trust, indeed, I pray, that such a thing didn't occur."

The earl cursed heartily and at great detailed length. Mr. Crittaker was impressed, but was wise enough not to compliment his lordship on his fluency. His lordship had been a major in the army, selling out only six weeks earlier when he'd come to take his place as the VIII earl of Chase.

The earl finally ran himself out of verbal bile. He said, "How is it that you just now remembered the Duchess?"

Mr. Crittaker tugged at his cravat, a somber creation that immediately unfastened itself with his pulling. "It was Mr. Spears who remembered."

"Spears," the earl repeated, then smiled. "My uncle's valet, now mine, reminded you about the Duchess?"

"Mr. Spears took a liking to her when she was just a little mite, that's what he called her," Mr. Crittaker said. "It occurred to Mr. Spears that something might have 'slipped through the crevices,' as he phrased it, my lord. He had believed that Miss Cochrane was perhaps in London at his lordship's behest, but of course she wasn't, but Mr. Spears couldn't have known that."

"I see," the earl said, and appeared to withdraw himself into deep thought. Mr. Crittaker didn't move. He wanted to pull on his ear, a habit he'd had since boyhood, and it took all his concentration to keep his hands at his sides.

The earl said finally, "It appears I must make a short trip into Sussex. I will leave in the morning and fetch Miss Cochrane back with me."

"Very good, my lord."

"Oh, Crittaker, your cravat is a mess. Also," the earl's voice dropped markedly, "if something has happened to Miss Cochrane, you will be finding yourself a new employment."

The earl continued his perusal of the glowing embers in the fireplace, kicking one with the toe of his boot.

Forgotten! Good God, Crittaker had simply forgotten her. It froze his blood to think of the Duchess alone and unprotected for two damned months. On the other hand, he'd not given her a thought either, nor for that matter, had anyone in the house save for Spears. Marcus hadn't seen her in five years, not since that long ago summer when his two male cousins had drowned in a boating race. He wondered if she'd grown as beautiful as he'd believed she would then.

Not that it mattered. She was his bastard cousin. But he owed it to his uncle to see that she was taken care of. What would he do with her? Ah, that was the question.

The Duchess was the topic of conversation the following afternoon in the snug and very cozy Green Cube Room at Chase Park.

"The Duchess," Aunt Gweneth said in the general direction of the Twins, speaking in her precise way, for she always prided herself on her enunciation, "is quite the most beautiful girl I have ever seen."

"But you haven't seen many girls at all, beautiful or otherwise, Aunt Gweneth," Antonia said, looking up from her Mrs. Radcliffe novel. "You've never ventured beyond York. However, I do hope she's all right. How perfectly awful to be forgotten. She must be very hurt."

"Marcus will take care of her," Fanny said. "He can do anything. Yes, he will make her feel better about her being forgotten. I would I could have gone with him. I could have kept his spirits up."

"I do wish you would get over your unfortunate infatuation with your cousin," Aunt Gweneth said, looking up at Fanny. She thought of the new earl, Reed Wyndham's only son, now the earl of Chase. And he'd been in the fighting in the Peninsula! He could easily have been butchered by those damned French, or by those guerrillas that seemed to abound in Marcus's few letters to his uncle over the past three years. But he'd survived, thank God, even though she doubted that James had thanked anyone heavenward. So many dead babes, so very many, and all of them male. She would have sworn to anyone who had bothered to ask her that her brother would remarry the day after the countess had been placed reverently in the Wyndham family tomb, the primary consideration being whether the girl was likely to be a good breeder. But given the opportunity, he hadn't remarried, to her great surprise, and now he was dead.

She would give Marcus credit for the consideration he'd shown his twin cousins and her. He had, in truth, surprised her greatly, for in her experience, gentlemen had the sensitivity of toads. She would also allow that Marcus was a handsome man, had much of the look of his uncle, with his thick dark brown hair and heavily lashed blue eyes. Ah, and that chin of his, stubborn as a demented mule, at least that had been what it depicted in James. In Marcus? She remembered James referring to Marcus as the devil's own son, and smiling slightly. She sighed. They still all had yet to see either the limits of his good nature or the depths of his irritation. He was taller than his uncle, towering over even Spears, his uncle's valet, who had consented, his voice at its driest, to take over, and doubtless improve upon, the appearance of the new earl. Spears, Gweneth had heard Sampson say, believed the new lordship to have a good amount of potential and grit, the latter commodity something he would have dire need of.

He'd only been here at Chase Park for four weeks now, having left his widowed mother in Lower Slaughter where she refused to budge from Cranford Manor. He was the head of the Wyndham family, this new earl who still couldn't seem to remember to answer to "Chase" rather than simply "Marcus Wyndham," only son of a second son with no particular prospects for anything save a life in the military. Life was uncertain, Gweneth thought, and served up wretchedly unexpected dishes on one's plate.

"I am not infatuated with him," Fanny said as she poked her needle through a piece of very poorly stitched embroidery, whose dubious platitude would be eventually rendered as *Home and Heaven*. "It is just that he is wonderful. He has been very kind, Aunt, even you admit that, and you remember how Papa always went on and on about how Marcus didn't have pure blood, whatever that means."

"Marcus does have pure blood, Fanny," Gweneth said, her voice sharp. "It's just that it isn't your papa's blood, such a pity."

"I hope nothing is wrong with the Duchess," Antonia said, oblivious of almost everything except her novel, effectively camouflaged by a tome of Dr. Edwards's *Daily Sermons*. "Two months alone. You don't think she went back to Holland, do you, Aunt Gweneth?"

Her twin sister, Fanny, identical down to the split thumbnail on her right hand, put down her embroidery, and said, "If Papa were alive, he would have provided her a Season in London to find a husband. He would have provided her with a dowry. Do you think she went back to Italy, Aunt Gweneth? She isn't from Holland, Antonia."

Aunt Gweneth shook her head, even as she said, pain and anger deep in her voice, "Your papa was most unfortunate in his choice of mounts. The brute killed him."

"The brute was his only mount for eight years, Aunt," Fanny said. Her lower lip trembled as she added, "Papa loved that horse. I remember once when it started raining and he took care of his horse before he took care of Antonia and me."

Gweneth didn't doubt that her brother had done exactly that, not for a moment. He rode to the hounds all the time, and took risks that made even Spears raise an eyebrow, but nothing had ever happened to him, not even a fall, until six weeks ago. He'd turned in his saddle to shout insults to a long-time friend riding behind him when he struck his head on a low-hanging branch of an oak tree—since cut down in a spate of reprisal—knocking him off his horse, killing him instantly.

Within three weeks of the fatal accident, Marcus, twenty-three years old, stationed in the Peninsula with his army battalion, was informed that he was the new earl of Chase. The VIII earl of Chase. Gweneth wondered if Marcus still felt like he was walking in his uncle's shoes, treading down his uncle's huge ornate central staircase, gliding across his uncle's rich Turkey carpets—in short, if he still felt like an intruder.

"I wonder if Marcus will give the Duchess a dowry and a Season to find a husband," Fanny said as she rose, shook out her skirts, and walked to fetch a scone from an exquisitely formed silver tray service.

Antonia snorted. "She doesn't need a dowry, just a chance for the gentlemen to see her. All of them will be on their knees, begging for her hand in marriage. This heroine in Mrs. Radcliffe's novel is ever so beautiful and kind and sweet and good, but she's as poor as a church mouse. There are already three gentlemen who hold their hands over their hearts when she passes by."

What drivel, Gweneth thought. If there was ever a gentleman with his hand over his chest, it wasn't from undying love but from indigestion after imbibing too much brandy. "Fanny, you will eat just one scone and when you chew on it, don't converse with us. Maggie remarked to me the other day that your gowns were getting a bit snug around your waist. You and Antonia are near an age where you should begin shedding your baby fat, not anchoring it on. As for you, Antonia, I sincerely doubt that Dr. Edwards's sermons include gentlemen eyeing young ladies. Mrs. Radcliffe, indeed. Your mama wouldn't have liked that at all."

Antonia's lower lip trembled. Gweneth sighed. "Why don't you read a passage aloud for Fanny and me?"

PIPWELL COTTAGE, SMARDEN, KENT
JUNE 1813

Marcus pulled his raw-boned bay stallion, Stanley, to a halt in front of Pipwell Cottage, as it was called by all the locals, dismounted, and tied the reins to the iron tethering post. He was weary to his bones, angry at the delay, and ultimately, so relieved that at last he'd found the Duchess that he wanted to fling himself to the ground and kiss the dirt, then strangle her for causing everyone such distress, particularly himself.

He'd gone to Rosebud Cottage in Winchelsea over three months before to fetch her, only to find that she was gone, long gone—no one knew where. At least she'd had a servant with her, a man, but surely that was odd, an eighteen-year-old girl traveling alone and living alone with a man, servant or not, old or not.

It had taken him three months to track her down. He wondered if it would have taken three years if Spears hadn't chosen to involve himself. In ways still mystifying to Marcus, Spears had traveled to Winchelsea, where Marcus had already questioned everyone in the bloody town, offering bribes and making threats. Then he'd gone on to London. He'd stayed in both places for merely two days, then returned to Chase Park, bowed formally to Marcus and gave him a slip of paper that had said simply: Pipwell Cottage, Smarden, Kent.

She'd been alone, except for that man servant, for nearly six months.

Marcus calmed himself. He'd found her. At least Pipwell Cottage wasn't a slum property. It looked charming in its early summer plumage, and there were at least a dozen oak trees and lush, green maple, larch, and lime trees as well. The small yews lining the path leading to the front door were neatly trimmed, the granite slab path itself smooth and firm beneath his feet. There were myriad plants behind the yews and set in symmetrical beds as well, roses and dahlias he recognized, but others too, huge blooms and giving a riot of color. The cottage was painted white, the window boxes white as well, trimmed with red paint. It was a very snug little property. Too snug, too prosperous.

However did she pay for it? He again dismissed the recurring thought that she, like her mother, had a protector. No, he thought, not the Duchess. Too much pride in that girl, much too much.

He realized as he strode to the front door, with its window boxes on either side dripping with roses and hydrangeas and primroses as purple as the black eye he'd given to Jimmy Watts eighteen years before, that all he wanted was to find her healthy and well fed.

He knocked and continued to pray.

Badger opened the door and stared at the young gentleman who was staring back at him.

Marcus blinked in confusion, and said slowly, "You live here now, sir? You are the owner of the cottage? The Duch—Miss Cochrane has moved away?"

"Aye, I live here," Badger said, not budging an inch from the doorway.

Marcus cursed, earning a spark of interest from Badger. "You were in the Peninsula then, sir?" Badger said.

"Yes, but now I'm a damned earl and I had to sell out."

"May I be allowed to ask your lordship which damned earl you would be?"

"Chase, the earl of Chase."

"That," Badger said slowly, readying himself for a fight, "is quite impossible. You'd best take your leave, sir. I won't be asking you again, if you take my meaning." He moved to stand more squarely in the doorway and Marcus saw those huge hands of his curl into fists.

Marcus, no fool, knew the man was ready to spring for his throat. But he didn't understand why. "It's true, I'm the new earl of Chase. The, er, eighth earl, not the seventh. I had hoped Miss Cochrane still lived here. I have come for her, you see. She was forgotten after her father's death, and then when Mr. Crittaker remembered her, I went immediately to Winchelsea but she was gone. It's taken me another three months to find her and now she's gone again."

Badger eyed him up and down. "You're Marcus Wyndham?"

"Yes, I am."

"The old earl called you the devil's own son. You are he?"

Marcus grinned. "My uncle never minced matters. Aye, I'll own up to it."

"You're telling me that her father is dead?"

"Yes, he died nearly six months ago. He was thrown from his horse and died instantly. She's still here then? You are her servant?"

"So that's why no one came for her. Strange that neither of us considered such a possibility. I assume it was an accident?" At the young man's nod, Badger said, "The Duchess used to speak of you when she returned from Chase Park. Actually, she said only that you were the one who named her Duchess, and that you were the devil's own son. I don't believe, sir, that she has much liking for you."

Marcus laughed. "I don't care if she hates the very grass I tread upon, just tell me that she is all right."

"Aye, she is just fine."

"She is eating sufficiently?"

"Aye, she eats enough."

"But how does she afford this cottage?"

"That, sir," Badger said, suddenly as austere as a bishop, "you'd best ask Miss Cochrane. If I may ask, sir, why are you here?"

"Would you like to invite me inside? I do need to speak with her, as you just suggested. Incidentally, who are you?"

"I am Badger. I look after the Duchess as I did her mother before her. I am her chef as well."

"Ah," Marcus said. "You cook?"

The huge, ugly man nodded and finally stood aside for Marcus to enter. He did, striding into a small entryway. A staircase rose just beyond him, leading to the upper floor of the cottage. He smelled roasting meat just off to his left, potent and rich. His stomach growled and his mouth began to water. He thought he heard a woman humming a neat little tune.

"Wait here, sir," Badger said, and left Marcus without a backward look. He opened a door to the right and disappeared through it, closing it behind him. The humming stopped abruptly.

Marcus tapped his riding crop against his thigh. He was hungry, tired, and couldn't believe that he'd been left to stand in a narrow hallway by a man who was a maid and a chef, but a man who spoke English like a little Etonian gentleman.

At least she was all right. At least she wasn't alone. But who was paying for this cottage? Her food? Her cook?

When the door opened again, Badger said, "You may come in, sir. Miss Cochrane will see you now."

Like she's the bloody queen, Marcus thought, irritated. The room was small, but pleasant. It had a lived-in feeling, that's what it was, a very welcoming feeling, and felt wonderfully cozy. There were stacks of London newspapers on the floor beside a blue brocade settee. Odd that he saw those newspapers before he noticed her, stacks and stacks of them.

It had been five years.

She was the most beautiful girl he'd ever seen in his life. She'd more than fulfilled the promise he'd seen in her when she was thirteen. It wasn't that she was gowned gloriously because she wasn't. She was wearing a simple muslin of dark gray, its collar nearly to her chin, the sleeves tapering down her arms to button tightly around her wrists. Her black hair was in fat plaits interwoven atop her head. She wore no jewelry. There was a smudge of ink on her cheek. She was standing utterly still, just looking at him, not moving even a fingertip. He remembered that stillness of hers, the aloofness, the serenity that sat so oddly on the shoulders of a young girl.

She was more beautiful than she should be. He said, "What are you doing with all those newspapers?"

"Hello to you, Marcus."

"Ah, hello, Duchess. It's been a while."

She merely nodded. "Badger tells me that my father is dead and that was why no one ever came for me. Odd, isn't it? Dead or alive, I was still forgotten."

"Yes, Crittaker nearly choked himself to death when he informed me of it over three months ago. I'm sorry it happened. I am here to fetch you back to Chase Park with me."

She frowned at him, still not moving. She didn't even offer him her hand or her cheek to kiss. She was his damned first cousin, for God's sake, yet she was standing six feet away from him, and her frown was becoming more pronounced.

He realized in that moment that he'd given her a profound shock. First her mother and now her father, both of them dead within weeks of each other.

"I'm sorry about your father. He was my uncle and I was fond of him. He had a quick death, there was no suffering."

"Thank you for telling me that. I thought he had forgotten me, that he no longer wanted me since my mother had died."

"Now you know he did want you at Chase Park. He had no say in what happened to him."

Badger appeared in the open doorway. "The duckling is perfect now, Duchess. It sits on a platter with small boiled potatoes around it and some fresh green beans. I decorated the potatoes with snipped-off bits of parsley. I also made some apple tarts, your favorite. Would you care to have dinner now? Would you like to have his lordship join us?"

She nodded, clearly distracted.

"Are you hungry, sir?"

"Yes, I have ridden hard all day. Is it possible for someone to see to my stallion?"

"You will have to see to your own horse," she said. "Badger hasn't the time to do it."

"I see," Marcus said. He turned on his heel and strode out of the small drawing room.

Badger called after him, "There is a shed behind the cottage. You may stable your horse there."

Marcus didn't say anything further. He was perfectly capable of looking after Stanley, but what he wasn't used to, what he couldn't seem to accept, was the fact that the Duchess was living alone with a man who spoke the English of a gentleman, was also her chef and decorated a roasted duckling with boiled potatoes and parsley. Even though Badger was ugly as a gnarly old oak and old enough to be her father, still, it just wasn't right. What was going on here?

She didn't look on the verge of starvation. She'd been humming when he arrived and she had a spot of ink on her left cheek. And she looked so beautiful he'd just wanted to stand there and stare at her, at least until Badger had come in and announced that dinner was served. As far as he knew, there had been no provision at all for her in his uncle's will, thus his growing fear over the past four months. As far as he knew, she had nothing.

What was going on here?

3

MARCUS PUSHED BACK his plate, sighed with pleasure, and folded his hands over his lean belly. The Duchess had finished some time before and was simply sitting there, calm and composed, not ruffled in the least by his presence, as if having a man to dinner was a daily occurrence. She merely waited: waited for him to finish, waited for him to speak, just waited as silent and calm as she had always been since he'd first met her when she'd been nine years old. She was slowly turning her wineglass between her fingers, a wineglass of good quality, he saw, surely a wineglass made of fine crystal that clearly cost a few guineas. It must be part of an expensive set. Who had paid for them? The man who ate evening meals with her?

He said easily, with deep appreciation, "Badger is a chef of great ability. The parsley was a nice touch. Greenery enhanced the paleness of the potatoes and highlighted the duck."

"Yes, it was a touch of artistry. He is a man of many abilities."

"Such as?"

She merely shrugged, looking as unruffled as could be, dismissing his sharp question as an impertinence, as he supposed it was.

"You're looking well," he said. "Everyone was very worried about you."

After they'd finally remembered she even existed, she thought, but said only, "Thank you. You have quite grown

36

up yourself. Were you a gentleman of leisure before my fath—before the earl died?"

"Oh no, I was a major in the army. I had to sell out after my uncle's death. I didn't want his damned title, though I know he never believed that, and I honestly didn't care that I was his nominal heir. Like everyone else, I believed he would remarry after my aunt died in childbed, and continue to try procreating a male child. Undoubtedly he would have succeeded if he hadn't died."

"It is odd. I wonder why he didn't remarry."

"He was killed only seven months after my aunt died. To have remarried before a year—well, perhaps eight or nine months given his need—would have laid him open to censure. My uncle was conscious of others' opinions."

"He visited my mother often after the countess died. Indeed, he spent most of his time with her. He'd changed so much after Charlie and Mark's deaths. At least those last months were very happy."

Marcus wasn't particularly surprised to hear that. After all, his uncle was always a lusty man who paid to have his mistress constantly at his disposal. However, he didn't say this aloud, not to his uncle's bastard daughter. He only nodded. He said abruptly, "Do you resemble your mother?"

"Yes, but as you probably have noticed, I have my father's eyes and his black hair. My mother's hair was incredible, all gold and blond." She paused a moment, then said easily, "I know what you're thinking. A man has the same mistress for twenty years—it boggles the mind. My mother was always beautiful, always charming, always here for him. She never carped at him, never demanded. She loved him, you see."

"Yes, I see," he said quietly. "I'm sorry, Duchess."

"Your apple tarts," Badger said, coming quietly into the small room. Marcus wondered if he'd overheard their conversation and picked his moment of entry. If he had, it wasn't badly done.

"Thank you, Badger. They look delicious," she said, smiling up at him. She said to Marcus, "You will be quite prepared to give up all your wealth after you have tasted Badger's apple tarts."

Marcus smiled, and forked down a bite. He closed his eyes. "My tongue couldn't offer an insult if it tried," he said, grinning. The Duchess merely nodded, saying, "It's difficult to believe that you really didn't care, that you didn't want the title and all the wealth that goes along with it."

He shrugged. "I didn't care, it's true. I was quite content with my life as it was. I didn't want to sell out. I was only the son of a second son, but I was needed. I like to think that I made a difference, that my judgments affected the outcome of at least a few events. At least I pray I saved some lives and didn't stupidly waste any."

"Did you spend all your years in the Peninsula?"

He nodded. "I joined up in August of 1808, right after Charlie and Mark drowned. The Spanish refused to have us help them in Spain so we went directly to Portugal, to Figueria de Foz, near Coimbra. My commander was Wellington." He paused, then looked a bit embarrassed. "Sorry for boring on about it."

"Please continue," she said, and nothing more.

He looked at her askance because no woman before in his life, including his mother, had ever wanted to know what he'd done. He leaned forward, saying slowly, "Napoleon subdued Spain then headed to Lisbon, traveling through Talavera and Elvas."

Suddenly the Duchess said, "Didn't Napoleon say, 'I shall hunt the English out of the Peninsula. Nothing can for long withstand the fulfillment of my wishes'?"

"I believe he said something like that," Marcus said, frowning at her.

"Do go on."

He winced, remembering, saying to her, "There was this awful mid-winter crossing, led by Sir John Moore through the Galician mountains, but we managed to outrun the French. There was little food, the animals—" He shook his head, looking at her now, hating those damned memories, seeing the faces of his men, of officers he'd called friend, so many of them dead now, and he'd not been able to do anything to help. "No," he said, "that is quite enough tonight."

"What do you think of the armistice made by Napoleon after he beat the Prussian armies at Lützen and Bautzen?"

Marcus shrugged. "We will see how long it lasts. None of the men I know think it will go much beyond the summer, if that."

"Is it true that Wellington wishes all his generals to avoid fighting Napoleon directly, that Wellington always tries to go up against his marshals?"

He was truly surprised, for few people knew of it. "How do you know of this?"

"I read," she said flatly, and he knew that he'd insulted her, treating her like a lady, in other words, like a bit of fluff with nothing noteworthy between her beautifully shaped ears.

"Yes, you're quite right. Wellington has said that Napoleon's presence on a battlefield is worth forty thousand men, not just men, soldiers."

She sat forward, resting her elbows on the table. The candlelight was soft, the room quiet, the apple tarts sitting unnoticed on their plates. "That is excellent. I'd never heard that. Is it also true that it wasn't the Russian winter that defeated Napoleon but rather the Russians themselves?"

"Yes, but there are arguments about that. Needless to say, all who deem Napoleon the greatest military leader of all time blame the vicious Russian winter. I have heard it said that the Russians learned from Napoleon's victories and copied him, thus defeating him at his own game."

"And don't forget that his supply lines broke down. Imagine the distances from the West all the way to Moscow! It quite boggles the mind to imagine how much food would be necessary, and clothing and equipment."

"Yes," Marcus said, "imagine." He couldn't help himself, he was staring at her and continued to stare at her. Did she have a protector who was in the army or navy? Is this how she knew so much? He said abruptly, "How long will it take you to be ready to leave?"

"Leave? I beg your pardon?"

"You are coming back with me to Chase Park, naturally."

"There is nothing natural about it that I can see," she said, and to his surprise, he saw her hand clench into a fist. The Duchess making a bloody fist? No, surely he was seeing things, not something so violent as a fist, not the bloody Duchess. Whatever had he said to ruffle her serene feathers? He couldn't imagine that bloodless, elegant hand fisting.

"You should have been living at Chase Park for the past six months. I have apologized for what happened. There is nothing more I can say. I've spent the past months trying to find you. Now that I have, I'm here to offer you a home, proper chaperonage, and if you wish to go to London for a Season, you will certainly go. I will also see that you have a sufficient dowry. With your looks and your show of interest in military matters, I daresay that you will have many offers of marriage, at least from lonely officers home on leave."

She merely looked at him, still again, her hands smoothed out on the white tablecloth. He noticed ink stains on her fingers, and said, "If marriage is what you want. But what else is there for a lady?"

"No," she said calmly. "No, I don't want marriage. This is home now. It is kind of you to search me out, but a long time has passed and I find that I am become self-sufficient. I have no need of a Season or a dowry. Or a husband. There are things for a lady, Marcus, other than marriage."

"How have you become self-sufficient? Is there a soldier you met after your mother's death? Is it he who has told you—" Marcus shrugged then, his mouth shutting, but his meaning was quite clear, appallingly clear.

She smiled at him, but it was a cold smile, one that held infinite secrets and a serious level of anger. But as usual, there was no sound of anger in her cool voice. "That, sir, is none of your business. Your line of reasoning is interesting, however. My knowledge of military matters or my interest in such occurrences as Napoleon's failure to survive in Russia obviously can't spring from my own brain, but it has to come, rather, from another—specifically, from a military man who is doubtless keeping me in this charming cottage, just as your uncle kept my mother in Rosebud Cottage."

He hunched forward and smacked his fist onto the table. "Damnation, Duchess, I didn't mean that. Are you forgetting that I am your cousin? That I am the damned head of the Wyndham family and am thus responsible for you now?"

"You are my cousin, true, but I am nothing but a bastard. You owe me nothing at all, Marcus. Certainly you aren't responsible for me. My father was, but like most men he must have believed himself immortal. Thus, he made no provision for me. However, I find now that I quite enjoy being on my own."

"You are eighteen years old. You are a gentlewoman. You cannot be on your own."

"I am nearly nineteen, and the fact remains that I am on my own and I am a bastard. Don't put respectable icing on this particular cake, for it doesn't fit."

He felt equal parts of anger and frustration. Here he was, a perfect knight errant, and the damsel was refusing his assistance. The devil of it was she didn't even appear to be at all in distress.

Suddenly, she laughed. "I can see exactly what you are thinking. You have gone to all this trouble to save your poor bastard cousin and she is turning you down. Goodness, she is turning you down after feeding you probably the best dinner you've enjoyed in many a long evening. I'm sorry, Marcus, but there it is."

"No, it isn't. You will pack your things and you will return with me to Chase Park. I would never serve your father and my uncle such a turn. I would like to leave tomorrow. Can Badger have everything ready?"

She didn't appear to be paying any attention to him. She was looking off into space, her eyes narrowed in profound thought, or something. All of a sudden, she began to hum a tune he'd never heard before. "Excuse me," she said abruptly, and rose from her chair. "Don't go away, Marcus. I shall return very soon."

She was gone from the small dining room, leaving the earl of Chase there with a half-eaten apple tart on his plate and a look of utter incomprehension on his face wondering how the devil she was managing. And now she'd run out on him without a by-your-leave.

"Would you like a brandy, my lord? Or perhaps port or claret?"

"Port," he said. He sipped at the port, waiting for her to return. Fifteen minutes passed and there was no sign of her. He said to Badger, who had just come into the small dining room to clear the dishes from the table, "What is she doing?"

"I couldn't say."

"Of course you can but you won't, will you? Come, Badger, how the hell does she afford this cottage? How does she afford to have you? There's a man, isn't there? He's a military man and he's footing all the bills."

"You will speak to Miss Cochrane, my lord."

"I wish to leave tomorrow. Can you be ready, Badger?"

Badger straightened to his full height, which would make many a short man envious. "You will discuss this with Miss Cochrane." Then he softened, adding, "You must understand loyalty, sir. You were in the army. There is little more precious than absolute loyalty."

Marcus sighed and set down his port. "You're right, naturally. Do you think the Duchess would mind if I tracked her down now?"

"I believe I hear her returning. Ah, sir, it is doubtless difficult for her, just learning that her father had been dead for six months, learning that he did want her and didn't forget her, that instead the rest of you forgot her. There has been too much death for her in the past months."

"She has hidden it well," Marcus said. "No tears, no sobs, nothing. No pleas, no explanations, no pleasure in seeing me or agreeing with anything I say."

"Naturally. What would you expect from her?"

"I don't know anymore," Marcus said slowly, now lifting his port and swirling the dark red around in the crystal glass, a quite well-made crystal glass. Damnation, he wanted to strangle her.

"Go gently, sir." Marcus watched Badger hold open the door to the dining room as the Duchess came back in.

"Forgive me for taking so long," she said, adding, "Would you like to remain here or come with me into the drawing room?"

"Here is fine. What were you doing?"

"Just a bit of this and that, nothing to concern you."

He felt frustration rising to new heights and announced with the heavy hand of a complete autocrat, "You will come home with me and that's that."

"No, but thank you for your feelings of guilt or responsibility or whatever it is you're feeling that engenders such a fist on the reins. Listen to me, you are absolved, Marcus, please believe me. From you I learned that my father did want me. That is important. I thank you for that. Now, I'm sorry but there is nowhere for you to sleep. In Biddenden, very near to the sign of the Biddenden Maids—"

"Who the devil are the Biddenden Maids?"

"You didn't come through the village? No matter. They were Elizabeth and Mary Chalkhurst and they lived in the twelfth century. They were Siamese twins. In any case, the

Chequers Inn is not to be despised, but it is small, but perhaps not too small for the new earl of Chase." She rose and smiled at him, not much of a smile, but something.

He stood and strode to her, looking down at her, knowing his stance was intimidating but not caring. "I will be back tomorrow morning." He left her without another word. Badger was waiting in the small entrance hall. He opened the door and silently ushered him out.

"The Chequers Inn will stable your horse, my lord," he said.

"That is something," Marcus said, shaking his head. "Siamese twins—remarkable."

When Marcus rode to the cottage the next morning, it was to see the Duchess dressed in an outmoded gown of faded gray, the sturdy cotton coming nearly to her chin, down on her knees, her hands gloved, digging in a flower bed.

He dismounted, tied Stanley to the tethering post, and walked to her. "I didn't know you were a gardener."

She looked up at him. The sun was behind her, a halo around her head. Her forehead was covered with perspiration and there were two dirt smudges on her face. She looked lovely, more than lovely, damn her. "Yes, I enjoy it very much, as did my mother. Only I have more the green thumb than she did. I had the time, so why not?"

"How do you suddenly have the time? Does this mean that you won't suddenly jump up humming and leave the roses?"

"It's always possible."

"I want you to give me an honest answer, Duchess."

"If I feel like it."

He wanted to box her ears. He came down on his haunches beside her. "How are you supporting yourself?"

"You no longer believe there is a man in the background?"

"No, and I never did. Not really. You wouldn't do that. But God, it makes no sense, surely you must see that.

You're naught but a young girl and—"

"It has been five years, Marcus. You really have no idea as to my character or lack thereof. Of my talents or lack thereof. In short, you know nothing at all about me."

"The Twins miss you, as does Aunt Gweneth. They want you to come home with me."

She smiled down at her filthy gloves, at the rich black earth that nurtured her precious roses. "You have become a very handsome man, Marcus, a very eligible gentleman. Since you are the earl of Chase, you will doubtless be sought after by every single female in this fair land. You will be marrying soon so that you may go about the business of breeding an heir. I cannot imagine your wife wanting me anywhere around. I'm a bastard. It would behoove you to remember that."

"I'm not even twenty-five yet! For God's sake, give me a few years before I must leg-shackle myself."

"Forgive me. I quite understand your consternation since I share the same reluctance. You must admit that my unusual upbringing could easily leave a girl with a somewhat cynical view of dealings between men and women, particularly married men and unmarried women."

"None of this matters, dammit. Listen, Duchess, you cannot remain here, living alone with a man despite the fact that he is your servant. Your reputation will be in ruins. You were raised to be a gentlewoman. It is what you're meant to be—a gentleman's wife, the mother of his children. I wish to give you that future. It's what your father would have done. Please, you cannot remain here."

She remained still and silent, her gloved hands now resting quietly in the earth. That earth was black and thick and rich.

He rose quickly, so furious with her for her damned silence, her stubbornness, he was for a moment without words. Then he bellowed at the top of his lungs, "What do you do to keep this damned snug little cottage?"

Very slowly she stood up and stripped off her gloves, tossing them to the ground beside her. "Would you like some breakfast, Marcus? It is still very early."

"I will strangle you," he said, looking at her throat, covered completely by that hideous faded gray gown. "Yes, I will strangle you, but after breakfast. What will Badger prepare?"

$=4=$

TWO BLOODY MONTHS, he thought, wadding up the single sheet of paper, containing only two paragraphs to him by her grace, that damned girl he himself had christened Duchess so many years before. How dare she?

He read again, feeling his face grow red:

My lord,
   It was kind of you to send grapes from your succession house. Badger has quite delighted in preparing them in various dishes.
   Give my regards to Aunt Gweneth and the Twins.

And she'd signed it, "Your servant"—nothing more, not Duchess, not her name, nothing. Not even *obedient* servant, which she wasn't, damn her eyes.

He looked up to see Crittaker standing in the doorway, obviously afraid to say anything until Marcus recognized him.

"What is Miss Cochrane's name?"

"The Duchess, my lord."

"No, no, her real name. It was I who named her Duchess when she was nine years old, but I have no memory at all of her real name."

Crittaker looked nonplussed. "I don't know. Shall I ask Lady Gweneth?"

"Don't bother. It really isn't important. I just received a letter from her. She received the grapes. Badger is cooking with them. She is fine, I assume. She says nothing more. I suppose I will write her back, but I would rather kill her, or at least maim her, or strangle her just a little bit, to get her attention."

Crittaker backed out of the door. "We can review your other correspondence later, my lord."

Marcus grunted, picked up a piece of foolscap, and dipped his pen into the onyx inkwell atop the desk. He wrote:

Dear Duchess:

I am more pleased than I can tell you about Badger's pleasure with the damned grapes.

I trust you are well though you didn't say. I am well, Aunt Gweneth is well, the Twins are well, though Antonia is ordering novels from Hookhams in London and telling me that she has developed a fondness for sermons and that is what comprises her orders. Fanny is gaining flesh and Aunt Gweneth has told her that no gentleman will want to speak to her if she has more than one chin. I don't suppose you will tell me what you are doing to earn sufficient funds for the cottage and food and Badger—

Your servant, Marcus Wyndham

He'd written too much, he thought, she didn't deserve all the words he'd bothered to write her, but nonetheless he carefully folded the paper and slipped it into an envelope, writing her direction in a neat hand. He dipped his signet ring into the hot wax he'd prepared, and pressed it on the envelope.

He turned back to the *London Gazette* and read the latest war news. Schwarzenberg had crossed the Bohemian Mountains and tried to storm Dresden. However, the French had turned the city into a fortified camp and they'd beaten off the poorly coordinated allied attack. Of course then Napoleon had arrived with more French corps and Schwarzenberg

ended up losing thirty-eight thousand men and retreating to
Bohemia. Thirty-eight thousand! Marcus couldn't take it in.
Good God, so many soldiers, slaughtered through incompetence, men now dead who shouldn't be. He ached to return
to action but he knew that until he married and produced
an heir that he couldn't take that kind of risk. He owed it
to the four-hundred-year direct line of Wyndhams.

Damn.

He turned in his chair and yanked the bell pull. Crittaker
showed his face around the door within two minutes. Marcus
sighed and allowed himself to be drowned in estate business
for the next three hours. At least he knew enough now about
his uncle's various business dealings not to make a complete
ass of himself.

PIPWELL COTTAGE
NOVEMBER 1813

The Duchess simply stared at the letter. She couldn't take
it in. She read it again and then once more. She called
out faintly, not realizing that she'd yelled, "Badger, please
come here, quickly."

She heard him crashing through the kitchen, through the
hallway, and into the drawing room. He was breathing hard
and obviously alarmed.

"I'm sorry, please, come here and read this. I can't
believe it. It is absurd, surely a jest. It is—" She fell to
a stop and thrust out the letter to Badger.

He looked from her white face to the letter. He read it
through, whistled softly, then read it again, and yet one
more time.

He seated himself beside her on the settee and took her
hands in his. He said quietly, "Well, this is a shock. It seems
that everyone was looking for you. It took the earl only two
months to find you, but this gentleman took considerably
longer. He claims he's been searching since last May. Well,
now he's found you."

"Marcus doesn't know about any of this."

"No, and that's appropriate, I think. This solicitor fellow is a realist. He knows that your position is automatically precarious, that everything rests upon his speaking to you and not allowing the earl or any of the family to get to you first. He is a wise man."

"He wants to visit me next Monday."

"Aye, rightfully so." Badger patted her hands then rose, sniffing like a hound on the scent. "My ham Galatine smells too potent. It is beyond what is gratifying. Perhaps the grated black pepper wasn't of the best quality as old shark-fin Freeman assured me. Well, I can add more basil and perhaps just another pinch of rosemary, then it will be perfect. I am pleased, Duchess, that your father didn't forget you. He did well. I will remember him more easily now."

"I wonder if there is more," she said.

"We will see when this Mr. Wicks person arrives," Badger said and left her alone to return to his ham.

Mr. Wicks was very old and very thin and had an unmistakable gleam of kindness in his rheumy eyes. His smile, with its half complement of teeth, was also kind and it robbed her of much of her wariness.

"How do you do," he said and gallantly bowed over her hand. "How pleased I am to have finally found you. I must say you have a charming property. My, how I should like some tea, and you, I imagine, young lady, wish to hear all about this unusual, but highly gratifying, situation."

The Duchess invited him in, gave him tea, and sat forward in her chair, her hands clasped in her lap.

"Your name, as I told you in my letter, is now Miss Wyndham. Your father married your mother last November, two months before he was killed. He immediately hired me to have you legitimized. It was finalized at last in May. I couldn't contact you before then since it wasn't yet completed, for one of the Wyndham family could have stopped it, thus ensuring that you would remain dispossessed. But it was completed and now you are a true Wyndham. Then in May, my dear Miss Wyndham, I couldn't find you. I hired a Bow Street runner and he managed, finally, to track you here to Smarden."

She was looking utterly shocked, something he well understood. "My mother told me nothing of this, sir, nor did my father. I thought your address to me as Miss Wyndham was just a kindness, perhaps even a misapprehension on your part."

"Actually, my dear, you are now a lady, right and tight, but I thought that would make only more confusion than necessary. You are an earl's daughter and thus a lady, just as are his other daughters, Lady Fanny and Lady Antonia. No, your father told me that he was holding it all a secret from you until you were finally his legitimate daughter. I'm so very sorry that your parents died so suddenly, leaving you alone and unprotected and unaware of what they had done to make things right for you. They both loved you very much."

"Yes," she said slowly, staring beyond his left shoulder, "they did make things aright for me." Had her father really loved her? Yes, she supposed now, yes he had. She lowered her head and cried. For the first time since Marcus had told her of her father's death, tears rolled down her cheeks to drop onto her folded hands. She made no sound, just cried and cried. It was Badger who came into the drawing room and handed her a handkerchief, saying to Mr. Wicks as he did so, "She is always forgetting to carry a handkerchief with her. I tell her to just stuff one in her pocket, but she never remembers. That's right, Duchess, cry all you want to. The handkerchief has been waiting years for just this occasion."

"Thank you, Badger," she said. Her face was pale, her nose red, her eyes watery, and Mr. Wicks thought she was quite the loveliest young lady he'd seen in many a year. He said, "You have your father's eyes and hair. I met your mother but one time. She seemed a remarkable woman, so bright, just as are you, and so very beautiful that I stared at her, I fear, stared and stared, and your father just chuckled and said that it was all right, that every man who had ever laid eyes on her stared. And you are at least her equal in beauty. Now you will take your rightful place in society, Lady Duchess. *Lady Duchess*—how odd that sounds, but your father insisted that was your name even when I questioned it. He said, if I remember correctly, 'Yes, Wicks, it's Lady Duchess she is and nothing else. She's a young woman of great charm and character who will change things around her if she is given the chance, and I intend that she have her chance.' Thus, my lady, you are no longer a bastard, you will no longer be expected to live in retirement. In short, you will now do just as you wish." Mr. Wicks sat back and beamed at her.

"But I am quite content as I am," she said. "I'm pleased that my parents married, truly I am, but I don't see how it will change my situation, which, in any case, doesn't need changing. Let me assure you that the current earl, my cousin, Marcus Wyndham, also tracked me down and invited me to come and live at Chase Park. He also offered me a Season and a dowry. It was I who refused his offer. I do appreciate all the precautions you took, Mr. Wicks, but Marcus would have been pleased about what my father had done. He wouldn't have tried to stop it. You should have told him."

"Possibly," Mr. Wicks said, and sipped delicately at his tea. "However, when it comes to my fellow man, I've learned, my dear, always to tread on eggshells. Now, there is more to tell you, much more. The current earl is an honorable man from what I've learned about him. I've heard he's also a trusted friend, a brave soldier, intelligent and loyal, but he is no longer an army man. He has new responsibilities, new expectations, new modes of behavior required of a gentleman of his class. Perhaps he is still a man to admire, a man to trust. However, it doesn't matter now because even if he were so inclined, there is now nothing he can do about it. As I said, there is more." He coughed lightly into his hand, then raised his head and smiled widely at her. "Allow me to congratulate you, ma'am. You are now an heiress."

CHASE PARK
DECEMBER 1813

Marcus pulled Stanley to a halt, dismounted quickly and tossed the reins to Lambkin, his favorite stable lad, who worshipped the ground Stanley trod his hooves upon. "Rub him down well, Lambkin. I've tested his mettle today. He's blowing hard."

"Aye, milord," Lambkin said, already patting Stanley's nose and crooning unrecognizable sounds and words to the stallion. "Aye, my handsome beast, ye've given 'is lordship a fine ride, 'aven't ye?"

Marcus smiled and left the stable. It was a warm day, the sun bright overhead, and here it was the middle of December. There was much work for him to do, but he'd seen the sun shining into his bedchamber and known the work could wait, for being England, being Yorkshire, the beautiful weather wouldn't. He'd said as much to Spears, who had merely nodded and said, "I have laid out your riding clothes, my lord. The tan riding breeches, I believe, would be most stylish this morning. And the blue superfine jacket. Your Hessians are more discerning of your facial features than that mirror."

"How did you know I would go riding?" Marcus shrugged into his dressing gown, a relic of his winters in Portugal, the elbows so shiny with wear that any day now the material would split.

Spears merely smiled and said, "I have already ordered your bath, my lord. Would you like me to shave you?"

"You ask me that every morning and the answer is still no, Spears. I refuse to become so lazy that I cannot even wield my own razor."

"Very well, sir, I have sharpened it for you, as usual. I found with your late uncle—he wouldn't allow me to shave him either—that when finally he hit his cups with too much vigor, he was blessedly thankful that I was here to wield the razor for him."

"Thank you for telling me. I will, as my uncle did, wait for the overindulgence before I give over my throat for the razor. Incidentally, Spears, I heard you singing a song— I thought at first it was in my sleep, I was just on the edge of awakening, you know. I don't believe I've heard it before."

"It's a clever ditty indeed, my lord." Spears smiled, then sang out in a rich baritone:

"Napoleon gave us thirty days
To bag our men and go away
But he misjudged the soldiers' guns
And now he gives us thirty-one."

Marcus grunted. "Your voice is better than the song, Spears. At least it rhymes. Napoleon gave us thirty days when?"

"To leave Berlin, my lord. Schwarzenberg had commanded Bernadotte to protect the city, but as you know, Bernadotte gave orders to abandon Berlin and would have if his subordinate Bulow hadn't talked him out of it."

"Ah, but it isn't all that accurate, Spears. There was nothing about thirty or thirty-one days. Well, perhaps there were a few jests about it, but it wasn't a fact."

"It is lyrical license, my lord, surely the prerogative of a ditty writer. I understand this ditty writer is quite the popular man in the army ranks. The men are singing his little trifles as they march along."

Marcus was smiling, finding himself singing the silly little song when Sampson opened the great doors to Chase Park and bowed him inside. Marcus was at last used to the deference and the endless services heaped upon him by his staff. He thanked Sampson, as was his wont, and said, "I suppose Crittaker is awaiting me in the estate room, a woeful look on his hangdog's face and a pile of papers for me to review."

"Yes, my lord, I believe that is quite accurate a description. I heard him shout some twenty minutes ago, shortly after I delivered your lordship's mail to him. I immediately went into the estate room with the repellent thought that he had succumbed to an apolaustic outburst, which, I might add, would have been vastly inappropriate, but he hadn't. It is evidently a missive of grave importance, my lord, and he had inadvertently, in his shock and surprise, given verbal vent to his, er, feelings."

"What the devil does apolaustic mean?"

"It refers to the giving of enjoyment or pleasure. It is an act of self-indulgence, my lord, something to be avoided unless one is lucky enough to so indulge."

"You're quite right, Sampson, I should have boxed his ears had he done it in my presence."

"Rightfully so, my lord."

Marcus, now thoroughly intrigued, didn't change, but rather strode directly to his estate room, flung open the door and said, "Tell me, Crittaker, with no tumult or stewing, exactly what news made you vent your, er, feelings."

Mr. Crittaker said nothing, merely handed Marcus a single sheet of paper.

Marcus read and read again, sucked in his breath and said, "My God! This is quite beyond anything I could ever have imagined. Do feel free to indulge in another fit of apolaustic behavior, Crittaker."

"Apolaustic, my lord?"

"You heard me, man. Surely you know the meaning of apolaustic. You are my secretary, after all, and it's your duty to be up on all meanings of all words I may use."

Crittaker was silent as the clock on the mantel, broken now for over seventy-five years. He looked to be in agony.

"It appears that the Duchess will be coming to us short-ly," Marcus said, looking through the narrow windows that gave onto the winter-barren east lawn. "That is, she will be coming to us for at least a short time. She doesn't say that she will remain. Though she will remain, if she isn't com-pletely stupid. I suppose I will see to it that she does remain. She is a woman. I am a man. She will obey me for I am the earl and her cousin and it is her duty to do as I tell her."

"Mr. Spears believes it will be a close call, my lord."

Marcus rolled his eyes. It seemed that his butler, his sec-retary, and his valet had formed a coalition. "The Duchess is proud, I agree, but she isn't stupid, at least I trust not, in this particular instance."

"Spears said that pride many times exonerates a greater stupidity than a blank brain."

Marcus carefully folded the letter, slipped it into his pocket, and took himself upstairs to change his clothes. Well, Duchess, he thought to himself, at last you will have to come to me. It wasn't until later that he reread the letter once more and focused on the final sentence. "Mr. Wicks wishes to see you on Thursday following my arrival. You doubtless already know this."

What the devil did his uncle's London solicitor want? Was there more afoot than he knew? But what?

She arrived at Chase Park one week before Christmas. The deadline had been the first of January 1814, but she had decided to have it over and done with. Badger stood beside her on the great front steps holding one small valise for her, and she was in the process of lifting her gloved hand to knock on the evil-looking lion's head knocker that had quite terrified her as a child, but of course, she'd never let on that it had.

Before her hand descended the door was opened and she was faced with a beaming Sampson.

"Miss Duchess! Ah, Lady Duchess! What a pleasure, a wonderful event, do come in, yes, do come in. Who is this person?"

"This is Badger. He is my—valet."

"Ah, well, no matter, doubtless his lordship will sort out everything to your satisfaction. He is awaiting you in his library. Do come with me, Lady Duchess. Your, er, valet—"

"My name is Erasmus Badger, sir."

"Ah, yes, Mr. Badger, I will take you upstairs myself to introduce you to Mr. Spears, his lordship's valet. Perhaps the three of us can come together later and discuss, er, things."

Badger looked at the Duchess, but she merely smiled that cool, aloof smile of hers. "Go along with Sampson. His lordship can't very well slit my throat in his library."

She walked quietly into the huge intimidating room. Marcus stood behind his desk. He didn't move when he saw her standing in the doorway, merely said, "You came."

She nodded. "I had to. I wrote you that."

"Yes, to be a Wyndham of Wyndham, you had to show your face here before January 1, 1814. But that makes no sense. You are either legitimate or you're not. You are not without sense, Duchess. There is more, isn't there?"

She wouldn't tell him the rest of it, tell him the real reason she was here. She couldn't serve him such a blow. She would let Mr. Wicks do it. She simply raised her chin, saying nothing.

Marcus grunted, threw down the sheaf of papers in his right hand, and came around the massive desk. "Congratulations on the marriage of your father and your mother."

"Thank you. I only wish I had known, just a clue, perhaps before—"

"Well, now you do and you're home where you belong. It's nearly Christmas. I plan to take the Twins and Spears out to cut a Yule log for the drawing room. Would you care to accompany us?"

He saw, perhaps for the first time since he'd known her, a leap of something very excited in her blue eyes, then it was gone, and she was nodding coolly, saying, "Thank you, Marcus. You are very kind. I apologize for being here, in advance, truly, I'm sorry if my now being legitimate is distressful to you."

He said, his voice harsh, "Nonsense, Chase Park is now your home, just as it is mine. If you hadn't been such a stubborn twit, you would have been living here for the past six months instead of—" He broke off, shook his head, then, as if he couldn't help himself, he said, "How did you earn money to keep that damned snug little cottage? And what about that very nice crystal?"

"When would you like to cut that Yule log?"

"In an hour," he said, looking at her white neck, his fingers clenching and unclenching. This gown was stylish, a pale cream muslin, the neckline not to her chin, but lower, just giving a hint of her bosom, which looked quite enticing to him. "Dress warmly and wear stout boots. Do you have warm clothes and stout boots?"

"No, I fancy I will have to wear only my shift and a pair of slippers. I have sufficient clothing, Marcus. Don't worry. You aren't my guardian. Also, I pray you won't forget that you have only five years on me. In short, cousin Marcus, we are both quite young and indeed, too young to beset each other."

"What the hell does that mean? You're still eighteen. I will very likely be appointed your guardian—despite my meager number of years—so I advise you, Duchess, not to raise the level of my ire any further."

"Your ire, Marcus, is of no concern to me. I'm here because I must be here. There is nothing more to it. And I now am nineteen."

"And will you deign to remain?"

She gave him a small smile, an infuriating small smile, turned, and left the library. She didn't close the door. He heard Mrs. Emory saying with surely too-great exuberance, "Hello, Duchess, and welcome! Oh, excuse me, miss, it's Lady Duchess now. Let me take you to your room. The earl has assigned you the Princess Mary Chamber, and very lovely it is, you remember, of course."

"Of course," the Duchess said. "I remember it quite well. It is kind of his lordship to select such a superior accommodation for me."

5

THERE WAS SOMETHING to be said for a Christmas at home in the bosom of one's family, Marcus thought, as he sipped the warm nutmeg-tart mulled wine, felt the heat from the burning Yule log upon his face. He turned then to look at his assembled family. His last Christmas had been spent around a campfire with fifty of his men, shivering in the Galician hills, wondering if the new year would bring them into battle and into death.

He realized that he hadn't bought a gift for the Duchess, not that she deserved it. Well, he had time, still five days until Christmas. Tomorrow, his uncle's solicitor from London would arrive. He frowned, wondering what else his uncle could have done. Legitimizing the Duchess was a fine thing, he had no argument with that, though he realized quickly that Aunt Gweneth now looked at her a good deal differently. He couldn't imagine why she would disapprove of the newly bona fide lady and approve of the bastard. Odd, that.

Aunt Gweneth said, "Duchess, Marcus told us that you were living in Smarden, in Pipwell Cottage, with a man. Really, my dear, such a thing is most peculiar and leaves your reputation open to slurs, given your unfortunate antecedents."

The Duchess smiled a very small but pleasant smile, those long narrow hands of hers quiet in her lap. "I have never believed my antecedents to be unfortunate, ma'am, merely difficult in this tender society."

"Nonetheless, you have had a man living with you."

60

"Yes, his name is Badger, and he was my butler and my chef. He's a remarkable man. Actually he still is my, er, valet."

"Still, it is not at all what one would expect from a lady," Aunt Gweneth said, but Marcus, horrified at how prissy and prudish she sounded, and realizing that he must have sounded exactly the same way, interrupted swiftly, saying, "It makes no more difference, Aunt. The Duchess is here now. Nothing more need be said about it."

"But that man accompanied her here."

"Yes," the Duchess said calmly, then remained quiet, sipping at her mulled wine. "Perhaps Cook should speak to Badger, for his mulled wine is the best I have ever tasted. He has secret ingredients he won't tell anyone about. I remember my mother used to plead with him, telling him that she could sell the recipe and make us all rich. He laughed and nodded, but refused to tell her."

"I can vouch for Badger's culinary expertise, Aunt Gweneth."

"Dear Marcus, the man lived with the mother and then with the daughter. He speaks the most beautiful English. Surely you cannot allow a man with such pretensions to influence the household. Why he apes his betters, and it isn't the done thing, Marcus. And she says he's still her valet? Her *valet*? That is utterly preposterous, unbelievable, and you, as the head of the family, surely can't allow it to continue. I don't want to see the Wyndham name swimming into any more disrepute than it already swims."

A very dark eyebrow went up a good inch. "Our name is in disrepute? Why is this? Perhaps you believe, ma'am, that I am the cause of this so-called disrepute since I am merely the son of the second son?"

"Don't be a nodcock, boy, it doesn't suit you. No, certainly not. The disrepute we are currently experiencing is the Duchess's being made legitimate. Add a man valeting a girl and the result is obvious to predict."

"Ah, well, Aunt," Marcus said, "I beg you to think, rather, that my uncle and the Duchess's father, came to see what was right and did it. As for this valeting business—"

The Duchess interrupted him in an unruffled, utterly serene voice. "It is done, dear ma'am, and I fear there is no going back now. I trust the disrepute will die down in time. But this does disturb me. Do you honestly believe Badger's excellent English to be pernicious?"

"No, she doesn't," Marcus said, giving Aunt Gweneth a look that shut her mouth quickly. "Particularly when Spears rivals him in elocution and delivery."

"Marcus, that is all well and good, but you cannot allow him to remain here as her valet."

"Valet," Antonia said, lifting her head from her current novel, a hideously ill-written story of a constantly weeping Medieval heroine and a hero who cleaved everyone he met in half with his magic sword. "He is your valet, Duchess? How very interesting. Does he arrange your hair? Does he draw your bath? Will you introduce him to me tomorrow?"

"If you like, Antonia."

"Badger will remain," Marcus said firmly. "In exactly what capacity I have yet to determine."

"I believe," the Duchess said quietly, "that it will be up to me to determine Badger's position."

"Hardly," Marcus said. "You may now live here at Chase Park, but you are not the master. Directing many servants on a vast estate is quite different from directing one servant in a cottage. However, I will discuss it with you, as well as with Badger. Incidentally, Duchess, I am pleased you came to reason and are now making Chase Park your home. Do you care to tell me why you changed your mind?"

The Duchess evidently didn't care to tell him anything. Her expression didn't change. Her white hands remained utterly still in her lap. Then she raised one hand to set her mulled wine on the low table beside her. She was so bloody graceful, he thought, watching her. Every movement she made was smooth and elegant. He suddenly saw her in his mind's eye on her knees, bent over, gardening, the smudges of dirt on her face, tendrils of hair on her damp forehead. She'd still looked utterly composed and lovely. It was always the same with her. He wondered then if she felt anything deeply, if she ever shouted or cried or sulked, or if the elegant serenity, the utter calm, was all there was to her, that it was her in fact.

Fanny looked longingly at a tray of lemon-seed cakes, caught Aunt Gweneth's frown, and turned miserably away.

The Duchess said, "Would you like an apple, Fanny? They're quite delicious. I just finished one myself."

Fanny shrugged, then caught the apple Marcus tossed to her. She rubbed it on her sleeve, earning her a disapproving look from Aunt Gweneth. Marcus smiled at the Duchess, but she didn't regard him.

"The hour grows late," Aunt Gweneth said some minutes later. "I think it is time for you girls to go to bed."

"All right," Antonia said, closed her book and yawned deeply. She said to the Duchess, "You're our half-sister. Marcus told us all about it. You're no longer our cousin from Holland."

"That's right. After your dear mother died, our father married my mother. He made me legitimate."

"You were a bastard," Fanny said, no guile showing on her face or sounding in her voice. "How very odd. I remember Antonia and I used to argue whether you were from Italy or Holland. It was difficult because we had never heard you speak either language."

"Yes, I was a bastard, until last May to be exact."

"Really, my dear, you needn't blare it so loudly," Aunt Gweneth said. "It would make people believe that you weren't ashamed of your unfortunate birth."

"Since I had no say whatsoever in my birth, ma'am, why should I ever feel shame about it?"

"Still—" Aunt Gweneth said, but was interrupted by Antonia, who said, "Now you will be able to find a husband. You won't have to pretend anymore that you're not a real lady."

"Just imagine," Fanny said as she chewed on her apple. "You were a love child. How very romantic."

"Bosh," Antonia said. "You're stupid, Fanny. Now, Duchess, you won't have to stay here because now you're all right and tight and legal. You won't have to stay here for Marcus to order you about."

"I, order you about, Antonia? Come, if I were such a tyrant, would I allow you to read that nauseating pap that is currently sitting in your lap?"

"Well, perhaps not," Antonia said, grinning at her cousin, "but still, Marcus, your rules do seem to multiply by the day. It must be that you and Aunt Gweneth make up new ones after Fanny and I have gone to bed. But Fanny and I will continue to bear with you. You haven't been the earl all that long and we quite understand that you must fit your own boots into it. Now, then, Duchess, will you go to London?"

"It's possible. Perhaps I shall go to London after Boxing Day. Why not?"

"Will Marcus give you money?" Fanny asked, looking still at the lemon-seed cakes, the chewed-down apple core in her hand. "London is ever so expensive, you know."

"We will see," Marcus said, his voice testy as hell. "Now, off to bed with you girls. No, Aunt Gweneth and I won't sit here and devise new despotic rules to test your fortitude. Aunt Gweneth, you may excuse yourself as well. Duchess, please remain for a moment longer, if you will."

A short while later, she looked at him from a goodly distance, saying nothing, merely standing behind a winged chair, one graceful hand smoothing rhythmically over the soft brocade as if it were Esmee beneath her hand. Odd, but even Esmee, the most independent of felines, lay quietly beneath the Duchess's hand when she chanced to pet her.

There was a slight flush on her cheeks from the warmth of the fire. "Yes, Marcus? You wished to say something to me?"

"Why did you say you wanted to go to London?"

"I said perhaps I would go. After Boxing Day."

"Do you need money to allow you to go?"

"No, I daresay that I won't need a sou."

"So, I had allowed myself to believe that you came here because your finances were strained beyond their limits. But it isn't so, is it? Not if you can afford to keep yourself in London. If keep yourself is indeed what you would be doing."

"Badger will be with me, naturally."

"You won't go. I forbid it. You will wait to go to London when I do, which will be in late March. Aunt Gweneth will accompany us and will provide you chaperonage. You will have your bloody Season. If you find a gentleman I deem appropriate, or if I discover a gentleman for you whom I deem suitable, why then I will provide you a dowry and you can marry."

"Nonsense, Marcus. Pray cease your outflow of orders. Tyranny doesn't become you."

"It is hardly nonsense and I'm not a bloody tyrant, no matter what the Twins say. There are many so-called gentlemen in London eager to sully a lady's reputation or take liberties with her person. You have no idea of how to go along. You're young and green. You would quickly make a fool of yourself. I won't allow that to happen. You're now a Wyndham, after all. You will go to London with me and I will point out all the scoundrels to you."

She said mildly, "If you aren't careful, Marcus, every female of your acquaintance will convey you bound and gagged to the Quakers in Bristol. They are the most strict of their sect, it is said. It is said they never see themselves unclothed, always dressing and undressing with their eyes straight ahead and bathing in the same way. I cannot imagine how it is done. Such modesty must require a great deal of practice and resolution. Truly, Marcus, you must mean well, but do not concern yourself with me."

"I have already set my guardianship of you into motion. It shouldn't take long to finalize."

"I don't think so," she said, then infuriated him by smiling into the fire, calm and unruffled as ever.

"You have no say in it, damn you!"

"Oh, I daresay that I shall have more say than you can begin to imagine."

"How?"

She remained silent.

"How did you support yourself? There was a man, wasn't there? There's a man awaiting you in London, isn't there? Why did you come back here if your plan was simply to leave again? Did your father make it a stipulation of your legitimacy?"

"That is an abundance of questions, Marcus. I will address the first. You seem to believe that ladies are singularly incompetent. Cannot you imagine that one of us could support herself through honest means?"

"Not you. You're a lady. You were raised to be a lady, to be a man's wife, nothing more. It isn't that you are incompetent, no, certainly not, it is just that you were raised to do nothing, except—" He stalled, seeing the endless hole beneath his feet he'd so eagerly dug for himself.

She said coolly, kindness reeking in her soft voice, "Decorate a gentleman's arm, perhaps?"

"Yes, and bear his children and see that his home is comfortable and well run. Perhaps keep flower beds if you wished."

"All that doesn't require some proficiency, some skill?"

"Not the kind of skill that would bring in groats. And yet, you seem to—" He stalled again. His words sounded utterly pompous and condescending. He sounded like an ass, but he wouldn't take the words back. Perhaps he'd even get a rise out of her this time. Maybe even make her raise her voice just a bit. That thought made his eyes glitter. But it was not to be.

"Marcus, what do you do to earn groats?"

He stared at her, then said more calmly than he imagined possible, "I was a major in the army. I earned money."

"And now that you are no longer in the army?"

He ground his teeth, there was no keeping it from her and he didn't care.

"Is there a rich lady keeping you in style? Obviously a nobleman can't earn groats, why his blood would quickly turn from blue to black."

"There are many responsibilities I have now, as you well know. I have to oversee all the properties; I am caretaker to more houses than you even know about; I am responsible for every man, woman, and child who works on all estates owned by the Wyndhams, I—"

"In short, you inherited everything."

"You know very well the title means little to me, but I will fulfill my duties as I must."

"Marcus, how old are you?"

"You know very well that I am twenty-four."

"So very young to be as you are," she said, then had the gall to shrug.

"And just how is that? Concerned for your well-being? Knowing that I am the one responsible for this damned family, as I said? Ah, don't try to turn this to me, Duchess. As I was saying, all your, er, abilities don't bring in groats. There was no inheritance to make you independent. Yet you had enough to rent that damned cottage, to—" He stopped on purpose this time, his eyes glittering anew. Perhaps now he'd see a fist again. Wouldn't that be something?

She had the further gall to shrug again. She said not another single word, and he waited, hoping, but there was not even a glint of anger in her cool blue eyes.

He gave up, saying, "Your Mr. Wicks will be here tomorrow. What do you say about that?"

"I imagine that Mr. Wicks will wish to speak to both of us. Do you plan to be here?"

He would have liked to tell her he was going to Edinburgh, but he didn't. "I'll be here. Now, I'm going to bed. I will see you at breakfast."

"Good night, Marcus. Sleep well."

He grunted. She stood silently, watching him stride out of the magnificent drawing room, over three ancient and rich Turkey carpets, past some furnishings that dated back to before Henry VIII. She paused a moment before leaving the Green Cube Room and looked up. All the beams in the vast ceiling were intricately carved, showing the family coat of arms in too many places as well as a series of interesting geometric patterns that struck her as designs for their own sakes. In between the beams various scenes were painted, beginning with Medieval tableaus and moving up well into the sixteenth century. There were beautifully painted figures of men and women, the colors still rich and vibrant even after so many years, the expressions on their faces still clear as well. Where the beams met the top of the wall, there were an abundance of smiling cherubs, too many, all pink and white, gazing with dewy Classical eyes upon warriors with swords and shields, painted like a foot-wide swatch of mural at the top of the walls. This last addition had been made only in the last century by an earl of Chase with more guineas than discrimination. The former older scenes were much better executed, the men and women depicted in a far more realistic manner, down to the lute strings of a Medieval young man playing for the lady before him.

The Duchess looked back down into the fire. What would Marcus have to say to her after Mr. Wicks's visit? She remembered him as such a wild young man, forever leading Charlie and Mark into the most appalling mischief. But then he'd bought a commission in the army and had been out of her life for five years. She wondered if he would still be as wild as a winter storm instead of the moralistic bore he'd become upon gaining his coronet if he were still in the army. He'd been the devil's own son, that's what her father had called him with a good deal of fondness, perhaps even respect. At least before Charlie and Mark had died there'd been fondness. She wondered what her father would call him now.

Whyever did he feel it his duty to prose on and on instead of laugh and view his new station in life with optimism and pleasure rather than grimness and a dour sense of duty? She wondered what he was doing now—hopefully he was taking deep breaths—for he'd left nearly on the verge of apoplexy.

Actually, Marcus was only on the verge of profound brooding. He allowed Spears to assist him out of his coat, which he normally didn't do. He wasn't helpless, for God's sake. He remembered his batman, Connally, who'd spat on the floor of the tent, staring at his coat even as he held it for Marcus to shrug on, as if it were a snake to bite him. Poor Connally had been shot, going down beneath his horse, crushed to death. Marcus said now under his breath, "Bloody girl. She'll end up strangled if she doesn't change her ways, that or fall into the arms of a scoundrel."

"May I ask what ways, my lord?"

"Your ears are a great deal too sharp, Spears. All right, the Duchess has secrets. She breeds them, she holds them tightly to her bosom. She won't tell me the truth about how she kept that damnable cottage, how she paid Badger, how she bought food, how she—"

"I quite understand, my lord."

"She just stands there, looking all calm and unruffled, and giving one of those stingy little smiles of hers and doesn't say anything. I can't even make her angry and the good Lord knows I pushed and baited and mocked. I did my damndest. Why won't she tell me anything?"

Marcus pulled away from Spears's ministering hands to pull loose his cravat and fling it onto the massive bed. "She has the damnable gall to inform me that she intends to leave for London on Boxing Day. I set her aright on that, I tell you."

"May I ask what your lordship set aright?"

"I told her I would soon be her guardian. She will do what I tell her to until she's twenty-one. If I can push it through, she will be under my control until she's twenty-five." Marcus stopped, frowned down at his left boot that was proving recalcitrant.

"Sit down, my lord, and allow me to remove it."

Marcus sat, saying, "Even if I managed to be her guardian until she was twenty-five, she would probably marry the first man to ask just to spite me. But she would never raise her voice, no matter what I did, Spears, oh no, she wouldn't deign to do that. That is doubtless beyond the scope of her emotional repertoire. No, she would just look at me like I was a seed in her garden, an unwanted seed that would sprout a weed."

"Surely not that sort of seed, my lord. You are, after all, the earl of Chase. Perhaps you would be contemplated a bulb, not a seed."

"Or maybe even a worm."

"All things are possible, my lord."

"She's a damned twit. Are you mocking me, Spears?"

"Certainly not, my lord. The very thought offends deeply. Your other boot, my lord."

Marcus stuck out his other foot, still mulling and brooding and sprinkling all of it with an occasional curse. "This bloody Mr. Wicks who's coming on the morrow, what the hell does he want? What's going on?"

"I daresay we will know soon now, my lord. I recommend, my lord, that you allow Mr. Badger to remain at Chase Park. He's a man of excellent skills and his brain is of the first order."

"He was her damned chef."

"Yes, I will speak to Mrs. Gooseberry. Perhaps she can be, er, cozied into allowing Mr. Badger to prepare an occasional meal for the family."

"You miss the point, Spears. She was living with Badger, alone, together. It isn't done. She's barely nineteen years old."

"Your lordship surely realizes that Mr. Badger could be her father. He loves her deeply, just as a father ought to love his offspring. He would never harm her. He would protect her with his life."

So would I, Marcus thought, then cursed. He was now standing naked in front of a blazing fire, his hands outstretched to the flames.

"Would you care for a nightshirt tonight, my lord? I understand from Biddle, the second footman who has lived here his entire life, indeed, whose family has lived here for six generations, that tonight will bring frigid temperatures."

"No," Marcus said as he scratched his side. "No nightshirt. The bloody things belong on women, not on men. What do you think this Wicks fellow wants, Spears?"

"I couldn't say, my lord. However, if you would care to get into bed, you could spend some time thinking about the possibilities. You would be warm rather than cold."

Marcus said nothing, merely climbed into the huge bed, sinking down instantly into the cocoon of warmth. Spears had used a warming pan and Marcus sighed with pleasure. It was quite unlike lying between the two thin blankets on the floor of his tent in Portugal.

"Is there anything else your lordship requires?"

"Humm? Oh no, thank you, Spears. Oh, have you seen Esmee?"

"Esmee, the last time I came into rather close contact with her, my lord, was stretched on her belly in front of this fireplace, sleeping quite soundly."

"Ouch! Here she is, Spears. After you warmed the sheets, she must have decided this was softer than the damned floor. It's disconcerting when she wraps herself around my belly."

"She's a very affectionate feline, my lord."

Marcus grunted at that and Spears appreciated his lordship's obvious verbal restraint.

"Sleep well, my lord. We will see this Mr. Wicks soon enough."

Mr. Wicks arrived the following morning at eleven o'clock. Marcus watched the old gentleman step gingerly down from the carriage. He couldn't make out his features for he was swathed in a huge muffler, a fur hat with ear flaps, and at least three scarves, all intertwined over his greatcoat, an immensely thick wool affair that nearly dragged the ground.

He walked back into his library, guessing it would take Mr. Wicks at least a half an hour to be divested of his outer garments.

When Sampson gently knocked on the door and entered quietly, Marcus merely turned and raised a black brow at him.

"Mr. Wicks requests that the Duchess be present, my lord. Actually, he, er, insists she be present."

"He does, does he? Well, I suspected as much, truth be told. Have her fetched, Sampson."

"She is here, my lord, speaking right now with Mr. Wicks. She is assisting him out of all his layers of gear."

"Ah, so kind of her," he said, feeling testy and sounding sarcastic because he didn't know what was going on. Well, actually he did know. Obviously Mr. Wicks had come to inform him of the amount of money his uncle had settled on her. Who cared? He would have settled money on her himself, in any case, as a dowry. He said, "When the Duchess has completed her disrobing of Mr. Wicks, do show them in, Sampson."

It was, in truth, another ten minutes before Mr. Wicks, a scrawny, quite old, rheumy-eyed gentleman, walked into the library, the Duchess at his side. The old man looked around him with great interest. The library was a wealth of history, Marcus thought, feeling a surge of unconscious pride. He looked at the Duchess. There was no expression whatsoever on her face. She looked serene and calm as the damned mistress of the Park, as if Mr. Wicks were the vicar here to discuss an excursion to the lime wells near Bell Busk for the orphans.

But Mr. Wicks was a London solicitor of some renown. He was the man Marcus's uncle had hired to legitimize the Duchess. What more was there other than a monetary settlement? Odd that his uncle had hired an entirely different solicitor to deal with this matter rather than one of the distinguished Messieurs Bradshaw, solicitors for the Wyndhams, father to son, for the past eighty years.

What the devil was going on here?

6

"THIS IS MARCUS Wyndham, the earl of Chase, Mr. Wicks. He is my cousin."

"My lord," Mr. Wicks said, his voice surprisingly vigorous for a gentleman of his advanced years. Marcus also saw the sharp intelligence in the old gentleman's eyes at that moment. He realized that he would be a formidable opponent, no matter what his age. "It is a pleasure to meet you, sir. Er, it perhaps seems strange to you that I must see you as well as Miss Wyndham."

"Actually, now, she is a lady. However, Lady Duchess Wyndham sounds a bit farfetched."

"I agree," she said. "Let us simply retain Miss Wyndham or perhaps even Miss Cochrane."

"No," Marcus said. "No, I won't allow that. You are now a Wyndham and that is what you will be called. I like Lady Duchess."

She gave him a slight smile, looked down at her white hands lying still in her lap. She said nothing more.

Marcus looked away from her to the solicitor. "Perhaps, Mr. Wicks, you would care to be seated near the fire. You can tell us what you must from that vantage."

"Thank you, my lord. The weather is a bit brisk today and I find that the older my bones survive, the thinner they become. Now, let's begin."

Marcus sat beside the Duchess on an exquisite old Queen Anne settee, beautifully sculpted, covered with pale cream and dark blue brocade.

"Now, my lord, you are fully aware that your uncle, the

former earl of Chase, married Mrs. Cochrane and legitimized the child of their union."

"Yes, I approve of his action. However, why wasn't I
informed immediately?"

Mr. Wicks didn't hesitate, but said frankly, "It was my
agreement with your uncle. All was to be finalized before
any of the Wyndham family was informed, including his
youngest brother's wife and her family currently residing
in the Colonies in a place called Baltimore, and, naturally,
your mother. This was to protect Miss Wyndham, er, Lady
Duchess. Surely that is understandable, my lord."

"Yes, certainly," Marcus said, rising quickly and striding
over to the fireplace. "Had I known before the legalities were
completed, I would have posted immediately to Smarden and
strangled her in her bed and thrown her body over the Dover
cliffs. Yes, it makes a great deal of sense to a brigand of my
stamp."

The Duchess cleared her throat. "He's merely jesting,
Mr. Wicks. Unfortunately, after the death of Charlie and
Mark, my father took a dislike to his lordship, because he
was alive and they weren't. Then, of course, all his wife's
babes died. This must have been the reason for his behavior,
not because he didn't believe Marcus honorable, but simply
to rub his nose in it, so to speak. Marcus, it's true. I trust
you will not think of it further."

"Don't you believe it, Duchess. He blamed me for not
being there to save them, that, or die with them. I was close
by, over at the Rothermere Stud, but not close enough. I
saw that as full measure of my perfidy, my lack of honor.
He quite hated me, Duchess."

"Surely you're exaggerating," she said.

"Am I, Mr. Wicks? Did my uncle tell you rather how
fond he was of me? How delighted he was to see me
succeed him?"

"Perhaps it is best if I address that a bit later, my lord.
Now, sir, you must wonder why I requested your presence."

Marcus merely inclined his head, an action that made him look older and strangely, quite forbidding.

"There's no easy way to say this, my lord."

"Then spit it out, Mr. Wicks."

"The former earl left all monies, all properties, all houses, and all possessions not entailed specifically to his successor, namely you, my lord, to his daughter, Josephina Wyndham."

There was utter silence. Marcus stared at her for a long moment, then said in a too calm voice, "Josephina? That is quite the ugliest name I have ever heard. You must thank me every night in your prayers that I renamed you Duchess."

Mr. Wicks looked at sea, and twitched his papers about nervously. "Did you understand what I said, my lord?"

"Yes, certainly, sir. You have just told me that I am a pauper. A pauper living in this great mansion, but a pauper nonetheless. I have been stripped of everything. If he had chosen to beggar his family in a more efficacious manner, why, I couldn't begin to imagine what it would be. You see, Duchess, I wasn't at all mistaken about my uncle's true feelings for me. Did he bother seeing to his own daughters, Antonia and Fanny?"

"Yes, my lord. He left each of them ten thousand pounds. But that was in his previous will. That will still stands, including all the bequests to servants, other retainers, and the remaining Wyndham relatives."

"So I was the butt of his vengeance—I, his heir."

"Not entirely, my lord. It is just that now, Lady Josephina is, well—"

"Don't refer to her by that repellent name. She owns everything except for Chase Park, I believe. Is there anything else entailed to me, Mr. Wicks?"

"Yes, my lord. The London house on Putnam Place is yours, rather it is yours for your lifetime."

"I quite understand. Aught else?"

"There is a hunting box in Cornwall that is entailed, near

St. Ives, I believe, and some two thousand acres of rich farmland. There is nothing else, my lord. I'm sorry."

"There is not a single bloody sou for the upkeep of this monstrosity of a house?"

Mr. Wicks said slowly, "Your uncle, the former earl, feared that you would simply consign him to the devil if he left you nothing to keep up the entailed properties. Thus, he has left me the trustee for all the Wyndham properties, monies, houses, possessions. I am also Lady Duchess's trustee and guardian until she reaches her majority. When she reaches the age of twenty-one, she is to act in joint trusteeship with me to oversee all the entailed Wyndham holdings. The incoming principle from all the Wyndham holdings is excellent and continues to grow each year. There are properties in Devon, Sussex, and Oxfordshire. However, my lord, the monies are not within your discretion."

Marcus said nothing. Indeed, he looked rather bored, dismissing both them and the killing blow struck him by his uncle, long-dead, no longer here to gain his vengeance.

He crossed his arms over his chest and leaned a negligent shoulder against the mantel. He laughed then, a very soft, bitter laugh. "You were wrong, Duchess. Will you now admit that he hated me? Will you admit that this is no simple nose-rubbing? The bastard—no insult intended to you, Duchess—the bloody damned bastard hated so much that I would succeed him that he has turned me into a poor relation, dependent on Mr. Wicks here for the very bread I eat, for any repairs I deem necessary to make, for the payment of all our servants. And doubtless dependent on you, his bastard, for any crumbs you would wish to throw my way, all this because of his hatred for me. He has crushed the hopes of his own progeny and future Wyndham generations."

Mr. Wicks looked unutterably depressed. "Let me say, my lord, that I argued vigorously with your uncle, but he wouldn't be swayed. He did hold you in remarkable dislike,

I will admit that. However, he did agree to leave you a, er, quarterly allowance."

Marcus looked primed for violence. "No wonder you all but laughed at me last night, Duchess, with me going on and on about becoming your guardian, providing you a dowry, protecting you as I now must protect my family. Now you have everything. Now you no longer need a man to see to your needs. Yes, you must have found all my prosings quite entertaining."

"No, I did not. You must allow me to explain, Marcus."

To her surprise, he managed to say with the utmost calm, "I don't think so, Duchess. Well, I believe that I will consider this. Good day to you, Mr. Wicks."

"But, my lord, there is more. You must stay! You must listen to me!"

"Even more than this? I think not, Mr. Wicks. I think I am quite up to my craw with your revelations." He nodded to her, then strode from the room, not looking back.

Mr. Wicks shook his head. "It wasn't an honorable thing your father did, my dear. Certainly making you legitimate was well done of him. Providing you a substantial dowry would have been proper, but this—leaving you everything and leaving his lordship an allowance, nothing more, leaving him the supplicant for any funds he will need—it is abominable."

She was staring, unseeing, at the toes of her dark blue slippers that peeped from beneath her gown. "You didn't tell me all of it, Mr. Wicks. You gave me no hint of what my father had done. You simply told me that he had left me quite a rich young lady, nothing more. What he has done is reprehensible. I won't allow it. I won't be a party to it." She looked at him full in the face now and her look was fierce. "Listen to me, sir. I fully intend to undo all that he did. Marcus doesn't deserve to be served such a turn. I refuse to allow him to be beggared. The nerve of my father blaming Marcus simply because he wasn't there, possibly to drown along with his cousins.

"You and I controlling his purse strings? You and I giving the earl of Chase an allowance? No, it is hideous. I will see it undone immediately."

She rose and began pacing. He'd never seen her so animated before. She turned suddenly and said in a deep commanding voice, "See to it, Mr. Wicks. You can leave me something, but all the monies, all the other houses and properties, any and all holdings must be returned to Marcus."

Mr. Wicks said very gently, "I'm sorry, my dear, but I cannot."

"What do you mean you cannot?"

"Your father foresaw that you could possibly react in this manner. He knew you were good-hearted, loyal, if you will, to your cousin. He said that if you refused the complete inheritance and all responsibilities it carried with it, then it would all be turned over to the wife of his youngest brother who died some five years ago, the wife and children living in the Colonies."

She took the sheet of paper from him and read: *Mrs. Wilhelmina Wyndham of Fourteen Spring Street, Baltimore, Maryland.*

"There is quite a large family, I understand. Three children born of the union."

"But I have never heard of this Wilhelmina, who would be my aunt."

Mr. Wicks cleared his throat. "Well, it seems the late earl's youngest brother was what one calls a gamester, a bad penny. He lost everything, including an inheritance from a distant aunt, and his father ordered him gone. He went to the Colonies. There he met Wilhelmina Butts and married her. To be blunt, Grant Wyndham was your father's favorite brother, despite his dispossession by your grandfather. He thought it would be a great joke to bring his rakehell brother's family back here, give them all the money—that is, ma'am, if you refuse to accept the responsibilities he's laid upon you.

"You see that your hands and mine are tied. I will assure you, Duchess, that I would never treat his lordship as a pensioner, despite my issuance of a quarterly allowance for his personal use. I won't treat him like a poor relation. I won't be a tyrant about funds that he needs for maintenance or repairs for the entailed properties or lands. In short, I will consider his pride of the utmost importance."

"You don't know Marcus, Mr. Wicks. No matter your assurances, your kindness and understanding, he won't accept it, ever. Marcus is a very proud man, but he's even more than that, he's perhaps excessively principled and holds himself to the highest standards. He's actually quite magnificent."

Mr. Wicks looked at her oddly, but just for a moment, then said, "Perhaps he won't accept this. But then again, duty is a powerful thing. Does he want to see a vast estate gutted? I hope not. I do fear, however, and I said this to your father, that after I have gone to my heavenly reward, the man who takes my place may consider himself a very powerful being indeed and treat the earl like some sort of indigent charity. I fear that. As I recall, your father merely rubbed his hands together and laughed."

"You have considered this a great deal, Mr. Wicks. Have you found no way out of the mess for Marcus?"

He brightened at that. "Oh yes, indeed, there is a way, yes. Your father, after he laughed, told me what he planned, but you and the earl won't perhaps be inclined to, er, follow through with it."

"And what is that, pray?"

"Your cousin must wed you before eighteen months have passed after your father's death to undo what will come to pass. Indeed, the two of you marrying would cancel out everything I have told his lordship. Your father wanted your blood in future earls of Chase. He said it would help to dilute Marcus's tainted blood."

"Marcus's blood tainted? That is utter nonsense. Do you so quickly forget that I am a bastard?"

"Nonetheless, it is what your father wanted above all things. He wanted your sons to succeed Marcus." Mr. Wicks shrugged. "He felt that if you refused, then he didn't care if the earldom fell into ruin. That's what he said, ma'am, he didn't care. This all happened after your mother's death. He changed, an alarming change. He simply didn't care anymore about anything. I was more than alarmed, but he simply didn't care. I remember he said to me when it was all done, 'Wicks, Bess is gone, my wife, the only woman I ever wanted, is gone. She never came to Chase Park where she always belonged, and she should have, if there'd been any justice. Let my nephew wallow in his own bile, I care not. Let him taste just a small bit of the injustice God meted out to me.' "

She sat perfectly still, saying nothing, not flinching, making no movement of any kind. She'd spoken forcefully, but always with that underlying control. She was, he thought, far too young for such control.

She said finally, her voice as pensive and calm as a dove's song on a midsummer's night, "My father died last January. This means that we must wed by June."

"Yes, that is so. By June sixteenth, to be precise."

"Why didn't you tell Marcus of this—this way out of his difficulties?"

"I tried, but he walked out. He is shocked right now, unable to believe what his uncle has done to him. I will tell him this evening. However, my first concern is with you, my dear. If you have no desire to wed with your cousin, you must tell me now. Thus, it would be an academic exercise. It is entirely your decision."

She rose slowly, every movement she made graceful and pure. She smoothed down her skirt, gently turned the bracelet on her right wrist.

"I lose everything if I don't wed Marcus?"

"More accurately it is if you refuse to comply with the terms of his will. Regardless, you will receive fifty thousand pounds. As I said, my dear, regardless, you are a very rich young lady. But it won't change the earl's dilemma. Rather than you, all the rest will go to these Colonials. They will live here in England if they choose, rich and without a care, and he will have an allowance."

"Marcus is a very poor young man if he and I do not wed by June sixteenth."

"Yes, my dear."

"Like Marcus, Mr. Wicks, I'm a bit overturned. I will see that you are shown to your bedchamber. We observe country hours here. Dinner is at six-thirty. If you would be so kind as to come to the drawing room at six."

She smiled at him, a slight smile, more a shadow of an expression, but nonetheless, Mr. Wicks was drawn to that semblance of a smile, and smiled back at her.

"Until later, Mr. Wicks," she said. "If there is anything you require, please inform Sampson."

"Thank you," he said and watched her walk gracefully from the library. He marveled yet again how a girl so very young could be so very composed and sedate in the face of what she obviously considered to be appalling news. He wondered how fond she was of her cousin. She had certainly defended him, had demanded that her father's infamous instructions be undone. That must denote at least some positive feelings on her part. He wondered further if the present earl of Chase liked the Duchess enough to marry her if she were willing, or if he disliked her so very much to tell her to go to the devil and take all her damned groats with her, or if he simply hated the situation so very much, felt so very humiliated by the complete destruction of his world, that he would tell her to go to the devil despite what he felt for her.

The earl appeared to be a proud young man. From the description given to him by the former earl, Mr. Wicks had initially been given to understand that Marcus Wyndham was a dissolute and disreputable young buck, bordering on malevolent. In short, a man worthy of no consideration whatsoever. He'd realized soon enough that it was spite on the former earl's part, or even a mental sickness brought on by the Duchess's mother's death.

He played again and again in his mind the scene in which he would inform the earl he would have to wed the Duchess to save his hide.

She certainly wasn't an affliction to the eye.

She was, however, born a bastard. Some people felt that nothing could ever change that.

Time would tell.

The earl appeared that evening promptly at six o'clock, dressed in severe black, his cravat simply but elegantly presented, his linen white as the young man's teeth. He was remarkably handsome, Mr. Wicks thought, looking at him objectively. Also, he appeared to have learned a measure of the Duchess's control. There was no hint in his expression, no clue in anything he said to anyone assembled, that everything he was growing used to had gone up in smoke. He was polite, nothing more, but then again, he was the earl of Chase, and wasn't it proper that such a nobleman not be overly confiding or intimate?

Mr. Crittaker was present. Mr. Wicks realized within five minutes that the man was smitten with the Duchess. He tried to hide it, but there was such sloppy emotion in his brown eyes that Mr. Wicks wanted to kick him or shake him, or both. He wondered if the earl was aware of his secretary's affliction.

Dinner passed smoothly. Lady Gweneth Wyndham, the late earl's older sister, was the hostess, and was passing gracious even to a mere solicitor. She did say, however, during a course that included potted pigeons flavored too strongly with nutmeg and roast lamb with white beans seasoned with too much garlic, "Marcus, you really must do something about that blasted Esmee."

Marcus looked up, a black eyebrow raised. "Excuse me, ma'am?"

"Your cat, Marcus. Mrs. Gooseberry said she stole a huge

slab of broiled lamb. That is why, she said, that there were more white beans than necessary in this particular dish."

"Esmee has always been remarkably agile," Marcus said. "I assume she escaped with her booty?"

"Oh yes, leaving Mrs. Gooseberry to holler and drive Sampson to the brink of overset nerves. He doesn't like to hear anyone hollering, Marcus."

"It's true. Perhaps it is time for Badger to make his way to the kitchen. He's a remarkable cook."

"He makes an excellent roasted buttock of beef," the Duchess said, looking at her fork that held some overcooked white beans. "The pastry he makes to wrap the roast beef in melts in one's mouth. Also, Badger is a diplomat. Would you like him to prepare a meal for you, Marcus?"

He didn't look at her, saying into his goblet of rich red wine, "I will tell Sampson that Mrs. Gooseberry needs a respite from the cat and all her machinations. Badger may prepare a buttock of beef for us tomorrow night. She may visit her sister in Scarborough."

"She doesn't have a sister in Scarborough," Aunt Gweneth said.

"Then she could benefit from the fresh sea air all by herself," Marcus said, then shrugged, obviously dismissing the problem. He was the earl, the master here, even though he currently believed himself to have been deposed, dispossessed. Mr. Wicks couldn't wait to speak to him. He disliked leaving things, no matter for how short a time, in such a muddle.

The earl didn't dally over port. Instead, joining the family in the huge drawing room, he continued civil. If he was more quiet, more aloof than he usually was, Mr. Wicks didn't know it since he had just met the young man. He said finally, at nine o'clock, "My lord, if you and I could please meet for just a few minutes in your library? It is critical to your situation that you understand everything fully."

Marcus raised an eyebrow, saying very quietly, so that only Mr. Wicks could hear him, "Ah, you mean, sir, that

I had no right to send Mrs. Gooseberry to Scarborough? Must I ask permission from you, sir?"

"No. Please, my lord, come with me now."

Marcus shrugged, said good night to the company, and led the way from the drawing room. He didn't realize the Duchess had come also until he turned to face both her and Mr. Wicks in the library. He said, his voice harsh and raw with fury, "What the hell do you want, Duchess? Get out of here. Go count your bloody groats. Write a letter to the man who was keeping you and tell him to take his congé with Mrs. Gooseberry in Scarborough. Ah, I see, I can no longer afford to raise my voice or tell you what to do, can I? If I offend you, then I will find myself living in a ditch."

"I ask you exercise just a bit of restraint. There is a solution. Please listen to Mr. Wicks, Marcus."

"Damn you, can't you ever—" He broke off, shook himself, and sat down behind his desk, his posture insolent. "All right, Mr. Wicks, what more wondrous news do you have for me? Am I to live in the dower house, or perhaps the tack room?"

7

"NO, MY LORD," Mr. Wicks said, looking earnestly at the young earl. "Please, I beg you to listen to me with an open mind. I ask that you forget your anger, your sense of betrayal, at least for the moment. There is a solution, you see, one that perhaps you will not find onerous or distasteful."

"A solution to this bloody mess? You mean my dear uncle destroys me then gives me a gun to shoot myself out of my misery?"

"No, my lord. It involves marriage."

"Ah, the proverbial heiress, eh? That's an interesting key to stick through the bars of my cage. Well, you mean my uncle didn't forbid my marrying an heiress? How very poorly completed his revenge was, to be sure. So I merely hie myself to London, look over the Cits' daughters currently up for sale, and make my selection. Then I have her, her blessed groats, and my gentleman's allowance. It is a charming thought, Mr. Wicks, so charming a thought that I do believe I will shortly puke."

"Marcus, please listen."

"Duchess, I am very close to smashing that amazingly ugly Chinese vase over there on its damned pretentious pedestal. I understand my uncle was quite fond of it. Yes, I am nearly over the edge. I suggest you take yourself out of here. I wouldn't want to bruise your—"

"Be quiet, Marcus. I can't leave, for this involves me as much as it does you."

She'd at last gotten his full attention. "What the hell does that mean?"

"She means, my lord, that your uncle allowed you a way out. Yes, you are to marry an heiress and he selected her for you. You need go to no trouble, my lord, you may simply wed with the Duchess."

Marcus just stared at him. Mr. Wicks wet his lips, wanting to give more arguments, but the look on the young earl's face held him quiet. There was blood in his eye. Yet he continued silent. The Duchess, however, as was her wont, was more silent. Absolutely unmoving, her eyes calm on his face. The stillness of her was amazing, and disconcerting. It occurred to him in that moment that her very composure, her unshakable calm in light of these extraordinary developments, was far from reassuring the earl. They were infuriating him.

Finally, after more minutes than Mr. Wicks ever wanted to live through again in his life, Marcus said with mocking insolence, "Marry *her?* Marry Josephina?" He looked her up and down, his eyes resting first on her bosom, then lower to the line of her thighs and hips. "Marry someone with such an ugly name? I can't imagine whispering love words to her, whispering *Josephina . . . Josephina.* I daresay I would shrivel like last spring's potatoes, that, or laugh myself silly. Surely it is all a jest, Mr. Wicks. There is a trick here, another blow from my uncle. Come, spit it out."

"No, it is no jest, my lord. There is no more. Could you not simply continue calling her Duchess? Surely you don't find that name ugly, you gave it to her, after all. Listen my lord, you must think carefully about this, there is so very much at stake, you must—"

"It isn't just her damnable ugly name, Mr. Wicks. This same girl has ice water in her veins. Just look at her, sitting there as still as a bloody rock. She isn't even *here.* She's probably thinking about her bloody flowers if she's thinking about anything at all. All us mere human mortals don't interest her. Someone could come up and put a placard around her neck and still she wouldn't stir. Birds could probably roost on her head and she still wouldn't move, wouldn't acknowledge that anything was even different.

"By God, she feels more for the roses in her garden than she ever would feel for another human being. I don't believe so, Mr. Wicks. Not in my bloody lifetime." Marcus stopped, struck a pose, then added, "Actually, I don't think she feels a bloody thing for her roses either. It must be their beauty that draws her, their cold beauty, like velvet to the eye. But, by God, you touch the things and you've got yourself scarred from the thorns. Yes, I can understand that she would find roses of interest, but a man? Can you begin to imagine how distasteful she would find a man, Mr. Wicks? We aren't nature's most splendid specimens. All that hair, our very size, our endowments that—"

"My lord! Please, moderate yourself. I know all of this is something of a shock to you, but you must recognize that it is a solution, it is—"

She'd pressed herself hard against the settee in shock, but it was on the inside, deep on the inside. She didn't allow herself to move, she barely breathed. Ah, but she felt the bitter angry words wash over her and through her and it was too much, it was far too much. And poor Mr. Wicks, trying so vainly to moderate Marcus's rage, an impossibility, she knew that. He was passionate—quick to joy and quick to anger. But still she hadn't imagined that he would say such things. But she should have. He was a strong man, a proud man, and now he was a man pushed too far. She simply looked at him, at the ugly sneer that distorted his well-shaped mouth, at the utter fury that held him in its grip.

Marcus continued, seemingly oblivious of his stunned audience, of the damage he was inflicting, "Can you imagine her in your bed, Mr. Wicks? Do think back, sir. Say, twenty or thirty years. Surely you had lustful thoughts then. Ah, and she is so beautiful, is she not? A glorious creature to behold, not only that face of hers but that body, all tall and slender yet with breasts and hips that tantalize any man unfortunate enough to be looking at her with more than appreciation for, say, a painting in his mind.

"But can you imagine how she would greet you if you were her husband? She would stare at you calmly, so detached that it is difficult to imagine that she really has substance, aye, she would stare as if you were some sort of rodent that really had no business being even in the same room as her. She would try, however, not to look too repelled. Perhaps she would even give one of her stingy smiles—paltry things, those meager smiles of hers—to show that she was completely aware of her upcoming sacrifice. Then she would calmly march to the bed and stretch out there, on her back, unmoving, probably as cold on the outside as she is within. God, it is a repulsive thought, Mr. Wicks."

Mr. Wicks tried, she gave him that. He cleared his throat, but there was desperation on his face, a tremor in his voice. "Listen to me, my lord, I understand this is all such a shock to you, that—"

"I would much prefer a woman to run screaming from me than to just lie there and bear all my repellent men's acts in silence, unmoving, perhaps whimpering like a little martyr, whilst I had my vile way with her."

Mr. Wicks cleared his throat loudly, continuing as if Marcus hadn't spoken. ". . . and thus, my lord, it makes you a bit resentful, a bit intemperate in your speech, perhaps a bit bitter and—"

"Bitter, Mr. Wicks? I assure you, sir, that bitter doesn't even begin to cover what I'm feeling. Resentful? Now there's a bloodless word I haven't ever heard applied to myself."

"My lord, your uncle wanted the Duchess to be your countess. He wanted his grandchildren to have her blood as well as yours. Surely you can understand that."

"Another exaggeration, Mr. Wicks, if not a downright falsehood. My uncle doubtless believed that her exalted blood, in direct flow from his own precious body, would reduce the corruptness of my blood in any possible issue, at least dilute its monstrous effects. Ah, yes, I see from your expression that is exactly what my dear uncle believed."

"Marcus."

It was her voice, quiet and contained, so very soft, as if she were a nanny wanting to bring her recalcitrant charge back in control. "Marcus," she said again when he remained silent. "Please try to understand."

"Ah," he said, interrupting her with a negligent wave of his hand. "I suppose you want to wed with me, Duchess? You are willing to sacrifice yourself on the altar of your father's revenge? Forgive me, but I can't believe that, even though I can see that you're ready to nod. Not to speak and say yes, but nod, perhaps sigh with resignation, which is quite a feat of emotion for you, but I'm not that much of an idiot.

"But wait, perhaps I have underestimated you again. Is it that my dear uncle also served you a bit of a turn, forced your hand, so to speak, Duchess? Perhaps your inheritance is somehow connected to all this? Will you lose all your groats if you don't marry me?"

"No," she said.

He waited, the good Lord knew he waited for her to say more, to say anything to reduce the humiliation of this entire situation, to tell him that she wanted to marry him and it had nothing to do with what her father had done to him, well, it had, but it wasn't important to her. He waited for her to perhaps scream at him for his vicious insults, for spewing out words surely fit only for street harlots, but she just sat there, staring down at her hands, utterly motionless, like a damned marble statue.

"She will gain fifty thousand pounds, regardless of your decision, my lord. However, if either of you refuse to wed the other by June the sixteenth of 1814, then your uncle's family from Baltimore, Maryland, will inherit everything that isn't entailed."

"I see. So the Duchess does have something to lose, quite a lot of something, I would say. What is a paltry fifty thousand pounds compared to being the mistress of an immense and old estate? Yes, wedding with me might be a consideration. Now, if my uncle's family inherits after June sixteenth, after I've gutted the vast Wyndham estate in only a very minor way—just the entailed property— certainly not all that important except for Chase Park, ah, then I'll be obliged to ask Auntie Wyndham for money to make repairs on anything else that needs to be done on my meager share of things?"

"No, my lord. Forgive me if I was unclear. I would be the one."

"May I know the amount of my allowance?"

"I believe it to be in the neighborhood of two hundred pounds a quarter."

"Two hundred pounds!" Marcus threw back his head and laughed. Deep, black laughter that bubbled up, that made his shoulders shake, that made her hurt so much for him that she wanted to scream, to plead with him to trust her, to know that she would make everything all right for him, but of course, she said nothing, she didn't know what to say. She had no practice, no knowledge of what to say.

"Did you hear that, Duchess? Two hundred pounds! This is very close to what I earned per year in the army. Good God, I would be bloody rich, a nabob with a title." And he laughed and laughed until his eyes teared. "All I would have to do is hold out my hand to Mr. Wicks here. That and hold my head up in society, hell, more important, I would have to look at myself in the mirror.

"Perhaps I could stand outside his office, join a line of beggars, and look properly humble and subservient whilst my hand was out, my expression set in modest line, my eyes downcast, so that he would give me my allowance and perhaps not accompany the guineas with a lecture on how not to be wasteful. I would wear those woolen mittens with the fingers cut out so that I could better snag the groats he tosses to me. I wouldn't want to lose any of my grand allowance, now would I?"

"Actually, my lord, your allowance would be an automatic thing, the funds sent directly to you each quarter."

"Ah, so Mr. Crittaker would see my allowance and see to its disposition. Good God, I forgot about Crittaker. Is he still to be my secretary? Surely one as poor as I has no need of a gentleman's secretary. Well, Mr. Wicks?"

"Your uncle was very fond of Mr. Crittaker, my lord. His wages are to be taken care of for so long as he wishes to remain with you here at Chase Park."

"To be taken care of," Marcus repeated slowly. "What an interesting sound that all has. Like your mother was taken care of, Duchess. How you were perhaps taken care of in that cozy little cottage of yours in Smarden. I see then that it is just if I wish to do anything, change anything, that I would find my place in the beggar's line."

She waited, her hands now fisted in her lap. She stared at them, at the white knuckles, and forced them to open, to calm, for if she didn't, her belly would certainly cramp into awful pain and she would be ill.

Then he said, his voice raw from all his laughter, "Well, Duchess, are you willing to carry through with this damnable charade? Will you wed me and become my countess? Are you ready to save me from this endless ignominy? Are you ready to suffer me in your bed and bear countless little boy babies who just might look like me rather than you? Did my uncle leave a provision for that, Mr. Wicks? Any male child that looked like me would be disinherited? God, that's a revolting thought, isn't it? What if they had my temper, my fits of emotion, my hairy body? What if they resembled me rather than you, Duchess, the most soulless creature I've ever met?"

She opened her mouth, yes, now she would tell him, but he suddenly yelled, "No! I don't want to hear your mewling protests, all very calmly stated, I'm sure. Actually, Duchess, I wouldn't wed you if you held the last loaf of bread in all of England and I was starving. What man would want to bed such a cold-blooded bitch, despite her newfound legitimacy, despite her groats? Not I, madam, not I. I'm not as scheming as your father. Actually, Mr. Wicks, I have just decided that the earldom will become extinct upon my death. I wonder if my bloody uncle ever considered that eventuality."

"Your aunt Wilhelmina has two sons, my lord. Were you to die with no issue, the eldest son, Trevor Wyndham, would inherit the earldom."

"Trevor? Good God, that name is as absurd as hers. *Trevor*. Is he effete, Mr. Wicks? Does he mince and waggle his fingers, wear patches on his cheeks? Does he chatter and giggle? Does he pad his calves to make them fill out his trousers? Does he have buckram wadding in his shoulders to make him manly enough? By God, *Trevor!*"

"I truly don't know the character of your aunt Wilhelmina's offspring."

The earl cursed, but there was little heat in it. Then, very slowly, he smiled. "No matter. Let a fop be the next earl. Let him mince about in the House of Lords. Perhaps he's even a pederast. If he is, I shall have a painting commissioned of him and I will place it next to my uncle's. The two of them can visit each other for all eternity. And I, well, I shall have two hundred pounds a quarter. Fancy that—I will be rich. These past ten months of playing a role that didn't at all suit my character will soon be forgotten. Count on it, Mr. Wicks. This precious earldom is already becoming a faint echo in my mind."

He strode then from the library, not looking back, still laughing that raw black laughter.

Mr. Wicks looked down at her, shaking his head. "I had not expected such excess, such vehemence, such a lack of measure."

"Marcus always spoke his mind when he was a boy," she said, her voice dull in its acceptance. "I have just never heard him speak it as an adult. He's gained fluency and tenacity. He's gained more range. It was something I always admired in him. Of course, Marcus always belonged, he was a true Wyndham even though he refuses to accept that he was. He could be angry, outrageous in his behavior or just plain sullen if the mood struck him." Yes, he'd always belonged until her father had done him in.

She saw that Mr. Wicks was quite distressed, shaking his head, mumbling, "I still cannot believe his insults to you. You have never harmed him. Indeed, you wished to set everything aright. He didn't even give you a chance to speak. You would have accepted him, wouldn't you, Duchess?"

"Yes, I would have accepted him, but he was very angry, Mr. Wicks. He wasn't ready to listen to any acceptance even if I'd shouted it in his face."

"I do not like anger, it leads to unfortunate conclusions, usually conclusions not wished by either party." He shook his head. "To insult you as if you weren't a proper lady, as if you were—"

"Still a bastard?"

"You're being purposefully obtuse," Mr. Wicks said sharply, and she saw that he was really quite pained on her behalf. She tried to smile, but it was a pitiful effort.

"What he said to you wasn't what a gentleman would ever utter, it was ugly and utterly unjust—"

She just shook her head, saying nothing, just shaking her head slowly, back and forth. "It doesn't matter," she said finally. "Truly, sir, you are kind to be upset for me, but it doesn't matter."

"But there is so much at stake here. Surely he will see things differently in the morning."

But he didn't.

In the morning, the VIII earl of Chase was gone.

His valet, Spears, was also gone.

WYNDHAM TOWNHOUSE, BERKELEY SQUARE, LONDON
MAY 1814

She smiled as she opened the window wider, leaning out so she could better hear. She saw them then, three soldiers, slightly drunk, singing at the top of their lungs, their arms entwined around each other, probably to keep themselves upright. The ditty was about Napoleon, upon his abdication.

"He bid a fond adieu to all his old Guard.
They cried and moaned, like pigs swilling lard.
But at last he's gone, dragged off Elba way,
To molder like hay from December to May."

It was a catchy tune, she thought, still smiling, even sung off-key. The rhyme wasn't all that remarkable, but it fit in with the melody just fine. They reached the chorus now and their voices became louder and merrier.

"And it's hidey ho, off ye go, to Elba where ye'll stay.
It's up with the anchor to sail ye away, far away
To Elba where ye'll die and rot, forever and a day."

To her absolute delight, they no sooner finished that ditty than they broke into another, this one about Wellington upon receiving word that Napoleon had abdicated. The two were meant to go together, surely.

"He was pulling on his boots so it was said,
planning the next campaign, all in his head.
Then the messenger came all out of breath,
shouting, 'No more death, no more death.'

"And Wellington said, 'Leave me be, leave me be,
I'll put on my shirt and then I'll see.'

"But the messenger grinned and danced with guile,
shouting, 'Listen, milord, he's choked on his bile.
Napoleon's eaten his hat, tossed down his sword.
We'll now go home and all be bored.'
'Hurrah, Hurrah,' said Wellington.
'By God, we've done it, by God, we've won!
No more battles, no more glory,
I'm England-bound to become a Tory.' "

She was grinning like a fool at the lilting melody, and
the way the soldiers were butchering it and having such fun
doing it. They enjoyed it, that was the point. She drew back
into her bedchamber as the soldiers passed out of her sight
and her hearing, down the street and around the corner,
their voices becoming a faraway echo.

The words weren't perfect, oh no, but to sing about
what Wellington had supposedly said, it was warming,
at least to her. There was another song, this one short-
er, but she'd heard it several times already when she'd
been out walking with Badger in St. James and had
seen it being sold at Hookhams. Both the words and
the music had been hastily printed, and thus reading
it was difficult, but evidently enough people managed well enough. It was about the French Senate,
manipulated by the astute and cunning Talleyrand, who
had doubtless convinced the Czar to vote in old Louis
to become king, and now that fat old idiot, brother
to the late King, would now become Louis XVIII.

And now, wherever he was, Marcus was safe. He'd been
safe since April 6, the day Napoleon had abdicated, no, that
wasn't true, there'd been another huge battle at Toulouse
and a myriad of small skirmishes. God, how she'd prayed
he hadn't been in Toulouse, the loss of life in that needless battle had been staggering. Surely he wouldn't have
been there, surely. Spears would have gotten her word
somehow.

Soon she would know exactly where he was. Soon, she would have him, the stupid fool, for time was growing short.

She walked to her small writing desk, opened the bottom drawer, and pulled out Spears's last letter. Unfortunately the letter was dated at the end of March. He'd written that he and his lordship were off on an assignment and he didn't know where they were being sent. He would inform her, he concluded, when he was able. He ended by assuring her that his lordship continued in his stubborn ways, but even a stoat could be brought about to mend his manners, perhaps. He finished by saying that all hell was breaking loose now.

What did that mean? It made her shudder. What if he had been wounded or killed after Napoleon's abdication? She'd searched the papers for war news, for the notices of deaths. No word of Marcus. She wouldn't believe he was dead, never, for she knew that if anything had happened to him, Spears would have managed to get back to her, yes, yes, he would, she must believe that or go mad. No, he was well. She folded the letter and slipped it back into the desk drawer.

That evening, a balmy spring evening so enjoyed by lovers, as she sat alone in the magnificent drawing room of the Wyndham townhouse in Berkeley Square, she realized she had to devise a plan, a campaign really, just as Wellington was always doing, mostly with outstanding success. Once she found Marcus, she couldn't really see him succumbing to reason, despite all the private conversations she'd created, first playing herself and then playing him. No, it would take more than words and sound reason. With Marcus, it would require an assault, the use of guile and cunning. Not a frontal assault, but an assault that would allow for no unforeseen deviations by his clever and equally cunning lordship. She rose, rang the bell cord, and waited for Badger. She hummed the ditty she'd heard earlier, treasuring the melody and the words alike.

When Badger appeared in the drawing room, she grinned at him, not at all a stingy grin, and announced blithely, "I've got it now, Badger. *The Plan.* Are you all set to leave the moment we hear word?"

"I've been ready for three weeks, Duchess," Badger said, grinning back at her. "His bloody lordship doesn't stand a chance if you've finally got a plan."

"No, he doesn't, the fool."

8

HE'D BEEN AN ass, a complete sod of an ass, and he wished he could forget it, but he couldn't seem to, even though so many days and weeks had passed. It was always there in the back of his mind, ready to spring back and shout it to his face, like now. Damnation, but he'd been bloody unfair to her. Not that she'd shown any particular pain or distress when he'd shouted all those things at her—calling her cold-blooded, frigid, for God's sake—insulting her until if he'd been her, he would have killed him. Dead, right on the spot, but she hadn't, she'd just sat there, looking at him, saying nothing, damn her beautiful eyes, damn her control. Control, something he'd lost completely.

He hated being an ass and realizing it and feeling guilty about it. And he'd done nothing about it. He'd not written an apology to her, for surely what her father had done wasn't her fault, no, he'd done nothing at all. God, he wished she were here right now and he would . . . What would he do? He didn't really know. He hoped he would apologize for spewing his venom and bitterness on her.

He shook his head. He looked up to see his friend North Nightingale, Major Lord Chilton, come into the vast chamber. He waited until North was close then said, "Ah, here comes Lord Brooks with two of his bootlicking aides, the chinless sots. They were right on your heels."

"Where they belong," North said, and smiled, that dark

saturnine smile of his, and looked around the immense room with its thirty-foot ceilings and its gilded and lavish gold-and-white furnishings. Marcus was used to the opulence. North wasn't yet used to the heavy splendor of it, the oppressiveness of it. The room was in the former Parisian mansion of the Duc de Noaille, now on loan to Wellington and his staff. Czar Alexander was just down the street, in the even more splendidly decadent mansion of Talleyrand; he was Talleyrand's guest, no surprise, Wellington had remarked to Marcus and North shortly after Napoleon's abdication, since Talleyrand wanted to manipulate Alexander, and having him under his own roof with access to his remarkable cellars, would aid him enormously, as it indeed had.

"Yes, but they're not all that bad, Marcus—the aides, that is. I heard them singing that new ditty about Talleyrand and how that wily and ruthless old fox is maneuvering not only the Czar but also the French Senate to bring back fat old Louis. They sang rather well as I recall."

"He's got no more sense than a goat, does Louis, but at least he's the rightful ruler."

"And no more presence than a pompous stoat. Ah, but Talleyrand succeeded, and Louis is now on the French throne. Lord, but I never want to tangle with that man. It's said that his mistresses put shame to a legion's numbers."

Marcus looked bored. "I've sometimes wished," he said after a moment, keeping an eye on Lord Brooks and those two eavesdropping aides of his, "that Talleyrand were English. Castlereagh is a brilliant diplomat; men trust him, but still, it seems to me there's just too much honor in Castlereagh, not enough guile. He has difficulty, I've seen, lying directly into another man's face."

"A failure indeed," North said, and unobtrusively poked Marcus in the ribs, for Lord Brooks appeared to be coming over for a chat.

"My lords," Lord Brooks said, all amiability as he looked them over, as he did on a daily basis. He was an older man with a fierce tuft of white hair, a large nose, and a brain that was exceeded only by his height, which was just barely over five and a half feet. "So, we now have Louis XVIII as the French king. I believe it an excellent thing that Napoleon has retained his title of emperor, don't you?"

Marcus thought it the height of stupidity, but said nothing, merely began sorting through some military dispatches.

North said easily, shrugging, "Emperor of what, isn't that a question that gives one pause? Ah, yes, he is now the sovereign ruler of Elba, an emperor of boulders and beaches and a few scrubby trees."

Marcus said, "Don't forget all those French and Polish bodyguards. And he does have a navy, Lord Brooks, the brig *Inconstant*."

"You perhaps dwell too lightly on an occurrence that surely justifies more sober reflection," Lord Brooks said, looked at both men as if he would like to strike his glove on their cheeks, then strode back to his aides.

"What did that mean?" North said.

"God knows."

"God cares, I'm sure. We'll be more careful in the future, Marcus. It doesn't do to insult the man. He's proud as the devil and hates to be shown his stupidity, a deadly combination."

They laughed, but not too loudly. There was no point in further angering Lord Brooks.

"I'm bored," Marcus said. "Bloody bored. I don't know what I want to do but it isn't this."

"I know. There's nothing but the diplomats dancing around each other now, making promises, breaking them when the dawn breaks. Lord, I sometimes hate diplomats and all the endless games of diplomacy. Ah, Marcus, do smile at Lord Brooks, the old bastard."

"More intrigue," Marcus said. "I have this feeling he came over here to discover if we know anything he doesn't know. I can't count the times I've been approached by underlings of Talleyrand, Metternich, Czar Alexander, to reveal any secrets I might have on Wellington's stand on this or that, or *opinions,* as those damned diplomats phrase their requests. Well, damn all of them."

"Amen," North Nightingale said. "Your arm looks a bit stiff today, Marcus. You're moving it awkwardly."

"I know. Spears never leaves me alone. Every morning he watches me lift my heavy sword, up and down, up and down, very slowly, fifty times to get the arm back to its full strength. Then he massages it. This morning I believe he must have overdone it a bit, it hurts like bloody hell."

"Still, despite his enthusiasm, it seems to help. It's been just a matter of weeks since you took that bullet at Toulouse. Trust Spears, he's a good man."

"Christ, North, at least I'm alive with but a stiff arm. We lost four thousand five hundred men, not just casualties, as the war ministry says so glibly, and all because a messenger can ride only so quickly to inform Wellington that Napoleon abdicated four days earlier. The damned waste of it. So many men, dead for naught." He unconsciously rubbed his arm again.

North watched Marcus close and lock the desk drawer, then stare down at the small golden key as delicate as a fine piece of jewelry, so insubstantial it looked. Yet Marcus always kept it with him. There had been two robbery attempts in the past two weeks. Even if a thief ripped the drawer open, he would only find outdated papers, for the secret drawer was well hidden.

The two men left the mansion and spent the next thirty minutes walking along the banks of the Seine, breathing in the clear early evening air, before crossing the western tip of Ile de la Cité on Le Pont Neuf—actually the bridge wasn't new at all, indeed it was the oldest bridge in Paris. They strolled down the Boulevard Saint Michel, speaking desultorily, cutting over to the Boulevard Saint Germain to where their rooms were located in a large early eighteenth-century mansion, the Hôtel Matignon, at number 57, Rue de Grenelle.

Marcus waved to a fellow officer, crossing the street at a diagonal from them. "We have our own battalion here in the Faubourg Saint Germain."

"Don't forget all the Russian soldiers here as well. Last night I had my window open, more fool I. I could hear them singing in their incomprehensible language until nearly dawn, drunker than asses. How the devil do they manage to get up and go about their duties?"

Marcus shook his head. "I've seen them staggering in at dawn and up again at seven o'clock. And the number of prostitutes has grown to staggering numbers, the randy bastards."

"None of them owes any of their wages to you, Marcus. How is the fair Lisette?"

"Fair as usual. I leased a very charming apartment on the Rue de Varenne for her. Her appreciation moved me."

North laughed. "I'll just bet it did."

She was beautifully skilled, Marcus thought. He said aloud, "You know what I really like about Lisette, other than the obvious things? She's always talking, chattering really, flitting about the chamber, always moving, telling me jests, laughing, always laughing. She's never silent, never like—"

"Like what? Like who?"

"Like the damned Duchess, if you would know the truth of it."

North Nightingale looked at the fast-flowing Seine in the distance. "You're a fool, Marcus."

"Stow it, North. I'm a lucky man, so very lucky. Do you know that in my pocket at this very minute is a bank draft for two hundred pounds? My quarterly allowance for being the bloody earl of Chase, all duly notarized by Mr. Wicks. It's taken long enough to catch up to me. I do wonder how Mr. Wicks found me."

"I do too. You've managed to keep yourself hidden from everyone else in England. You won't turn down the funds will you, Marcus?"

"Hell, no. A goodly portion of it goes to Lisette's upkeep."
He smiled at that, wondering what Mr. Wicks would say
if he knew the old earl's groats were being spent on his
hated nephew's mistress. Well, the old bastard had had his
own mistress, the Duchess's mother. Odd, how it seemed
different, given the Duchess.

Where was the Duchess? Back at her damned cottage?
Or reveling in her fifty thousand pounds in the middle of
London society, entertaining gentlemen who doubtless all
drooled on her, damn her beautiful blue eyes. He'd thought
about her many times, wondered about what was in her
damned mind, wondering, always wondering in those off
moments, if there had been a man to protect her, to pay
the rent on Pipwell Cottage, to pay Badger, to pay . . . God,
none of it mattered now, not her motives, not her, none of
it. His rage still burned deep and bright and strong. He never
would see Chase Park or her or any of the other Wyndhams
as long as he lived.

He wondered if the American Wyndhams had arrived yet
to take over all the unentailed properties. Aunt Wilhelmina
couldn't take possession, he recalled, until after the sixteenth of June.

Then it would belong to the Americans, at least all of it
would after his demise. *Trevor!* That damned bloody dandy
with his fop's name. Marcus could barely stomach even
thinking about that name and the man it called to mind. He
realized he had sworn to let that bloody Trevor inherit the
earldom. Yes, Trevor Wyndham, the earl of Chase. It had a
ring to it, a ghastly ring, but he accepted, even wanted it.

"Where the devil are you, Marcus? You've been silent
as the Duchess you've told me so much about."

"I've told you very little about the Duchess. Very, very
little."

"Just last week when you were quite foxed, you told me
a bit more than very little."

"Contrive to forget it. I have. I've forgotten her. I hope
she has a protector, she's her mother's daughter, isn't she?

Actually I was just thinking about my cousin Trevor—
Jesus, *Trevor!*—it's too nauseating to contemplate. I'm certain he's slender as a girl, with soft skin and hair, ah, but
just hair on his fop's head, nowhere else on his body. And
he probably lisps and wears his shirt points to his ears. He
probably has as much muscle as Lisette."

North laughed and punched Marcus in his good arm.
"Here we are at Lisette's charming apartment. Go relieve
yourself, Marcus, and try to enjoy yourself as well. Have
Lisette position you in a more charming frame of mind.
After all, I'm the one with the dark soul, with the black
meanderings, not you. See that she takes care of you and
I, well, I believe I will have a tidy little dinner and see
what else the evening has to offer."

The men separated and Marcus knocked on Lisette's
front door. He listened, hearing her light footfalls as she
ran to answer the door. Lisette never walked or glided.
She was never silent when he made love to her. Ah, how
he loved to hear her scream when he brought her to her
release. Not like that damned Duchess. Doubtless she'd be
silent as the tomb.

Lisette DuPlessis looked pleased to see her Major Lord,
as she called him in her lisping English—bloody foppish
Trevor probably said it just the way she did—only he
didn't have her marvelous breasts that drew his hands and
his mouth in rapid succession.

She took his cape, his cane and unstrapped his sword,
touching it lovingly. She ran her fingers over his scarlet
and white uniform, delighting in the feel of the fabric and
of him, just beneath it, speaking all the while, telling him
what she'd done since she'd last seen him, which had been
only the night before. She spoke to him now in French, save
for his title, and since his French was nearly as fluent as his
Portuguese, he had no difficulty speaking and understanding. Ah, but she'd taught him sex words over the past weeks
that curled his toes and made him hard as a stone.

He kissed her, then discovered he didn't want to stop.

Her breath was warm and sweet with the rich red Bordeaux she'd drunk. She was drinking too much, he thought, but for the moment, he didn't care. All he wanted was to be inside her. Her breathing quickened, and her hands, never still, never lingering, made him wild.

He wanted to go slowly, but Lisette knew men very well, despite her tender nineteen years. She knew he wanted her, knew that he was wild with lust—a young man was always wild with it—and thus, she accommodated him with aplomb, stripping off his clothes in a moment of time, drawing him quickly into her bedchamber and onto her bed, covering him, urging him to come inside her. He did and it was over too quickly.

He said finally, once his breathing had slowed, and his heart was nearing its normal pace again, "I'm sorry, Lisette. I'm a pig."

Her busy hands were busy on his back, stroking him, long deep strokes, sweeping over his buttocks to gently ease between his legs. She giggled, bit his chin. "True, my lord, but I will be understanding. Will you promise to do better next time?"

He grinned down at her, feeling all the grinding boredom of the day fall away from him. "Yes," he said, rolling off her to rise to stand beside the bed. "Yes, I will do much better."

"Already, my lord?" She eyed him with enthusiasm.

PARIS, HOTEL BEAUVAU, RUE ROYALE

Badger wouldn't meet her eyes.

She eyed him with growing impatience. "Come, Badger, did you find him? Do you know where he lives?"

"Yes," Badger said, nothing more, nothing less.

She waited. Obviously he was disturbed about something. He didn't want to tell her what it was. She walked to the gilded blue brocade settee and sat down. She said nothing more, merely waited. She began to sing in her mind, *Lord Castlereagh needs more bombast. He speaks too softly, never will he last. He needs to take lessons from Talleyrand, who has more guile than any man.*

It was a beginning. Actually Canning had sufficient guile for any two ministers. She started to hum, realized that the melody was too close to another, and paused, her brow furrowed, trying to think of a different tune.

Suddenly, without warning, Badger said, "He's got a mistress, damn his eyes for being young and randy and like every other young randy man!"

"Talleyrand?" she said, at sea. "Canning?"

"No, no, his lordship. I followed him and Lord Chilton— a man we want to avoid at all costs, Duchess, trust me, he's dangerous—they separated, and his lordship went in to see this young girl who greeted him and I know she was his mistress because she hugged him and kissed him and drew him inside this narrow building on the Rue de Varenne. Her hands were all over him, Duchess. He must live there, with her, or at least visit her all the time, nearly."

"Well," she said reasonably, keeping some distinctly hateful feelings at bay. "He doesn't have all that much money. He must practice economies, I suppose. Two households would doubtless place a strain on his budget. But I will wager you, Badger, that he has his own apartment. Marcus wouldn't live with a mistress. I don't know why I'm so certain, but I am."

"You shouldn't be so damned understanding."

"He is perfectly free to do exactly as he pleases and with whom he pleases. At least at this particular moment he is. Does Spears live in this apartment as well?"

"I don't know."

"There, you see, he does have his own lodging."

"Again, I don't know. I hung about for a good two hours, and then he came out with her on his arm and off they went to one of those Frog restaurants that pride themselves on serving that nasty tripe covered with even nastier sauces. Animal entrails! Jesus, it makes me shudder. No, I didn't see Mr. Spears."

"We must find him before we begin *The Plan*. Spears must approve. I'm so pleased Mr. Wicks at least told us Marcus was with Wellington's staff here in Paris. Even that upset his lawyer's innards."

"I know. Tomorrow morning, early, I'll go back to the apartment and see where the earl goes."

"Make it *very* early, Badger. He has his own lodgings."

"His arm is stiff."

"What do you mean?" She was sitting forward, suddenly rigid, suddenly very afraid. "What do you mean?" she asked again.

"I asked around, all discreet. He was wounded in the final battle, at Toulouse."

"Oh God. Did you—did you see any pain on his face, Badger? Do you believe he has suffered? Oh God."

Badger looked at her full in the face. This was odd, he thought, but hopeful. "I don't know. Don't worry, Duchess. Tomorrow, no matter what else, I'll find Mr. Spears. Shall I bring him here?"

"Oh yes," she said, but she appeared distracted. Good God, he thought, she's thinking about his lordship being wounded. It bothers her. Glory be, this was better than he'd ever imagined. If only they'd heard from Mr. Spears before they'd left London.

Spears said in his patented bland voice, "Did you hear, my lord, that when old King George—while held in the kind restraining hands of his two wardens—was told the Allies had marched into France two months ago, he asked who commanded the British forces. He was told it was Wellington. Old George shouted, 'That's a damned lie. He was shot two years ago.' "

Marcus grinned. "Poor old mad George III. If he ever becomes lucid and discovers his son is the most scorned prince in history, it would likely split his spleen and push him into eternity. Before he became as raving mad as a jackdaw, he wasn't all that bad a ruler."

"I think he knows, my lord," Spears said. "Yes, many believe the stupidity and endless greed of the son led the father into insanity. Now, my lord, it is time for you to bathe and dress. I believe you're commanded to attend the festivities at the Hôtel de Sully."

Marcus grumbled and cursed, but nonetheless, he was garbed in immaculate evening wear, and on his way in a hackney coach to the Marais, to the Hôtel de Sully on the Rue Saint Antoine, for a diplomatic ball. He didn't believe he'd mentioned the ball to Spears, yet he'd known. The bloody man always knew everything. Marcus just shook his head and leaned back against the surprisingly clean squabs of the hackney. No surprise, really, for Spears had seen to the fetching of the coach, as well as everything else, curse his eyes.

Spears waited patiently until he saw his lordship well ensconced in the coach and on his way. He donned his cape and hat and took himself to the Rue Royale.

To his surprise and displeasure, she answered his knock. "Duchess," he said formally. "Why are you not in the drawing room? Why did you answer the door? It is not done. Mr. Badger shouldn't allow this. I will speak to him about this."

"Pray do not, Spears. Badger is preparing our dinner and Maggie is doubtless preening. I believe she is seeing a Russian soldier this evening, not an underling, mind you, but a man of standing, and doubtless of grand good looks. She says she has a vast interest in Russian history and this young cossack is just the man to teach her. Oh my, let me take your cape and hat. Don't look so disapproving, Spears. I'm not helpless just because I'm no longer a bastard."

"It simply isn't done," he said, stepping away from her, "but I can see that you will continue to disagree with me. Now, this female, this Maggie, she's the one who saved Badger's life in Portsmouth before you sailed to France?

The woman who saved him from being run over by a runaway mail coach?"

"Maggie saved him all right. She yelled and knocked him right out of the way. She says she doesn't know why she did it, she just did. She's an actress, you know, and she tells me she's quite good. However, she was temporarily, er, without acting employment, and thus I offered her a position as my maid, something she's never done before, but as she says, she's bright and willing and Paris is ever so exciting. And so she'll give me a trial."

"That is quite the oddest thing I've ever heard. She doesn't sound appropriate as your personal maid."

"I think, Spears, that Maggie will change your mind. I like her. She's different, somehow whole and unsullied, despite her rather colorful background. There is kindness in her and the sweetest devilment imaginable."

Spears divested himself of his own outer garments. His attitude was stiff. It wasn't her duty to see to him. If she were lax in matters of propriety, he most certainly wasn't. He would speak both to Mr. Badger and to this Maggie, who was a sweet devil.

"Do come into the parlor or *salon,* as the French say. I want to hear everything. First, why didn't you write me? I had to find out from Mr. Wicks that Marcus was here in Paris. Then it took Badger nearly three days to find him."

"I know," Spears said gently. "I will tell you every-thing."

"His arm, Spears, is he all right? Why didn't you tell me he'd been wounded? Why didn't you write to me or send a messenger?"

Spears was silent a moment, then shook his head slowly. "I had no wish to worry you." He sighed deeply. "I fear it still gives his lordship a lot of pain. The bullet fragments are still embedded, you see, in his upper arm. Many times he can't sleep with the pain. Naturally he refuses to be quacked. He won't even allow a tincture of laudanum in a cup of tea. I have, of course, many times ignored his wishes to do what is best for him."

Her face was perfectly white and Spears quickly added, his voice smooth and persuasive as a vicar's, "But for the most part, it continues to heal. A physician could do nothing really. The fragments are very, very small and they eventually make their way out of the arm, which sounds rather disgusting, but it happens and it's a good thing it does happen. It's just a matter of time until he is perfectly fit again, Duchess."

"Time grows short."

"Actually," Badger said from the drawing room doorway, a huge wooden ladle in his hand, "time runs out in exactly two and one half weeks. I, for one, hate to leave things to the last minute. Last minute endeavors never succeed."

"Mr. Badger has told me of your plan, Duchess. It will work. We will contrive." She believed him. He would make a splendid Foreign Minister, she thought, and took his arm as they walked into the dining room. There was no one to remark that the very rich young English lady, who had no chaperon and whose personal maid was upstairs arranging her glorious red hair in preparation to drive a young Russian cossack mad, was eating in the splendidly decorated dining room with her cook and an earl's valet.

The Duchess didn't hear a thing from Spears until the following evening.

"His lordship," Spears said with admirable control, and with two bright spots of color on his lean cheeks, "got into a fisticuffs last night. He is in bed with two cracked ribs, a black eye, and nearly an entire set of bruised knuckles. All his teeth, however, and thank the good Lord, are unharmed, still white and even and whole. He was also grinning like a sinner."

"How could he fight with his arm still hurt?"

Badger laughed. "Mr. Spears, did he tell you how his opponents fared?"

"Yes. Evidently one of the English officers called him the

Dispossessed Earl, and his lordship beat the, er . . . he gave better than he got. He was hurt because this opponent had friends. It was one-sided, you see. His arm wasn't harmed, Duchess. It was unfortunate that Lord Chilton was occupied elsewhere, or his ribs just might have survived."

"I see," the Duchess said, her voice faint. "However does anyone know about the stipulations of my father's will?"

"These things have a way of spreading," Badger said. "Like the plague."

"That is an excellent analogy, Mr. Badger. Very apt. Any news that titillates precludes secrets. His lordship's, er, mistress is with him, at his request. She very prettily asked me to provide her with the appropriate nostrums. I left her gently daubing his lordship's brow with a soft cloth dipped in rosewater, and humming one of those new ditties to him, by that English fellow."

"His mistress with him?" she said, her voice thin and high. "Soothing his fevered brow?"

"I do not believe his brow is fevered. Despite his injuries, his lordship was giving her many, er, interested looks, which bodes well for his general feeling of well-being. However, despite his lordship's wishes as regards her, I will nonetheless contrive to send her back to her own dwelling this evening. It may be very late, but it will be done." He gently flicked a piece of lint from his dark blue jacket sleeve. "You will be relieved to know she isn't a harpy, Duchess, nor is she always pestering his lordship for baubles and jewels and the like. Indeed, I believe she cares as much for his lordship as a creature of her stamp can care for anyone."

Like my mother, she thought, but said aloud, "I am delighted to hear it. Actually, relief is an emotion I'm not feeling at the moment, Spears. Perhaps I should invite her to tea to thank her for her restraint."

Spears turned away, hiding his very small grin, saying over his shoulder, "Perhaps it isn't such a good idea. She would expire with shock."

"That would be a good start," the Duchess said.

Rancor, Spears thought. It was indeed rancor, a goodly dose of it.

He said, "Her name is Lisette DuPlessis."

The Duchess said nothing to that.

"His lordship likes her name. He thinks it sweet."

"I don't trust Marcus," the Duchess said finally, looking over Spears's right shoulder. "I don't want to chance leaving this business until the last minute. I agree with Badger. I want to complete the matter tonight."

"If his lordship will allow me to remove his mistress from his bedchamber."

"You said you would contrive."

"That's right," Badger said. "Mr. Spears will see it done, Duchess. Don't worry. With his lordship at less than his full strength, it should make things easier. Also, Lord Chilton is at Fontainebleau and thus won't be in our way."

She remarked to the heavy brocade draperies, so typically golden, and so typically French in their heaviness and opulence, "His lordship is incapable of making anything easier. It isn't in his nature. If you both believe otherwise, you don't know him well."

9

IT WAS DARK. There was no moon, no stars to lighten the sky. Rain clouds bulged thick and heavy. Even as they spoke, it began to drizzle sullenly. There were no people on the Rue de Grenelle. A few candles were lit in the huge mansions, but not many.

Literary salons, she thought.

Men enjoying their wives or mistresses, Spears thought.

Mincing French chefs preparing menus, Badger thought.

The Duchess pulled her cloak more tightly about her neck. "No, don't say it," she said sharply to Badger. "I will not hang back and wait for you to whistle to me. I'm staying with you and I'll hear no more about it. No more arguments."

They walked the last few steps to the earl's lodgings.

"He's asleep," Spears said, pointing to a third-floor window that was completely dark. "I didn't give him all that much laudanum, but enough to send him into a stupor."

"What if he can't speak?"

"Don't worry, Duchess," Badger said. "We will sprinkle his lordship's face with some of his mistress's rosewater until he's conscious enough to do what he's told."

She shot Badger a look, but held her tongue. Damn Marcus for making all this intrigue necessary. She realized, even as she damned him for it, that she was enjoying herself. Hugely.

"It is nearly three o'clock," she said. "I have timed this two times now. Everything is on schedule. The official

114

you bribed will be here in ten minutes. What is his name, Badger?"

"Monsieur Junot. A hungry little man with a wife and four children. He was pleased enough to accept your proposal. Strange as it sounds, since he's a bloody Frog, I trust him."

"He will see that everything is duly recorded in the public registry?"

"Indeed he will. You will have the papers, all signed right and tight."

She nodded, stepping back for Spears to unlock the door. It made a prodigiously loud grinding noise. But Spears didn't seem to be concerned. He stepped inside the dark entrance hall, paused, and listened. Then he walked toward the staircase to the left, the Duchess and Badger behind him. She stumbled once, her foot hitting a table leg. Another horrendous noise, but Spears, again, seemed not to be at all concerned.

They were midway up the narrow staircase, walking as quietly as vicars in a brothel, when suddenly a candle was shone in their faces from above them, and a man's mocking voice said, each word in a loathsome drawl, "Well, well, do I have a quiver of thieves here? No, I daresay you, Spears, would not choose to rob me in the middle of the night."

"My lord," Spears said very gently, "do put down the gun. Perhaps your fingers aren't all that steady at the moment."

"Certainly they are. The two of you made enough noise to awaken the dead. Besides I wasn't asleep. Is that you, Badger? Whyever—no, wait, there are three of you. Good God!"

Marcus simply went silent with surprise. "You," he said at last. "May I inquire as to why you are here, in my lodgings, at three o'clock in the morning?"

"Yes," she said.

"Yes, what, damn you?"

"You may inquire, if you wish."

"You and Badger and Spears. Do I scent a conspiracy here? Surely not. What kind of conspiracy would bring together the three of you? Why Spears, are you that concerned that I won't be able to afford your wages on my allowance? I showed you the draft from Mr. Wicks."

"No, my lord, I'm not concerned, nor does our presence here have anything to do with robbing you, my lord. Now, may I suggest that I assist you back to bed? Surely your ribs are protesting. Are not your knuckles very sore tucked about that gun?"

Marcus said very slowly, enunciating each word, "I want to know what is going on and I want to know this instant. Not in the next instant, in this instant. Well, no, I want to know in the instant I designate. Now, let us go downstairs to the drawing room. Spears, you may lead the way and light some candles. Duchess, you've scarce opened your mouth—not that I expected you to in any case. As is your wont, you've merely sprinkled me with a mere smidgen of words. Badger, take her arm. I don't wish her to go break her neck falling down my stairs. If there is any neck breaking to do, I will be the one to do it. Go, now, all of you."

She felt Badger take her hand and gently squeeze it.

She felt her heart thud heavily. He'd heard them because she'd clumsily fallen against that table. Well, it was her own fault, no one else's. Nothing was easy with Marcus. Nothing. Why was he awake? Obviously the laudanum hadn't been enough.

He was behind them. He was wearing only a dressing gown, his feet bare, his black hair tousled. How, she wondered, her heart thudding even more heavily now, had she noticed all that?

Spears had lighted a branch of candles. He held it high, stepping back as the Duchess and Badger stepped into the small drawing room. He lowered it slowly to a tabletop when Marcus came in.

She turned to face him and saw that he was still pointing the gun toward them. It was an ugly thing with a long barrel, an obscene hole in the end of it.

"Sit down," he said, waving the gun toward a settee.

They sat, the Duchess between them.

She saw then as he walked toward them that he was in pain and that he wasn't standing upright. His ribs, she thought. She said aloud, "You should be in bed, Marcus. Surely this isn't good for your ribs."

He laughed, then stopped immediately, sucking in his breath at the sharp pain it brought him.

"My mother," he said. "Is that why you're here, Duchess? To minister to my wounds? To coo at me?"

She just stared at him, unmoving. "Like Lisette?"

He grinned. "So Spears told you of my ministering angel? Ah, she just removed herself not very long ago, Spears."

"But I—"

"I know. You doubtless put something in that tea you gave me to drink. But you see, I wasn't thirsty. What I wanted was Lisette, again."

"Please, my lord."

Marcus waved the gun to silence his valet. He stared hard at the Duchess. "No, I can't imagine you ever cooing, even to your bloody roses. But you felt you had to come in the middle of the night to care for me? You feared I wouldn't be pleased to see you and thus toss you out if you came in the light of day? You could only come when I was drugged senseless by my utterly loyal valet?"

"I came for another reason, Marcus. I will tell you if only you will sit down before you fall down. Please, Marcus."

"I don't want to sit down."

She rose and walked to him, her eyes on his face, shadowed in the candle light, but she saw the haggard lines, the black eye and swollen jaw. "You're not well, Marcus."

He just stood there, watching her walk toward him. "Stop right there, Duchess," he said pleasantly. He reached out his left hand and gently closed his fingers around her throat. "Tell me, do I inherit your fifty thousand pounds if you stuff it?"

"I believe so, though I don't think my father even considered that. Perhaps it would go to the Americans, I don't know. I will write to Mr. Wicks."

"I could simply strangle you on speculation."

"I don't believe that either Spears or Badger would allow you to do it, Marcus."

"They don't know you as well as I do. If they did, they would cheer my actions."

"Actually, you don't know me at all."

He shrugged, wincing. Any movement seemed to bring renewed pain to the continuous dull throbbing in his ribs. "Actually, I don't care. Now, why are the three of you skulking about in my house? The instant has come and I am frankly tired of all this. Tell me now."

At that moment, there was a gentle knock on the front door, a sly knock, a surreptitious knock. Marcus, surprised and taken off guard, turned toward the sound. Both Spears and Badger were on him in an instant. He struggled, but he was weak and he hurt and the two of them bore him to the carpet quickly enough. Spears very gently removed the gun from his right hand.

"My lord," he said gently. "I fear you must drink a bit of tea now. All right?"

"You're fired, Spears."

Badger said quietly, "Duchess, it is Monsieur Junot. Let him in."

The following ten minutes were fraught with silence so thick she thought she would choke on it. Spears and Badger had to pry open Marcus's mouth. He struggled to the point she knew he was hurting himself. Yet still he fought them. Finally they managed to pour a goodly amount of tea laced with laudanum down his throat. Monsieur Junot stood over them, holding a candle, saying not a single blessed thing.

He appeared to be enjoying himself.

Marcus fell back. She saw that he was fighting the drug, but he was losing. She hated this, but she knew it was no time to have an attack of scruples. Nothing had changed. True, he had complicated things, made all of them jumpy and feel guilty, but he'd succumbed in the end. There was no other way to save him, the damned stubborn sod.

She gently touched her fingertips to his swollen jaw. "It will be all right, Marcus. I promise you. Don't worry, just lie still, please."

He said in a slurred voice, "I will kill you, Duchess."

"Perhaps you will want to, but you won't."

"I don't know what you're doing, but I will kill you."

Monsieur Junot approached. "Is he ready for the ceremony?"

Spears looked into the earl's vague eyes, saw that he was more compliant than he'd been but a moment before, and said, "In two more minutes."

In four more minutes, Monsieur Junot said in a jovial voice, "It is done, my lady. You are now the countess of Chase. Fancy how he said I do when Mr. Spears gently nudged him. Now, he will have to write his name on the certificate."

Spears guided the earl's hand, but he did write his name and it was legible and strong. She signed her own beside his. Then she rose and dusted off her cloak. She took a slender gold band from her pocket and slipped it over the knuckle of her third finger. "Good," she said, and smiled at all of them in turn. "It is done."

"Yes," Badger said, rubbing his hands together. "No more Dispossessed Earl."

"I wonder," Spears said, "if his lordship will remember that he dismissed me when he awakens."

Monsieur Junot laughed. "This is quite the most interesting night I have spent since my house was very nearly shelled by Russian cannon two months ago."

Marcus opened one eye. He saw soft white hangings overhead. That couldn't be right. Even if he were in Lisette's bedchamber, there were no hangings over her bed. There was a huge mirror.

He slowly opened the other eye. Bright sunlight poured through a wide window to his left. It was morning sunlight, late morning, if he wasn't mistaken. He was wearing his dressing gown, he knew that, and it was odd, for he wore nothing at all to bed.

He sat up, shaking his head, clearing the odd muzziness from his brain. He was in a lady's bedchamber. The furnishings were all fragile-looking and gold and pale green, everything looked soft and vague. It was not a man's room.

He stilled, hearing footsteps outside the door opposite the bed. He watched as the door slowly opened.

The Duchess came in, carrying a tray on her arms. She turned and gently closed the door with her foot.

"You," he said. "So it wasn't a dream. You came to my house last night, in the middle of the night, and you were up to no good. What was the no good?"

"Good morning, Marcus. I've brought you breakfast."

"Spears and Badger were with you. I remember now, there was a knock at the door and those two bloody bastards knocked me down and took the gun. Then—" He paused, his brow furrowed, trying to remember. "You drugged me."

"Yes, but it was necessary. You're a stubborn man, Marcus."

He fidgeted and she said kindly, as would a nanny to her two-year-old charge, "Can I assist you?"

"If you don't leave this instant, Duchess, I will relieve myself in front of you. Men have no sensibilities, not one speck of modesty." She didn't move, just stared at him, and he threw back the covers and swung his black hairy legs over the side of the bed. She made no sound, just turned about, set his tray on a table, and left the bedchamber.

When she returned, he was seated at the small table eating the breakfast she'd brought him. The brioches were delicious, warm and flaky, the coffee hot and strong. His dressing gown was securely fastened around his waist.

"How do your ribs feel?"

He grunted and drank more coffee.

He looked like a brigand with his black eye, the heavy

beard stubble, his tousled hair, and the bruises along his jaw.

He continued to eat and drink. He paid her no more mind.

She seated herself opposite him and poured herself a cup of coffee from the lovely Meissen pot.

He said then, in a voice she recognized as the eye of the storm, "I will kill you, Duchess. After breakfast."

"But you don't yet know why or if you would still want to."

"I'll want to. It doesn't matter, it—"

"I'm your wife."

She watched his hand holding a butter knife become perfectly still. He had a brioche halfway to his mouth. It remained halfway. He shook his head, then winced from the pain it brought him in his ribs. He looked over at her, then shook his head again.

He said very politely, "I beg your pardon?"

"I'm your wife. We're married."

Still he couldn't take it in, he couldn't make the words take on sense. She thrust out her hand toward him. He stared at it, bewildered, then watched her waggle her third finger.

He saw the plain gold band.

He said, still staring at that finger with its ring, "You said that you're my wife?"

"Yes, Marcus. I can explain everything if you will allow me to."

"Oh yes, I will allow that. Then I will kill you."

"We drugged you. I insisted because I knew you would never agree. You're much too proud, too stubborn. You would have never listened to reason."

"Spears assisted you."

"Yes, as did Badger. I hope you won't blame either of them. They believed strongly in what we did. They didn't want to see you lose your inheritance because of—"

"Yes, Duchess? Because of?"

"Because you're such a stubborn sod. And because you somehow imagine that this punishes my father, who is dead and doesn't know a thing. And because you dislike me so very much."

"I see. So first, Spears tried to drug me, but he didn't know that I wanted sex with Lisette more than his lukewarm tea, and didn't drink it. Thus I heard the intruders break into my lodgings. I should probably have shot all of you."

"We had only until June sixteenth, Marcus. Otherwise the American Wyndhams would have inherited everything. I couldn't allow that to happen. Surely you must see that."

"May I ask how long you've been planning this?"

"Since the morning you ran away."

"I didn't run away. I left an intolerable situation." He stopped, leaning back in his chair. He looked at his fingertips tapping rhythmically on the tabletop. "I didn't want to ever see Chase Park again, you know."

"You don't have to, but you own it. You now have no more worries. There will be no more allowances, no asking Mr. Wicks for permission to do this or to do that. Everything is in your control now, Marcus. Everything."

"And the only price to pay is having you for my wife."

He'd said it calmly, quietly, but she felt herself stiffen nonetheless. There would be more, she could practically hear the words forming on his tongue. She didn't have long to wait after she said, "I hope, I pray, that having me as your wife isn't too heinous a prospect."

It was as if she were purposefully asking for insult, she thought, and wondered what he would say. He said, "It is a prospect that I am still unable to credit. Yesterday, I was a single man with his very charming mistress, content with his two-hundred-pound quarterly allowance. This morning, I awaken to find myself back in the earl's boots. I had thrown those boots away, Duchess. I didn't want them back."

"Then why did you fight the man who called you the Dispossessed Earl?"

He roared to his feet, nearly toppling the table. One coffee cup fell to its side. She watched the coffee drip onto the table and run in a thin quick line to the edge and then to the floor.

"How the hell do you know about that, damn you? Ah, it was that bloody Spears! I'll kill him after I've seen to you. Good God, have all of you been planning this?"

His face was white, his hands tight fists. If his ribs hurt, she doubted he felt it. He was finally furious. He was finally over the edge. Very slowly, she rose to face him. She splayed her fingers on the table. "Marcus, you don't have to keep me as a wife. Indeed, I had intended to go back to London at the end of the week to spare you the sight of me. What I wanted to happen has happened. Everything is as it should have been. Surely you can forgive me, or at least forget me without too much anger."

"You damned sacrificed female goat! I won't have it, Duchess. You have tricked me, manipulated my valet, drugged me, all to give me back what I didn't want. Don't you remember what I told Mr. Wicks? I don't want it, none of it. That damned pederast, Trevor, will become the next earl." He paused and rubbed his fingers over his jaw. "Well, that can still happen, can't it? My thinking processes aren't quite sharpened yet this morning, doubtless because of the dose of laudanum you forced down my throat.

"But I'm thinking now. Yes, Trevor could easily be the next earl. After all, I would have to force myself to bed you, probably many times, to get you with child. And what if it were a girl you birthed? Then I would have to force myself to take you again and again for the male child." He stopped again this time because he saw that her face was perfectly white. But it didn't matter. He didn't care. "To bring myself to seek out your bed would require more than I have, Duchess. It is true what I said to Mr. Wicks. Whispering love words to a bloody inert woman would shrivel me into oblivion. Is your flesh as cold as you are, Duchess? Would you perhaps sob softly whilst I

had my filthy way with you? No answer. Well, what did
I expect? How did you bring yourself to say your vows
during our eminently forgettable marriage ceremony? Yes,
just look at you, all tight and stiff and cold.

"I would have to lay Lisette there beside you so that I
could look at her while I took you, hear her laugh and moan
and scream so that I could force myself to even touch you."
He was doing it again, he thought vaguely, hurling insults
at her again, insults that had to cut deep. But this time she'd
done it, she'd gone too far—drugged him for God's sake—
and he refused to take them back or apologize. Besides, it
was possible that what he said was true.

Oddly, although she knew intense pain at his words, she
felt no anger. She said then over his harsh breathing, "You
don't know that, Marcus."

"Don't know what, curse you?"

"If you would need your mistress there to stimulate
you."

He shook his head, his right hand lightly stroking over
his ribs. But the pain dulled, oh yes, dulled to practically
nothing when he looked at her perfidious face again. "I
don't believe this, any of it. I will spend the day determining
if I wish to strangle you. Send me Spears. I have a meeting
with Wellington and have no wish to miss it."

She merely nodded and left him.

=10=

HOTEL BEAUVAU, RUE ROYALE

BADGER LOOKED CLOSELY at her, not saying anything for the longest time, waiting for her to speak, but, of course, she didn't. She was the most self-contained individual he'd ever met in his life. He'd always believed her inviolate—that's what her mother had always said—but now he wasn't so sure. The thought of her with Marcus Wyndham, the thought of that man as her husband, a man who was outrageous in his speech, who said, in fact, anything it pleased him to say, who gave way to rage and anger with the speed and precision of a battlefield surgeon, worried him profoundly. But then the young earl got over it, and cleanly, realizing of course that he'd strewn insults and hurtful words in his wake, but not knowing the power of them. Badger shook his head and said finally, "Duchess, I heard him yelling."

"Oh yes, his yelling. He is quite good at it, but for the most part, he was fairly quiet. Then he saw me again when he was on the point of leaving." She drew in her breath. She'd meant to stay out of his way once she'd left him to his breakfast, but she was worried about his injuries, and thus had returned to his bedchamber. Her hand was raised to knock on the door just as he'd opened it. He looked like a banged-up demon, she thought, with his black eye, the swelling in his jaw.

"You're a little late, Duchess," he'd said in that sneering

voice of his that made her wonder who this man was, for surely Marcus wouldn't sneer like that. "I'm not naked anymore. Indeed, I am leaving this house. I assume it is yours?"

"Yes, I rented it before I came to Paris. You may remain here, if you like, Marcus."

"Why? Do you mean you told my landlord that I had been shot and was no longer in Paris? Did that bastard Spears bring all my clothes over here?"

"I don't know."

" 'I don't know,' " he repeated, his voice thick with sarcasm. "This was all your plan, wasn't it? What the hell do you mean, 'I don't know'?"

"If Spears did bring all your clothes here, then don't you think you'd like to remain here? Perhaps you would like to dine with me this evening?"

He looked down at her from the intimidating height he'd attained during the past five years. She realized with a start that she came only to his jaw. "Have dinner with my wife? That's a novel idea. A wife, a commodity I hadn't ever considered. Well, yes, I did, didn't I, for all of five seconds when dear Mr. Wicks gave me my ultimatum. It sounded damnable to me then and now it makes me want to puke. No, I believe I will be spending the evening with my mistress."

"I wish you wouldn't, Marcus. I ask that you come back here and let us speak about the future."

"The future? You think you have changed everything, don't you, Duchess? Well, I don't know what I'm going to do, but whatever it is, it won't include you. Good day, madam."

He stomped down the corridor, stopped, wheeled about, and shouted, "Don't wait up for me, will you. God knows, Lisette is a greedy puss, and in her bed I intend to forget you and all you've done to me."

Hurtful words, she thought. Marcus had never learned brakes for his tongue.

She now said aloud to Badger, "For the most part, he preferred to stomp this time rather than waste his breath. Though when he does yell, the neighborhood must enjoy the drama." She sat down in a window seat, her hands folded quietly in her lap. "I imagine that everyone in the house heard him slam out of the front door."

"Yes. Did he agree to, well, anything?"

She gave him a ghost of a smile. "Do you mean is he delighted that I am his wife?"

"I shouldn't go that far yet with a man like the earl."

"No you shouldn't. I believe, actually, that he informed me that he would be spending the evening and night with his mistress. You know, Badger, the one who has the pretty name and isn't, according to Spears, a harpy."

"He wouldn't! That's . . . why that's—"

"He is quite remarkably upset with me. As for your part and Spears's part, I believe that will blow over. I am beginning to realize that his lordship is like a short-lived typhoon. Quick to rage and quick to a smile."

Badger wasn't so sure about that, but he just shrugged, saying, "Do you believe he will return here tonight?"

"I doubt it. I told him I would be leaving for London on Friday."

"Will he be willing to accept your gift to him?"

She said nothing, merely turned and lifted the heavy gold brocade drapery and gazed out onto the street. "He has no choice; at least I could do that much for him. But he doesn't appear to see it that way. He just kept saying that he didn't want the damned earldom."

"That could present a problem, Duchess."

"Oh? Whatever do you mean, Badger?"

"Annulment."

She looked puzzled, then her brow cleared. "I understand. Forgive me for being so slow. I read about it in the *London Gazette,* a certain Lord Havering annulled the marriage of his daughter to a Major Bradley."

"Do you know what it means, Duchess?"

"It means that Marcus can cancel out our marriage? That it can all be undone?"

"That's what it means, but it isn't possible if he, well, if you and he consummate your marriage."

No betraying flush rose on her cheeks. Her expression remained contained. She said only, "Oh, dear. That could present a problem, couldn't it?"

"Aye, if his lordship thinks about it, if he realizes he can annul the marriage, both Spears and I fear he would act before he realized what he was doing. Men who feel betrayed will do stupid things. Actually, with his lordship, I should say he can't stand not to be in control. So for him this is beyond betrayal since it hits at the heart of what he sees himself to be."

"Oh dear," she said again. "You are doubtless right, Badger. Oh dear." She rose and shook out her skirts of pale yellow muslin. "Another plan then. But first things first, Badger. You know where Lisette lives?"

"Yes," Badger said, eyeing her closely. "Her full name is Lisette DuPlessis."

"Good," the Duchess said and left the drawing room.

The narrow building set in a lovely residential neighborhood on the Rue Varenne looked inviting, the Duchess thought. At least it must look very inviting to Marcus, and inviting enough to Lisette since she agreed to let Marcus have her live there. Since it was early summer, the trees were thick and full, shading the street. She nodded to Badger, saw that he would argue, and repeated, "No, you will remain here. Stand under that oak tree yon and look French."

He blinked, saw that elusive smile of hers, and stepped back to lean against the tree trunk.

A very homely young maid answered her knock. She believed I would be a gentleman, probably Marcus, the Duchess thought, as she nodded and held out her visiting card.

"I would like to see your mistress, please," she said. *Mistress,* she thought, smiling inside, *how very apt language was upon occasion.*

The young woman gave a mighty frown, eyed the Duchess carefully, then tossed a head of remarkably fine blond hair. She left the Duchess standing on the doorstep.

She stepped inside a small entrance hall, closing the door behind her. The maid didn't look back. In front of her a narrow staircase rose to the second floor, then wound up to a third. She heard women's voices speaking rapid French. She sat down on a single chair in the entrance hall and folded her hands in her lap, and waited, something she was very good at doing.

Five more minutes passed. She heard more conversation, something about changing clothing. The Duchess wondered if Lisette were wearing something very alluring. She trusted Marcus wouldn't show up on the doorstep while she was here.

Lisette was more or less what she expected. She was young, quite well formed in the bosom, appeared to have a waist the size of two male fists pressed together, and didn't boast all that many inches in height. The impression was one of innocence and the knowledge of Eve, surely a potent combination. The Duchess then saw the wary look in her dark eyes.

"Oui?" she said, coming slowly down the stairs. She was wearing a frock that didn't shout her profession, at least to the Duchess's eye. It was a soft dark blue muslin, banded with a lighter blue ribbon beneath her breasts.

The Duchess rose and smiled and said in passable French, "My name is Josephina Wyndham, Lady Chase. May I speak to you for a moment?"

Lisette started to speak, then shook her head. "Come into the drawing room."

The Duchess didn't hesitate. Only the truth would serve, and she spit it out quickly with no digressions, speaking as quickly as her French would allow, finishing finally,

". . . So you see, I must consummate my marriage with his lordship else he could annul it and then all would be lost, for him, that is. I was told that you were an honest woman, Mademoiselle DuPlessis, that you weren't out to . . . well . . . take all his money. Would you help me save him?"

Lisette could only stare at the beautiful young woman sitting so calmly opposite her. "You are truly married to him? You truly drugged him? All of this is true?"

The Duchess nodded. "It is true, all of it."

"I can't imagine Marcus standing for it. *Mon Dieu!* A woman getting the better of him. It would not be a happy thought for him. It would wound his male dignity to eternity, I think. Ah, it is glorious what you did." This brought out a wicked smile that the Duchess saw before Lisette lowered her eyes. "My Marcus, he must be truly enraged. He must be beside himself, you, a girl, outsmarting him. He is a man who must be in control. Is he even now tearing Paris apart with his bare hands?"

The Duchess smiled, she couldn't help herself. "I imagine he would if his ribs weren't so very sore. Perhaps he will after he has healed. However, I hope that by next week he will see more reason than not, and realize that what he now has he won't want to give up again."

"And what would you like me to do?"

"I would like to give you ten thousand francs to change your lodging and not see Marcus again. I do not wish you to be hurt financially for your assistance in this matter, thus I willingly give you the francs so that you can find a new lodging and a new gentleman that you like."

"I see," Lisette said, her mind racing. Ten thousand francs! It was a great deal of money, surely enough to tide her over until she had a new protector, one of her choice, one like Marcus, not one she had to settle for. She wondered if she would find another man like Marcus, a man who was an excellent lover, a man who enjoyed a woman's pleasure, a man who knew more ways to pleasure than even she, Lisette, had yet experienced. She looked over at Marcus's new wife, a young lady who really was quite lovely and quite nice, but there was such innocence about her, such an air of frankness and simplicity. Marcus would surely eat her for his breakfast. She had drugged him and married him? All to save him? It was all a very strange notion to Lisette. Then she sat back and thought about this entire strange interview. She found herself beginning to laugh. "I am sorry," she said after a moment. "It's just that a wife coming to see a gentleman's mistress— it has never happened to me before. It is too much." She wiped her eyes and smiled at the Duchess. "And you aren't jealous. If you don't approve of me, you hide it well. Don't you care anything about his lordship?"

"Oh yes," the Duchess said, "but that isn't the point, don't you see?"

"Yes, perhaps I do see," Lisette said slowly as she rose. "His lordship will be here in three hours. That is his normal time. I have much to do if I am to be gone before he arrives."

The Duchess rose. She pulled a small slip of paper from her reticule. "Here is the address of a new lodging in the Faubourg Saint Honoré. There are many embassies there, many gentlemen of wealth and influence. The apartment is very close to the Elysée Palace, a center of power."

Lisette walked to stand face-to-face with the Duchess. She said, "I have never met a lady like you before. You are too young to be as you are, so very understanding, so accepting of the fact that I have slept with the man you have married. I am fond of Marcus, but he is like a volcano. You appear to be more like Lake Como, all calm and clear, with no waves."

The Duchess smiled. "Perhaps. However, what is important here is that Marcus not annul our marriage. I do thank you for your help, Mademoiselle DuPlessis."

Lisette said, "Next to the Elysée Palace, you say? Excellent, just excellent." She paused, then very gently she laid her hand on the lady's sleeve. "Marcus is a good man. Don't let him hurt you, madame."

"Because he is who he is, it is impossible for him not to hurt me." With those confusing words, the Duchess left her husband's mistress, her husband's former mistress.

She left the door to the drawing room open. She heard him come in the front door, slam it and yell for Spears, then Badger, and when neither of those two very intelligent gentlemen responded, he stomped into the drawing room. He looked like a very handsome bandit in his officer's scarlet-and-white uniform, his sword strapped to his waist. Uniforms should be outlawed, she thought. It made men look too splendid. Just now Marcus looked dangerous and splendid, an unlikely combination, but it was true.

He stopped in the doorway when he saw her, seated next to the fire, a book in her hands. She was dressed charmingly, even he realized that, in a gown of gossamer yellow muslin, her beautiful black hair loosely braided and wound through with yellow ribbon on top of her head. She wore no jewelry.

Except for that plain golden band on her third finger, that damned wedding ring she'd shoved on her own finger. He certainly hadn't done it, damn her.

She smiled at him. "Would you care to have dinner now, Marcus? It's very late, but Badger prepared dishes that wouldn't be ruined if you weren't here earlier, which, of course, you weren't. Or would you care to change and bathe?"

Marcus stopped himself. With great difficulty, he managed to keep his mouth shut, managed to keep the furious words unsaid, at least for the moment. He strolled into the room. He pulled off his cloak and tossed it over the back of a chair. He walked to the fireplace and stretched out his hands to the flames, for it was an unseasonably cool evening for early June. It would rain later, the air was thick with moisture.

"How are your ribs?"

"Yet another question, Duchess?"

She said nothing more.

"Yes, my ribs are better. There is still pulling, but I hadn't really noticed them all that much. As you know, I intended to visit my mistress this evening. But it is such a very odd thing."

She remained studiously silent. He said in a low furious voice, "Couldn't you at least flinch? Perhaps raise a flush on those pale cheeks of yours?"

She said nothing.

"It seems Lisette is gone. No one was able to tell me where. She left in the early afternoon in a very nice carriage, all her valises piled atop. Do you find that strange, Duchess?"

"Should I believe it strange, Marcus?"

"Where did you send her, Duchess?"

She said without hesitation, "I sent her nowhere, Marcus."

"I see," he said. He looked down at his hands. Slowly, he unbuckled the sword from around his waist. He gently folded the leather belt, laying the sword carefully over it in a chair. Then he straightened, his back to the fire. He leaned his shoulders against the mantel. He crossed his Hessians. Spears kept them so clean he could see his face reflected in them, even after a long day. He saw that he was frowning, that he looked ready to explode. He forced all expression from his face, then said, "It seems as well that my own lodgings are bereft of my belongings. I could have gone to a friend's apartment but I decided that you were right. You and I need to talk about the future." He saw it then, the exquisite relief that flooded her face.

She rose swiftly. "Could we dine first, Marcus? I am very hungry."

"Certainly," he said politely. He extended his arm to her. "Madam."

She sent him a wary look and he saw it. It pleased him. It pleased him inordinately. For the first time since he'd come to her small cottage in Smarden a year ago, he felt himself in control. All because he'd held his fury inside. All because she no longer knew what to expect from him. He smiled down at her, saying nothing. Let her wonder what was in his mind without shouting it at her.

He seated her at one end of the table and took himself off to the other. The food was already there, between them, beneath silver domes to keep it hot.

"Badger has outdone himself," Marcus said, closing his eyes as he slowly chewed on the chicken with orange and tarragon. "The onion is sweet, the Stilton cheese utterly perfect—pale at the rind and pale yellow and creamy inside."

"I was just thinking that same amount of detail myself," she said, staring at the Stilton cheese she hadn't touched. What was he planning to do?

"Wherever did Badger find such delicious oranges?"

"At Les Halles. He spends several hours there every morning."

"Ah, yes, *le ventre de Paris*—the belly of Paris for the past six hundred years." He forked down more chicken, made ecstatic rumbling noises as he chewed, then smiled at her again. "You don't appear to be enjoying your dinner, Duchess."

"I ate a tremendous luncheon," she said.

"Were you busy today? Perhaps you were shopping? Visiting friends? Visiting mistresses? Visiting your new husband's former lodgings to remove all traces of him?"

"I didn't do all that much today, Marcus."

"Ah, yet again I asked more than one question which gives you the perfect chance to answer none of them. Eat your chicken, Duchess."

"I am waiting for Badger's London buns. They're delicious. He says it is the quality of the lard one uses that makes the difference, he says—"

"I will have to wait," Marcus said, sitting back in his chair and lacing his fingers over his belly. "I have quite stuffed myself."

"You were hurt. You need food to regain your strength."

"You want fat on my manly charms, Duchess? You don't really care, then, for you say nothing. Well then, this dining room is quite charming, as is the rest of the house. Since you are now a very rich young lady, I fancy you didn't even blink an eye when you were told the rental."

"It is rather expensive, but as I told you, if you wish it, I will leave for London. If you wish to remain here, why, you are very rich yourself now, Marcus, you can well afford it."

"Yes, I am rich now, aren't I? It is interesting that during the ten months when I believed myself to be the real earl as opposed to the temporary earl, I never forgot the value of money and what it was like to consider purchases. I doubt I will change now. I was just thinking of the poor American Wyndhams—all for naught, the poor sods now have nothing at all."

"They didn't deserve to have anything," she said. "It is all yours. It was all meant to be yours."

"Oh no. It was meant to be Charlie's and if not Charlie's then Mark's."

"They died, Marcus, five years ago. It was no one's fault, certainly not yours."

"How very interesting. You blame your father."

"Yes."

He realized in that moment that he couldn't bear it, none of it. The Duchess, sitting at the opposite end of the table, her face in the shadows, but her damned voice sounding like a serene Madonna's, no, he couldn't bear it. He rose and tossed his napkin onto his plate. "I'm going out," he said, and strode toward the door of the dining room.

"Marcus."

He paused, then said over his shoulder, not turning to look at her, "Yes? Am I forbidden to leave the house once I'm inside it? Will I find your bully boys on the front doorstep waiting to shackle me and drag me back inside?"

"Marcus, we haven't spoken yet."

Now he did turn to face her. In a voice that held no passion, no anger, naught of anything she could hear, he said, "I fear I am not up to it now, Duchess. There are things I must think about, things that concern only myself and only my future. Surely you must understand that?"

She was very afraid that she did. The words were choking in her throat, but she couldn't make herself ask if he was now considering an annulment. She said nothing, merely stared at him in silence until he turned again and strode quickly from the dining room, from her.

11

BADGER TUGGED ON his right earlobe. He opened his mouth, then closed it again. He tugged more, then said finally, "Mr. Spears, it worries me nonetheless. We have discussed this and we are in agreement. I understand the need, indeed, but she is very innocent. It was her mother, you see, and the situation she was in. She was a mistress, Mr. Spears, and thus her daughter was a bastard. She sought to protect the Duchess, and that, in her mind, meant keeping the girl appallingly ignorant."

"Mr. Badger, I realize this situation is not one that either of us would wish, but you must stop pulling on your poor earlobe, it's getting quite raw. The strain these two have created is enough to drive a sane man to immoderate drink, or to yanking at his earlobe. Would you like a brandy, perhaps? No? Well then, it must be done and you know it. His lordship just might be seeing to an annulment this very moment. She would be most upset were he to succeed. She is willing to do it. Indeed, she must do it. I will myself ascertain his lordship's mood this evening before she proceeds."

"And if he's in a ripping foul mood?"

"Then, Mr. Badger, she will have no choice but to wait. I wouldn't trust him with her if it were so."

"Damned bloody young fool! I should like to snaggle him in an alley and pound that stiff pride out of him."

Spears sighed. "He is a young man, Mr. Badger. Young and strong and proud and he sees her as the source of all his problems."

"But she saved him!"

"Yes, but it changes nothing. In his view a man should do the saving, and if he isn't able to, then no one should, particularly a female."

"Poor little mite," Badger said.

"Then she had the gall to inherit that fifty thousand pounds, leaving him in a most humiliating position. An allowance, Mr. Badger, an allowance! For the earl of Chase. Could you think of anything that would belittle him more than that?"

"But none of it was her fault!"

"Certainly not. But she was there, don't you see? She went from being a harmless bastard to being a legitimate heiress, and the heiress part took all that belonged to him, *by right*. Ah, it makes no matter what is in his mind. She will do what she must. She always has."

"She shies from nothing, I'll say that," Badger said, rising from the comfortable rocking chair near the fire in Mr. Spears's sitting chamber. "Well, she shies but she makes herself act."

"Do let me tell you, Mr. Badger, that the chicken with orange and tarragon was superb."

Badger nodded, still clearly distracted. "But Mr. Spears, what if he hurts her?"

"She will bear it. And then it will be done."

The Duchess was wondering if she hadn't suddenly stepped over the edge of sanity and become quite mad. She paused at the closed door, listening, but hearing nothing.

Was he already asleep? It was just past midnight. If it were a normal night, she certainly would be sleeping by now.

It was a reprieve if he was.

She shook her head. She didn't want him to be asleep. She wanted him awake and willing. A reprieve would only put it off and she was afraid to put it off. Marcus was unpredictable, he was slippery, she had no idea what he

would do and when he would do it. Very quietly, she turned
the brass doorknob. The well-oiled door eased open with
no betraying creaks or groans. There was a sluggish fire
still burning in the fireplace, casting off shadowy light.
She stepped quickly into his bedchamber, quietly closing
the door behind her. The room was warm, which was a
relief, she supposed.

The carpet felt thick and soft beneath her bare feet.
She followed the line of his discarded clothing beginning
from near the fireplace toward the bed. She saw that his
sword was still in its scabbard fastened to its leather belt.
The belt was carefully wrapped and laid atop a table. She
very nearly tripped over one of his Hessian boots that
stood drunkenly at right angles to the bed. His cloak was
spread on the floor, looking for the world like a black bat
in flight.

She stood beside the wide bed, staring down at him.
He was asleep, lying on his back, one arm flung over
his forehead, the other at his side, palm up and open.
There was a single sheet covering him and it stopped at
his waist.

He was big, his chest covered with black hair and hard
with muscle, as were his arms. She realized he looked as
splendid out of his uniform as he did wearing it. She
smiled before she realized that she hadn't yet really begun
to sift through their differences. She could see him outlined
beneath the sheet, the largeness of him, and that was surely
something to think about.

She saw that his ribs were green and blue with faint tinges
of yellow. She wondered if they pained him much.

It was then she wondered what to do. She thought of
the book Badger had handed her silently that afternoon,
not quite meeting her eyes, just mumbling, "This might be
of some assistance, Duchess. There are, er, drawings."

"Drawings, Badger?"

"Yes, drawings. Did your mother tell you anything about
what happens between men and women?"

She very slowly shook her head. Badger said, "Look through the book, Duchess. If you have questions, I'll ask Mr. Spears to see you."

She thought, on the face of things, that he looked better than any of the rather crude drawings that filled that strange but very informative book. She lightly touched her fingertips to his jaw, still bruised, covered with black stubble. Then she lay her palm over his heart, feeling the steady thudding against her flesh. His hair was crisp and curling beneath her fingers. He moved then, turning slightly, then falling back again. His arm came down to rest over his belly.

What to do now?

She wasn't afraid, just stymied, for unlike any of the male drawings in the book, Marcus was asleep. There was no eagerness, no leering smiles to be seen on his face. He certainly wasn't ready to leap on her like many of the men in those drawings.

He opened his eyes and stared up at her. His eyes were blurred and vague, but his voice was sharp. "By all that's strange and beyond strange. You of all people, in my bedchamber. What do you want, Duchess?"

"You," she said. "I want you, Marcus."

He said nothing, merely smiled at her, and closed his eyes again. His breathing was deep and even in but a matter of moments. It was then she realized that he hadn't truly been awake. But he'd sounded awake. So, it was up to her, completely up to her.

She wiped her damp palms on her dressing gown. Slowly, knowing there was nothing more for it, she untied the sash at her waist and slipped the dressing gown off her shoulders. It pooled at her feet. Her nightgown, she thought. She had to do it. In a moment, she was still standing there beside him, now naked. She felt the warmth from the fire against her back.

She leaned over him and touched her mouth to his. "Marcus," she said. "Please wake up. I'm not all that certain what to do. I mean I am certain what has to happen, but I'm not certain how to make it happen. Please wake up, Marcus."

He smiled at her words and said softly. "Ah, Lisette, won't you let me get any sleep at all? You're more greedy than a bloody man." His hands came up and cupped her loose breasts. She sucked in her breath, but managed to hold herself still. He was kneading her breasts now, lifting them, massaging them, filling his hands with her, all the while, his eyes were closed. She saw the outline of him change beneath the sheet. She knew what that meant. It meant that this particular part of him, the most important part in terms of what she had to accomplish, was more awake now than not.

But he believed she was his mistress.

Suddenly, his hands moved from her breasts to encircle her waist. He lifted her over him, pushing at her legs so that she was straddling him, her hands supporting herself against his chest, her hair coming over her shoulders to touch him. His hands were again on her breasts, and he was moaning softly as he caressed her.

She was too terrified to move.

"What is this?" he whispered, then laughed over a moan. He slipped his hand beneath her buttocks and drew the sheet down. She felt him hard beneath her. The heat of him was incredible. She hadn't imagined anything like this.

He breathed deeply, and now both his hands lifted her and she felt him stiffening, felt him now hot against her, and didn't know what to do.

"What is this, Lisette? You're not ready for me yet you want me to wake up and pleasure you again? Hold still, yes, that's right, just hold still and let me enjoy you." He pulled her forward so that she was lying on his chest. He found her mouth and she felt the heat of him, the sweet warmth that made her open her mouth immediately, wanting the taste of him, and his tongue touched hers and she jumped slightly, and he laughed softly into her mouth. She focused on his tongue, on the movement of his lips until suddenly his fingers were on her, pulling gently at her flesh and easing inside her. She cried out, she couldn't help it, but he soothed her, stroking her hips, as if she were an animal, she thought wildly, and he sought to calm her. His fingers hurt but he didn't stop what he was doing, going in and out of her, stretching her, and she raised her face, biting her bottom lip to keep quiet. She knew what he would do. She wasn't stupid, but she didn't want it, for the pain was building now, raw and deep and she'd felt him before he'd pulled her forward to lie against his chest, and she knew he was much larger than the two fingers inside her. Now she felt the dampness of herself and it was embarrassing, but she didn't have time to consider that because he was pushing her upright again, over him, then lifting her and she felt him hard and pushing against her and suddenly he was inside her and he was groaning with his pleasure in it.

She didn't want to cry out. She refused to. She splayed her palms on his chest, closing her eyes and her mouth as he deepened inside her, deeper and deeper until he was pressing against her maidenhead and she felt it, actually felt him there, pushing harder and harder until, with no warning, he threw back his head and gritted his teeth, his hands tightened around her flanks and he lifted his hips even as he brought her hard down on him.

A cry ripped from her throat, she couldn't help it. The pain, the deep burning, was horrible. Surely he could go no deeper into her, but then he did and she didn't think she could bear it further.

He was lifting her and lowering her now, rhythmically, his fingers digging into the soft flesh of her hips, and he was breathing hard, jerking his hips, and she opened her eyes and looked down at his face. There was a dark flush on his cheeks, his eyes were closed and his lips were parted. He appeared to be in pain. That made two of them, she thought, then all rational thought dissolved when he quickened his thrusts until he was frantically jerking into her, his legs and chest heaving, and his breath was catching in his throat and he groaned loudly, his head thrown back on the pillow now and she was crying, she tasted her tears in her mouth, the salt of them, felt the pain of his fingers digging into her hips and the endless pain of him deep inside her.

Then it was over. He was utterly still beneath her. He sighed deeply and his head rolled to the side. His hands fell from her. She felt his legs sprawl beneath her. He was still deep inside her, but the pain had lessened now for there was wetness from him, his seed, she knew, and it helped, at least it helped reduce the intense pressure inside her.

She felt the rumbling in him as his chest heaved slightly, and again he opened his eyes. He frowned up at her. "Duchess," he said. "By God, it's you, isn't it, Duchess? Pretending to be Lisette this time. Why are you here? Why am I inside you? This can't be, it can't. I'm dreaming. Yes, it's a dream." His mouth closed. He shuddered then fell perfectly still once more. She felt him come out of her, and very slowly she slipped off him to stand beside the bed. Her legs were sore, the muscles of her inner thighs trembling.

The single sheet was tangled around his knees. She stared down at him, at his flat belly, at the tangle of black hair at his groin, at his sex, soft now, but wet with himself and with her, she supposed, and with her blood. She shuddered and quickly pulled the sheet back to his waist.

She jerked her nightgown over her head, then pulled the dressing gown over it. She didn't cry until she was in her own bedchamber, huddled beneath a mound of blankets. She couldn't seem to get warm.

She fell asleep, a sleep fraught with phantoms that had no faces, that brought her pain, she knew it was pain, yet she couldn't seem to move, and they were laughing and laughing. Then suddenly, she was more awake than she was the moment before and she felt more warmth than she should feel. She turned into the warmth, the flesh that felt so wonderful pressed against her. This wasn't a phantom and if it was from her dreams, then she would hold it tightly to her for there was no pain here, no faceless fear. Large hands that were stroking down her back, pulling her closer, molding her to him, and she felt the thick hair of his chest against her breasts, and then lower, the heaviness of him, and he had her hips in his hands and pushing her rhythmically against him. She awoke with a start.

It was no phantom spun from her dreams. It was Marcus. He was in her bed and he was naked and she was naked as well. What had happened to her nightgown? His hands were sifting through her hair as he kissed her neck, the lobe of her ear. He blew softly at the tendrils of hair in his way. He kissed her chin and then her mouth, and she didn't know what this was, this immense warmth and urgency that was beginning to invade her. She felt her legs pressing against his, hers so very smooth and his hard with muscle.

"Marcus," she whispered, and she pulled his head down to hers and kissed him. "Marcus," she said again into his mouth. "I'm not Lisette. I'm not your mistress."

"Yes," he said. "Yes, I know." He was kissing her deeply now and his hands were on her breasts veiled with her hair—her body remembered the pleasure of his fingers on her flesh, remembered very well, but then he was going lower, his hand between their bodies and he was touching her, feeling the dampness of her, and she felt that smile of his, touching her mouth, and then he was on top of her and she felt the weight of him pushing her down, the heaviness of his legs, but his hands were beneath her hips, drawing her upward, and he slowly eased into her. She heard his breath catch, felt him going deeper and the pain wasn't so bad this time, but it was there despite the dampness still within her, and she tried to pull away from him, but he held her tightly until he came over her and she felt him touching her womb.

"Not again," she said, for he was beginning to move and stretch her and she was still very sore, but he wouldn't slow. "Not again," she said against his throat, hearing his breathing sharpen and grow more urgent. "Please, Marcus, it hurts." She felt his frenzy even before it became wild movement, before he jerked and shuddered as if in the throes of a cataclysm of something she couldn't begin to understand. She cried out, "No, Marcus. Please, not again. There's no need. Please, Marcus, no!"

"There's every need," he said, his voice raw and deep, "every need because . . ." His harsh breathing overtook his voice. He continued until he found his release. He was quiet over her for but a moment. Then he pulled slowly out of her. He rose to stand beside her bed, staring down at her. He'd lit a candle and she opened her eyes to look up at him. She was sprawled on her back, her legs parted.

"Why did you do that?"

"Why not?" he said and shrugged. She saw no anger in his eyes, no expression on his face. He continued, his voice hard as his body. "Since you already took me once why shouldn't I return the favor? Don't you think I'm a gentleman, Duchess?"

She struggled to pull the covers over herself.

"There really is no need. I've felt your body and looked at it. Do you think I've never seen a naked woman before? Do you believe yourself such a treat of originality? Such a feat of creation? You're only a woman, Duchess, nothing more." He struck a naked pose, his long fingers stroking over his jaw. "Of course, this is the first time I am really seeing you, for that first time, it was dark and I was only conscious enough to . . . well, I don't want to be crude, do I? And this time we were beneath all those covers."

She left the covers at her waist. She said nothing. She felt her heart thudding wildly, but she held herself quiet, knowing she did it automatically as a protection against his words, and knowing just as certainly that her silence wouldn't keep him from saying anything he wanted to say. He was like that.

She saw that he would leave. He couldn't, not yet, not until she was certain he understood. She said quickly, "I had to do it, Marcus. Surely you realize that. You did not seem averse."

"I thought you were Lisette. Had I realized it was you that first time—" He shrugged and her eyes fell from his face down his body, and he knew she was looking at him and he merely shrugged again. "You had to do it. What an odd thing for you to say. Why? Surely you, of all women, of all bloody virgins, wouldn't willingly want to take a man. You're so cold I doubt you would ever have consented to have me inside you unless . . ." His voice stopped cold. He stared at her.

"The one time was necessary. You're safe now, Marcus, you're safe from yourself and your perhaps unthinking anger . . . that is, you can't now annul the marriage."

"So," he said. "I thought that, but I didn't want to believe it, even in my muddle-minded state, but I couldn't believe that I could think such perverse thoughts. Goodness, Josephina, you even forced yourself to be impaled on me. And I helped you because I believed you to be Lisette. Yes, that worked mightily in your favor, didn't it, Duchess? If I hadn't come awake, wanting her again, why I never would have realized what had happened until the morning. But I saw your blood all over me and on the sheets as well, your precious virgin's blood, a commodity Lisette hasn't shared with a man in many a long year. But I did wake up. You're right, there'll be no annulment now." He looked at her another moment, and his expression was hard and unyielding.

"Marcus," she said, and she lifted her hand to him.

He just shook his head. "I doubt I would have annulled this marriage, Duchess, despite what you have done. I'm not all that stupid. Even I wouldn't whistle a bloody fortune down the wind all for the sake of pride."

"But you gave me the impression that you would, you made me think—"

He just smiled, not a very nice smile. "I was angry," he said, as if that explained everything, excused everything. "Now, it is done. No annulment. Don't misunderstand me, Duchess. I still believe that bloody pederast Trevor can still be my heir, or if he begets any little pederasts, then they can. Don't believe your precious blood will flow through the next earl. Never would I give your damnable father that satisfaction. If I father a child, then it will be as illegitimate as you are—were. And, unlike you, he will remain a bastard.

"No, no annulment, Duchess. Your simple mind can now be at ease again. You have made your ultimate female sacrifice. And here I was crude enough to force myself on you again. Well, that's a man for you. And I am your husband."

"Do you truly want to be my husband?" She heard the plea in her voice and hated herself, for she knew he wouldn't hesitate to dash her into the rocks, and he did.

"I wonder what that means?" he said, still stroking his jaw, his voice sounding mocking in his scorn. "Does that mean I must be civil to you at the breakfast table? Does that mean I must force myself to take you occasionally? As I did tonight? I must tell you, Duchess, that first time when I believed you were Lisette, ah, that left me blank-brained with lust and pleasure. This second time, knowing it was you, well, consider it an experiment on my part, an experiment to determine if you are as cold as I believe you to be."

"I'm not cold."

"You, Duchess," he said very precisely, the hated drawl more pronounced, "hated my touching you. Don't deny it. It was difficult for me to bring myself to climax with you yelling at me to 'stop, stop, please Marcus, do stop.' Very difficult. I had to keep thinking of Lisette and the way she cries out and squirms against me and caresses me with her mouth and her hands."

She closed her eyes against him. "I didn't hate you touching me. You woke me up and you hurt me again.

Surely that doesn't make me cold. I didn't know how to caress you and touch you. And I didn't yell at you to stop. I just didn't understand, Marcus, and I was afraid."

"Well, let me be more simple for you, Duchess. Understand this, you forced your way into my life. I cannot force you out of it now, but I don't have to accept it. Do go back to England, Duchess. You don't need anyone hanging about you, particularly a husband. You are so self-contained, so very independent, and now you're a countess, no longer an ignominious former bastard. But I beg you not to take a lover. There will be no progeny from this union, as I told you. I couldn't punish your father in life, but, by God, I will make certain that he has no children from your womb. I slipped tonight, taking you that second time, but no more. Yes, Duchess, go to London, and do enjoy yourself. You are rich and you are now titled. Even the greatest sticklers should admit you to society.

"But first, why don't you tell me where you have stashed Lisette?"

She had won; she had lost. There was no hope for it. She said, calm as the soft summer breeze outside her window, "She is in an apartment just down the street. There are embassies along the Rue Royale and that meant men of power and influence and wealth. I gave her ten thousand francs, Marcus."

"You spoke to Lisette?"

She nodded.

"What did you tell her? Jesus, you told her all of this debacle?"

"Yes, it's the truth. That I was afraid you would annul the marriage and I couldn't allow that to happen. She understood, Marcus. She is fond of you and she wanted what was best for you. She was willing to help me help you."

"Not even a small showing of wifely jealousy, eh?"

"There was no room for it."

"I see. Didn't you even remark her abundant bosom and make a comparison to yourself?"

She closed her eyes and said, "Yes."

"But no jealousy. Didn't it bother you—after all—you are my wife at your own behest, that I have suckled Lisette's magnificent breasts? That her body gives me immense pleasure? It didn't bother you at all? You are silent again. Your nobility is beyond anything that I would ever have expected, beyond anything I ever wanted. I suppose you paid for her new apartment?"

"Yes. It is at Number Forty-seven Rue Royale."

"Thank you, Duchess. Now, it is too late to visit her tonight so I will take myself back to bed. Good night, Duchess. Thank you for an enlightening episode."

"It was enlightening," she said. He didn't turn. She watched him stride naked from her bedchamber. She saw the anger radiating from him. There was nothing specific to point to. It was something she simply felt. She'd always felt him—when he was joyful as only a boy of fourteen could be, when he was dashed down, again, as only a boy of fourteen could be, beginning when she was nine years old, the first time she'd met him, but she wouldn't think about that because it wasn't important now. She'd won, for he'd breached her maidenhead. He'd consummated the marriage. He was safe, finally, despite his rage, he was safe. She wondered if he truly wouldn't have considered an annulment. He was probably lying to himself when he said he wouldn't have.

It was Badger who awoke her the following morning, not Maggie. He had a tray on his arm. He handed her the wrinkled nightgown from the floor, then turned his back while she pulled it over her head and smoothed it down. She allowed him to assist her into her dressing gown, then drank down the thick black coffee. He said nothing until she had taken two bites from the warm brioche.

"Do you not wish some butter and honey?"

She shook her head. "No, this is fine, Badger. The brioche are wonderful. Did you bake them?"

Badger waved away her words. "His lordship is gone. Mr. Spears said the earl was pulling on his boots when he went in to wake him. Mr. Spears said he was very quiet, not overtly angry that he could see, just very quiet. Mr. Spears, naturally, couldn't question him. He did ask him when he would return and his lordship said, 'Ah, I live here now, Spears, don't you know? But I—'" Badger folded his lips into a thin straight line.

"Please, Badger, tell me the rest of it. Nothing he would say could possibly surprise me. Please understand, I am quite used to Marcus's rages and his insults."

"He said that he now knew where you'd sent Lisette and he would doubtless spend a good deal of time with her."

She took another bite of brioche.

"Shall I send you Maggie? I heard her humming when I passed her door. Her hair is redder this morning, if such a thing is possible. She is a piece of work, isn't she?"

"Yes," she said. "She makes me smile. Ah, Badger, please inform her that the three of us will be leaving for Calais by noon, no later."

He stared at her, opened his mouth, then closed it. He said ten minutes later to Spears, Maggie beside him, "It's over. Your master and my mistress have bungled it royally. We're returning to London. I will send you our address when we arrive."

"You won't stay at the Wyndham townhouse?"

Badger shrugged. "I have no idea, Mr. Spears. She won't tell me anything. But I think we will. She let the lease go on Pipwell Cottage in Smarden. I can't see her traveling to Chase Park, not now in any case."

"Thank God for that," Maggie said fervently.

He grinned down at her. "You'll like the townhouse. It's in the middle of everything that is exciting and fun. I'll have to assign you a footman to keep all the young bucks away."

"I surely hope so, Mr. Badger," she said, all demure as a nun, and winking at Spears. "But perhaps you shouldn't act so hastily—with the footman and all."

However, Spears didn't see her wink, which was just as well since he was looking austere as a hanging judge. "I will correspond to you as well, Mr. Badger, as soon as I understand what is happening here."

"His lordship is a bleater, Mr. Spears."

"Yes, Maggie, it would appear so, at least for the moment. I will take care of him and we will see. Good journey to you, Mr. Badger, Miss Maggie. Mr. Badger, I look forward to your veal and bacon terrine."

"And what will you look forward to with me, Mr. Spears?"

"Why, your pert rejoinders, Miss Maggie, what else?"

"How unoffensive of you, Mr. Spears."

=12=

BADGER STOOD IN the doorway of the drawing room, saying nothing, merely looking at her. She was writing and humming as she wrote, quicker and quicker, which meant that it was coming easily now. A blessing, he thought, for she'd been so silent, so very withdrawn, damnation, so very *broken*, since their return from Paris some weeks before.

He waited patiently, grateful that she had something important to her to give her thoughts another direction. She looked up, jumped slightly at the unexpected sight of him, then smiled. "Do come in, Badger. I was so immersed in this. It happens sometimes, which is good."

"I know, I know. It means everything is flowing freely out of that clever head of yours."

"Clever? Well, that's an interesting thought, isn't it? Odd, isn't it. Now I do it because of the fun of it, not because I have to pay the rent or buy eggs or try to pay your wages."

She'd always paid him, despite his protests. She'd always paid him first, even before paying the rent on Pipwell Cottage. He'd hated it but he'd known it was important to her; paying him proved to her that she had control over her life. He said, clearing his throat, "I heard the ditty about Czar Alexander and the Grand Duchess Catherine. Goodness, what a harridan she is. She certainly deserves her treatment in the song. In this case, I must admit I felt sorry for the Prince Regent. He might be a fat selfish sod, but he's an English sod and not one of those feudal tyrants in Russia who kill peasants because they don't like the smell of them."

"It's true. Grand Duchess Catherine really outdid him in rudeness, crudeness, and lewdness." She laughed and it warmed him to his toes. "Isn't it marvelous that all those juicy words rhyme?"

"Yes, and they roll off the tongue. I hear it everywhere I go."

"The Czar is just as horrible, rude to the Prince Regent, hobnobbing with the Whig opposition who in truth think him a fool. He deserves a ditty all to himself, I think."

"Possibly," Badger said. "But he didn't force himself into that all-male banquet at the Guildhall like the Grand Duchess did. Then she insisted that all the music be stopped because it made her sick. I should have loved to be there."

"I too. Can you imagine the Regent having to plead with her to allow the musicians to play *God Save the King?*"

"Yes," he said, "and she complained loudly through the whole thing. I have been thinking, though. There are other subjects than the state of diplomatic affairs, though those buffoons give as much credence to incompetence and self-aggrandizement than the gentlemen and ladies of the *Ton* give to frivolity and sin."

She laughed again and he wanted to shout for the sweet sound of it. "You've a good point there, Badger. Hmmm, perhaps I should read other parts of the *London Times* and the *London Gazette* with that in mind."

"You used to read all of the papers, every single word. Perhaps it is time again. I came to speak to you about something else, Duchess."

She merely cocked her head to one side, her quill still held in her right hand, poised above the piece of fools-cap.

"It's his lordship."

She became utterly still, almost as if she were trying to draw into herself, to protect herself. "What about him?"

"Mr. Spears has written to tell me it is possible that his lordship will be returning to London soon."

"I see. Has he sold out again?"

"I don't know. Mr. Spears didn't say, so I must assume that he hasn't."

"Very well. This will require some thought. Ah, is that the front door knocker?"

It was. Nettles, the London butler, allowed Mr. Wicks to present himself a very short time later in the drawing room. He gave her a low bow and a frazzled smile.

"Dear Mr. Wicks, what is the matter? Do sit down, sir. Should you like a cup of tea? Brandy?"

"No, no, my lady. It's . . . oh dear, this isn't good, but I had to come tell you immediately so that we could make plans. I'm so very sorry, Duchess, er, my lady, that—"

"Please, Mr. Wicks. Calm yourself. Nothing could be that dreadful. Do sit down and tell me about it."

In his agitation, he was actually pulling on a straggly lock of grizzled white hair. She waited, her silence meant to calm him, to steady his nerves, and it did. She was good at soothing nervous animals, nervous humans, all except Marcus, her husband. All she could do to him was make him want to murder her.

Finally, he managed to draw a deep breath. Then, unable to help himself, he blurted out, "The American Wyndhams are at Chase Park!"

"The Americans. Oh yes, my father's youngest brother, my uncle, gambled and wenched until my grandfather wanted to throw him in Newgate, but then to top it all off, Uncle Grant went to America and had the gall to marry an American, which finally got him disinherited, and he went to Baltimore to live, which was her home."

"Yes, yes, and Grant Wyndham is dead. But his wife, Wilhelmina, isn't, nor are the three offspring. There is Trevor, James, and Ursula. Oh dear, you already know all of this. They're all at Chase Park."

"Tell me about it, Mr. Wicks."

"I wrote to them, my lady. I had to because I believed back in April that the earl, er, your husband of three weeks now, wouldn't marry you and that the Americans would inherit and thus I had to write to them and tell them of their probable good fortune, and now they're here. They never wrote me back, they never came to see me in London. They just went directly to Yorkshire, to Chase Park."

"How very odd. How did they know where the estate is, I wonder? You did say that Uncle Grant is dead. He would have known, surely, but his wife?"

Mr. Wicks shook his head distractedly. "I don't know, but I do know, Duchess, that I must leave now, today, no later than tomorrow morning. I must go to Chase Park and I must explain to them that there is nothing for them, nothing at all. It is a dreadful coil. Why didn't I simply trust you to bring his lordship about? I'm a dolt, Duchess, a bloody dolt."

He stopped cold, shocked that he'd spoken so, with such unplanned emotion.

She merely smiled. "Perhaps you should have waited, but you didn't. Indeed, you did what you believed the proper thing. No matter, Mr. Wicks."

"I'm relieved the earl isn't here and thus, perhaps, if the good Lord still believes me an obedient servant, the earl won't find out about it."

"It wouldn't matter if he were here or if he did find out. You did what you believed was right, Mr. Wicks. Don't chide yourself further."

She rose and shook out her skirts. "Well," she said more to herself than to Mr. Wicks. "Life does dish up odd things on one's plate." She turned to him, holding out her hand. "I will come with you, Mr. Wicks. Please don't worry. We will face the dreaded Americans together. I wonder if Marcus would declare the name Wilhelmina as ugly as Josephina."

*   *   *

Marcus Wyndham, VIII earl of Chase, arrived at the Wyndham townhouse in Berkeley Square on the twenty-sixth of June.

Nettles took his lordship's cloak and hat. "My lord," he said with more formality than before, for now there was appropriate substance in his lordship's pocketbook, no longer just the title, "her ladyship left with Mr. Wicks for Chase Park just yesterday morning. She was accompanied by Badger and that red-haired maid of hers, Maggie."

"I see," Marcus said. "Spears," he said, turning to his valet, who appeared to be closely regarding the elegant baseboard molding in the entrance hall, "do see to our things. I wonder if there is anyone here to prepare the meals since Badger went with my . . . went with the Duchess."

"I have instructed Mrs. Hurley to resume the responsibilities, my lord. Her ladyship told me to see to it quickly since it was possible that you would be arriving here shortly. If I may say so, my lord, her ladyship has seen to everything in a very nice way—so considerate she is—if you don't mind me saying so."

"No, not at all, Nettles."

Heartened, the butler added, "She is a very restrained lady, my lord, allowing no familiarities, as if anyone would ever attempt such a thing in any case. Now, my lord, would you like a glass of port, perhaps, in the library?"

Marcus took his port and went instead to the master bedchamber at the end of the corridor on the second floor. It was a massive room, hung with dark draperies, spread with even darker carpets. The furnishings were very old, but they sparkled with wax. He wondered if his wife's meddling hands had rubbed in the lemon wax.

He said to Spears, who was gently folding his cravats and placing them in a drawer in the dresser, "I wonder at the timing of all this."

"Timing is an unpredictable thing, my lord, or so I've always believed."

"I wonder why she left for Chase Park with Mr. Wicks, of all people."

"Ah, my lord, I do have a letter, given to me by Mr. Nettles, who was given it himself by the Duchess to give to me and finally for me to present to you. You understand?"

"Certainly, Spears. Where is this letter that couldn't have been given directly to me but had to go from the Duchess to Nettles to you and then to me?"

"It is here, my lord."

"A circuitous route always arouses suspicions," Marcus said as he tore open the envelope. He read, cursed, then laughed. "Well, this is very interesting. It seems the American Wyndhams are at Chase Park, for Mr. Wicks, doing his duty, mind you, wrote them and told them of their perhaps good fortune come June sixteenth. They came to England and now they are at Chase Park, arriving evidently precisely on the sixteenth. The Duchess and Mr. Wicks have flown after them. Ah, yet again, she meddles."

"She is your wife, my lord. It is not meddling, it is the duty of a wife to see to her husband's interests whilst he is unable to see to them himself."

Marcus gave his valet a grunt, then began to pull off his clothes. "I would like a bath, Spears."

"Yes, my lord."

He had one leg out of his trousers when he said, "I wonder why they went to Chase Park. Surely Mr. Wicks didn't tell them that was also part of their probable inheritance."

"It is a mystery, my lord."

"One would have expected them to stop here first in London and see Mr. Wicks. Then perhaps he would have directed them to the Essex House, in Clampton, a very nice property that I saw with Charlie and Mark some years ago. Unentailed, of course."

"Now all the property is yours, my lord, including Essex House."

"I know."

"Will you be remaining home this evening, my lord?"

"If you must know," Marcus said now, pulling on a dressing gown, "I am going to White's. A number of gentlemen are dining together."

"I suggest, my lord, that you not imbibe overly. I further suggest, my lord, that we ourselves leave for Chase Park on the morrow."

"Your suggestions be damned, Spears. I have no intention of going to Chase Park. Mr. Wicks got himself into this mess, let him extricate himself. Doubtless the Duchess will be of invaluable assistance. Why else would she have accompanied him if she hadn't intended to meddle? No, don't answer that. In any case, I have to meet with Lord Dracornet at the War Ministry tomorrow."

"I will see to your bath, my lord."

"Good. Don't try to change my mind, Spears. I won't go to Chase Park despite the fact that the namby-waist, Trevor, just might be the future earl." Marcus looked around the rapidly darkening bedchamber. "You know, perhaps I should inform Mr. Wicks not to send the American Wyndhams to the rightabout entirely. Perhaps I should tell him that dear Trevor just might be the earl someday. Perhaps I should tell him to encourage that mincing fop, Trevor, to get himself an heir just in case. Yes, I should make that communication to Mr. Wicks."

"The Duchess, my lord? Your *wife?*"

"Oh, she is fully aware that any offspring she bears will be not of my seed and thus will not succeed to the title."

He listened to Spears suck in his breath. Ah, consternation from his unflappable valet. It felt good. He smiled. He was still smiling when the two footmen entered the bedchamber, carrying buckets of hot water for his bath.

He was lathering his hair when he chanced to see Spears looking at him with the tight-lipped disapproval of a bishop at an orgy. It made him feel even better.

He saw Spears open his mouth and quickly said in a voice as chill as Gunther's ices, "No, Spears, I will not go to Chase Park. I don't care what either Wicks or the Duchess do. I plan to enjoy myself immensely here in London. I plan to install a mistress over in Bruton Street or perhaps in Stretton Street, close enough to here so that I can stroll over at my leisure. Yes, that's what I'll do."

"My lord, it would seem that such activities would require more time than you currently have, what with your duties to Lord Dracornet. Surely you will be too busy with the upcoming discussions about the Congress in Vienna this fall."

"Oh no, not at all. I'm not a bloody diplomat, Spears, indeed, all the diplomats involved in this program will be intriguing until the world comes to an end. They will lie and they will do anything to gain what they want. No, it isn't for me. Damn, if you're going to stab someone, do it to the man's face.

"Lord Castlereagh did inquire as to my wishes about the Congress and I told him that I had other things to do. Actually, I came near to kissing his boots in my politeness, but I did indicate that I wouldn't be able to attend, as much as I wanted to. As to Lord Dracornet and my duties here in London, I have asked for a temporary leave since I have to assume my new duties as the VIII earl of Chase. Not only just new, of course, but also now endowed with appropriate funds. I believe Lord Dracornet was so relieved that I am no longer destitute, no longer a peer embarrassment, that he was most sincere in his best wishes to me."

"I see, my lord. Your lordship has many other duties as well. Your estates are vast. Surely you recall in your ten months as a real earl how much time is required to see that everything runs smoothly."

"Oh yes, I remember, Spears. No, you can keep any further arguments to yourself. I'm not going to Chase Park. The last female in the world I wish to see is the damned Duchess."

"She is a countess, my lord."

"Your wit ripens, Spears. Go away and leave me alone. Forget Chase Park. That's the last place I'll go."

CHASE PARK

The Duchess stared at Wilhelmina Wyndham. Surely she couldn't have heard her aright. "I beg your pardon, ma'am?"

"I said that the grouse hereabouts could be infected with vile parasites."

She hadn't said that, of course, but the Duchess let it go. "I will ask Badger to carefully examine all grouse before they are allowed into the kitchen."

Wilhelmina Wyndham nodded. She turned then to gaze about the huge drawing room. "All this is just as my husband described it to me. He painted pictures for me—all in words, naturally—and I could see Chase Park in my mind. At last I am here. You wondered why we came here immediately and didn't go to London first. I knew exactly where Chase Park was and I wanted to waste no time coming here."

She said gently, "But ma'am, even if Marcus and I hadn't married, Chase Park would have remained the earl's, for it is entailed."

"Yes, I know. You think Americans are fools, but we're not. This was my husband's home. Surely you don't believe I wouldn't want to visit here?"

"Of course you would want to and you are welcome. Chase Park is very impressive and its history is quite remarkable, but surely you will want to visit London before you return to America?"

"You are nothing but a slut. I won't heed you."

The Duchess blinked hard. "I beg your pardon, ma'am?"

"I said that you're in a rut and if I must plead to stay here, why then, so I shall. I won't leave you, Josephina, you would be ever so lonely. You don't mean to say that we are not welcome here?"

"Naturally you are welcome, ma'am, I just told you you were, but Chase Park is not your home. As Mr. Wicks told you last evening, there is no inheritance now that his lordship and I have wed."

"I think you're a conniving bitch."

The Duchess heard her well enough this time, but she was so utterly taken aback that she couldn't think of a thing to say. She just looked at her, waiting to hear what she would say now, but Wilhelmina merely shrugged and walked toward the grand double doors. "Yes," she said now, "it must be nice to be very rich."

"Indeed."

Wilhelmina smiled and said gaily, "What do you think of my boys?"

Boys? Trevor was all of twenty-four, Marcus's age, and James was twenty. "They are very charming, ma'am. Ursula is also very nice."

"Ursula is a girl and thus of no worth, of no more worth than you are, damn you."

"Excuse me?"

"I said that Ursula is a girl of excellent birth, certainly of as good a birth as you are, you sweet lamb, you. I believe she will make a brilliant marriage, don't you think?"

She had a pounding headache. She merely nodded, thankful that her aunt Wilhelmina was willingly taking herself off. She quickly went out the eastern side door and hoped to lose herself in the Chase gardens, beautiful now in midsummer, all the roses blooming wildly, hyacinth with their bell-shaped flowers scenting the air, mixing with the perfume of the roses and the daisies and the huge-blossomed hydrangeas. Lilac trees with their lavender clusters were so sweet now that they clogged the senses. She walked to an ancient oak tree, so twisted and bent that it could be a meeting place for witches on All Hallows' Eve. She seated herself on the wooden bench beneath its lush green canopy of branches, leaned back against the trunk of the tree, and closed her eyes. It seemed as if she'd endured Aunt Wilhelmina for more than a decade and not just a day. Well, actually, a morning and an evening. Not even a full day.

Mr. Wicks was in a state of retreat, for Aunt Wilhelmina had all but attacked him the previous night.

When they'd arrived the previous afternoon, Aunt Wilhelmina had greeted her and Mr. Wicks as her guests. It was the strangest feeling to see Aunt Gweneth standing back, clearly deferring to the woman with the aging but still beautiful face with her head of hair so blond it was nearly white in the sunlight. Aunt Wilhelmina was unexpected, but then again, so was Trevor, the effete sod, the damnable pederast, the lisping dandy, according to Marcus. She smiled remembering Marcus's contempt. *Trevor! By God, a pederast, a mincing fop!*

She supposed she'd expected to see a pretty young man with his mother's fair complexion and blond hair. She supposed she had even expected him to lisp and wear his cravat so high it touched his ears. Well, Marcus would be in for a surprise. No, there would be no surprise, for Marcus wouldn't come to Chase Park, not as long as she was here.

She wondered if he had returned to London.

The Twins and Ursula found her ten minutes later. At least her headache was reduced to a dull throbbing.

Antonia announced, "I have decided to marry Trevor, Duchess. He is much to my liking."

Ursula, a small fourteen-year-old girl with her mother's fair coloring, a sweet girl with pretty features that surely would mold into beauty in four or five years, said, "Trevor is unhappy. He won't want to marry you yet, Antonia. Besides, you're only fifteen. At least for three more months. Trevor is quite old now."

"Old! Trevor is quite a young man!" Antonia was flushed with the heat and with the audacity of such a statement about her newly appointed idol.

Ever practical, Fanny asked, "Why is he unhappy?" She took a big bite of the apple she held in her hand, the loud munching the only sound for at least a minute. At least it wasn't a sweetmeat, the Duchess thought. It seemed to her that Fanny's face had thinned out over the past months. She and Antonia were growing up. She felt ancient at the moment.

"His wife died," Ursula said.

Her mouth fell open in surprise. "He was married, Ursula?"

"Yes, Duchess. Her name was Helen and she was very nice, quite the prettiest girl in Baltimore, only she was sickly, Trevor said. She died in childbed, after a bad fall from her mare, the babe passing away with her. It happened only four months ago. They were only married for a year and a half. Trevor went away to New York, I think. He came back to escort us here to England because Mother wrote him a letter and begged him. James didn't like it because he wanted to take Father's place and see to our welfare. He didn't speak to Trevor for at least a week. I don't think Trevor even noticed. He was with us in body, but he was still away, if you know what I mean."

"Yes," the Duchess said. "I know exactly what you mean, Ursula." Goodness, she thought, overwhelmed, you simply never knew anyone, their secrets, what they'd endured, what they were really like.

"By the time I am eighteen," Antonia said with all the confidence of a girl who was rich, had an immense dowry, and who had been deferred to all her life, "Trevor will be over his unhappiness. Then he will marry me and I won't die in childbirth because I ride a horse quite nicely and I'm healthy as a stoat. Aunt Gweneth says so."

Fanny took the last bite from her apple and flung it into the pond that lay just beyond the huge old oak tree, sending several ducks flapping away, quacking loudly in surprise. "Perhaps I will take James. I just wish he were a bit older. Boys are so callow. They need to ripen, like wine, at least that's what Papa used to say. Remember, Antonia? Papa used to tease Charlie and Mark whenever they remarked upon a pretty girl. He told them they were still vinegar, that it would take some years to make them vintage port."

Ursula laughed. Antonia looked stricken. The Duchess said easily, "I can see him teasing the boys, Fanny. It's good to remember your brothers with pleasure and laughter."

Ursula said, "That's why the earl is an upstart, isn't it? Since my cousins died—"

The Duchess said calmly, "Marcus is your cousin too. He is the earl of Chase. Your father and his father were brothers. You will give him your respect, Ursula, and you will look to him as the head of the Wyndham family, which he is."

"Yes, ma'am."

"I suppose you can begin with that respect business now. It is Ursula, isn't it?"

The Duchess didn't move. Then, very slowly, she turned to see Marcus leaning at his ease against the oak tree. How long had he been standing there, listening and watching? She stared at him silently.

"Yes, my lord."

"You may call me Marcus, since we're cousins."

"Yes, Marcus."

"No fond hello for your husband?" He strode to her, stared down at her bent head a moment, then lifted her limp hand and kissed her fingers.

════════13════════

MARCUS FROWNED AT the sound of that damned valet of his humming. Then Spears broke into song, his deep rich baritone echoing in the huge bedchamber as he neatly folded Marcus's socks.

> "She's more rude than the Regent,
> She's more boring than a stoat.
> She's as lewd as her brother,
> She's as crude as a goat.

> "Ah, yes, crudeness, rudeness, and lewdness,
> Three great qualities.
> The Grand Duchess Catherine—
> She royally claims all three."

He couldn't help it, he smiled now. He'd heard how Czar Alexander had choked, spitting up his wine on his royal white gold-buttoned tunic when he chanced to hear some citizens beneath the bow street window of White's, singing at the top of their lungs, the words stark and clear as they'd strolled up St. James Street. He'd roared with rage, claimed he would slay the bastards, but was restrained by the unflappable Henry, the majordomo of White's for longer than Marcus could remember, and by the Duke of Wellington himself.

"Ah, my lord, you have seen the Duchess?"

"Yes, but just for a moment. She was in the garden with the bevy of young girls."

165

"Is she well?"

"Why shouldn't she be? Wait a minute, Spears, have you learned something I should know through that damned spy network of yours?"

"No, my lord, it is just that when I last saw her, she wasn't happy. You hadn't been even passingly civil to her."

"She didn't deserve civility, passing or otherwise. As for you, you traitorous sod, you should have been fired."

"I appreciate your lordship's restraint." As he spoke, Spears gently laid six freshly ironed cravats flat in a drawer.

"Are you mocking me, Spears?"

Spears straightened. "I, my lord? Mock you? Certainly not, my lord. The very thought deeply offends."

Marcus grunted, saying, "When I saw her, I didn't at first gain her attention. You see, she was exhorting Ursula to give me full respect for I was the head of the Wyndham family."

"Since you are the head of the family, it is most appropriate for her to point that out, my lord."

"I suppose so, but why did she say it?"

Spears stilled his task of straightening the brush, comb, and nail file on top of Marcus's dressertop for a moment, then said gently, "Why would she not say it, my lord?"

"Oh shut up, Spears. You're not a bloody vicar. It's none of your damned affair. It was never any of your damned affair until you and Badger were impertinent to stick in your noses. I should have you transported to Botany Bay."

"Ah yes, my lord. A nasty place, I've heard. Now about the garden, my lord, and what the Duchess said?"

"Oh very well. I said something then—made my presence known—and she turned into stone—nothing new in that. Now, I'm going riding. I hear that bloody effete sod, Trevor, is out marching one of my horses over my acres. Doubtless he's marking off boundaries to see how rich he will be."

"But you said he would be rich, my lord. Either he or his progeny."

"Go to hell, Spears. This is different. This is now, and I won't have the bugger treating Chase Park as if he's the earl. I will put a stop to his insolence. I wonder if the peacock uses a sidesaddle."

"It is an interesting speculation, my lord. Will you be back for luncheon?"

"Yes, if I can find the fellow. I think I'll bloody his nose, no, that would make him shriek and perhaps cry. That would never do. No, I'll offer to lead his horse back to the Park for him. Surely he'll be fatigued by the time I find him. I wouldn't want the poor little dandy to overtire himself."

"Most considerate of you, my lord."

The Duchess was hungry but she didn't want to go into the dining room and face Aunt Wilhelmina. But poor Mr. Wicks didn't stand a chance around that formidable lady so she knew she couldn't leave him alone. She shuddered, remembering how Mr. Wicks had told her in a trembling voice how Aunt Wilhelmina had come to his bedchamber— *bedchamber!*—and proceeded to get everything out of him that she wanted to know because he was so startled, so taken aback, so incredulous. In short, Aunt Wilhelmina was a force to be reckoned with.

Where was Marcus?

He'd kissed her fingers, then smoothly introduced himself to Ursula, hugged Antonia and Fanny, then taken his leave, not looking at her again, or tossing her another meager word.

She sat in her place at the table. Aunt Gweneth had insisted she take the countess's chair, that it was only right. She'd merely been residing in that chair until the true countess could occupy it. She'd been charming since the Duchess and Mr. Wicks had arrived, treating the new countess of Chase as if she'd been a bastard again. The

Duchess was vastly relieved. The last thing she wanted was
Aunt Gweneth's nose out of joint. The earl's chair at the
other end of the twelve-foot table was empty.

No Marcus. She noticed that Trevor was missing as
well. At least Mr. Crittaker was here, speaking kindly to
Ursula.

She nodded to Sampson to begin serving the luncheon.

Aunt Wilhelmina said in a carrying voice, "Where is my
nephew, the one who's set himself up as the new earl? He
has yet to introduce himself to me."

"I met him, Mama," Ursula said as she forked up a bite
of turtle soup. "He is very handsome and ever so big and
nice. His hair is as black as the Duchess's and his eyes are
a light blue too, just like hers."

"They are related," Wilhelmina said. "They should not
have married. It is not natural or healthy. Any offspring
could be gnomes."

"Really, ma'am," the Duchess said easily, "it's all perfectly legal. The Church doesn't object, after all."

"The Church of England," Aunt Wilhelmina said with a
goodly dose of contempt. "What do those old fools know?
If a man has a title and money to bribe them, they'll bend
any rule that's ever been written. That's what happened,
isn't it?"

"I assure you, ma'am, no bribery was necessary. Actually, his lordship and I were married in France. It is very
Catholic there, ma'am. Even the civil requirements are as
strict as those of the Church."

"The French," Aunt Wilhelmina said and snorted, just
like Birdie, the Duchess's mare. "It is all understandable
now. Perhaps I had best ask if your marriage is even valid
in England."

"I assure you, ma'am, that it is. Mr. Wicks will also
give you assurances. He would, I daresay, even give you
the assurances here, at the luncheon table, rather than in his
bedchamber. Now, everyone doesn't need to hear more of
our chatter. I suggest that we eat."

"You're a stupid shrew and a bitch."

"You didn't . . . no, no, surely no. Excuse me, ma'am?"

"I said all of this has come out of the blue and everything's gone off without a hitch, for you. What else could I have said?"

Evidently as Aunt Wilhelmina's indignation increased, her ability to match her cover-ups to her insults lessened.

"He should have come to meet me," Wilhelmina said. "The new earl shows no respect. It shows his lack of breeding."

That was probably true, the Duchess thought, at least the respect part. "You will enjoy his company at dinner, ma'am," she said easily. She raised her glass and Toby, the footman, poured her more lemonade. "Thank you," she said and smiled at him.

"He should die."

"I beg your pardon, ma'am?" the Duchess said, ignoring the gasp from Mr. Crittaker, who was sitting next to Aunt Wilhelmina and thus could hear even her muttered words.

"I said the earl would cry over this ham. It is too salty and the pieces are sliced too thick."

Mr. Wicks sent the Duchess an anguished look. He took another bite then excused himself. The Duchess knew poor Ursula couldn't budge from her chair until her mother gave her permission to do so. As for Fanny and Antonia, they looked too astonished to budge.

She ate slowly, chewing thoughtfully as she looked at her young cousin James, who was just her age. He would probably be as large a man as Marcus when he reached his full growth. Now, though, he had still a boy's slenderness. His hair was fair and slightly curly, his eyes a wonderful dark green, and his chin was square as the devil, stubborn, if she didn't miss her guess. He was also very quiet, perhaps sullen, his eyes on his plate, eating one bite after the other without pause. He seemed oblivious of all of them. She remembered Ursula saying that he was angry because he wanted to be the man of the family, not Trevor. She noted the very beautiful onyx ring on the index finger of his right hand. It was set in an intricate gold design. She wondered idly where he'd gotten it.

The time crawled. She had no more thought, idle or otherwise, she was too bored, too itchy. She wished Marcus would come in. She just wanted to look at him. She also wanted to look at his ribs and his arm to see that he'd healed properly.

Finally, when she knew escape was now possible, she smiled and rose. "Forgive me, but I have business to see to. If you will all excuse me."

"She thinks she's royalty, the stupid bitch."

"What did you say, Mama?"

"I said her gown is lovely, and looks quite rich."

Mr. Crittaker choked on the muffin he was eating.

She walked sedately from the breakfast room, though, truth be told, she would have preferred running.

She went to the small back morning room she had taken over, and set herself to reading the *London Times*. She read the society pages, trying to find some amusing tidbits, but failed. It held only a mite of her attention for about ten minutes. She kept thinking about Marcus, wondering where he was.

She couldn't wait to see what he made of that mincing fop, Trevor.

Marcus slowed Stanley to a canter, enjoying the fresh summer air on his face. The sun was high overhead, a bit warm, but no matter. Where was that wretched coxcomb, Trevor?

The gall of the man, stealing his ill-tempered stallion, Clancy, despite Lambkin's assurances that the brute was mean and vicious and not to be trusted. Lambkin had said the American gentleman had just laughed, mounted Clancy without a single problem, and ridden off to the east. So Clancy had been feeling charitable, more's the pity. Ah, but it never lasted. He hoped his cousin wasn't dead, yet.

Marcus had been riding over three hours now, and still no sign of that poaching sod, Trevor. He'd stopped to speak to his tenants when he chanced upon them, feeling oddly warm inside when they greeted him enthusiastically and welcomed him home. The men had asked him all about the damned Frogs, finally beaten down into the ground just as they'd deserved, flattened by our British troops, aye, and about that tyrant, Napoleon, the king—no, bloody *emperor*—of the clobbered Frogs. His tenants treated him as if he'd been the one to make Napoleon abdicate single-handedly. The wives had smiled at him and given him cider. The children had regarded him with favorable awe.

It had felt good, damned good. For the first time, he'd felt like he really belonged here. As the master of Chase Park, as the earl of Chase. Maybe.

Marcus realized he was hungry. Where was Trevor? Had Clancy finally turned into himself again—treacherous bugger—and thrown him? Was he dead at this moment? A nice thought, that. No, he'd probably sprained his ankle and was limping gracefully back to the Park, one white soft hand pressed against his brow. Maybe he was even quoting some of Byron's poetry to romanticize his trifling complaints.

Marcus snorted, then chanced to see someone riding toward him from the north. He pulled Stanley to a stop and waited.

It couldn't be the fop, Trevor. No, as Clancy got closer, he saw that the man riding toward him was big, as large as he was—that is, the top part of him was. Maybe he was a dwarf with short legs, but Marcus didn't think so. The man rode as one with that brute, Clancy, swaying easily in the saddle, in complete control, his gloved hands holding the reins easily. Damnation. It had to be that bloody Trevor.

When Clancy got close enough, Marcus, absolutely furious, feeling like a damned fool, shouted, "Why the hell didn't you change your bloody fop's name?"

The man didn't answer until he'd pulled Clancy to a well-mannered halt directly in front of Stanley's nose. He grinned, a white-toothed grin that held mockery, an infuriating understanding, and a good deal of humor. He shrugged, then said, in a soft southern Colonial drawl, "I presume you're my cousin Marcus? The earl?"

Marcus stared at the man, a man with vibrant, nearly harsh features, strong nose and jaw, thick black hair and eyes as green as the water reeds that grew thick in the pond in the Chase gardens. He was muscular as hell, his body powerful, obviously an athlete, his posture indolent yet bespeaking authority. He simply didn't look like a Trevor, damn his sod's eyes.

"Yes. Why didn't you change your name? Good God, man, *Trevor!* It's enough to make a real man puke."

Trevor laughed, showing dimples that didn't look at all effeminate, but rather powerfully charming. Marcus would wager this man was a terror with women. He wanted to hate his guts, but he found he couldn't. He even found himself smiling back at those damned dimples. Trevor said in that lazy drawl of his—stretching out endlessly, like thick honey, just taking its time—that should have made him sound like an affected half-wit, but didn't at all, "It does tend to lead people to think of me in a different way," Trevor Wyndham said easily. "That is, naturally, until they meet me. I believe my late father, another one of your uncles, thought it an elegant name. That aside, in all honesty, it is better than the other names he and my mother landed on my head."

"What are they?"

"Horatio Bernard Butts."

"Good God," Marcus said blankly. "Butts?"

"Yes, Butts was my mother's maiden name. Awful, isn't it?" Trevor Wyndham stuck out a strong black-gloved hand. "A pleasure to meet you finally, cousin."

Suddenly, Marcus began to laugh. He threw back his

head and laughed louder. His cousin was content to watch him. Finally, Marcus wiped his eyes, then took his cousin's proffered hand and shook it vigorously. "The image I've had of you ever since Mr. Wicks told me about the American Wyndhams—good God. I've referred to you as a mincing fop and damned coxcomb, and much worse. Forgive me, cousin. If you like, you can smash me in the stomach. Just not my ribs, they're still sore from a small contretemps I had in Paris."

"A contretemps? I would say you're a dirty fighter, Marcus. Perhaps we can find some ruffians and see which of us is the dirtiest. No, I don't believe the Duchess would like that. Nor would she like me to strike you. I daresay since you've been married such a short while, she still believes you the most handsome, the most noble, the most exquisite of all God's creatures."

Marcus grunted, looked vaguely uncomfortable, and Trevor raised a thick black eyebrow.

"I would also say that the Duchess is quite the most beautiful woman I've even seen."

"Have you been to London? To Paris?"

"No, but I am a man and I'm not blind. You don't think your wife is immensely lovely?"

Marcus grunted again, saying nothing, his anger at her simmering and bubbling like a witch's caldron just beneath the surface. He'd just met his bloody cousin, who, it turned out was a man and not a fop, but he'd be damned if he would spill his guts to him. How dare he carry on about the Duchess as if she were even remotely available to him?

"Needless to say, my mother was rather perturbed when our Aunt Gweneth informed her upon our arrival that you had married—before the magical date of June sixteenth. She was prostrate with a headache for a good four hours. She quite contemplated the topic until I took over her headache from her."

"I did not know you were here at Chase until three days ago. The Duchess had left me a message and I followed."

"The Duchess said you were in Paris, seeing to the restoration of the Bourbon."

"Yes, consider him restored. As for the rest of it, there will be a congress convened in Vienna this fall. It will probably be as entertaining as the shows at Astley's Amphitheater."

His cousin cocked his head.

"Ah, Astley's is a theater of sorts where you will find men and women doing tricks on horseback, girls going into the audience selling oranges and themselves, men harassing bears to make them dance, that sort of thing. The children love it and the young men go there to ogle the scantily clad females."

"In Baltimore we have a similar sort of entertainment. It's called *The Fat Man's Chins*."

Marcus laughed.

"It's odd," Trevor said thoughtfully. "You look a lot like me. Except for the eyes."

"Yes. You're as dark as a sinister midnight. Our uncle, the former earl, called me the devil's own son. Does that apply to you as well, cousin?"

"Perhaps. Recently, at least." Trevor shrugged, then shook his head at him, dismissing unpleasant thoughts, Marcus thought. He continued, "Your lands are impressive. I borrowed Clancy, though I thought your stable lad, Lambkin, would explode with fear believing this nice fellow would dash me beneath his hooves."

Trevor leaned over to pat Clancy's chestnut neck. Clancy, the perverted bugger, snorted and nodded his great head.

Marcus wished he could punch the damned horse in his nose. He said, eyeing the stallion with disfavor, "He isn't known for his sweet temperament. Let him near a mare and he turns into Attila the Hun ready for an orgy. However, you seem to have him well in hand."

"I have a way with horses, actually I have a way with most animals. A gift, I suppose. Sometimes an embarrassment, particularly when a lady's little lapdog bites her mistress to free herself and comes leaping up on my leg, barking her head off. Incidentally, Lambkin seems to worship your every footstep."

"Lamb's a good lad and excellent with the horses. My uncle didn't like him. Why, I don't know."

"Probably because he's lame," Trevor said. "I've seen it before."

"I hadn't thought of that. Maybe you're right."

"My brother, James, has my mother's fair coloring and very green eyes. My father's eyes were a much darker blue, like the Duchess's. Ah, forgive me. It makes sense since the earl was her father."

"Yes," Marcus said curtly. "You appear to know most of the machinations that have landed upon my head."

"Yes. My mother is excellent at badgering people into telling her everything she wants to know. Your Mr. Wicks was no exception. He scarce presented her a challenge. She told me this morning that after everyone had gone to bed, she went to his bedchamber last night, and he was so flustered, he spilled every scape of information he had. Don't worry yourself, cousin—"

"Call me Marcus."

"Marcus, don't worry. I will convince her that there is absolutely nothing here for her and remove her as quickly as possible. I've a mind to see London again and I think Ursula and James would enjoy themselves, perhaps even at this Astley's of yours."

Marcus pulled on his earlobe, a habit that Badger had. "I don't mean to pry, Trevor—Good God, that name still curdles my tongue!—but there is no financial problem with your family, is there?"

"None whatsoever," Trevor said, his voice becoming quite cool, odd considering that the drawl was still in full force. "My mother simply came without considering that it would be highly probable that you and the Duchess would marry. I tried to make her wait, but she refused. I had no choice, really, but to accompany her here."

"Why did she wish to come to Chase Park? Even if the Duchess and I hadn't married, the Park is entailed, and thus it wouldn't have been part of our uncle's legacy."

"I don't know. But she insisted. Father spoke so longingly of Chase Park, perhaps he created this myth in her mind and she had to come. Perhaps she is just nosy. Who knows?"

Marcus laughed.

"There is also the Wyndham legacy."

"The what?"

"My father spoke of the Wyndham legacy, his voice always low and whispery, as if he feared someone would overhear, as if it were some sort of dark secret and no one else could know about it. He said that someday he would come back and find it and we would be richer than the mandarins in China."

"I have never heard of it. My father never mentioned such a thing nor did the former earl, at least not that I know of. This is very curious. Did your father give you any clues as to what kind of treasure?"

"I don't think he knew, even though he spoke of jewels and gold pieces, that sort of thing. But he told my mother of the clues he'd pieced together before our grandfather kicked him out. It was old, he'd say, buried long ago, buried back in the reign of Henry the Seventh, just before Prince Arthur died, when the future Henry the Eighth was just a lad, a golden little boy, he'd whisper, riches beyond belief and all belonging to the Wyndhams. And you'd lean toward him, half-afraid and utterly held by his voice and his words. Then he'd change it the next week and claim it was buried during Henry the Eighth's time or Queen Elizabeth's. Who knows?"

Marcus found that he had to shake himself. Trevor continued in his cool, drawling voice, "You know, of course, that Aunt Gweneth and my father corresponded until his death, then it continued with my mother."

"No, I had no idea. However, I haven't been back here the five years since Charlie and Mark died. I came back only after our uncle died and I became the earl. The Wyndham legacy, huh? A treasure from the early sixteenth century? It all sounds like a bloody fairy tale to me."

"It does to me as well. But my mother believes it."

"Shall we go back to the Park?"

Trevor nodded, giving Marcus a lazy smile. He said in that drawling voice, "If nothing else, I can sit and just look at the Duchess. It warms a man's cockles to see such character and loveliness in one female person."

"You need spectacles," Marcus said, turned Stanley, and dug his heels into his stallion's sides. The two men rode side by side in silence back to the Park.

=14=

MAGGIE FASTENED ELIZABETH Cochrane's pearls around the Duchess's throat, stood back, and studied her in the mirror.

"Lawks," she said, complacently patting her own brilliantly red hair as she saw her own image with its vibrant mass of ringlets above the Duchess's head.

The Duchess smiled, wondering who the lawks was for. She said as she lightly fingered the pearls, "My mother used to tell me that pearls had to be worn often against the flesh otherwise they would lose their luster."

"Lawks," Maggie said again, fingering one of the pearls at the back of the Duchess's throat. "These oyster pellets must have cost his lordship a bloody fortune, I'd say."

"You'd probably say right, Maggie."

"Now, Duchess, I didn't ever think anyone could have hair as gorgeous as mine, but yours is passable-looking, it surely is, despite that sinful black color, maybe even because of it since your skin is whiter than that Yorkshire cheese I've seen, that looks wonderful but tastes like a rotted bladder. Yes, all that black hair provides distraction, and distraction is important for the stage."

"Thank you, Maggie. You're probably right."

"Yes, you're quite passable-looking too, beautiful even, if I stretch it just a little bit, and I know his lordship will think so too."

"You believe his lordship will stretch it, Maggie?"

"Stretch what, Duchess?"

Marcus stood in the now open adjoining doorway between

178

the master's bedchamber and the countess's bedchamber. She grew very still, unable to look away from him. He was dressed in immaculate black evening wear, his linen stark white, his cravat crisp and beautifully tied, thanks, undoubtedly, to Spears and his magic fingers. His thick black hair was a bit long, curling over the top of his cravat. His blue eyes, however, were cold, colder than the freezing winter of last year that froze the Thames. She tried to smile at him, tried to recognize within herself that he was here and he was sleeping in the bedchamber through that single door, just a thin simple door, that was all, and now he was here, looking at her, and she managed to say calmly, "Maggie thinks I can go beyond passable-looking if you stretch it."

"Aye, but you, my lord, as her husband, would stretch it to beautiful."

"Would I? I wonder. You've tricked her out well, Maggie. You may leave us now."

"Just a moment, my lord," Maggie said with oblivious disregard of the fact that the earl himself had dismissed her. "Let me put this lovely shawl over her shoulders. It's fair cool at night and I won't want her to catch a chill. There, Duchess. You look bloody fine now. I approve."

"Thank you, Maggie. Please don't wait up for me."

Maggie just nodded, then, to Marcus's utter astonishment, she winked at him, then walked out of the bedchamber, all the while touching and patting that flaming red hair of hers.

"Where the devil did you find her?" he asked, staring in bemusement at the now closing door.

"Badger did, in Portsmouth. She found him, actually. She saved him from being run down by a mail coach. I needed a maid and she needed a position. It seems she was between acting jobs. That's what she is, you know, an actress. Actually, she is very competent and I find her amusing."

"She winked at me!"

"Well, she's never been a maid before. She was probably

quite used to men looking at her and admiring her, perhaps even more. Perhaps she forgot herself for a moment and was seeing you as a possible leading man in a play."

More like a possible protector, Marcus thought, but said aloud, shaking his head, "Jesus. The countess of Chase has an actress for a personal maid." He added with a grin, "I will admit she does have panache."

He'd actually referred to her as the countess. She felt something hopeful sprout in her, but then he turned away from her and began pacing the floor.

"You shouldn't allow her to call you Duchess. Surely it's an impertinence." This observation he tossed over his shoulder. "Everyone calls you Duchess. You're not Duchess, you're a countess, you're a *my lady*."

"I don't really care," she said, watching him closely. "How is your wounded arm?"

"What? Oh, my arm. It's fine. Actually, it still gets a bit sore if I use it too much."

"And your ribs?"

He looked at her now, stood there with his arms crossed over his chest, his legs spread, and just looked down at her. He was so big. She knew he was trying to intimidate her, but how could he when she'd known him since he was fourteen years old? As she recalled, to a nine-year-old girl, he'd been overpowering even then. "What is this? Wifely concern?"

"I suppose so."

"My ribs are well again."

"That's good."

"I met Trevor. He was riding Clancy. He looked like a bloody centaur."

She smiled, actually smiled, more than one of her meager little liftings of the corners of her mouth, and he knew she knew he'd made a complete and utter ass of himself. He persevered. "Trevor is still a wretched dandy's name."

"Perhaps, but he is a man with nothing at all effete about him. Don't you agree?"

"Yes, dammit. It's ridiculous to pin such a ridiculous name on a man who is my size."

"Yes, but right now, I really don't care." She paused a moment at the surprised look on his face, then said, "It's good to see you, Marcus. I was hoping you would come here."

"I hadn't intended to, but, well—" He shrugged, and for a moment, she would have sworn he looked vastly uncomfortable, even embarrassed.

"Regardless, I'm glad you're here. Your Aunt Wilhelmina is a difficult woman, a puzzle really. Your young cousin Ursula is very nice, I'm sure you realized that when you met her this morning in the garden. James is my age, perhaps a bit older, and I have no idea what he's like. The look on his face is decidedly morose. Something is wrong there. As you saw for yourself, Trevor is quite a lovely man. He's kind."

"What do you mean he's 'lovely'?"

"He's big and very strong and handsome."

"I want you to watch what you say around him, be certain not to be overly friendly. He might try to take advantage of you. You're very innocent and he is not."

"I'm a wife now, surely I'm not all that innocent."

His eyes dilated. "Yes," he said slowly, "yes, you are. No, don't argue with me in that reserved well-bred way of yours. Tell me why you're glad I'm here."

She became perfectly still and he hated it. He shouldn't have reminded her that she was reserved. She'd become a bit more open with him, spoken freely, without restraint, but now her hands were folded quietly in her lap. Slowly, very slowly, she raised her chin and looked at him squarely. It seemed to him a mighty effort. Then she said baldly, "You're my husband. I missed you."

"Your husband," he said, sarcasm evident in his repetition. For a moment he'd forgotten her perfidy, but now she'd fanned those perfidious embers back into a roaring orange flame. "Don't you find it odd that we're married, Duchess? I've known you since you were nine years old, skinny with knobby knees, and so very solemn you could have been a pillar in the Norman abbey in Darlington. Yes, so quiet you were, so aloof, so very reserved and watchful. I saw the future beauty in that somber, too quiet child. And I called you the Duchess and everyone then saw the same things I did, and thus it became your name, even to your red-haired maid who's an actress and looked at me as if she'd like to bed me and have me buy her a bauble in return."

"Yes," she said. "And when I was only nine years old, you were fourteen and proud and strong and the devil's own son. My father was right about that. You led Charlie and Mark into some disgraceful mischief. My father always knew it was you who led them, always. Do you remember when you, Charlie, and Mark made a stout pine casket and filled it with stones and laid it on the floor in front of the altar in the church? When people filed in for the Sunday service, there it was, that coffin, just lying there with a rough bouquet of flowers on top of it, and everyone was afraid to open it." She smiled a very small smile down at her folded hands, then added, "I looked up to you ever so much, but still you frightened me."

"Frightened you, Duchess? I'm sorry, but I can't imagine you ever being frightened of anything. If anyone threatened you, you'd just freeze him with one of those still, blank looks of yours. One of those inhuman looks that make a person silent as the grave. Why would you be frightened of me?"

She looked away from him then, and he realized she was embarrassed.

"Why?"

She said in a voice that didn't sound at all like her, a low voice, muffled, reticent, "You belonged here. You were strong and confident and you belonged. Even now you belong although you're fighting it with all your absurd misplaced pride. I never did belong."

He didn't want to deal with that, not now, there was

too much else to think about. He said shortly, "Well, now you're the damned countess of Chase. Surely you believe that you belong now. More than I do, truth be told, for your father gave you everything that wasn't nailed down with the entailment. Doesn't everyone treat you with respect and deference?"

"Yes, everyone has been most kind. When Mr. Wicks and I arrived three days ago, I will tell you that I was nervous. After all, I am the former earl's bastard, no matter how you cut the cake, a former bastard who is now the mistress. But everyone has been generous. I am grateful for that."

"But not dear Aunt Wilhelmina."

"Her behavior is frankly strange and leaves one's mouth gaping open. I daresay you will gain her measure very quickly. It is time to go to the Green Cube Room, Marcus. It is time for you to meet her and James."

"Very well. No, no, don't move. Good God, you're showing too much cleavage, Duchess. Here, hold still."

He strode to her and she rose to meet him. He rearranged her shawl, tying it first in a knot and setting it directly between her breasts, then pulling the knot to the side so that the long part of the shawl draped low over the front part of her gown. It looked frankly ridiculous, but she said nothing, didn't move, her arms hanging limply at her sides. Still displeased, he tried to pull the gown up, but it wouldn't move, for it was banded snugly beneath her breasts. For a moment, she felt the warmth of his fingers against her flesh. If he noticed where his fingers were, he gave no indication of it, saying with a frown, "I still don't like it. You will have it altered. I trust your other gowns are not so very revealing. Doubtless that mangy dog Trevor will ogle you. You will give him one of those cursed cold looks with your chin up to the ceiling, like he's so lowly he's beneath your slipper."

"Do you believe he would prefer being a mangy dog to a bloody fop?"

But now Marcus was looking at her breasts. Then he looked at his fingers that had touched her. He didn't say anything. She saw his eyes darken, saw his pupils enlarge. His cheeks flushed. Slowly, he lowered his fingers and lightly skimmed them over her bare shoulder. He looked utterly absorbed. Those calloused fingertips moved slowly, so very slowly, to touch the top of her breasts. She felt a shiver of warmth, felt a shaking response from deep within her and leaned toward him, pressing her flesh against those tantalizing fingers. He whipped his hand away. She was motionless for a moment, knowing she had to regain her sense, knowing that she hadn't behaved as she should have. She'd simply done what her body had wanted her to do and he'd found her unacceptable. She finally managed to say, "It is time."

"Yes," he said in a low voice, still looking at her breasts. "I suppose it is time, Duchess."

It was very late. She yawned, then realized that she couldn't manage the buttons at the back of her gown. She stood there before her mirror for a moment, wondering what to do. She wondered until the adjoining door opened and Marcus walked through, wearing an old burgundy velvet dressing gown. His feet were big and bare.

She froze. "What are you doing here?"

He walked up to her, stopped just inches away, and smiled down at her. "I'm your husband. I'm also the master here. I can be anywhere I please."

"I see," she said, her eyes on the lapels of his dressing gown. She saw the bare threads threatening to pull apart, particularly at his elbows.

"I doubt it."

"What do you think of Aunt Wilhelmina?"

He frowned a bit. "She is unexpected. She was all charm and sweetness to me, but I don't trust her. As for Trevor, I was right. He stared at your breasts and don't try to deny it. And James, he was staring too, but he is more concerned with his own troubles than with your attributes. It went off all right. Everyone behaved himself. It's fortunate that there are so many tidbits of interest right now, what with the political situation and all the entertainment our foreign visitors are providing us. Have you heard that ditty about the Grand Duchess Catherine? With the rude, crude, and lewd? She and her brother, Czar Alexander, and their antics, will provide dining conversation for another three months."

"I have heard Spears singing it. I think it a clever ditty. He has a beautiful voice."

"He thinks so at any rate. As I said, Aunt Wilhelmina acted normal, at least as much as a Colonist can act normal, their speech being so slow you want to yell at them to just get on with it. Yes, the evening went off just fine."

The evening hadn't been all that painful, she thought, as she nodded slowly. She had, however, been surprised when Aunt Wilhelmina had oozed charm all over Marcus. He was right about that. And she'd watched him, she couldn't seem to help herself. She'd looked at his beautiful mouth, listened to his deep voice, his deeper laughter, the way he chuckled off-key, and couldn't seem to keep her eyes off his hands, large hands with black hair on the backs, and those long fingers of his, fingers that had touched her, caressed her.

"Would you please unbutton my gown, Marcus? I cannot seem to manage it."

With any other woman, he would have believed it an invitation. But not with her. Not with the Duchess. His wife. She turned, lifted the thick glossy black hair that was in a loose pile down her back. It hung there in deep ripples, for she'd just pulled the braids apart and smoothed them through with her fingers. It was a style that suited her, those fat braids interwoven with ribbons in a coronet atop her head. Her face was too fine, too well-sculpted for all those clusters of ringlets over the ears. No, this style suited her to perfection. He unfastened the row of small buttons that marched up her back. The gown was quite pretty, the dark blue the precise color of her eyes. Still, it was cut too low.

When the gown gaped open, he took a step back. "There," he said. "You're free of it."

She turned to face him. He didn't move. There was no screen in the bedchamber. "I have to change now, Marcus. Would you please leave me for a while?"

"No. But I will get in bed."

She stared at him, words shoved together into a meaningless mass in her throat. She watched him walk to the bed set on its foot-high dais, watched him walk in his bare feet, big feet that were really quite beautiful, watched him pull the covers back, unsash the dressing gown, shrug it off, and naked as a black-haired god, climb into the bed. He pulled the covers to his waist, fluffed the pillows behind his head, and settled himself. Now he watched her.

She wasn't stupid. He wanted to have sex with her. But still there were no words in her mouth or in her mind. Her mind was filled with the sight of him, standing there, for just an instant really, shrugging off that dressing gown, showing her his long muscled back, his man's flanks, his man's buttocks and long, thick legs. She swallowed. She supposed she'd considered this, but not really, not to this point, not to where he was actually in her bed, and he was awake and sober and appeared to want this. To want her.

She felt a surge of hope. She stared at his chest with its mat of thick black hair, at the obvious strength and power of him and said, "You want me to be your wife now, Marcus?"

He merely smiled at her and crossed his arms behind his head. "Get undressed, Duchess."

Slowly, she pulled the gown off her shoulders, eased it past her hips, and let it drop to a soft pool of blue silk at her feet. She slid her hands beneath her chemise and pulled the dark blue garters down her legs and unrolled her stockings. She kicked off her slippers and pulled the stockings off her feet. Dressed only in her chemise, she stepped out of the clothing and walked slowly toward the bed.

"You didn't want me before," she said, stopping a foot from the dais. Her black hair fell and framed her face, a face now very pale in the dim light. Maggie her maid had been right. The contrast of all that sinful black hair against the white flesh of her arms and legs and the pure white of her chemise was starkly beautiful. She was exquisite, this wife of his who had drugged him and married him while he was in a stupor and who had come to his bed and made him take her virginity so that he couldn't, in a state of enraged stupidity, if he could have ever been that abysmally stupid, annul the marriage.

"True," he said, "but I'm a man. Since you are my wife and have no say in the matter, I might as well avail myself of you. It's certainly more convenient than riding into Darlington and finding a comely wench there to see to my pleasure. Not that I'll gain much pleasure from you, but I'll make do. I'm not that bad off, so even a modicum of pleasure will suffice me. Now, come here. I want that chemise off you."

"But you said you didn't want a child from me. You said you would gain vengeance against my father by not allowing a child of mine to inherit the earldom."

"That is what I said. I meant it."

"I don't understand."

"Undoubtedly you don't, but you will soon enough. I do ask that you not cry or moan or whimper when I take you, Duchess. If you must lie there like a piece of silverware, then I will make do, but no sounds, if you please."

"You won't call me Lisette, will you?"

He laughed, not a very pleasant laugh. "Oh, indeed not. But perhaps I will call you Celeste."

She paled even further, flinching deeply, but none of it showed in her face, for it was all inside her. She didn't move. "You were only in London for a single night."

"Yes. So?"

"This Celeste person, you were with her for just that one night?"

"Yes. She was quite talented. Not so much as Lisette, but she's from Bristol where there were naught but rough seamen to practice on. Doubtless it will take her another year or so to perfect her skills. Her breasts were quite impressive. I couldn't hold them and my hands are quite large. Not that it mattered really. Now, come here, Duchess."

There was pride, after all, and he'd just pushed her beyond what she could excuse, beyond what she could bear. "No, Marcus. I don't think so." No, she couldn't bear any more of it, not another word. She turned on her heel, her bare heel, grabbed her dressing gown from the end of the bed, and walked quickly to the door, jerking on the dressing gown as she went. Her hand was on the doorknob when she felt him behind her, touching her, his right hand over her head against the door. She tried to jerk it open but it didn't budge.

He leaned down, his left hand lifting her hair and he kissed the back of her neck.

She stood very still, her dressing gown loose about her for somehow, somewhere, the sash had disappeared. He blew his warm breath against her ear and gently nibbled the lobe.

She didn't move, didn't make a sound. She was holding her breath.

Very gently, he turned her around, laced his hands beneath her hips and lifted her. He carried her to the bed and laid her on her back. He stood above her, naked, but she didn't look at him, she couldn't, she was too frightened and far too excited. She was aware of his size, his power, the way he filled her vision, if she would but look at him. He didn't say anything. He jerked the dressing gown off her, then turned and smiled. "Now the chemise."

He lifted her hips and jerked it up to her waist, then pulled her upright, bringing her face against his chest, and tugged it over her head.

He eased her back down and stretched himself out next to her on his side. He didn't touch her, just looked at her face.

"So cold, so contained," he said, then stroked her hair from her forehead and back from her ears. "It is what a man expects from a wife, who is also a lady, I suppose. It is considered well-bred to be cold and contained, having no ill-bred feelings to betray any bodily pleasures. But still it is a disappointment. You have very nice ears, Duchess." He kissed her ear, his tongue tracing its outline.

She sucked in her breath, but held herself perfectly still.

"Don't ever again wear a gown like the one you wore tonight," he said in her ear. "It's beautiful and obviously expensive, but it's still a tart's gown."

"You mean it is a gown my mother would wear?"

He paused a moment. "I didn't say that."

"You're afraid I will be a tart, that it's in my blood, that it's already beginning to come out, at least in my clothes."

"Perhaps, I don't know. Hold still now." He leaned over her and her breasts were pressed against his chest. He closed his eyes a moment at the feel of her. His hand fell to her face, his fingers tracing over her cheekbones, her nose, smoothing her eyebrows, then moving to stroke her throat. "You are so white," he said, leaned down and kissed the pulse in her neck. Then his mouth was on hers, hot and pressing, and she gave no more thought to Lisette or to Celeste; she gave it no thought at all. She opened her mouth and gave him her own warmth and her excitement that was building deep inside her, pounding in her, wanting to be free, to shout, but she tried to hold it down, tried and tried.

His hand was caressing her breast now, tugging gently, making that pounding go deeper and deeper until she didn't think she could bear it. She slid her arms around his back, fascinated by the warmth of his flesh. He was now hers, this man who was also her husband, and at least now, in these few moments, he held no contempt or anger for her, just wanting and need, and it was enough, it had to be enough.

He raised his head and stared down at her. He saw the flush on her cheeks, saw the pulse pounding in her throat. Her arms were tight around his back, her hands stroking downward to his flanks.

"Duchess," he said and came over her.

She moaned words that wouldn't speak themselves, she couldn't hold it in, at the feel of him against her, the heat of him, and she opened her legs for him.

She heard him suck in his breath, she saw him rise over her, looking down at her body, his breathing harsh and raw now, and then he was touching her with his fingers. Suddenly he shook his head. He stared at her until she was trembling with the excitement of it, then he lifted her hips and then his mouth was touching her belly, his tongue harsh and wet and hot on her flesh, and she didn't understand, but she didn't care, for the pounding was building and building and there was no stopping it now. She knew if it did stop, she would shatter somehow.

She cried out, her hands now on his shoulders, wildly kneading his flesh, then in his hair, tugging, and he went lower then and sealed his mouth against her and she screamed with the shock of it, the immense power of it. Screamed and moaned and lurched wildly, her head thrashing on the pillows.

The feelings were beyond shattering. Never had she believed such a thing possible, but it was and she was in the midst of it, and it went on and on and she let those feelings fill her, knowing somehow they would overwhelm her and she wanted that. She reveled in the nearly painful sensations that rocked her deep, expanding to enclose all of her, not just her body, but her mind and her hearing and her smelling and it was hard to breathe even. The wildness controlled all of her senses, and for those moments she was naught but feeling, naught but mad frenzy, willingly trapped in those wondrous sensations that shook her and made her cry out. His mouth burned into her flesh, so very hot, pulling on her, then soothing her, and slowly, very slowly and gently as the feelings retreated, softening now, but they were still there, deep yet easing now, but somehow waiting still, and he reared up, and she saw him staring down at himself and at her, saw his hand on himself, then move to open her for himself, and he came into her fully and deeply.

She screamed, bucking upward, nearly heaving him off her, grabbed him around his neck and brought his mouth down to hers. She felt the weight of him, the strength of him and she felt his tongue deep in her mouth just as his sex was deep inside her belly. It didn't last long, just a few moments and she felt him tense and drive even more deeply, even more fiercely, and then she took his moans in her mouth and she held him against her. She never wanted to let him go, never.

═══ 15 ═══

IT WAS HE who left her, pulling away to stand beside the bed, his big chest heaving with the power of his release, a sheen of sweat making his flesh glisten, just standing there, staring at her, and she wanted desperately to touch him, just to touch her fingertips to his flesh, to slide them through the thick hair on his chest, to trace the contours of the deep muscles that shaped his arms and shoulders and his belly. She'd never known, never even considered that a man's body could be so very beautiful, so pure and strong, such an instrument of pleasure for her. She forced her eyes upward.

She started to hold out her arms to him, wanting desperately to bring him back to her, to feel the heaviness of him on top of her, to feel his warm breath against her cheek, her ear, but knowing now, realizing now as her brain cleared, that he was well and far away from her now. She was utterly alone. Slowly, saying nothing, for there was nothing to say, after all, she pulled the covers to her chin. She wanted to cover herself, to sink down under the protection of those covers, for he was gone now, almost as if he'd never been driving into her, making her quake and scream and heave like a madwoman.

He said, "Dammit."

That was odd, she thought, and frowned. "Why do you curse? Did I do something wrong?"

His eyes narrowed even more on her face. "I hadn't meant that to happen." She heard it now, the disgust in his voice.

Oh God, he was regretting all of it now. But she wasn't a shy tongue-tied maiden to be devastated. She had pride, but still it was difficult to keep her voice steady and calm, but she managed it, saying, "You didn't mean what to happen? You didn't want to stay with me?"

He shrugged then, and grabbed up his dressing gown. "Oh, I wanted to stay with you, Duchess, and that was my downfall, but it won't be again. Next time, I'll do what I must. Surely this one time won't matter, surely."

"What are you talking about, Marcus?"

"You'll see," he said, then grinned painfully. "Doubtless you'll see even before this bloody night is over."

She'd expected—she didn't know what she'd expected. Perhaps some new sign of closeness from him, for what he'd made her feel had been more than she could ever have imagined. It had been glorious and beyond wonderful, and she'd been part of him even though he was a man, a being so utterly different from her in thought and strength and body. Unlike her, he hadn't seemed to care or notice or feel anything other than his man's release. She could have been Lisette or Celeste or any of the now faceless women who would probably be in his future. She couldn't bear it. She was nothing to him—a wife, a convenience. She couldn't bear to look at him. She turned her head away from him.

Marcus stared at her as his heart finally began to slow. He'd never experienced such untidy surges of raw feeling before with any woman in his life. And now with her, the bloodless Duchess, who was cold and contained and frigid and . . . what bloody nonsense. When he'd caressed her with his mouth she'd been more frantic, more uninhibited, than any woman he'd known in his adult life. And when he'd come into her, she'd become frenzied again, pulling him deep, bucking and yelling and it had made him into a savage, grunting over her, wanting to devour her, to absorb her into himself. Fool that he was, he'd been a part of her frenzied pleasure and he'd lost control. By God, he didn't like that, didn't like what she'd made him do, didn't like what she'd made him feel.

He was lying to himself. He'd more than liked what she'd done to him then. But not now, not now that his brain had returned to functioning properly.

He said, as he flicked a fleck of lint from the sleeve of his dressing gown, not looking at her for he was going to lie to her now, not just to himself, "You surprised me, Duchess. You didn't just lie there and endure me. You didn't whimper or moan. Well, you moaned, but it was with pleasure not sufferance."

Actually she'd screamed like the most lascivious woman ever born. She said nothing. She'd pressed her fist into her mouth.

"You were willing. You were more than willing. You appeared to want me more than the most skilled harlot—" He broke off, then continued more slowly now, his speech measured, "I didn't mean that. Forget I said it. What I meant was that you were not pretending. I know women well and I know when a woman feigns pleasure. No, you weren't dissembling. I find that vastly incredible."

Tears seeped from her eyes and onto the fist stuffed in her mouth to keep all sound within her. She would die if he knew how he hurt her.

"I don't like it, Duchess. I don't like surprises and I don't like losing control. Is that what you wanted me to do? Lose control so that you would breed a son for this cursed earldom, for your cursed father who gave you what you wanted? Was it a deal the two of you struck? Well, it doesn't matter what your plots and plans may be. It won't happen again, not this way, in any case. I will see you later."

As soon as the adjoining door closed with a sharp snap, she sat up and snuffed out the candles on the table beside the bed. There were more on the dresser and she rose. There was his seed on her and her steps faltered for a moment. She bathed herself, then snuffed out the other branch of candles.

She was sore, but it was a wonderful sore, a drawing sort of feeling that made her feel again those hidden places that were deep within her. She pulled her nightgown over her head and got back into bed, burrowing beneath the covers.

She lay awake for a very long time. He didn't come to her again that night.

When she awoke, the sunlight was bright in her bedchamber. She blinked and yawned, her mind blurred, for she was feeling again the warmth deep inside her, remembering the softness, the frenzy, the utter losing of herself within her and within him.

"Good morning."

Slowly, she turned her head to face him. He was seated on the side of her bed, fully dressed in a riding habit and glossy black Hessians. One leg was crossed over the other. The softness was gone, the deep warmth naught but a senseless dream. She'd been a fool, naught but a witless fool.

"Did you sleep well?"

She nodded. "Yes, very well."

"A man who knows what he's doing can bring a good night's sleep to a woman."

"And vice versa?"

He frowned. "Yes, that is also true. And yes, I slept very well. Of course a man is much easier to please than a woman." His frown deepened. "I didn't wake up during the night. If I had, I would have come back to you."

He fell silent now, obviously brooding, swinging a booted foot. "You surprised me."

She waited. She wanted desperately for him to tell her that he was pleased, that he found he now wanted her. That he hadn't meant what he'd said last night.

"Yes, you were a great surprise. So wild you became when I put my mouth on you. When I came inside you I thought you'd throw me off you were so frenzied."

Surely he shouldn't be speaking so baldly about it, not now, not in the sunlight, but he was Marcus and he was her husband, and so she said honestly, "I felt things I've never imagined could be. I couldn't help it."

"No, I daresay that if you could have stopped yourself from being so very frantic and savage, you would have." He paused then, and she wondered what he was thinking. Then she wanted to scream at the unfairness of it. He'd said it last night. In a thin voice barely above a whisper she said, "You shouldn't have been so surprised, Marcus, that I acted like a harlot. After all, didn't you believe my gown last night was a tart's gown, like a gown my mother would have worn? Why shouldn't I react to a man like my mother undoubtedly did to my father? You called me savage and wild. Perhaps lewd and promiscuous would do as well, given the bastard I am, given my mother was a rich man's mistress, his bought whore."

"I do not find you amusing. What you are doing," he said coldly, "is giving over to melodrama. It doesn't suit you."

She only shook her head. She'd said it and he hadn't denied it, just steered clear of it. He rose and began to pace the bedchamber. She saw he was carrying a riding crop. He was slapping it against his right thigh as he paced. He turned then, saying, "That damned impertinent Spears was hovering over me this morning, indeed, it was he who woke me because in my dreams I could hear his breathing and see that vicar's disapproving face of his, and he was exhorting me not to be a sinner, and when I woke up there he was."

She said nothing.

"Silent? Yes, of course, you're always silent. That way, you never put yourself on the line, do you? You never have to take a risk. Well, it doesn't matter. Spears knew I'd been in your bed, doubtless doing despicable things to your fair person. He was concerned. No doubt Badger was outside the door anxiously awaiting a full report. I told him to go bugger himself. He drew himself up proud as the Prince Regent, only without the huge belly, and said in that insubordinate bland voice of his that he would fetch his lordship's bath. Then, I daresay, he left to confer with Badger, the disloyal sod."

He lightly slapped his riding crop against his open left hand. "Should I have told him that you were more than willing for me to be with you? Should I have mentioned your screams, the way you lurched and trembled and quivered when I touched you? No, I suppose not. Leave him with his belief that you are the Madonna reincarnated. You're silent. No matter. Your red-haired maid is wrong. You're beyond passable. There's no need for any stretching at all. You're bloody beautiful with that black hair of yours all tangled around your face, and your mouth looks red and swollen. Was I too rough with you?" He leaned down and planted an arm on either side of her. His breath was sweet and warm on her cheek. "Perhaps a bit swollen, but very soft too. I have things to do else I'd stay and kiss you and if I did, then those covers would be around your dainty ankles and I'd be freeing my sex and coming into you so fast you would surely faint from the boorishness of it. No, if I did that, I doubt strongly that you'd behave as you did last night. Yes, you would swoon."

She looked up into his blue eyes and said, "Perhaps not."

He jerked, looked uncertainly at her mouth, then forced himself to straighten. "I will see you later."

He was gone then and she was left to wonder what was in his mind. She'd surprised him a bit. That was something, she supposed. Maggie came in then, doubtless sent by Marcus, and soon she was bathed and perfumed and powdered and dressed in a becoming, quite modest morning dress of white cambric muslin with two deep flounces at the hem. The gown fell gracefully to her ankles where the ribbons of her white slippers were tied in a small bow over her white stockings. The gown also looked exquisitely sweet with its small puffed sleeves. A well-bred just-out-of-the-schoolroom gown fit for a shy debutante. Why had she ever considered the bloody thing? She knew the answer to that. She'd bought it when she didn't know a blessed thing about what went on between men and women, more to the point, what Marcus would do to her and make her feel.

She sighed and pulled the bodice down as far as she could, but there was no cleavage in sight. There were two rows of lace that reached nearly to the pulse in her neck.

Maggie said, "Whatever are you doing, Duchess? Don't ruin the line of this lovely gown. Ah, I see. You want to entice his lordship. Well, cleavage is all well and good, but not necessary, not with your other assets."

The Duchess laughed, a rueful, perhaps even wistful laugh, and Maggie fell silent for a moment, but only for a moment. "Now, you heed me. At least long hair is back in fashion. All those mincing little coiffure fools with their snapping scissors won't be balding any more ladies' heads. Let's keep the fat braids on top of your head with the tendrils dangling down to your shoulders. Those silly little ringlets you're supposed to pile over your ears don't become you, not as they do me. I was made to wear them, what with my brilliant glorious red hair, but you weren't.

"And stop worrying that he won't notice your other things. Men always notice things, particularly a lady's things, though they'll pretend not to, at least overtly, since they're supposed to be gentlemen, at least around ladies."

This monologue left the Duchess momentarily deprived of words. "I understand, Maggie," she said at last. "Thank you."

Maggie beamed at her and patted her own hair, all done up this morning in those impossible little ringlets on each side of her face that did indeed look quite alluring on her. "Now, you go downstairs and have breakfast."

*   *   *

Badger was waiting for her in the breakfast room, a smallish nearly circular room that was filled with bright sunlight pouring in through the big windows that faced toward the east of the house. The table wasn't large enough for all the relatives currently descended upon Chase Park and she imagined they'd dined in the formal dining room. She was thankfully alone. She could see through the lime, maple, and oak trees and the thick well-trimmed bushes to the stables.

"You are pale and too thin. Eat this porridge, it's from a Scots recipe and I made it myself."

She allowed him to seat her and eyed the steaming oats before her. "I hate porridge, Badger. I'm not thin. It's this silly little girl's gown that makes me look unsatisfactory."

He frowned and said, "I forgot. You've hated it since you were a little nit. All right, here are some sweet scones. Eat those. You look quite satisfactory, believe me, even in that virgin's gown. Some kidneys?"

"No thank you. Mrs. Gooseberry allowed you into her kitchen? I know how I look, Badger, in short, ridiculous."

"I believe his lordship asked Mrs. Gooseberry to take a nice vacation early this morning. I am now in charge of the kitchens. There are two other cooks and I will direct them if I don't wish to prepare the dishes myself. I am, I told his lordship, still your valet and my first duties are to you. He got that stubborn look on his face, but I'll say this for him, he did manage to hold on to his temper. You look like a tender pullet in that gown and that's how his lordship better treat you."

"The scones are delicious, Badger. His lordship will always do just as he pleases. You can't change him. I'm not a chicken, tender or otherwise."

"Exactly. Now that you've taken a nice bite of that scone, chew it. That's it. Mr. Spears and I will attempt to change him if it becomes necessary. Now, tell me what happened.

Mr. Spears is most worried because his lordship was being snappish and rude to him—"

"Yes, I know. Marcus told Spears to go—oh yes, to go bugger himself."

Badger looked shocked, his eyes nearly crossing. "You can't know what that means."

"Well, no, but it can't be very nice, considering it's from Marcus and he was quite put out."

"I won't tell you. Just never say it again, all right? Now, tell me what happened."

She took another bite of scone and nearly choked on it. "I can't, Badger. Really, it's very personal."

"He didn't hurt you again, did he?"

"He never really hurt me before. He didn't hurt me, no. Quite the opposite, in fact."

"Ah. How very strange. Or is it? Hmmm, I must think about this. Good God, you're blushing. You, the Duchess— who can freeze the wart off a face with just a look."

"Badger, it's true, you're more my father than my real father ever was, but surely you must realize that such references embarrass me to my toes. And I'm not cold, please, I'm not, truly."

"Yes, I can see that I could possibly make you feel uncomfortable. I'll tell Mr. Spears not to worry. I'll also tell him that you won't say such things as 'bugger' ever again. Duchess, you will tell me if his lordship does anything that is, well, beyond what a gentleman should do?"

"I don't know," she said, looking suddenly quite interested. She was wondering what that *beyond* could possibly entail. She'd become something last night she didn't know was possible, or perhaps if one called a spade a spade, she'd simply been loose as a tart. Maybe she was indeed a tart. How could she find out what she was? She looked at Badger, knowing she couldn't ask him, she'd die of embarrassment. Somehow she couldn't see asking Aunt Gweneth either. She could just see herself saying in a very calm voice that she'd lost all control, all desire to control.

She'd nearly burst with pleasure.

What was this *beyond* business? What else could there be? He could stay with her, hold her close and kiss her and fall asleep with her, but she knew deep down it wasn't that. She wanted to know very much.

"Meet me in that small morning room that you like, Duchess, and we will plan the menus for the week. I've a fancy to try my hand at some of those Frog dishes. Their *filet de truite poché à la sauce aux capres* wasn't bad, was it?"

"Ah, yes, the trout with capers."

"And I shan't forget the *pommes-noisettes.*"

"No, it would never do to forget the potato balls."

He grinned at her. "And perhaps some *asperges tendres à la sauce Bernaise.* Yes, that's it. Twenty minutes?"

She nodded. He patted her shoulder and took himself back to the kitchen.

"You surely shouldn't allow a servant such liberties, Duchess. Not only did he actually touch you, he was overly familiar in his speech. And he spoke *French.*"

"Did you hear all of it or just the last little bit?"

"Just enough, I daresay." It was Aunt Wilhelmina and she looked primed for battle.

The Duchess said, "It's a lovely day, don't you think? I'm going for a walk. What do you think, Aunt Wilhelmina, a cottage bonnet or a small round straw hat tied under my chin by white ribbons?"

Aunt Wilhelmina frowned at her in frustration and chewed on her bottom lip.

"Or perhaps I could change into riding clothes. Then I could wear that adorable black beaver riding hat with the short ostrich plume. What do you think?"

"I hope you get tossed from your horse because you're a bitch."

"*What?* Excuse me, ma'am?"

"I said, 'You should be careful not to get lost and thrown into a ditch.' "

"Ah, certainly. That's what I thought you said. It was just such a kindly sentiment that I was taken aback. It is rather early, isn't it?"

"Why don't you just go away?"

The Duchess just smiled at her, cocking her head to the side.

"I said, 'Why don't you go enjoy the nice day?' "

"Of course that's what you said. Such kindness from a relative I hadn't even heard of until Mr. Wicks told me of my father's legacy."

"Well, all of us wish we'd never heard of you, but we had, for Gweneth has written about you over the years. Everyone also knows that you married his lordship for the position and the money."

"Everyone? Could you be more specific, ma'am?"

Aunt Wilhelmina settled for an elaborate shrug. "My dear son Trevor said it was so and he is very smart."

Trevor had said that?

She managed to say calmly, "It isn't true. No, ma'am. Regardless, I inherited fifty thousand pounds. That is quite a sufficient sum. It was Marcus who would have been hurt had we not married, not me."

"Fifty thousand pounds! It's unheard of to leave a bastard such wealth!"

"I wasn't a bastard long after he left me the money. If you'll recall, Aunt Wilhelmina, my father made me legitimate, something I beg you not to forget again. You become tedious when you continually forget things. It quite makes me yawn. It quite sends me to sleep."

"The earl doesn't like you. He married you only because he had to. He'll take countless mistresses and march them all in front of your impertinent nose."

"Well, that isn't your concern, is it? After all, you will soon be gone, back to Baltimore, and I daresay I won't remember anything you said."

The Duchess left Wilhelmina Wyndham standing there, for once without another word to say or to reshape.

She met with Badger, agreeing to the menu he suggested with just two additions. "Remember those Roehampton rolls you used to make, Badger? Some of those, please. And yes, perhaps some salt cod with parsnips?"

He grinned at that. "Sorry, Duchess, no fresh cod, not today. Perhaps Wednesday night. I'll have to send a lad to Stockton on Tees to the fish market. Now you're certain those American relatives will like the jugged hare?"

"Oh yes, they're not at all provincial. Do send the hare to the table with some red-currant jelly and string beans."

He gave her a severe look. "Naturally. I have always used the old Lincolnshire recipe."

In another thirty minutes, she was in her black riding habit with its epaulets, tight waist, and high black boots, the small black beaver riding hat with its short ostrich plumes set jauntily on her head. She went to the stable to ask for the sweet-mouthed bay mare, Birdie, she'd ridden at Lambkin's suggestion two days before.

Trevor was just mounting Clancy, laughing at the stallion's efforts to remove him from his broad back, patting his glossy neck, enjoying himself and the horse's performance thoroughly. He saw her and called out, "Come with me, Duchess. I would like to ride to Reeth, an errand for my mother."

"That is a two-hour ride, Trevor."

"Yes, I know. Sampson gave me excellent directions. Come with me, Duchess."

"Just a moment, both of you." It was Marcus striding toward them, flicking the riding crop against his thigh. "I feel like riding and Reeth is a fine place to ride to. You would doubtless get lost, Trevor, and God knows the Duchess couldn't find her way to the next dale without me to show her the path."

Trevor arched his dark eyebrow a good half-inch. He said in such a pronounced drawl that she wondered how he could say everything he wanted to say before an hour passed, but he did, "Regardless of all the problems that would doubtless plague us, Marcus, we could have managed. However, it appears that you are set upon being the third in our party. Come along, my dear fellow, before Clancy here becomes enamored with the Duchess's mare and we find ourselves in the soup."

The three of them rode out of the stable grounds, through the park and down the long driveway lined with giant oak and lime trees. They turned their horses onto the small winding country road that led southwest. There was a good deal of silence, black silence. She breathed in the clean summer air, not caring that Marcus was in a snit. She even grinned when Marcus managed to insert Stanley between Birdie and Clancy. He was acting jealous, that was it. She was astounded and absurdly heartened. She smiled between Birdie's twitching ears, wondering how long he could contain himself.

It wasn't long.

"I don't like you going off with strange men, Duchess, without my permission."

═══16═══

SHE TURNED IN her saddle. "Strange? You believe Trevor is strange, Marcus? Exotic? Peculiar? Surely you just think his name is strange, don't you?"

"You know very well what I mean, madam. Don't bandy words with me, particularly not in this mongrel's presence. It gives him too much satisfaction."

"So I'm a mongrel, not just a strange man. That makes me feel more acceptable, cousin."

Marcus realized in that moment that he was being an ass. He managed to hold his tongue to bland topics until they neared Richmond.

Richmond lay just four miles to the east of the small hillside village of Reeth. They stopped at the Black Bull Inn for a glass of cider.

"Since I am with you, Duchess," the earl of Chase informed his wife as he closed his hands about her waist and lifted her from Birdie's back, "it will be acceptable for you to come into the taproom with us. If, however, you had accompanied this mangy hound by yourself, you would have had to wait out here in the stable yard so that everyone could see that you understood the decorum demanded by your station, and good sense."

"He is a considerate husband," Trevor said, grinning. "No, Marcus, keep your verbal darts to yourself. I'm thirsty." He said to the Duchess, "Does he always concern himself with what people think of you?"

"No," she said, "this is the first time. I rather like it. It makes him appear masterful."

"Masterful? Ah, that has a fine ring to it, doesn't it? What do you think, Marcus?"

Whatever Marcus thought he kept to himself. He strode ahead of them into the inn.

To her surprise, once there were two ales in front of the men and a ladylike lemonade in front of her, they began to discuss the war between England and America. It was as if now they were the best of friends. They spoke as would two soldiers concerned with strategy and tactics, not with politics or principles. They were perfectly amiable to each other as long as she kept quiet, which she did, content to look at Marcus, to listen to his voice, crisp and certain.

As they rode toward the spacious village green of Reeth, she said to Trevor, "This is one of the more charming of the Swaledale villages. See all the black and white houses? Are they not unusual? And there are many pottery shops. Reeth is known for its fine pottery."

He smiled at her enthusiasm and nodded. "The shop I must visit is on High Row."

Marcus frowned, but held his tongue.

"High Row is just on the western side of the green. Ah, yes, lead is mined in the nearby hills," she added, grinning at him now.

"More educational bits, Duchess?" Marcus said.

"I am pleased to be educated," Trevor said. "There is propriety in education. Such education a husband can't possibly object to."

"Well, let me see. If we had time, we would ride to Muker, it's the most rugged and remote of the Yorkshire dales. It's really quite savage. I picture the Scottish Highlands as looking something like Muker."

"A charming name—Muker."

She realized then that she was telling all this nonsense to Trevor just to enrage Marcus. She was surprised, somewhat disappointed actually, at his restraint. Had they been alone, by now he would be cursing, telling her to cease being a nitwit, any number of utterly Marcus-like things. She could picture his scowl, hear him muttering. But his face was set and cold. He did look disgusted, but he was admirably silent. She swallowed and looked away for a moment. Had he really been jealous?

The day was warm, but not overly so. It looked to rain, but she hoped it would hold off until the afternoon.

"So," she said to Trevor after they'd left their three horses in the grubby hands of a boy who'd handily snaggled the single pence Trevor had tossed to him, "it appears that Marcus has decided you're all right, despite your name."

Trevor laughed, tossing a smile toward Marcus. "Evidently he so admires my ability to handle Clancy here that he is quite willing to overlook my regrettable name. Isn't that so, cousin?"

"Clancy," Marcus said, "is an unaccountable stallion. There is no saying what sort of man he will tolerate."

Trevor just laughed again.

"Marcus does say what he means."

Trevor said, "It's a relief he's not one of Castlereagh's diplomats. England would surely be at war with the entire world."

She laughed, a sweet sound that made Trevor Wyndham start. It made Marcus feel vicious. Trevor said to her, "Did he tell you about the Wyndham legacy?"

"No, what is that, pray tell?"

Marcus said, "There is no need to regale her with all that nonsense. The only reason you've said anything at all is because you believe it's just a story, a fantasy, naught more than a silly legend."

"Very true, but it is interesting. Also, my mother believes it to be genuine. Listen now, Duchess, and learn about it." He told her about the treasure buried sometime during the sixteenth century, probably somewhere during the time of Henry the Eighth's marriage to Anne Boleyn, that unconscionable harlot, and how his father had told them story upon story about it, speculating what it actually was, but knowing, just knowing that it was wealth beyond anything imaginable, this mysterious treasure that was here, at Chase Park. It just had to be found. He told her that Aunt Gweneth had corresponded with his father and with his mother, after his father's death. "I told Marcus that my father couldn't really place it, but he did tell more stories about the time of Henry the Eighth than of any other. That is why we're here in Reeth. Mother believes that there is a clue to be found in this small Antiquarian shop on High Row owned by a Mr. Leonardo Burgess. My father and this Mr. Burgess were friends as boys and young men, and corresponded faithfully and enthusiastically over the years. Mr. Burgess kept an eye on things here, so my father said, and just last year, Burgess wrote to tell my mother that he'd discovered something. He seemed quite excited about his find. So, we are on a treasure hunt, Duchess. What do you think? Are you interested?"

"I think it's wonderful," she said and laughed aloud again. She thought she heard Marcus mutter under his breath, "The bloody fool, the damnable bloody fool."

"Surely though, Trevor, your mother can't want you telling all of us about the treasure."

"It doesn't matter," Trevor said, shrugging. "As I said, I don't believe it exists. I agree with Marcus entirely. It is a game to pass the time until I can pry my mother from here and take her and James and Ursula to London. But before I can do that, I must exhaust all possibilities. She must be convinced that there is no treasure and never was. I'm sure you've noticed that her mind is of a tenacious bent."

"But if there is such a thing and if we find it, why then, it would belong to Marcus. Surely your mother realizes that."

"That is why she wants to box my ears for spilling the treasure story. If she thought I had the two of you with me today, off on this most sacred of quests, she'd doubtless want to stick a knife in my throat. I suppose she planned to dig up the treasure beneath a full moon at midnight, pile it into a coach, and escape without you, Marcus, being any the wiser."

"I'll tell her as soon as we return," Marcus said. "A knife in your throat isn't a bad thought."

"Oh no, he won't, Trevor, don't worry. We'll stay mum. Your mother will never know that we've dipped our feet into her treasure hunt. And Ursula? What does she think about all this?"

Trevor shot her an odd look. "Ursula is a girl."

"This is incontestable. What does she think about the treasure?"

"I don't know."

"Girls do have brains, you know, Trevor, and imaginations. Perhaps they even have talents about which men have no idea."

"Yes," he said, his voice suddenly clipped.

"The Duchess is right. Girls have many things—talents included—that continually surprise men," Marcus said, his eye suddenly caught by a quite lovely young girl who was openly eyeing both him and Trevor. "That little lass over there, why she could be naught but a flirt, or she could willingly want to have a man pleasure her."

The Duchess clamped her mouth shut.

Trevor frowned at Marcus.

They walked in silence to High Row.

As it turned out, Mr. Leonardo Burgess was quite a surprise to all three of them.

Once they'd identified themselves, Mr. Burgess ushered them quickly into the dusty shop, pulled the curtains over the windows, and drew them back into the deep shadows.

"You'll not believe this," he said, shaking Trevor's hand with fervent enthusiasm.

"Probably not," Trevor said, then smiled, robbing his words of offense.

Mr. Leonardo Burgess was a bull of a man, completely bald, but sported a huge black mustache that he liberally waxed. He grinned as he spoke, showing crossed front teeth.

"I'm glad you've arrived, Mr. Wyndham. And you, my lord. I knew your uncle, but I've yet to meet your lovely

wife. My pleasure, your ladyship. Very nice, very nice.
Now, Mr. Wyndham, do allow me to tell you how sor-
ry I was to hear of your father's death from dear Mrs.
Wyndham."

Trevor's father had died five years before, but he nodded
gravely to Mr. Burgess. "Thank you, sir. Now, I understand
that you have come across something that will help us locate
the Wyndham treasure?"

Mr. Burgess drew nearer and lowered his voice to a near
whisper. "Oh aye, lad, I'm not stupid. I know you believe
this is all twaddle, all fevered imaginings on your father's
part and now on your mother's part. The old earl never did
anything but laugh contemptuously about it. But do I look
like a man who would suffer twaddle? There's still a cast of
uncertainty in your eyes. You believe me a meandering old
fool. Ah, no matter. Just wait until you see this." He turned
on his heel and sped as fast as his impressive bulk would
allow through a curtained-off entrance to a back room. He
returned shortly, cradling in his arms a very large book that
looked to be ancient. The cover was an illumination of a
thick cross with a beautiful rope of pearls looped around
it. The cross was red, the pearls a deep gray. The red
ink was faded and peeling, but still vibrant. It was old,
so very old.

"Come here, away from the light. The pages are so
fragile I fear they'll split and crumble. Now, look here,
all of you."

Mr. Burgess gently laid the book on top of a counter.
The Duchess breathed in the stale dust raised by the turning of each thick page. The pages of the huge tome were
done in beautifully executed script, some in a deep black,
others in royal blue, yet others in that same brilliant red
as the red cross on the outside of the tome. There were
more pictures—of animals grazing in fields with piles of
strange rock formations in the background, of priests blessing kneeling men and women in the square of a town, of the
inside of a small Norman chapel that surely looked familiar.

Finally, there were sketches of a magnificent abbey, drawn in stark black against a background of fierce heavy black clouds. Oddly, the next pages were of its lush grounds.

"I recognize this abbey," Marcus said, lightly tracing a fingertip over the outline of the building.

"Aye, I do myself, my lord. It is the Saint Swale Abbey, once one of the richest monasteries in all of northern England."

"Its ruins lie very near Chase Park," Marcus added.

"So that is Saint Swale," the Duchess said. "As children, Fanny, Antonia, and I would track each other like the wild Indians in America through the ruins."

"Aye, my lady. Listen now, Cromwell, that miserable jackal, put it toward the top of his list."

"Cromwell?" Trevor said. "I thought Cromwell was the fellow who led the anti-Royalist Roundheads and beheaded King Charles I back in the middle of the seventeenth century."

"Aye, Oliver Cromwell was the great-grandson of this Cromwell's nephew. Betrayal, greed, and power mongering flow in all their veins, curse the buggers, begging your pardon, my lady. The king—Henry the Eighth named Cromwell his vice-regent—made him more powerful than any man should ever be."

"So it was in Henry the Eighth's time. What is this about a list?" Trevor asked.

"The king was bankrupt. The easiest way to get all the wealth he wanted was to take the monasteries—they owed allegiance to the pope, after all—and not to Henry who was the head of the Church of England. Cromwell made up a list, beginning with the wealthiest of the monasteries. It was called the time of the dissolution, beginning way back in 1535 and lasting for three years."

"I begin to see where the legend of the treasure derives," Marcus said, stroking his fingertips over his jaw. "Many of the monasteries had great wealth, not only in land and buildings and holdings, but in jewels and gold collected over the centuries. And their religious artifacts were priceless even then—gold crosses encrusted with precious gems and the like. They knew Cromwell's men were coming and thus they hid as much treasure as they could."

"Exactly, my lord, exactly." Mr. Burgess beamed with approval on Marcus, until Marcus added, "I would have thought, however, that instead of burying all the loot, the monks would have taken it with them when they fled."

"They were holy men," Mr. Burgess said in a voice to rival a bishop's. "They didn't want their monastery's wealth to fall into the king's rapacious hands."

"As I recall," Marcus continued, "most of the monks were set adrift in the world after Henry sold off their monasteries to anyone with the money to meet his price. Many starved, for they had no notion of how to survive."

"Aye, 'tis true, the poor buggers, beggin' your pardon, my lady."

Bugger was a versatile word, she thought. If the monks were buggers, then surely it couldn't be so very bad, could it? Did monks bugger themselves as well as being buggers?

Trevor said, "So, you have a clue to tell where some monk buried his abbey's wealth?"

"Not exactly, Mr. Wyndham. What I have is the proof that there was a treasure buried."

Mr. Burgess turned another page. There was only script on this one. It was in Latin. He ran a blunt finger beneath the words as he said slowly, "The monk says that it was Beltane—the celebration of Beltane or the first of May is an ancient rite, still practiced in Scotland and here in northern England," he added to Trevor, then continued. "Aye, the monk writes that it was Beltane and the night was dark as a dead man's eyes, and the winds blew strong across the dales and whistled through the crags, threatening to uproot the trees in the maple forests. The fires burned too brightly and many became uncontrolled, the winds whipping the fires and the people into a frenzy. Many were burned and killed but they stayed, swaying with the ancient rhythms of the past and crying out in blind ecstasy, and performing the heathen rites of fertility that heralded the growth and rich heat of summer. He says that he and six of his brothers dragged the chest from the abbey, staying in the shadows as best they could for they'd heard that Cromwell had sent men there to prevent just what they intended to do. Look here. It also seems they were carrying a body with them, a large bloated body, he writes. This is very odd. What body?" He pointed back to the following text. "He writes they promised their Holy Father that the king would not have their abbey's wealth for his immoral uses."

The page ended. Mr. Burgess slowly lifted the page and laid it carefully down. The next page was a drawing of the raging Beltane fires, their flames shooting heavenward with wild-faced people staring upward at the shooting flames. And then it changed. The people were still pointing, or perhaps reaching for something, but now, strangely, they seemed to be inside a room, not outside with the Beltane fires. And they were looking upward.

Mr. Burgess gently lifted and turned that page. There was nothing more, only the obvious proof that someone had torn out one or more of the precious pages. Gently, as if he were touching the most precious of gems, Leonardo Burgess lightly traced his blunt fingertips along the jagged rips. "Someone tore out the next pages, all of them."

"I'll be damned," Marcus said.

"Indeed," Trevor agreed.

"But who?" the Duchess asked. "And when?"

"A long time ago," Mr. Burgess said. "There's yellowing at the edges. See?"

"I do wonder who," Trevor said. "In any case, the thief didn't find the treasure, else it would have been the news of the decade."

Marcus said suddenly, "You, sir, look very familiar to me. It's the way you hold your head, the way—"

"Aye, my lord. I believe I would be your half-cousin, and yours as well, Mr. Wyndham. Goodness," he added, smiling at the Duchess. "You're all my kin. My mother was born on the wrong side of the blanket, begging your pardon, my lady, thus she was a half-sister to your grandfather. Thus it wasn't difficult for me and your father, Mr. Wyndham, to be friends as boys and to keep that friendship once he'd left for the Colonies. The earl, naturally, didn't acknowledge me."

Marcus shook his bastard half-cousin's hand before they left the shop, assuring him of acknowledgment.

"Good God," Marcus said, shaking his head, as they walked back to where the young boy was patiently tending their horses. "I believe that there is some sort of precedent here." He said to the Duchess, "Do you think I am expected to continue in the tradition of producing offspring out of blessed wedlock? Will my ancestors' ghosts haunt me if I don't populate the area with my bastards?"

"That is all well and good, Marcus," she said, frowning at him, "but not to the point. What we learned makes me believe there is more to this treasure than fevered brains making up stories."

"I wrote it all down," Trevor said.

"And you," Marcus added to her, "sketched those drawings very nicely. I had no idea you had a lady's talents. You continue to surprise me. I don't like it."

"You have no idea of many things, Marcus," she said. "Or perhaps you do, you just don't want to accept them."

He saw the half-smile on her mouth and wished devoutly that Trevor was in Algiers. He wanted her. Quite simply, he wanted to jerk up that riding skirt of hers, brace her against a tree, and bury himself inside her.

He trembled. Damn Trevor.

She turned then to look up at him. The half-smile froze on her face but she didn't look away. She simply stared at him, unconsciously taking a step toward him. Marcus cursed.

Trevor, eyeing the two of them, quickly mounted Clancy and dug his heels in the stallion's sides. He called out over his shoulder, "Take care not to fall off a cliff."

Marcus cursed again and helped her to mount Birdie. "Just wait," he said. "Just wait."

She said slowly, not looking away from his blue eyes that were glittering brighter than the summer sky overhead, "I've a mind to find that treasure, Marcus."

"Which treasure?" he said, his eyes on her breasts.

══ 17 ══

MARCUS SAID ABSOLUTELY nothing throughout the two-hour ride back to Chase Park, staring straight ahead between Stanley's ears. She didn't look at him either, but her thoughts were of him, all of him and what he was thinking, what he wanted, what he would do to her. She spurred Birdie to a faster pace.

When they reached the Chase stables, he nearly jerked her off Birdie's back, grabbed her hand, and said low, "Come on. Now." He grabbed her hand and nearly ran to the stables, kicked open the door to one of the tack rooms, then slammed it shut again with the heel of his boot. There was a key in the door and he turned it, still not releasing her right hand.

She had never imagined that a man could be so very urgent in the middle of the day. And here they were, not five minutes from his bedchamber and his bed. He'd waited two hours, but no longer? It was fascinating. Maybe this had something to do with that *beyond* business.

She devoutly hoped so. Suddenly, she was doing more than hoping.

"Now," he said, turning to face her. He pulled on her hand, bringing her against him. His cheeks were flushed, his eyes narrowed, focused entirely on her. "Hurry, Duchess."

She was pressed to his chest, feeling the deep pounding of his heart. She closed her eyes, those two simple words of his roiling through her. "What do you want me to do?" She was whispering, feeling suddenly so urgent she could barely talk. She flattened her hands against his

216

chest, felt the pounding of his heart beneath her palm, and rose on her tiptoes. "Marcus, tell me what you want me to do."

He stared down at her, his look intent. "Just be you. I want to see if you will moan for me again, if you will scream and nearly buck me off you. I want to see if you will become frantic for me again."

She felt his large hands pulling open her riding jacket. He was holding his breath, she realized, when suddenly his hands cupped her breasts through the thin white lawn of her blouse. He closed his eyes, throwing his head back as he kneaded her through the soft material.

"Marcus," she said again. He hugged her to him. He pulled off her jaunty riding hat, then tugged the pins from her hair. "Ah," he said, and kissed her ear, blowing tendrils of hair from his mouth, his breath warm against her flesh, his fingers tangling in her hair.

"Do you want me, Duchess?"

She pulled him more tightly against her. She let her hands go down his back to his flanks. "I think that's quite the stupidest thing you've ever said."

He had to grin at that, but it was difficult. He had her undressed and flat on her back in a matter of moments. He stood over her, pulling off his boots and his buckskin trousers, looking at her face all the while he jerked off his clothes, and she lay there on her back, her riding clothes spread out beneath her, watching him, excitement rippling through her as he removed each piece of clothing. When he tossed his trousers aside and stood over her, his legs slightly spread, his sex free of his clothes, full and heavy, she said, "Please hurry, Marcus." She stretched out her arms to him, her eyes darkening. "Oh goodness, you're more beautiful than your stallion."

He cocked an eyebrow at that and came down on his knees beside her. "Stanley would hurt a mare when he took her. I would never hurt you. And I won't hurry, Duchess, at least I'll try my damnedest not to."

He leaned down as he spoke and his last words were a whisper against her breast.

She cried out, arching up against his mouth.

"Easy," he said, pushing her back, his hand flat on her belly. "Easy. It will be all right. Just be open for me, Duchess. Just open."

He wanted her mouth immediately and she gave him her warmth as she parted her lips and he touched her tongue. She arched again and she felt him trembling against her, his hand now moving from her breasts to her belly, kneading her, spanning her with splayed fingers, gently caressing her pelvic bones, then going lower, circling her, lightly touching the warm flesh of her thighs, then finally cupping her, his fingers caressing and so very gentle until he found her and began to move in a rhythm that made her forget everything but him and those fingers of his and his mouth on hers and the heat of him as he moved over her. This time, though, his mouth never left hers, and it was his fingers that brought her to a tension that threatened to shatter her, so intense it was. And just at that instant when she knew, just knew there could be no more for her, he came into her, hard and deep, and her body exploded into blazing light, sparking a pleasure so strong, so urgent, she screamed, her hands clutching at his arms, at his back. It was too much.

He was driving into her, drawing her upward to meet him again, when she managed to look up into his face, harsh in the dim light of the tack room, his eyes glazed, and suddenly, it seemed that he was in immense pain. His jaw was locked, his cheeks flushed, the flesh taut over his bones. He grew still. She could feel him deep inside her, heavy, jerking slightly. Then, in the next instant, he wrenched away from her, heaving, groaning as if he were in pain, cursing, his hands digging into her hips to support himself, and she didn't understand, couldn't begin to realize what he was doing until she felt the wet of his seed on her belly, felt him jerking over her until finally, he was on his knees between her legs, his head bowed, his eyes closed, his breathing ragged.

She said nothing, merely stared at him, the pleasure from such a short time before now as cold as ashes on a summer grate. She felt nothing but a vast emptiness that would consume her, she knew it as certainly as she now understood him and what he had planned the previous night but had failed to carry out.

She saw his seed on her belly. She held perfectly still. If she remained perfectly still, said naught, not a single word, maybe the pain would diminish, maybe he would say something that wouldn't tear her apart.

He rose, standing naked over her. "I'll get my handkerchief." She closed her eyes and turned onto her side, drawing her legs up. She didn't care that she was naked, that he would look at her, it just didn't matter. She felt him coming back down on his knees, felt his hands on her shoulder and hip, turning her back to him. She felt the handkerchief wiping his seed from her.

"Don't you dare cry, Duchess," he said low, his face bending close to her head. "Don't you dare weep your damned woman's tears and say that I abused you, that you didn't gain pleasure from me. You had great pleasure if your screams were any measure, and believe me, they were. I didn't cheat you out of anything save my seed, but you know I intended to do that. If you didn't understand what I meant, you do now. I told you that you won't bear any child of mine to follow in that bastard's footsteps. It is done. Get up now and get dressed."

He tossed the handkerchief beside her on her riding skirt. She watched him as he dressed, his movements as graceful as they always were, oblivious of her now, as if she had been naught but a receptacle for his man's lust, and since he was through with her, why bother then regarding her anymore. Then she saw his hands, hard and large, yet when they touched her, they . . . she closed her eyes. He was in full control, both of himself and of her. She had no control at all, indeed, at that moment, she had nothing.

Slowly, she sat up, drawing her now wrinkled chemise over her head. She stared at a beautiful Spanish saddle as she said, "Badger is preparing dinner himself tonight."

Marcus eyed her with some surprise. He shouldn't be surprised, he thought, no tears for the Duchess, no sign of anything, except when she wanted him to pleasure her. No, no sign of anything because emotion was too messy, it would reduce her in her own eyes to show anyone anything save her immense calm, that damnable aloofness of hers. He said, "What is he preparing?"

"Roasted lamb with apricot sauce. He says it takes too long a time to hash a shoulder of mutton properly so instead he has marinated the mutton all day."

Marcus grunted as he pulled on his coat. He walked to a chair, sat down, and pulled on his boots.

"He is also making a cherry and almond cake. It was always one of my mother's favorites. And cassia biscuits. They have castor sugar and currants in them."

He rose then and looked down at her sitting cross-legged on her riding skirt, his damp wadded-up handkerchief beside her, her chemise pulled over her head to fall only to her thighs, those white legs of hers so beautifully shaped. Her hair was tumbled about her head. She looked so lovely and yet so desperate in her calmness, he felt a stab of alarm. He shook his head. No, not the Duchess, she wouldn't feel anything that would interfere with the smoothness of her breath, save when he took her and stroked her. And that gave him power over her. That pleased him. He could shatter her calm in those precious minutes. He took a step toward her, then stopped suddenly, frowning. "Do you not think it a bit odd to speak about Badger's recipes so soon after having sex with me?"

"Would you prefer that I said nothing?"

"It is what you usually say. Holding cold and detached is your specialty. It is what I expected."

"I spoke about food to break the silence, to give you background noise while you dressed again. Would you rather I had spoken of something else?"

"Yes. Of me and what I did to you, of what I gave to you. Of yourself, and what I will teach you to do to me. Right now you are taking, Duchess, naught but taking. Are you willing to give as well?"

She looked beyond his right shoulder. "Do you know how pippins and plums are candied?"

"No, I don't know."

"You mustn't forget that a good cook, which Badger is, also knows how to use foods to prepare remedies for illnesses."

He hunkered down beside her. He took her chin in his palm. "Shut up."

She became still as a stone.

He kissed her, forcing her mouth open, but he didn't savage her, no, not at all. She felt his tongue gently come into her mouth, lightly touching hers, demanding nothing. She closed her eyes, forcing herself to ignore the burgeoning warmth deep in her belly. It was humiliating, that damned warmth that he drew so effortlessly from her.

Then he was gone, rising to stand over her. "Dress yourself. I imagine that all our stable lads know exactly what we've been doing. Come, I'll help you. There is straw in your hair. I suppose I should take that handkerchief. It smells of me and of you and I wouldn't want to make you remember that you are as wild as a mare when a stallion comes over her."

Suddenly, something else shattered deep inside her, broke wide apart, and rage such as she'd never felt in her nineteen years poured through her. She knew it was rage even though she'd never recognized it within herself before. Ah, yes, she knew, and she let it feed on itself, let it grow stronger and stronger still. She could feel the rage pounding in every part of her body, unleashing itself in her, pushing her and pushing harder and harder.

The stillness, the hard-won calm and serenity she'd shown to the world since that long-ago day when she'd heard the upstairs maid tell the Tweenie that she was a bastard flared bright and hot in her mind. She could see the two of them, hear their voices talking about her. She saw herself, small and so very frightened, so utterly alone in this huge mansion, seeking out her father's wife, knowing she would tell her the truth, just not realizing the depths of the countess's hatred of her, of her very existence. It was more than just hatred, it was vile and cold and contemptuous, what the countess of Chase felt for her, a nine-year-old girl who'd just found out she was a bastard. It spewed over her, drowning her in it and she hadn't been able to bear it.

And then Marcus had named her the Duchess and all that calm, that stillness, that haughty reserve that others applauded in her, indeed poured approval upon her because of it, seeped into her very soul. And she nurtured it as she would a precious rose in her mother's garden, until it was, quite simply, natural. It became her, and she a reflection of it; she was it. She became the Duchess.

Until now. The rage bubbled and flamed. She was stripped, everything in her naked and hard and cold and eager for violence. She stared at him, letting her rage at what he'd done to her continue to build.

She rose slowly to her feet, smoothing down her wrinkled, soiled chemise. She saw that her hands were shaking, but not with timidity, but with the cleansing sweet anger. And it was sweet, that rage that she'd buried deep as her very soul so many years before. She watched him as he walked back to his chair and sat down. He crossed his legs and his arms over his chest.

"Dress," he said. "You might try some feminine wiles on me, I'd like to see if you have talent for it. You don't understand, Duchess? Well, dress slowly, tease me with a toss of your head, raise your breasts, perhaps show me some cleavage, move your hips in a seductive way. Are you capable of such a thing? I wonder."

She just stared at him, this man to whom she'd given herself, this man she'd saved, truth be told, she had saved him, saved the future of the Wyndham line, and he was a tyrant, a fool, a savage who had humiliated her more than she'd believed one human being could humiliate another. He'd withdrawn from her because of his hatred of her father. He'd treated her like nothing more than a vessel for his lust and even that he hadn't allowed. He scorned her womb because it represented a tie to the uncle he hated so very much. He scorned her for it, even though she'd been naught but a bastard, and perhaps that was why he did. He simply didn't care what he did to her. And he knew she would simply accept whatever he meted out to her.

She realized that his hatred of her father wasn't close to the rage that consumed her now, this fine rage that was making her mind cold and hard and so very clear. She stoked it with memories from her childhood and more recent memories of his humiliating treatment of her.

She even smiled as she looked around the tack room, smiled even as she felt the rage turning inside her to something more forthright, something pure and cold as ice, something really quite vicious. If she'd had a gun, she would have shot him. She grabbed a riding crop from the desk, raised it high and ran at him, yelling in a wonderfully demented voice, "You damned bastard! You think I will remain silent and allow you to humiliate me? You think you can treat me as you would a person of no account at all? I hate you, do you hear me, Marcus, you bloody damned bastard! Never will you abuse me again and take it as your right, your privilege, never again!"

She struck his chest and shoulder with the riding crop. For an instant he didn't move, just stared at her, unwilling to believe what he'd just heard from her mouth or the pain from her slashing riding crop. He simply couldn't connect this virago, this frenzied creature, to the Duchess, to the female he'd known for ten years.

She was panting hard, as if she'd been running until she was ready to vomit with the strain, panting and heaving. "You want me to act the seductress? Prance in front you as if you're my master, my owner? You're a filthy bastard!" She struck him again and he felt his riding jacket split open, felt the lash cut through his lawn shirt to his flesh beneath.

He roared and jumped up. "Enough, damn you! What the hell is wrong with you? Just a moment ago you were as placid as a stupid cow, sitting there silently as you always do, obeying me, quoting Badger's menu to me, for God's sake. Nothing on your mind save what you deemed appropriate and proper."

"Don't you dare call me a stupid cow, you fool!" She struck him again. He lunged for her, but she jumped back just beyond his reach, hitting out at him again, missing this time, but if she had connected, it would have slashed through his flesh.

He stopped cold in his tracks. He couldn't believe what was happening. The proof was in the pain of the two slashes she managed, but still . . . He said, his voice colder and harder than what he'd used to get his men into battle, "You won't strike me again, Duchess, not again. I will make you regret striking me at all."

"You try it and I'll gullet you, you stupid, ungrateful sod. God, to think that I saved you, that I felt that I owed you your heritage. You don't deserve anything, Marcus, save a beating that will bring you to your knees, humiliation, in short, God, that's what you deserve, that's what you need!"

She threw the crop at him, grabbed up a bridle and began swinging it at him with all her strength. She felt the instant the metal bit struck his flesh, felt the iron bit strike his skull, and it was clean that blow, clean and pure and he deserved it. She watched him weave where he stood, his hand on the side of his head, and he stood there just staring at her utterly disbelieving, then he dropped like a stone to his knees, then keeled over onto his side, quite unconscious.

She was panting hard, feeling stronger than the mightiest Amazon of legend. She gently laid down the bridle, went down on her knees and felt his heart. The beat was steady. He would be fine, the damnable bastard. God, she hoped he would have a headache to rival the worst bellyache she'd ever suffered.

She rose, smoothed down her chemise once more, then quite calmly, dressed herself. She gave him one last look, smiling at the two rents in his clothes from the riding crop and left the tack room, quietly closing the door behind her.

It was raining, the afternoon prematurely dark, the wind blowing hard, the branches of the maple and lime trees tearing at themselves. "It is like Beltane night the monk wrote about," she said aloud, then laughed, throwing her head back and letting the rain wash over her face and hair. She felt wonderful. She felt strong. She felt whole.

18

THE GREEN CUBE Room was cozy with its fire blazing and the heavy draperies drawn across the windows. It was late afternoon and she was alone. This time, it felt quite good to be alone. She spared only a passing thought for Marcus. If he was conscious, then what was he doing? What was he thinking? Perhaps he was staggering back to the house even now. Perhaps she should go and meet him. No, if she did, she'd laugh in his face. Instead, she smiled into the flames, feeling herself grow as warm on the inside as on the outside.

"Hello, Duchess. You're alone. May I speak to you?"

She turned slowly and looked at Trevor. How very handsome he was, she thought, and not at all a fool or an idiot like her husband. "Do come in," she said.

He stopped beside her chair, then moved to stand beside the fireplace, leaning his shoulder against the mantel. "You know, Duchess, you can speak to me. I also know that I'm more a stranger to you than not, but then again, strangers aren't bad sorts sometimes. They can be trusted. They can be discreet. Something bothers you."

"There is nothing wrong with me," she said. "At least not anymore there isn't. Why would you possibly think that?"

"Your stillness," he said slowly. "When you become silent as a stone and as unmoving as that beautiful painting over the mantel, I know that you are distressed."

To his surprise, she laughed. "Actually you're very observant, Trevor, but my stillness now, well, it's not the kind of stillness it was yesterday or even this morning or even two hours ago. Now it is just simple stillness because, frankly, I'm tired. So, believe me, sir, there is nothing at all wrong with me now, nothing at all."

"You're right," he said slowly. "Something has changed, you're different somehow. I was thinking when I saw you sitting there, so still, so quiet, that Marcus has known you since you were a child, yet he never realized your quiet pose was just that, a pose, a shield you'd fashioned over the years to protect yourself from hurt. He sees it as arrogance, as your way of playing the queen and keeping the peasants at their distance. It enrages him, you know."

"You are more than observant, you're frightening. As you said, something has happened, and that girl you just described has thankfully fallen behind the wainscoting. She no longer exists. If I am silent now, or overly quiet, it is because it is what I feel like being. God, life can be quite satisfying, can it not? I will see you at dinner, Trevor."

The Duchess rose from her winged chair and walked from the room, whistling one of the military ditties she'd heard Spears singing. He could but stare. What had happened? He wondered where the hell Marcus was.

"What were you speaking to that little trollop about, Trevor?"

He raised his eyes to his mother's face as she walked briskly into the room. "She isn't a trollop. She's the countess of Chase. She is a lady and she has a kindness I've never before seen in another person." He paused a moment at his mother's loud *hrmmph,* then added, "Indeed, if you don't find some conciliatory remark to flit out of your mouth, it's possible that she will simply order us out of here."

"She wouldn't dare. She's a bastard and the earl doesn't even like her. She has no power here. She is nothing. Besides the earl finds me quite to his liking."

Trevor could only stare at his fond parent. She was actually patting the tight sausage curls over her left ear. He sighed, saying, "I assure you that Marcus is quite fond of the Duchess." He wished he could add that Marcus's fondness had quite likely extended itself to very physical demonstrations a short time ago, but he held his tongue. If Marcus had done the job even adequately, why was there such a transformation in her now? There was an unleashed power in her that she couldn't hide. It was controlled, but now it would be loosed when she chose. He found it fascinating. But what had happened to bring about this change in her? Surely Marcus couldn't have bungled his lovemaking all that badly. Maybe, he thought, just maybe it was that Marcus hadn't bungled anything. Maybe she was a pleasured woman and that had made all the difference in her, for her.

Trevor eyed his mother. He realized that he didn't know his mother all that well. Since his eighteenth year, he'd not lived at his parents' home in Baltimore. He'd made his home in Washington. Indeed, he'd fought like the devil himself when the British had landed and stormed the capital. He'd turned twenty-two during those blood-soaked weary days, then when it was all over, he'd gone back to Baltimore and married the richest most beautiful girl Baltimorean society had to offer a hungry young man. Her name was Helen and she was more lovely than her legendary namesake. He saw her in his mind's eye—dead, lying there on her back, her eyes open, her flesh like gray wax.

"I'm going to be twenty-five next Tuesday," he said to no one in particular.

"I thought you were only twenty-three, Trevor. Mayhap twenty-two."

"No, Mother."

"I have told my friends that you are younger."

He grinned, realizing that his age made her too ancient and she suffered for it. "I won't tell anyone back home," he said. "Now, have you seen James?"

"He's off somewhere, doubtless by himself. The boy is driving me quite distracted. He is silent. He is withdrawn. I wish he would do something."

Actually, Trevor knew the source of his younger brother's discontent. He'd finally spilled the beans to his older brother. It seems he'd fallen in love only three days before they'd sailed to England. He missed Miss Mullens and blamed his family for forcing him to leave her.

"I will speak to him, Mother."

"Good. Now, tell me again everything Mr. Burgess told you. Then I will formulate a plan. I will get the treasure away from here, you'll see, and none of them will be the wiser. Oh why, Trevor, did you tell the two of them about the treasure? You're an unnatural son. But I will win, you will see, my son who is too old, surely, I will win."

The Duchess sat by her window, staring down on the drive. There was nothing to see, for the storm had blackened the summer sky and bloated black clouds hung low overhead. It still drizzled. She thought it a beautiful sight. She shivered with the beauty of it. She looked up when the adjoining door opened and Marcus strode into her room, all healthy and big and looking like a lord, which, of course, he was. She'd wondered where he'd been, if he had a splitting headache, if he'd been on his face, moaning with the pain she'd brought down on his head. Goodness, that made her smile, and she did now, watching him come forward, wondering what he would do. Would he scream at her? No, Marcus didn't scream, he bellowed, he roared.

She couldn't wait. Never again would she let him reduce her to a silent mass of nothing at all. Perhaps he'd brought a pistol with him and he would shoot her. She waited now to see what he would do, excited, her eyes narrowed, her pulse quickening. She would fetch a gun. She still wanted to shoot him, in his right arm.

It was as if he knew what she was thinking. "No," he said easily, "my head only hurts in a dull sort of way, lucky for you, madam. I woke up and lay there on the tack-room floor for a few moments, just thinking about what you'd done. Now, it is time for dinner. You look quite adequate.

The gown is still too revealing, but it is better than the other one."

"Thank you," she said, and looked away from him, back out onto the drive. "I don't suppose you puked up your guts. I hoped you'd have a headache and a goodly dose of nausea from that blow I struck you. Did I manage to slash through your clothing to your flesh, Marcus? Did I mark you? A nice angry welt perhaps? I wanted to mark you, very badly."

He thought of the two welts she'd struck him with that riding crop and said, "You're wearing no jewelry. There is the Wyndham collection, you know. I have no idea of the individual pieces in it, but it's bound to be something spectacular. I will have them fetched from the safe in the estate room. You may select what you wish."

"Thank you, Marcus. Not even a single red slash mark on your strong man's flesh? I'm disappointed. I must become stronger. I do want to mark you. I want to mark you forever and whenever you see that mark, you'll know I was the one who did it and perhaps you'll even remember the pain of it." She rose and shook out her skirts.

"I don't want your bloody jewelry." Evidently he wasn't going to speak of what had happened in the tack room. He walked to her now, stopping within inches from her face. He cupped her chin in his palm and forced her to look up at him. "The Wyndham jewelry is also yours. If you don't want your jewelry, I really don't care." He looked down at her silently now, brooding, then said, "I will never think of the tack room in quite the same way again. I will picture you lying on your back, your hands caressing me, drawing me closer, your legs parted for me. I will see your head thrown back, arched up, moaning and crying out."

She merely smiled, cocking her head to one side, a coquettish cocking, she hoped as she said, "It is probably in my blood, my harlot's blood. Perhaps it would be the same with any man. Perhaps I did you a great disservice by forcing you to marry me. Who knows? Perhaps if another man touches me, I will immediately toss up my skirts and moan for him as well. I am sorry that is all you remember from that encounter. I would prefer that you remember pain, Marcus, a lot of pain. A bit of humiliation as well. Bested by a woman. I do hope it grates and rubs."

"Don't try to bait me, Duchess. Now, I haven't forgotten what happened after you turned into a wild woman for me. You took offense at nothing at all, struck me with that riding crop, then knocked me out with that damned bridle. Yes, I felt pain from your unprovoked attack. I simply haven't yet decided what you deserve in return."

"Doubtless I will be the first to know, once you've made up your mind." She smiled at him again, a full, wide, white-toothed smile. "I will do it again when you behave like a damnable bastard. Don't think I won't. No more will I be a placid cow. You try to hurt me in return and I swear to you, Marcus, that I will make you very, very sorry. Believe me."

He whistled. "So, the serene, silent princess is no more. What has been spawned in her place?"

"Most certainly you will see, being who and what you are."

He stared at her, and she would have sworn that there was a flame of interest, no, more than interest, it was puzzlement and it was fascination. The damned man, what did he want from her? He said now, obviously dismissing her and what she might be, "What did you do with the sketches of the drawings in the monk's book?"

So be it. She'd meant it. No more would she simply take the verbal pain he piled on her head. No more. She actually felt quite good at this moment. She fetched them from the marquetry table drawer and gave them to him, smiling all the while. He smoothed them out and stared silently down at them. "This scene in the village square. If I'm not mistaken, it's Kirby Malham. See the stone cottages in the background and that little hump-backed bridge across the water? That could be the River Aire."

"What is its importance? Why is the priest blessing the people?"

"I don't know. I am certain that this sketch is of Saint Swale's Abbey, no doubt about that. And Mr. Burgess—our interesting relative—also thinks so. I believe I'll explore the ruins tomorrow. I haven't been near them in years. Like you and the Twins, Charlie, Mark, and I would sport in those small monks' cells, contriving all sorts of vile tortures."

"I believe Trevor plans to visit them tomorrow, when it stops raining. Both he and James."

"Damned bounder. He knew, damn him, he knew that I wanted you right at that moment, and if it hadn't been raining buckets, he would have gone about his treasure hunting without me."

"He knows that if there is a treasure, it will belong to you, Marcus."

"He is, I am forced to admit, a gentleman, mayhap even honorable, in the way of the stiff-necked Colonists. But his name still irritates."

Marcus laid down the sketches, turned, and took her in his arms. He leaned down and kissed her, his fingers tightening on her chin to hold her still. She didn't move, not because she was silent and serene and calm, but because she wanted to see what he would do. He misunderstood her, not a surprise for he was a man and used to seeing her only one way for a good ten years. He raised his head and laughed. "All calm again, silent as that candle, though you're showing no flame and I did just kiss you. Tell me, Duchess, was your virago's temper an act? I'm tempted to insult you into another rage just to see what you will do. Right now you play the frigid virgin, or is it the disdainful queen? But if I had but a few more minutes with you—" He sighed and stepped back. "There's no time for me to do a proper job with you now. Ah, there's that smile of yours, that damnable mocking smile. But know it, Duchess, if I had the time and if, naturally, I was in the proper mood, I would have you yelling and bucking within minutes. However, it's time to face our Colonial relatives again. You said that Badger was preparing mutton?"

"Yes, with apricots. And you hold a quite high opinion of your seductive skills, Marcus. Don't forget—" She actually laughed, a low very seductive laugh. "I am my mother's daughter. You're just one man, perhaps not all that skilled with women, I am too inexperienced to judge properly. It's true that my body seems to respond perhaps too much to you, but there it is. There's a world full of men, charming men, handsome men, skilled men, who just might find me utterly delightful. Perhaps one of them will give me a child. Who knows? Oh, yes, Badger didn't have time to hash the mutton. No, he didn't."

He laughed, dismissing all her fine talk—the bloody fool—took her hand, and laid it in the crook of his arm. He patted her hand. Let him think she would fold, like a sheet in the hands of the upstairs maid.

She knew she'd hurt him, at least a bit. Wasn't he planning retaliation? Surely he wouldn't ignore what she'd done. He'd try something, indeed a man like Marcus wouldn't allow another person, particularly a feeble woman, a token wife who'd saved his damned hide and had thus, obviously earned his contempt and his indifference, to get away with what she'd done to him. She'd struck him repeatedly with the riding crop then hit the side of his head with a bridle. What was wrong with him? Ah, she knew Marcus better than he knew her, at least as of today, she knew him better. She was ready, just let him try his worst.

"I think Mr. Badger is wonderful."

"He's a servant, Ursula. Pray mind your tongue and remember who you are."

"I'm an American, Mama."

"You are the granddaughter of an earl. Mind your tongue."

Trevor said easily, "I would say that Ursula has got it right, Mother. All of us are Americans. I fought the British, despite my antecedents. Besides, that isn't the point here. Badger is a man with more talents than most I've ever known."

Marcus said to Ursula, "What do you think of Spears?"

"Mr. Spears is ever so kind and patient. He has a beautiful singing voice. Today I heard him singing a song about Lord Castlereagh and the upcoming Congress in Vienna. It was very funny even though I didn't understand all of it."

"I believe I heard the Duchess humming it as well," Trevor said. "Do you remember the words, Duchess?"

She gently lay her teacup back on the exquisite Meissen saucer and recited:

"Vienna's the place to make your mark.
Bring enough groats so they'll roll over and bark.
    Tallyrand will cede France for a bagatelle;
    Castlereagh has most of Portugal to sell.
Don't forget to lie through your teeth.
Dance on your tongue, not on your feet.
    It's time to steal; it's time to play;
    By all that's holy, it's the diplomat's day."

"How the devil do you know that ditty?"

She slowly turned her head toward her husband. "Why shouldn't I know it, Marcus? I am a sentient human being, truly, despite what you or others may think. Don't you think it clever? I myself believe the writer of these ditties to be beyond clever. There's real talent in them."

"There have been many of them and it seems that Spears knows all of them. But you are a woman, Duchess. How do you know it, and by heart?"

"Ursula just told us that Spears was singing it. I do listen occasionally. I have an excellent memory. Most ladies do, Marcus."

She was lying and he simply didn't know why. She was mocking him, another unexpected result of the attack in the tack room. She'd changed, but perhaps not. Damnation, but she fascinated him. He frowned at her even as he accepted a cup of tea from his worshipful cousin, Fanny, who fluttered her long eyelashes at him, eyelashes that would slay many a young gentleman when she had her Season in London in three years. Was it three years? He must remember to ask the Duchess. His wife.

"It's clever but you don't sing it well," Aunt Wilhelmina said. "Ursula here has a lovely voice. I trained her myself."

"Oh, Mother! The Duchess is perfect. Did you hear her recite the ditty? She's wonderful."

"Not all the time," Marcus said. "No, there are many sides to her, and after this afternoon, I have discovered that not all of them are what a man would expect."

She had no intention of staying in her bedchamber that night to see if he would come to her. He was a man who was used to being in control. Truth be told, she was afraid that if he touched her she would melt all over him. She couldn't allow that. She moved to the small bedchamber at the end of the east corridor known as the Gold Leaf Room and burrowed beneath covers that were old and musty and smelled of years of disuse. She couldn't sleep, but not because of the strangeness of the bed. When her thoughts weren't of Marcus and what the devil she was going to do, they were of the Wyndham treasure—what it was and where it was. A treasure from the time of Henry VIII. That there had been such a treasure she now accepted completely.

She sighed, threw back her covers. In a few minutes, she was walking quietly into the vast Wyndham library, her single candle casting little useful light throughout that room with its high bookcases that stretched from floor to ceiling. Where to begin?

She lit a branch of candles then began at the left-hand side of the door with the books at the very bottom.

A clock in the corridor outside the library chimed four strokes when she at last looked up. She had no idea it was so late. She held the huge volume in her arms, still not believing her luck. She felt elation at her discovery. When she'd come to the library, she'd really not believed she'd find anything. Ah, but she had. Carefully, she eased it down on the massive mahogany desk and gently separated the pages.

It was the same tome that Mr. Burgess had, all in Latin script and with those strange drawings.

She'd found it quite by accident just moments before when she'd dropped an incredibly old book whose pages weren't cut, but had still been dusted once a month by the industrious house staff, but never read. And behind that old book had been this tome, layers of dust on it, obviously not seen or read for as many years as it was old.

Who had hidden the book and why? She felt her heart begin to pound as she turned those final pages. The drawings were just a bit different, but to be expected since each tome had been done one at a time. St. Swale's Abbey still appeared unutterably depressing, drawn in such stark black, and the scene in that village square was as strange as the other. Slowly, she turned the page. There were final pages here, not ripped out as they'd been in Mr. Burgess's copy.

It was in Latin, naturally, and there were two more pages.

She leaned down, bringing the branch of candles close to study the words. She could make out some of them. There was the name Cromwell, ah yes, the vice-regent for Henry VIII, and something about men he'd sent, arrogant young men who owed their souls to their master, Cromwell. She skimmed her finger down the page, stopping when she recognized the word for tree and cistern. Defeated with the remaining text, she turned the final page and to her surprise, there was one more drawing. It showed an incredibly old oak tree, gnarled and bent, towering over an ancient stone well. There was an old leather-bound bucket attached to a chain from the crossbar above. There were piles of rocks in the background, not set at random, but rather planned. But what did they represent? The oak tree dominated and it was on a small rise. The sky was blackly ominous, seeming to bear down on the scene, the stroke of the quill strong, the stark black lines still as black as sin.

Then, quite suddenly, she heard something, naught but a small sound, perhaps just the wind whispering, but not here, not in this immense, closed library, but there it was again, that small sound, as if someone were breathing softly, but it was still in the back of her mind, not alerting her really until it was too late. She was turning when she glimpsed a shadow and felt a rush of panic just at the moment the pain against her temple sent her into blackness.

=19=

SHE OPENED HER eyes to see Marcus's face very close to hers. He looked worried, definitely worried. About her? No, Marcus didn't care enough about her to worry. She blinked and yet again she saw the lines of his face deepened, his blue eyes darkened even more. Why would Marcus be upset? It made no sense. Besides, he was blurry, so she had to be wrong. Without warning, a shaft of pain nearly sent her back into the darkness. She moaned with the shock of it.

"Marcus," she said. She raised her hand, but felt him gently draw it back down. "Shush," he said. "Just hold still. I know it hurts. You've a huge lump behind your left ear. Hold still, all right?"

She wanted to speak, but knew if she did, the pain would redouble in its force. She nodded and closed her eyes against it.

She felt his fingers on her face gently pushing the hair from her forehead, smoothing it behind her ears. Then she felt a cool, wet cloth cover her forehead. "Spears said that soft muslin soaked in rosewater would help reduce the pain. Badger says that you can't have laudanum yet, not until we're certain you didn't scramble your brains with that blow you took."

He cupped her cheek in his palm then, and without thought, she turned her face ever so slightly to press against his warm flesh. "That's right, try to relax. When you're better you can tell us what happened. James found you unconscious on the library floor, the candles guttering on the desk above you. It was the candlelight that brought him into the library. He thought you were dead.

"I must say, Duchess, you gave me the fright of my life, not to speak of what poor James felt. He was stammering with fright, white-faced as any famous castle specter. Don't do that again. You must have fallen and hit your head on the edge of the desk. It was after four in the morning when James found you. What were you doing there? No, keep quiet, I forgot. Just be still. We'll sort all this out later. Keep your eyes open for me. That's right. And relax. Badger says we're to keep you awake. That's why I'm carrying on like a crazed magpie.

"Now, tell me how many fingers I'm holding up."

She saw the fingers, blurred, but she saw them. She wet her lips and whispered, "Three."

She gasped with the pain that simple word brought her.

The cloth was lifted from her forehead and another laid gently in its place. It felt wonderful. She wished she could tell him that it felt so very good, but the pain was leaching at her senses and she knew just keeping awake would require everything in her.

She felt his large hand against her breast, heard him say quietly, "Her heartbeat is slow and steady, Badger. Stop hovering, man, she's fine."

"I know, I know," she heard Badger say. "I knew her heartbeat would be strong. No surprise there. She's a strong girl, she always was. Keep the covers to her chin, my lord. We'll keep the lass warm and quiet. But awake. She must stay awake."

She realized then she was safe. No one could strike her again, not with Marcus and Badger here with her. She heard Spears say as he walked toward the bed, "I have prepared the mixture you detailed, Mr. Badger. If you can gently move her head, my lord, I will apply the mixture to the lump."

"It will reduce the swelling and make the pain lessen," Badger said.

"I don't want to hurt her," Marcus said, but then he moved her head on the pillow.

She didn't realize she was crying until she felt someone wipe the tears off her cheeks and gently daub at her closed eyes. Marcus said very softly, "Gently now, Duchess. Spears has the lightest fingers of all of us. It will hurt though, but then it will be better. That's what Badger promises. If he's wrong I'll let you smack him on the side of the head. That will make three of us with headaches."

Spears applied the salve. Suddenly she felt nausea twist and roil in her stomach, adding to the dreadful pounding in her head. She swallowed convulsively.

Badger said, "Breathe deeply, Duchess. That's right. It will make the sickness go away. No, don't fight it. Do as I tell you. Deeply. Good."

When at last they gave her laudanum, she actually felt better, but Marcus wouldn't allow her yet to speak. "No, Duchess, I want you to sleep."

She managed to whisper to him, "Don't leave me."

He was silent for a moment, a surprised silence that went on so long she was afraid that he didn't know how to tell her that he didn't want to remain. Then, however, he said easily, "I won't leave you, I promise."

She took stock of her injuries. There was a dull thudding over her left eye. The nausea was gone, as was the debilitating pain from the blow to her head. Slowly, she opened her eyes. Marcus wasn't there and she cried out, panicked and afraid.

"I'm here," he said, and she watched him stride quickly back to her bed. "Shush, I'm here."

"You promised you wouldn't leave me."

"I just wandered to the fireplace, no destination further away than that. Ah, and once I did have to relieve myself, Duchess. But I sent Badger in to oversee your sleep whilst I was gone. How do you feel?"

"I did feel like a keg of ale that rolled off the wagon and splatted on the cobblestones. Now, the keg only has a small leak."

"I felt something like that," he said, then grinned at her, leaned down, and lightly touched his mouth to hers. His mouth was warm and reassuring. "Now, here's tea for you. Badger said you would be thirsty and this fancy herbal tea he mixed for you would be just the thing."

He helped her drink, then said, "Are you hungry?"

"No, nothing. The tea is very good."

"You promise me you feel all right now?"

"Yes, the leak is merely a small crack now."

"Good." His voice lost its sweetness and became a low furious roar. "What the hell were you doing in the library with guttered candles at four o'clock in the morning?"

She wanted to laugh but a small smile was all she could manage. "The Wyndham legacy. I went searching for clues and I found another old book just like Mr. Burgess's."

He frowned as he said, "You should have awakened me if you wanted to go treasure hunting. You won't go do anything alone again. Now, about that book—there wasn't one there when I got down to the library."

"Someone hit me and took it. Actually I guess someone saw me reading it and struck me down in order to take it."

"No," he said. "That's simply not sensible. You must misremember, Duchess. You must have slipped and fallen. You must have struck your head on the edge of the desk."

"I'm sorry, but someone did strike me, Marcus." She saw that he believed her, but he didn't want to. To accept it meant that someone in the house had deliberately hurt her, that someone was up to no good. She didn't want to believe it either.

"That cursed treasure," he said, and continued to swear as he plowed his fingers through his hair. "Where did you find the book?"

"Behind another one on a lower shelf that hadn't ever been read or moved, just dusted periodically."

Surprisingly, he said, "All right. You went to the library to look for a clue and you found the book. Were you in the library long? I went to your bedchamber and you weren't there. I was perturbed—about many things—but I didn't go looking for you."

"I went to the Gold Leaf Room but I couldn't sleep. As I said, I went to the library to search for a clue—I never even thought to believe I'd find the book, find anything that was important—but I did find it. Only someone else must have seen the candlelight. I didn't hear anything, not really, just this slight movement, this sort of whispering sound, but I was concentrating so hard on the text and the sketch—"

He gently touched his fingertips to her lips. "Don't get upset, you'll just make yourself sick. Close your eyes a moment and breathe deeply. That's right. Just relax, Duchess."

He studied her face as she stilled. She was very pale, terrifyingly so, but Badger had sworn to him that she would be fine. Just a bit more time, he'd said.

Her breathing evened into sleep. Slowly, he rose from the bed and stretched. He wanted a bath and clothes. He rang for Maggie and she came, her glorious hair becomingly tousled, for it was still early, barely eight o'clock in the morning. At least she was dressed now. Before she'd dashed in wearing a peignoir that a London mistress would be proud to own, a feathered silk affair of pale peach. Just who, he wondered, had bought that for her? Her taste was flamboyant, but really quite good. The peignoir was something a man would buy, expensive, but gaudy and screaming sex.

He sent her to search out Badger, who just happened to be with Spears in his own bedchamber, just beyond the adjoining door.

Damned meddlers, he thought.

* * *

She was sitting up in bed, still weak, but now she felt in control again. She hated being sniveling and helpless.

"You still look pale as death," Maggie said as she gently braided her hair. "But since you looked like death itself just this morning, what you look like now is an improvement."

"Thank you, Maggie."

"You must eat some more of the barley soup Mr. Badger made for you. It should taste quite delicious to someone who nearly stuck her spoon in the wall but didn't, and thus should be grateful to be able to eat anything at all. I took a sip but it didn't suit me. I'm well, you see, not sickly like you, Duchess. I don't feel like I'm going to puke up my innards, not like you do."

"I don't think I'll be sick now, Maggie. The nausea is gone."

"Well, that's a blessing. I don't fancy cleaning up that kind of sickness, mind you."

Marcus overheard the last of this and was hard-pressed not to smile. He lost the desire when he saw her face. She looked utterly defenseless. The aloof reserve was gone and in its place was a damned vulnerable look that made him flinch. He'd never seen her this way before and he realized that it scared him witless. He realized with a start that he would prefer her yelling at him, calling him a bastard and a sod, even sticking that chin of hers in the air again, anything but staring silently at him as if he weren't worth the words to say to curse him with, as if, somehow, she were afraid of him. No, she couldn't be afraid of him. Soon, she'd be as she had been and he knew it would take some getting used to, that passion of hers, that very loud violent anger of hers, but he wanted to see it again, he wanted to see her face turn red, watch her change from the aloof, bloodless creature into a woman as passionate out of bed as in it. She'd gotten in a quite good blow with that damned bridle.

And someone had struck her down. Someone in this household. And that someone had to be one of the damned

Colonists. Aunt Wilhelmina was his prime candidate, the miserable old besom.

"Hello," he said, walking to her bed. He leaned down and kissed her cheek. He searched her eyes, saw that they were clear and that pleased him. "You will appreciate that Badger and Spears together took Mr. Tivit beneath his arms and bodily assisted him from this room."

"I vaguely remember a fat little man with a red face and a loud voice. His black coat was dirty, wasn't it?"

"Yes, filthy. I'm glad you didn't see his hands. That's Mr. Tivit, and he's the local doctor, and a miserable one at that. Anyway, when he pulled out his bleeding instruments and brought over a basin to the bed, Badger told him to take his torture devices out of here and never show his face again. He appealed to me and I told him you were so weak now that if he took any blood from you, you would turn into a beautiful leaf and float away. He huffed, lamenting his wounded dignity all the way to the stables."

He lifted her hand, enclosing it in his large one. He felt warm, solid. "He is an old fool. I wouldn't have let him near you but Trevor sent for him, not realizing that he was an ancient relic and even as a young man he was a half-wit."

"Has anyone said anything about what happened?"

"Do you mean has Aunt Wilhelmina broken into tears and confessed all? I'm sorry, Duchess, no such luck. It turns out that James was downstairs on his way out the door to the stables. He had it in his mind that he would visit the ruins just at dawn, and search for the treasure. A romantic notion but one that would have probably just given him an inflammation of the lungs, given our damp mornings.

"Perhaps James struck you down and took the book and then raised the alarm. Perhaps he was afraid he'd killed you or that you would die without help. I don't know, Duchess." He paused a moment, then looked directly into her eyes. "Why did you leave your bedchamber?"

"I didn't want to stay. I was afraid you would come."

"I see," he said, his hackles rising, but he managed to keep both his voice and his expression calm. He'd been stupid to ask her that question given her current condition. No, he would ask it again when she was once more fit and he could yell at her and then toss up her skirts and drive her wild with pleasure. Just maybe she'd yell back at him and . . .

"Why are you smiling, Marcus?"

"Huh? Oh, I was just thinking about the obnoxious barley concoction Badger is right now mixing up for you. Esmee, my cat, even removed herself at the smell. That or it was Badger's singing whilst he stirred the mess that made her run yowling from the kitchen."

He was lying but he was good at it, and she didn't really mind. She'd lied to him herself once or twice in the past five minutes.

"Now, tell me about the book and those final pages."

She did, describing in detail that gnarled ancient oak tree and those stones that were piled up, not just in piles but constructed with a purpose in mind. And the well, with that leather-bound old wooden bucket, surely it was very, very old. And there were men and women there and they looked Medieval, if she remembered correctly.

He looked abstracted. He rose.

"Where are you going?"

He grinned down at her. "So, my company is preferable to no one else's, eh? No, don't worry, Duchess. Aunt Gweneth will be here shortly. She's very worried about you. She'll not leave you until I return."

Not five minutes after Aunt Gweneth arrived, all gentle worry and soothing fingers to smooth away her headache, Aunt Wilhelmina came into the bedchamber, swathed in dark purple, her impressive bosom well in the foreground like the figurehead on a ship.

"Oh dear," Gweneth said, "I don't believe dear Marcus wants more than just one visitor at a time, Willie. The Duchess is still quite weak."

The Duchess opened her eyes and stared into a face that had once been quite pretty but was now filled with discontent, and bright, dark eyes that were filled with a savage sort of delight at seeing her lying here on her back. *Willie?* Surely that wasn't quite the right name for her aunt. Surely a Willie was warm and giggly and kindness itself. It was just as odd a name on her as Trevor was on her eldest son.

"So, someone struck you down. What a pity."

"Yes, as you see. To get the book, the same book that Mr. Burgess has."

"You're lying. No one would strike you to get to that silly book."

"Really, Willie, the Duchess is ill. I beg you to leave now. She must rest."

"I wish she would die and good riddance to the whore."

Aunt Gweneth gasped. "*What?* What did you say, Willie?"

"I said I could cry and that I pray there'll be no more."

The Duchess closed her eyes and turned her head away from Wilhelmina.

It required but the Twins and Ursula, and they poked their heads into the bedchamber not two moments later.

"Mother, the Duchess must rest," Ursula said in a firm adult's voice. "Come along now. Fanny and Antonia want you to see the new bird feeder we've made. Mr. Oslo, the estate carpenter, helped us, but we did most of the work and we even painted it. It has the look of our house in Baltimore."

"Oh, very well. Do rest, Duchess, maybe forever."

"Willie!"

"What is wrong with you, Gweneth? I just told her to rest and get better."

"Mama, please come along now."

When they were alone again, Aunt Gweneth said softly, "Do forgive her, Duchess. She isn't always a diplomatic woman and her life hasn't been all that easy."

"You mean she was starving in a gutter drinking blue ruin when your brother married her? Or perhaps she was an orphan in a workhouse? I know, it was smallpox, wasn't it? Or do you mean that your brother—my uncle—beat her?"

"Well, no, not exactly. However, you've covered just about every possibility." Gweneth paused a moment, a brow raised thoughtfully. "That was well put, very well put indeed. You seem a bit different, Duchess. Ah, it's just that, well—Wilhelmina isn't a very happy person."

"She's a vicious harpy," the Duchess said, then sighed deeply. "I want to rest now, Aunt Gweneth, that's certain, but not forever."

"No, dear, certainly not. Whatever medicine Badger gave you, keep taking it. I like the vinegar in you, dear. It's such a change, but so invigorating, don't you think?"

20

WHEN SHE AWOKE, it was late afternoon. Badger was sitting beside her. He immediately smiled down at her and gave her some water, holding her head gently in the crook of his arm.

"You always know what to do. Thank you."

He merely nodded. "I heard about the invasion of that American person from Miss Antonia. Now, this person, who is only your aunt by marriage, will not be allowed to discomfit you again. Mr. Spears and I have worked out a schedule. Whenever his lordship isn't here, either Mr. Spears or Miss Maggie or I will be. You won't be bothered again, Duchess."

"And when they aren't here, why I will be. How do you feel, Duchess?"

She felt her spirits lift just at the sound of his voice. It was stupid of her, but true nonetheless. "I'm fine now, Marcus. If you wish, you can relieve your spleen. You can yell at me again with good conscience."

He frowned at her. "No, I shan't do that, particularly in front of Badger. Now, I will dine with you this evening, right here, then we will see tomorrow morning if you're ready to get out of bed." He continued to Badger, "I understand you forced my poor Esmee to eat some of the barley mixture you made for the Duchess and she died. Is that true?"

She laughed, a weak laugh, but still a laugh.

"That damned selfish cat wouldn't offer herself up to try my barley soup," Badger said. "Miserable beast, that

Esmee. I thought I'd caught her, but she twitched her tail right out from between my fingers. Mr. Spears said she sleeps with you, when you're in your own bed, that is."

"It's been known to happen. Esmee is fickle, just as is the Duchess."

"Esmee slept with me last night," she said. "Right in the bend behind my knees."

"She prefers my chest when she deigns to visit me," Marcus said. "She likes to knead the hair, damned creature. As for her volunteering for that barley mixture, she wouldn't ever offer herself up."

He slept with her that night, stretching out naked beside her, completely at his ease, as if he'd slept there for the past twenty years. Esmee had come briefly into the bedchamber, stared silently at them, then, twitching her tail, she went through the open adjoining door into Marcus's bedchamber.

He reached out and took her hand in his. She could feel the heat from his body. She felt safer than she ever had in her life.

"All this excitement left me with a gray hair, Duchess. I ask you to keep to your bed after this and not go searching out clues in the middle of the night."

"I don't believe you, Marcus. Let me see this gray hair."

"No, I shan't light a candle and have you poking about my scalp. You can find it in the morning."

"Did you discover anything?"

"No. Everyone claims to have been soundly in the arms of Morpheus. Also, I might add, the Wyndhams have excelled at the art of falsehood for centuries. None of us ever flinch or even blink an eyelid when spilling out a lie. Even you, Duchess."

Her fingers tightened over his. "You must be exaggerating, Marcus."

"Nary a bit. Now, I find this a mite interesting. Here we are side by side in bed like a good married couple should be, and I will admit that I'm harder than the bricks on the fireplace, but I won't attack you, not even when I know you like it so much."

Before she would have been silent as a tombstone. But now she giggled and bent back his thumb until he yelped.

"You become physical again. But my thumb, Duchess? Would you like me to give you pleasure?"

"No. Be quiet, Marcus. My head hurts."

He laughed. "Ah, the excuse of wives for centuries, or so my father told me. However, in your case, it just might be the truth. As I recall, my mother hit his arm when he said it. Good night, my dear."

"Did you go to the abbey ruins?"

"Yes. Trevor and James were there poking around, the damned sods. Even Ursula arrived shortly to do her own poking. It was a merry family, all wanting to find anything at all and keep it from the others. I don't like any of this, Duchess."

"Except for Ursula. She would run to you with anything she found. She idolizes you, both she and Fanny. You'll grow abominably conceited with all this guileless female attention."

"No, I won't accept that. Believe me, Fanny's infatuation is quite enough. One young girl fluttering her eyelashes at my poor self is unnerving enough. And here my wife is lying in her bed unable to protect me. And now you would protect me, wouldn't you? Or would you perceive that I was a bounder despite my innocence, and come after me with another weapon?"

"I would try to be fair. Now, you can rest easy. Ursula is very fond of me, so she wouldn't dream of trying to take you away from me."

"A relief. A right bloody relief."

The relief lasted for a full day and a half. She rested and mended and the lump behind her left ear disappeared. Maggie even washed her hair, removing all the oily salve Badger had made for the lump and Spears had remorselessly rubbed in three times that first day. On the second night, Marcus came into her bedchamber wearing only his dressing gown and she knew he was naked beneath it, but then again, why shouldn't he be?

She remembered how she'd left her bedchamber because she'd not wanted to face him. Well, she wouldn't ever leave again. Let him do his worst. She grinned at that. Just let him try to treat her like a vessel again, a vessel that he scorned.

"Hello, Marcus," she called out to him. "I am quite well tonight. Do you intend to exercise your marital rights? Will you heave over me? When you've had enough of me will you leave again and spill yourself on my belly?" She saw him clearly in her mind's eye, lifting himself over her, saw the intense determination on his face, saw him spilling his seed on her belly, not inside her, no, never there because he hated his uncle so much for his betrayal.

He paused, staring at her. She'd startled him yet again. He shook his head. He doubted he would ever get used to this new side of her.

She changed then before his eyes, now she was serious, dead serious, saying as he came to stand beside her bed, "You must have an heir, Marcus. Your pride mustn't get in the way of providing a male child for the next generation of Wyndhams. Why don't you just forget my father and what he did. It isn't important. It doesn't touch us."

"Oh yes, it does and it always will." Then he smiled at her. She wouldn't control him, no matter how her mind shifted and played and danced around him. He said easily, "Once you and your damned cohorts forced me to wed with you, you removed many of my options, Duchess. But not all. Let's get that nightgown off you. I'm tired of waiting."

In that moment, something deep inside her uncoiled and began to fill her. She felt herself growing cold and colder still, all of it inside her, deep inside.

"Very well," she said, and all that coldness she felt was in her voice, in her eyes as she stared up at him.

She said nothing more to him. Besides, he didn't want to talk, he wanted his pleasure and hers as well because she'd come to realize that it gratified his male vanity to make her cry out despite herself. He was gentle and insistent at first, then his mouth was on her mouth, then on her breasts and her belly, until finally he was caressing her, pushing her to pleasure. But there wasn't any. She lay there, and this time she did suffer him. She hadn't realized how very empty this lovemaking could be when she was not part of it, not part of him. But there he was, isolated from her, and she saw his growing passion mix with his frustration because he couldn't arouse her, and she didn't care. She just lay there, her arms beside her flat on the bed. She didn't even feel anger, just a numbness, just a waiting for him to finish.

He stopped finally, coming up to look down at her. He'd left the candlelight so he could see her face and her body, for both pleased him, he had told her several times before, then he would speak softly to her, going into vast detail and laughing softly when she would flush at the shocking words, words surely too intimate, and then he would carry his words into action.

This time he said nothing. And now he was looking down at her, studying her face, looking at her breasts and her belly. His face was flushed, his breath coming deep and heavy. He was swelled and ready for her. He started to speak, then shook his head at himself. Suddenly, he pulled her open to him and, lifting her in his big hands, went into her deep and hard.

She gasped at the feel of him but he didn't hurt her for he'd softened her, she couldn't deny that, but still she felt him deep inside her with none of the pleasure, just his differentness, the hardness of him, and his heaving over her, and she hated it, this separateness from him. She simply waited, not moving.

Then, just as suddenly as the first time, he pulled out of her and pressed himself against her belly.

And when he was done, he went back onto his heels between her legs.

She said, cold as the North Sea during winter solstice, "Are you now through with me? Ah, certainly you are. May I have a handkerchief, Marcus? I dislike your seed sprayed on me. No, don't worry, there are no weapons for me about to take to you though you deserve to be beaten quite thoroughly. No, just give me a handkerchief and take yourself off."

She'd begun sounding as unemotional as a stick and he wanted to yell at her. But now she was mocking him, laughing at him, and he didn't know what he wanted to do. She'd been utterly still beneath him. He'd wanted desperately to bring her to him but she hadn't responded. He hated it. He looked down at his seed on her belly. So she hated his seed on her, did she? He looked to her face. She looked utterly composed, no, more than that, she looked bloody amused now, but it was cold, that amusement of hers. She looked as if she didn't give a good damn. She looked indifferent. She could castrate him with her indifference. He hated her at that moment, hated her for being as passionate as he was before, hated her for making him as wild as a young boy, all the while lying there, thinking about nothing in particular, perhaps even wondering about characters in the novel she'd been reading that afternoon, or perhaps about Esmee, but not thinking of him, just lying there, enduring him, waiting for him to finish with her. He rocked back on his heels with rage, striking his fist on his thigh.

"I don't believe this. I'd rather have you shrieking at me like you did in the tack room. You lost complete control. You've good strong lungs. The good Lord knows I never wanted you for a wife and believe me, Duchess, I will use you only until I return to London. Then you won't have to suffer me further."

He was off her bed in moments, jerked up his dressing gown and was gone from her room, slamming the adjoining door behind him.

She rose and washed him off herself. She slowly pulled her nightgown over her head and smoothed it down. She tied the ribbons at her shoulders. When she was back in her bed, she moved to the far edge, for she fancied she could still feel the heat of him. And she was cold, for the deep rage was banked. Perhaps she should fetch one of her father's dueling pistols from the estate room. Perhaps she should simply be prepared. She could never outguess Marcus. Yes, she would be wise to be prepared.

The Duchess climbed over the low fence, careful not to rip her riding skirt. She looked about her, studying the details of the landscape. The Fenlow moor was off to the west, rugged and barren even in the lush warmth of summer. To the east was a dense copse of trees, firs and beeches, mostly. But directly in front of her were farms, spread out like richly embroidered squares, rich with growing crops under the summer sun, one after another, their boundaries stone fences or lines of carefully planted trees. There were small hillocks dotting here and there and trees and several small streams. It was a beautiful prospect, but she didn't care. It was a puzzle. These were just pieces and she didn't yet know which pieces fit where.

She just wanted to find that ancient gnarled oak tree, and thus she'd walked from a different direction today. She stopped and studied the stone fences slashing gray and thick across the horizon, most of them well maintained by the farmers, but some falling into disrepair.

She shook out her skirts and walked forward. Where the devil was that oak tree?

She reached the ruins of St. Swale's Abbey after a brisk twenty-minute walk. She'd been here every day now for a week and a half, looking through the rubble, searching, for what, she had no idea.

As to who had struck her down and taken the book, she didn't know that either. Nor did Marcus. Nor did Spears or Badger or Maggie, who refused to let her out of their collective sight. Even Mr. Crittaker and Sampson had joined their ranks. She was never alone in the house, never. Now her guard believed her to be resting as they believed her to have been resting for the past week and a half at this particular time. And that was why she was on foot. The stable lads were loyal to Marcus. Lambkin would have a fit if he saw her near the stables. If she took Birdie out, Marcus would know it within ten minutes.

She was on her knees in what she was certain had been a monk's cell, studying a small etched drawing low on one of the stones in the wall when suddenly from behind her, he said, furious, "What the devil are you doing here? Damn you, Duchess, you're supposed to be resting."

She turned slowly, unaware that there was a smudge of dirt on her cheek and that her hair was coming down, a thick plait curling over her shoulder. "Marcus," she said only.

"What are you doing here?"

"Looking around." She shrugged. "Come look at this etching. It's very faint, but I can still make out the lines. This is a monk's cell, I'm sure of that. Come on your knees and look."

He didn't. He grabbed her arm and hauled her upright. "You have bloody lied to everyone, haven't you?" He shook her. "You haven't been the feminine little lady reclining on her bed napping, have you? No, you've been here, digging about and wandering around alone, damn you." He shook her again for good measure. "Say something, anything. Shriek at me or yell. Yowl like Esmee when she's in a snit."

Suddenly, she turned perfectly white. "Marcus," she said, utterly disbelieving, "let me go. I'm going to be ill."

He was so surprised, he released her immediately. He watched as she fell to her knees and wretched. Soon she was dry heaving, for she hadn't eaten much. He knelt beside her, pulling back her hair, steadying her, for she was trembling now from the effort, weak from vomiting. He felt a shaft of guilt, sharp as an arrow. "I told you that you should be resting. Look what comes of it. Damnation, you're still ill from that blow. No wonder you didn't yell at me, or flail at me with your shrew's tongue, you were too busy swallowing your bile, and you failed."

He took out his handkerchief and handed it to her. She wiped her mouth, then crumpled it in her hand when her body shook with more heaves that left her sweating and shaky.

He cursed even as he lifted her into his arms. He was silent as a midnight moon as he managed to mount Stanley with her in his arms. He settled her in the crook of his arm, then kicked Stanley in his fat sides. To her surprise, he didn't ride back to the Park. Instead, after some minutes, he halted his stallion beside a slender thread of a stream bordered with thick water reeds.

He lifted her down and eased her onto her knees. He cupped the water in his hands and let her wash out her mouth. She then swallowed some of the water, clear and so cold that it made her lips blue. The water hit her belly and nausea struck her again. She moaned, clutching her arms around herself.

He ripped off the hem of her petticoat, wet it, and wiped her face. He carried her to the shade of a maple tree, eased down and pulled her back against him, settling her between his legs. "Hold still. Is your belly settling now?"

"I don't know."

"You feel weak and shaky. It's understandable. Just lie against me and keep quiet for a while. I'm tired of your damned protestations."

She didn't remember protesting anything. She closed her eyes.

He felt her ease, heard her breathing slow and deepen. He stared over the top of her head to the stream then beyond it, realized he wasn't seeing anything at all, and tightened his hold around her, leaning his head back against the trunk of the tree. It was warm. Bees buzzed about. He could hear larks singing.

He heard a cow mooing in the distance. Stanley was eating water reeds not many feet away, chewing noisily. He closed his eyes. When he awoke, the sun had moved a goodly distance toward the west. He must have twitched upon awakening, for she was now awake too.

"Don't move. First tell me how you feel."

"I'm fine now, truly. Thank you for helping me, Marcus."

"I saw you leaving the house and I followed you. Why the devil didn't you at least ride Birdie?"

"The stable lads would have told you immediately. Lambkin would probably have refused to saddle her."

"You have done this before today?"

"Yes, for over a week now. I want to find that oak tree with the well beneath it. It should be near the abbey, but I couldn't find it. But it must be around here, Marcus, someplace close. I've been so frustrated."

Very slowly, he lifted her onto his thighs and turned her to face him. "Listen to me. Hasn't it occurred to you that the person who struck you down in the library just might be interested in striking you down again?"

"Why? The person saw that book and I was in the way. I was struck only because of the book, Marcus."

"You can't possibly know that. Now, we're going back to the Park. No, don't try to move yourself. I'll carry you."

As he walked to Stanley, who was chewing vigorously, and ignored them, he said, "Are you still having headaches as well as belly nausea?"

"No, and I haven't felt ill before today, I promise you. It is odd."

"You will climb into your bed when we get home. No, don't stiffen up like a frightened virgin or draw in your breath to scream at me for my interference like a Milanese soprano. I have no intention of climbing into your bed beside you. I will come to you tonight though, so don't go haring off to another bedchamber. If you do, I'll search you out and I won't be pleased with you. Another thing, there will be no more lying there, wishing me dead or impotent, which would be worse."

"Why don't you just go back to London? To Celeste? Or you could have Lisette come to you here."

"Yes, I could, couldn't I?"

"You could try it," she said, chin up, eyes lighting for battle, for the nausea was gone now, thank God. "I wonder if you would be so stupid."

His eyes glinted and he was slavering to goad her but good, saying in a drawl that could match Trevor's, it was so slow and taunting in its slowness, "Do I take it that you are threatening me, woman? Are you saying that you would gullet me if I touch another woman?"

"Right now I am saying that you would be very sorry if you brought one of your women here. If you touched another woman—I will think about that and let you know. I believe a man should understand his options."

She said not another word, but she was smiling, curse those mysterious eyes of hers. He insisted on carrying her through the entrance hall for all to see, then upstairs to her bedchamber, where he made a grand production of seeing to her care.

=21=

"I WISH YOU WOULD lose all your hair."

"Huh? What did you say?" His hold around her tightened.

"I said," the Duchess said sweetly, smiling at him, "that I wished you would call for a chair. Surely you're uncomfortable just standing there like that."

He grinned down at her. "That wasn't bad, but you're no competition for Aunt Wilhelmina. Perhaps you simply haven't any talent for well-turned rhymes."

"Enough talent so I didn't starve!" She stared at him, clamping her hand over her mouth. She was a fool. It was the first time in her life he'd goaded her into unwise speech. In the past two weeks, he'd not goaded her in anything. She'd said just what she'd wanted, but now. She wanted to bite her tongue off.

But he didn't understand, at least he didn't realize what she'd just let slip. "So, we're back to the mythical man who supported you at Pipwell Cottage again."

"No, we're not. But just perhaps I was lying, as all Wyndhams lie, so you've told me. So perhaps there was a man. What do you think, Marcus?"

If he'd been a dog, he would have growled, but he got a hold on himself immediately, saying in that easy way of his that made her want to strike him and kiss him at the same time, "Well, I know he wasn't your protector. If you convinced some fool to give you money with no return with your favors, who am I to cavil? No, come on now, Duchess, I wasn't really serious." He gave her an unrepentant grin.

"Shall I undress you? Where are your nightgowns?"

"I'll see to her, my lord," Maggie said, coming into the room like a queen ready to fire off her troops. "You just leave the Duchess be. Look how flushed she is. You've been scolding her, haven't you, or teasing her? That can't be good for her, though, I, like everyone else, saw you bringing her in. We all believed you to be resting, Duchess. It wasn't well done of you to go off by yourself. That monster who struck you down just might have done it again."

"From the mouths of maids," Marcus murmured.

The Duchess closed her eyes. She wondered if she should tell Maggie that she was flushed with utter delightful anger. But she didn't. To her surprise, she felt fatigue wash over her. She was asleep within moments.

Marcus was true to his word. That evening after solicitously seeing her to her bedchamber and handing her over to Maggie, he took himself to his own bedchamber. He opened the adjoining door a half an hour later.

She was sitting in an overly plump chair in front of the small fireplace, staring into the sluggishly burning flames.

"Hello," he said. "Here I am just as I promised."

She spared him a glance. "Go away, Marcus."

"Oh no. I only just wrote to Celeste this afternoon. She won't be arriving for another four days. I will have to make do with you until then."

"You've been warned," she said, nothing more, just that. Then she folded her hands in her lap and ignored him, an enraging, indifferent, aloof act that the old Duchess would have performed.

He gave a martyr's sigh, leaned down, and scooped her up in his arms. He kissed her as she turned her head and touched her neck. "You smell wonderful, but then you always do."

"Thank you. Go away, Marcus. I will not be your vessel of the moment. I won't suffer the boredom of you in my bed. Go dream of Celeste."

" 'Vessel of the moment.' That sounds mighty odd, Duchess." He set her on her feet beside her bed, then, without fuss or more words, stripped off her dressing gown and nightgown. He set her away from him. "The good Lord constructed you quite nicely," he said, stroking his fingertips over his chin as he looked her up and down. "He had me in mind, obviously, for the size of you, and the shape of you, is just to my liking."

She looked indifferent, merely standing there, looking away from him, not moving. She sucked in her breath when he reached out his hand and lightly caressed her left breast. "Yes, you're made of beautiful shapes. This is very intriguing, Duchess. You are silent as the Duchess of yore, then you're not. I never know what to expect from you now."

"You never will know, Marcus, you damned sod."

He laughed even as his hand stroked over her ribs and her belly. She took a step back, then gave a sharp cry. She looked at him, her eyes wide and bewildered. Then she turned and ran from him.

"Duchess." He took a step after her, then frowned himself in consternation when she dropped to her knees and retched into the chamber pot. He went down on his knees beside her, holding her steady. "This is familiar," he said, pulling her hair back from her face. "I don't like it. You were ill this afternoon and now you're ill again. There is a physician in Darlington who has a fine reputation. I believe I will have him come here to the Park now, tonight in fact."

She was shuddering, huddling in on herself. He rose and fetched her dressing gown, wrapping it around her. He put her in bed, then said, "You lie still. I mean it, Duchess. Just lie still until I return."

He did return and in only five minutes. With him were Spears, Badger, and Maggie, wearing a gown of teal-blue satin with a décolletage that would send a vicar into shock. Marcus was saying as he entered the bedchamber, "She vomited this afternoon and again now. I know of this physician in Darlington. I want you, Badger, to go fetch him."

Badger cleared his throat and stared at his pale huddled mistress in the large bed.

Spears closely studied the small clusters of grapes carved into the edges of the mantel.

Maggie smoothed the luscious teal-blue satin over her hips.

Marcus frowned. "What the devil is going on here? Badger?"

Spears said to the Duchess, "Maggie will fetch you a biscuit to nibble on. It will help settle your stomach."

"How the hell do you know that?"

"Now, my lord," Spears said in an odious avuncular voice, "there is naught to worry about. We have all discussed the situation and there is nothing to concern us and therefore nothing to concern you. Her ladyship is performing a natural function."

"What bloody natural function? Do you so conveniently forget that she was struck down not two weeks ago?"

Badger said, "The Duchess is breeding, my lord. She is carrying *the heir*. The nausea and vomiting are natural. It will pass within a short time. Mr. Spears says another three weeks and she'll be perfectly fine again. Well, perhaps longer, but we know she's superior and thus the three weeks will apply to her."

There was utter silence in the room. From a great distance, Marcus heard the Duchess say, "I am fine, Spears. Please, Badger, Maggie, please leave now. It's important. Please leave."

The three marched out, but their pace was slow.

Marcus very slowly closed the bedchamber door. He then turned the key in the lock. "Are you going to be ill again? Do you need something to eat?"

She shook her head.

It was then he realized that she was utterly without color, her eyes dilated, her body hunched over itself.

"Did you know?" he asked, his voice as quiet as a leaf quivering in a breeze.

"No."

"How can I believe you?"

"You can't. You said yourself that all Wyndhams were excellent liars, myself included."

"You are carrying my child. That isn't possible. The three meddling idiots must be wrong. You vomited because of that blow to your head."

"Very well, it isn't possible. But for the sake of argument, let's say it's true. Now, is it to be an immaculate conception or have I cuckolded you? Ah, don't forget my generous lover at Pipwell Cottage."

He sliced his hand through the air. He looked bewildered, disbelieving; he looked like a man who'd just been shot but didn't yet feel the pain. "I don't understand this. It's true I took you a few times, a very few times, and I didn't have the fortitude to withdraw from you as I do now, but it takes much longer to impregnate a woman, surely it must take many, many times and many, many months."

"Evidently not."

He began to pace. She looked at his flapping dressing gown, his black hairy legs, his bare feet. He was beautiful, this man who didn't want her to have his child. Ah, she was pregnant. Her body had accepted his seed. On their wedding night? That second night he'd come to her? She wanted to sing and shout and dance. Instead she felt a stirring of the nausea and began to breathe deeply and slowly.

"You didn't have your monthly flow after we were married in Paris?"

She shook her head.

"You're a damned woman. Didn't it occur to you that something might be different? Namely, me, the man who spilled his seed inside you?"

"I'm not always as predictable as many women."

"You mean in that oblique way of yours that your monthly flow doesn't occur necessarily when you expect it to?"

She nodded, staring him straight in the eye.

"I don't want this child and you damn well know it!"

She held silent, though the words were near to breaking through, but she was concentrating too hard on not throwing up to speak.

"You did this on purpose."

Ah, he'd finally swung his axe. The look on her face was bleak and accepting, then just as quickly shifted to utter red-faced rage. Even then the old Duchess peeked through as she shrugged saying, "I wondered how long it would take you to fix the blame firmly on my head. My mother told me several times that a man couldn't bear to be in the wrong. She said a man would say whatever he had to say in order to put the woman in the wrong instead." Then, miraculously, even the rage disappeared. She actually smiled at him. "You will be a father, Marcus, and I will be a mother. I am pregnant with a child, our child."

"I refuse to accept that your bastard father has won. Forgive me. You're the bastard, but only by birth. He is one in mind and in act. I won't accept it, Duchess. Do you hear me? I don't accept that you're pregnant." He slapped his palm to his forehead. "I have done nothing to deserve this, nothing, dammit. I was quite happily going about my life when your father died and I had to be the heir, there was no choice for anyone. Then because he's bitter and twisted, he unleashed his venom on me. He hated me and he proved it, stripping me of all means to maintain and support all the Wyndham estates and properties, unless I married you, his precious bastard. You, the one woman in the bloody world I never wanted, or if I did want you from the time I was fourteen years old and randy as a young stoat, I wouldn't have any longer than it took him to humiliate me to my soul. And yet you forced me to take you.

"I want my life back in my control. I want you and your damned child out of it."

He stomped toward the adjoining door, only to draw up at her quiet voice. "I see. Do you wish me to leave tomorrow, Marcus?"

"I would that you leave tonight, right this bloody instant, but that would be cruel. You would probably faint on the front steps."

He slammed the adjoining door behind him.

She stared for a long moment at that closed door. Then, slowly, she lightly touched her stomach. She was flat, but inside her womb was her child, their child.

She was lying there, staring up at the ceiling, when there was a knock on the door. She rose and unlocked it. Badger, Spears, and Maggie stood there, Maggie with a small covered plate in her hands.

They said nothing, merely came into the bedchamber when she stepped back.

"Here, Duchess, eat there," Maggie said as she guided her to the chair in front of the fireplace.

The three of them took position about her, saying nothing until she began to nibble on one of Badger's fresh scones.

"I made them with small apple slices," he said. "And fresh cream. It is my Aunt Mildred's recipe."

"They're delicious."

"Your stomach is settling?" Maggie asked.

The Duchess nodded and continued to chew slowly as she stared into the fire.

Spears cleared his throat. "His lordship is a passionate man. He is a natural leader, a man of action. He despises dithering about. In all the battles he fought, his men trusted him above God. He protected them, drove them relentlessly, and they knew he would willingly die for any of them. They knew this and gave him their best."

Badger continued, "He is hotheaded, always has been, Mr. Spears tells me, even as a boy. Besides a leader, he is a man who is loyal to his bones. Sometimes, however, he isn't a cool thinker, not what you would call a measured scholar of philosophy. He reacts, then thinks. He can curse some of the most amazing composites I've ever heard. Then he's calm again and laughing."

"They say that we women are the ones to lose our calm and spit out whatever comes into our minds," Maggie said, hands on her silk-covered hips, "but it isn't necessarily true. Just look at you, Duchess, quiet and still as a clam. You never lose your head and scream foolishness. You're just the opposite of his lordship." Maggie frowned, then shrugged. "At least you used to be his opposite. It's strange, you're different, all of us have noticed it."

Spears said, "It is true that his lordship occasionally loses his temper and thus control of his tongue, but he will come around, Duchess. Even though you appear to have lost your magnificent reticence, at least when you now choose to lose it, you can't come near to his lordship in sheer undignified temper. He isn't an unfair man, he's just—"

"I know," she said. "He's just passionate and hotheaded and easily driven over the brink. But know this, all of you. He doesn't want the child. He's said that often enough, it isn't just something he decided tonight."

"He is a man. However, he isn't stupid," Maggie said, frowning. "Well yes, he is, for he is a man, after all, and all men must . . . well, that's not important here and now, is it? Now, his lordship must realize that babes follow lovemaking. Even as he cursed and ranted, he knew it would be natural for you to become pregnant, for his lordship is a lusty man—"

"Exactly," Badger said. "His temper, his insistence that he doesn't want an heir doesn't make sense. As Maggie said, he isn't stupid."

The Duchess became utterly white and still. "You don't understand."

The three of them looked baffled.

"You don't understand," she said again, slowly, then clamped her mouth shut.

"Well, regardless," Maggie said, "I know men, Duchess, and his lordship may be proud to the point of you wanting to strangle him, but he will come around. He will come to understand what is right."

"He will moderate his stand," Badger said.

"He will moderate his stand, or we will have to take action," Spears said, and Badger and Maggie nodded.

She looked at each of them in turn. Finally, she said, "Yes, perhaps we will have to take action."

"You won't run away, will you, Duchess?" Badger said.

She looked at him thoughtfully.

=22=

MARCUS CAME TO an abrupt halt at the bottom of the huge staircase that spilled onto the grand entrance hall of Chase Park. There in front of the front double doors were three valises and beside them stood Maggie, all trimmed out in a flaming red bonnet with a curling ostrich feather curving around to her chin and wearing a dark blue cloak. She was tapping an elegantly shod foot, tap, tap, tap. She was obviously waiting.

She was waiting for the Duchess.

He bellowed, "Where the hell is she, Maggie?"

Maggie turned very slowly and gave the earl a deep curtsy. "My lord, who the hell is she?"

"Don't you twit my nose, girl, or I'll—"

"That is quite enough, Marcus. Actually, I am here, but for just the next moment, then Maggie and I are away from Chase Park."

"You aren't going anywhere, damn you."

"But you were quite clear in your wishes. You wanted me gone immediately, but were afraid your consequence would suffer if it became known that you kicked out your pregnant wife in the middle of the night."

"It wasn't the bloody middle of the night. Now—"

"Thus, in the spirit of *bonhomie,* I waited until this morning. Good-bye, Marcus."

She turned on her heel, her chin in the air, as regal as the damned duchess he'd named her so long ago. Then, she tripped on one of the valises and went crashing down on her side.

He reached her in an instant, hauling her into his arms. "Are you all right? Say something, you damned scourge."

"I'm all right. How very embarrassing to be felled in the midst of such an excellent exit."

"Yes, that's what happens when your chin is in the air. However, I won't laugh, at least not just yet. Now heed me, Duchess. You aren't going anywhere. This is your home and here you'll stay." He shook her. "Do you understand me?"

"I'm not certain, Marcus. Perhaps you'd best shake me again. It makes me think more clearly."

He hauled her to her feet and stared down at her, his look as black and brooding as one of the quixotic Lord Byron's heroes.

"Why is Chase Park now my home? Why are you singing a different tune this morning? Truly, I don't understand you, my lord."

"It is your home until I tell you it is not, and even then perhaps it will still be your home, as arguments follow from the night unto the morning and things change in the hours in between. Do you now understand?"

"I will never understand you."

"I am a man. Men are not easily fathomed. Our feelings aren't sitting in the middle of a plate for all to comment upon and taste, not like you bloody women."

Maggie snorted behind him.

"Oh dear," the Duchess said in that tone of voice he now recognized very well, and he let her go without any hesitation whatsoever.

She ran out the door, down the deep wide marble steps, past a startled gardener who dropped his spade, fell to her knees, and vomited in the rosebushes.

Maggie looked him up and down. "You shook her on purpose to make her sick. I spent a good twenty minutes brushing her cloak from all her trips to that wretched abbey where she grubbed around on her knees looking for that wretched treasure, and now just look. Black dirt, worms, and God knows what else."

"I did not shake her for that purpose. However, the result just might be a dollop of common sense in that woman's brain of hers. Sampson! Ah, there you are, just behind me. You're becoming a lurker, just like Spears and Badger. Have her ladyship's valises removed back to her room. Do not delay. Once she is on her feet again, her brain just might be swayed again to perversity."

Maggie snorted.

Marcus went outside into a beautiful summer morning. The sky was a light blue with white clouds dotted here and there, the smell of cut grass heavy in the air, and his wife was retching on her knees in the rosebushes.

He waited until she was done, then picked her up in his arms and carried her back upstairs, not pausing to say anything at all to any of her cohorts. He passed Aunt Wilhelmina, who raised a brow and said, "Perhaps she has finally cocked it?"

"No, she hasn't. Good day to you too, Aunt Wilhelmina."

"Mama!" he heard Ursula say. "Really, you shouldn't say such awful things. She's the duchess and she's the mistress here."

"I? I said nothing at all untoward. I merely wondered if she had merely knocked herself up with all her activity."

"I could do better than that," Marcus said under his breath. She wanted to smile at that but she felt too wretched. "I don't like this, Marcus."

"No, I shouldn't like it either. Now you know that you must be calm and placid as a cow, and do exactly what I tell you to do."

He reached her bedchamber, frowned a maid out of the room in a near dead run, and laid her on her bed.

She took sips of the water he handed her. She groaned, grabbing her stomach.

He left the room and she heard him shout, "Maggie, get her some biscuits. Doubtless you packed dozens. Go, quickly!"

Not three minutes later, she was chewing slowly on a biscuit flavored with cinnamon. She sighed, finally relaxing.

"You don't want me here. Why are you being perverse? Is the vicar due to call on you? Do you fear he will see your wife leaving you?"

He was silent. He turned away from her and began his familiar pacing, back and forth at an angle between the bed and the winged chair, long strides in his black boots.

He was such a splendid-looking creature. She liked him in those tight buckskin breeches. She remembered how he'd looked in his uniform and sighed again. "I'm willing to leave, Marcus. As you know, I'm very rich. And you also know, even without the money my father left me, I can still manage. I obviously didn't get pregnant on purpose, that, I suppose, is impossible. But I am with child and there's nothing I can do about it." Suddenly she sucked in her breath and whispered, "No, surely not. You don't want me to do that."

"Surely not what? What don't I want you to do?"

"I have heard of women who try to rid themselves of their babies and many succeed. They stick things inside themselves. Sometimes they die too."

"Oh, for God's sake, Duchess, just shut up. Yes, I can certainly see you tripping into some back alley in York asking for an old besom to rid you of the child. Or better yet, why don't I drag you by your hair into a back alley? Just cease your asinine talk. You may be quiet or you may turn red raging at me. Just don't be a fool." He began pacing again, more quickly now, his steps longer, his heels clicking on the wooden floor. He was indeed very nice to look at, the sod.

"What do you want me to do, Marcus?"

Then he turned and he was smiling. "It seems that now I won't have to withdraw from you. The damage is done, so to speak."

She could only stare at him. "You said Celeste would be here in four days."

"I could have lied. I'm a Wyndham and it is a possibility that I didn't write to her instructing her to come. You possibly know I was perhaps lying, don't pretend otherwise. Since your bouts of illness come and go with neither rhyme nor reason, then I'd best enjoy you when a propitious moment is offered. Like now."

She didn't move for the longest time, nor did she speak. Then, very slowly, she rose from the bed, walked to the chamber pot, and retched.

"Well, hell," he said, kicked over a stool, and went to hold his wife until she sagged back against him.

"You know," he said, drawling out his words as he lightly stroked her hair from her face, "I just might have Celeste come after all. You are in no shape to offer me much of anything, fight or passion. What do you think, Duchess?"

"You just try it," she said.

He stared at her a long moment. She could see him thinking, sorting through ideas, then he said, "I think I'm beginning to see things more clearly. I don't think you had any intention of leaving Chase Park or me, did you?"

"Did you not see the valises? Wasn't Maggie all decked as fine as a nine pence? Was the carriage not there waiting?"

"Did you?"

Actually he was perfectly right. She was only pretending to leave, the valises had been empty, and Maggie, bless her actress's heart, had doubtless enjoyed herself immensely. She'd prayed he would come to grips with the existence of the child, prayed that if he thought she was leaving him, he would realize he wanted her, that he wanted both her and their child. Now she had no idea at all if she'd gotten what she'd prayed for.

She remained silent. She wouldn't give him that kind of ammunition. Her chin went into the air.

"You now offer me another challenge," he said, and his blue eyes glittered. "You like games, madam? Now that I know what you're about, you'll soon realize you haven't got a chance. You will be humiliated. You're a mere babe at this. You have no clue of proper strategy, no instinct for just what to do at any exact moment. Yes, a challenge from you—when you're not puking on the rosebushes—just might please me."

"I just might leave you tonight, at eight o'clock."

He laughed.

"I don't like it," Marcus said to Badger and Spears. "She's ill all the time. She's pale and she's thin as a damned stick. She's too exhausted to even get angry, and the good Lord knows I bait her enough when she appears well, goad her until if I were her I'd shoot me or stab me with a dinner knife, but she doesn't even take a nibble."

"That is worrisome indeed, for you are renowned for your bait, my lord," Spears said.

"I don't like it either," Badger said. "You are also renowned for your goads."

"Another two weeks," Spears said. "I understand your concern, but I have studied this thoroughly, my lord. Surely just another two weeks and she'll be much improved. Mr. Badger is preparing excellent dishes for her to eat, and what she is managing to keep in her belly is very healthful for her and the babe."

Marcus flinched whenever anyone mentioned the child. He still had no idea what he was going to do. Send her away when she was well again? To Pipwell Cottage? He cursed, which made both Badger and Spears regard him with some surprise.

"I had thought, my lord," Spears said, "that this was a meeting with a purpose, namely, to relieve your mind of your wife's continued illness."

"You sound as austere as my mother, Spears. Incidentally, when is my fond parent to arrive?"

"Mr. Sampson said she would be coming the third week of July."

"Oh God, can you just see my mother with Aunt

Wilhelmina? She and that harpy from Baltimore will have a fine old time. Poor Aunt Gweneth—she'll be buried along with the rest of us beneath the sweet poison darts those two will be flinging about."

"Your mother isn't at all difficult," Spears said. "She is amusing. She doesn't suffer fools, thus I wager that the harpy from Baltimore will quickly find herself at *point non plus*. I told Mr. Badger that she was fanciful, what with her adoration of Medieval legend and lore. Quite harmless, I would say, my lord, and charming."

"Not only Medieval, Spears. She believes that Mary, Queen of Scots, is just one step earthward of the Virgin Mary, Queen of Heaven. I fear that she and Aunt Wilhelmina together will send all of us to early graves. My mother is sharp-witted, you know. She quite terrifies me."

There was a cough at the door. It was James Wyndham and he was looking steadily at Marcus.

"Ah, James, do come in. Spears, Badger, and I were just conferring on the possible winners at Ascot next month. What do you think, *Elysian Fields* or *Robert the Bruce?* Both are strong in the chest and run faster than a storm."

"I have always thought that Robert the Bruce—the man— was just excellent. I should bet on him."

"Just so, Master James," Spears said. "Now, Mr. Badger, it's best that you get back to your kitchen. We will all endeavor to curtail our worrying."

"What are we having for dinner, Badger?"

"Baked cod and smoked mussels, my lord. Many other courses as well, but I won't bore you with the recital of them. Also, some glass pudding, a favorite of the Duchess's. It's light so her stomach shouldn't rebel. I might try another Frog dish, perhaps some *crème de pommes de terre aux champignons* would sit nicely in her belly."

"Potatoes and mushrooms? Yes, give it a try," Marcus said, half his attention on James Wyndham, who was regarding Spears and Badger as if he'd suddenly stepped into a Drury Lane play and didn't know his lines. Marcus supposed that the denizens of Chase Park weren't exactly what one would expect, not that he cared a whit.

When they were alone, Marcus said, "What's wrong, James? You look all tight in the jaw."

"I've been thinking, Marcus, thinking and remembering and thinking some more. When I found the Duchess unconscious on the floor, that book wasn't on top of the desk. I do remember that clearly. If you don't mind unlocking the library, I think we should look in that spot in the bookshelves where she found the first one. Perhaps there are more volumes that just might give us clues about the Wyndham treasure."

"Let's go," Marcus said. He fetched the library key from Sampson and he and James went into the gloomy room. Marcus threw back the thick draperies. Bright afternoon light poured into the room. "Let's open some windows as well. This place needs a good airing."

He turned to see James on his knees gently pulling out books all along the second bookshelf from the bottom. There were no volumes behind the outside books.

While James replaced the books, Marcus removed those on the shelf above. Still nothing.

They continued, saying nothing much, until James let out a cry. "Goodness, here's something, Marcus."

He pulled a very old thick book, that sent up billows of choking dust when he lifted it. It was set behind sermons of a certain George Common, an itinerant preacher of the early last century.

"It's just as old," Marcus said. "Here, James, put it on the desktop.

"Well," Marcus said after a few moments, "I'll be damned and redamned. Your brain is good, James, very good."

"My mother believes so," James said with a cocky grin. "I'll have to admit that she gave me the idea when she was carping on about the treasure and how to find it. And keep you from finding out, naturally."

"Let's see the back pages."

"Marcus, I know you suspect my mother of striking down the Duchess. I know someone in the house is responsible—but my mother? It's difficult to swallow."

"There's always Trevor or you or Ursula."

"I see your point," James said as he gently turned the pages.

Marcus looked at her closely, decided she was being honest, and said, "Very well, so your belly isn't going to revolt in the next two minutes. Here is the book James found. You'll note there are no pictures, just writing. I've gone through it completely and translated it as best I could. The monk or monks who wrote it and the other two tomes tells us here where to find the abbey treasure. His rhyme is about as intelligible and lucid as my translation of it.

"Look above to find your sign.
Look hard to find the number nine.

Take it to the shallow well.
Beneath the oak tree in the dell.

Bring a stout bucket and a cord.
Prepare to kill it with your sword.

Lean down deep but do beware.
The monster lives forever in his lair.

The Janus-faced nines will bring the beast.
But be quick or be the creature's feast."

"My translation is adequate at best, but what is this about a monster? The beast lives in the well? And a nine that is Janus-faced? A deceitful nine? That's a kicker, isn't it? What do you think, Duchess?"

"That oak tree and well I've been looking for—why, that's it, Marcus."

"Well, it can't be that simple. There's still this nonsense about looking up to find this number nine, whatever the devil that means. And the monster in the well—"

"My lord."

"Yes, Spears, what is it?"

"Mr. Trevor Wyndham wishes to see you."

"Shall I allow him in your bedchamber, Duchess? The bloody rake just might get the wrong idea. He's a man and he's got too much experience for my peace of mind and you're looking particularly fetching and vulnerable, a combination to drive any man wild with lust."

"Do show Mr. Wyndham in, Spears," she said. "My husband will surely protect my virtue."

He was huge and dark and excessively handsome, this cousin of hers. She realized that Marcus was regarding him with a vicious look and said, "Hello, Trevor. Have you come to see the book James found?"

"You look lovely, Duchess. You're feeling more the thing now? Has this boorish dolt been wearying you? Shall I remove him and perhaps challenge him to a duel of wit?"

"My wit, Trevor, will always make yours look like a withered stump. However, I have a dueling pistol that trains its sights automatically on bloody Americans. Particularly hungry Americans who look like slavering wolves at my wife."

"You mean, Duchess, there are other men just like me who slaver like wolves at you?"

"If there were others, they're long gone now. Being vilely ill tends to dampen ardor, I should say."

"Your repartee is grating on my nerves," Marcus said, rising. He found himself staring right in Trevor's eyes. "Damn you, I wouldn't have minded you being a fop, a mincing little dandy. Then I could have mocked you or ignored you, as the mood took me."

Trevor grinned his white-toothed grin, saying, "Sorry, Marcus, but the last time I was little I was five years old. Now, you two, James showed me the rhyme. Nothing else but that? An entire volume filled with nonsense about the abbey's woes with signing the Act of Supremacy, their

worries that King Henry would accuse them of owing their
allegiance to the pope and not to him, which was, naturally,
quite true. Then at the end, just that fool poem about the
treasure?"

"That's about it," Marcus said. "I can't imagine that
you'd have any ideas. You don't, do you?"

"Let me see the book and I'll tell you."

After ten minutes, Marcus said sharply, "Take the bloody
thing and give it to your mother. We've got the poem that
is surely an aberration of our mad monk's mind. There's
nothing else that James or I could see helpful. A monster
in a well, a nine that is Janus-faced—two nines together yet
facing apart. It seems like a mess of nonsense."

"It does, but I'll give it to my mother. She's nearly
bursting her seams with curiosity, and fury at James, of
course, for drawing you into it, Marcus. The poem will
keep her occupied, at least for a short time."

"Trevor," the Duchess said after he'd left her bedchamber,
"isn't remotely a fop."

"No, he's more the beast in the well, the bloody scav-
enger."

═══23═══

THE DUCHESS SLAPPED her riding crop against her boot. She felt wonderful, her belly was happy with Badger's scones and honey, and she'd ridden Birdie without incident all around the St. Swale's Abbey, to the north this time. She just hadn't found anything. No oak tree, no dell, no bucket, no well, nothing. Not even a monster of any repute, not even a nine that was just a simple nine, much less a nine that was front-faced and one that was backward.

But she wasn't cast down, oh no. She couldn't wait to see Marcus. The past three days he'd not come to her bed, but he hadn't avoided her; he'd been as assiduous in his attentions to her as a mother superior to the Virgin Mary herself. She wanted to pound him into the ground for not acting remotely like he should act, like he'd always acted since she'd met him when she was nine years old—irritating her until she was raging at him, mocking her, making her want to kill him and kiss him and tease him. No, he was acting like a reasonable man, a man who was calm and deliberate, a passionless man she disliked immensely.

She began to whistle a tune that had popped into her mind and still hadn't words yet to go with it. She had the idea though. It made her grin just to think of the Congress of Vienna and how Caroline Lamb and Lord Byron should attend. Just imagine what those two could achieve in the way of new boundaries for conquered countries.

She was still whistling when she turned the corner around a huge row of yew bushes that gave onto the front drive. There was a carriage with its four horses blowing and the door was open and there was Marcus helping down a very delicious piece of feminine confection, and this delicious piece was dressed elegantly in a traveling gown of dark green with a matching bonnet tied charmingly beneath her chin. One dainty foot was showing in a soft kid traveling boot of matching dark green.

She watched Marcus raise her gloved hand to his mouth, his eyes never leaving the woman's face. She heard a clear, sweet laugh. She saw the woman lightly stroke her gloved fingers over his cheek. She saw her go up on her tiptoes and kiss him right on his mouth.

She saw red.

"How dare you! Get your hands off my husband. Marcus, get your mouth off hers, you rotten sod!"

She skittered to a halt when the lovely creature turned to look at her, clear gray eyes wide with what? Puzzlement? Amusement? She didn't know.

"Oh," the woman said sweetly, "and who are you? Do you work perchance in his lordship's stables?"

"She does anything I tell her to do," Marcus said, and patted the woman's hand, "a good thing in a woman. Actually, Celeste, you can call her the Duchess. She's the wife of mine I wrote to you about."

Celeste!

The red she saw was turning more crimson by the moment. "You told me you probably lied, you wretched real liar! You didn't, you wouldn't dare bring her here, you rarefied lout. Gracious heavens, I'll kill you!"

She didn't think, just acted. She'd already struck him with a riding crop. She needed something else. There wasn't anything else unless she could rip a branch from that lime tree, and that damned branch was too high for her to reach. She sat down in the driveway, pulled off her riding boot, leapt back to her feet and headed straight at him, swinging it over her head.

She yelled as she swung, "I told you I would make you sorry. Oh, why don't I ever have a gun when I need it?"

She struck him hard on his shoulder. He quickly set Celeste away from him. "Now, Duchess, you have been ill, you know. I've been a saint these past days, allowing you to rest your fill, but I'm a man, Duchess. Surely you don't want to be a selfish wife, one who doesn't see beyond the needs of her own sick belly. Celeste here is really quite congenial. She'll see to me quite nicely. There's no reason for you to be upset or to worry."

"I haven't been ill in four days. *Four* days and you've acted like a man bent on obtaining sainthood through celibacy! You haven't even yelled at me once. You haven't even made me want to hit you a single time. You've been a bloodless fool and I've hated you." She swung viciously and the heel hit his forearm hard. Where was that woman? Ah, she was still hiding behind Marcus. No matter that she was a woman, she was a coward and the Duchess despised her for it.

Sampson and two footmen appeared on the top steps. From the corner of her eye, she saw one of the footmen take a step forward, only to be brought up by Sampson. Good, that meant Sampson was on her side. She hit him again.

Marcus backed up three steps. "Really, Duchess, your damned boot?"

"How dare you bring her here!" she shrieked. "You could have gone to London on business, like most bloody men, damn you. You could have pretended. You will pay for this perfidy, Marcus!" She struck him two more times with that boot heel, one a very gratifying thud against his right shoulder.

"Duchess, your aim is getting too good. Stop it now." He rubbed his shoulder and his right arm. "Aren't you tired now? All that hopping about on one foot—and your stocking is quite ruined—surely you're getting fatigued."

"I will remove your head from your neck, Marcus Wyndham! I'll strangle you with my ruined stocking. I have no intention of getting tired until you're writhing in death throes on the ground."

She raised the boot again, so enraged she was pounding with it. Then something got through to her. He wasn't angry, he was laughing. *Laughing!*

At her.

She stopped cold and stared at him. The woman was peeping out from behind him. She didn't appear to be the least bit perturbed or frightened. If the Duchess wasn't mistaken, the woman looked ready to break into hysterical laughter along with her bloody husband.

She raised the boot again, then very slowly lowered it. She sat back on the ground, pulled the boot on, and rose.

She raised her fist at him, then realized that he was nearly doubled over with laughter.

She jumped at him, flailing at him, hitting him as hard as she could, yanking on his hair. He had his arms around her, pinning her arms to her sides, and still she struggled. He held her there until she quieted.

"So, that once tranquil, speechless creature is well and truly buried. You've a strong right fist, Duchess. No, don't try to kill me again, consider me already suitably maimed."

"You bastard, let me go."

"Well, if I do, do you promise not to fetch a pistol and shoot me?"

She kicked him in the shin.

He grunted, then pulled her hard to the side of him. "Now, would you like to meet Celeste Crenshaw? Isn't she charming? She adores me, was perfectly willing to come all the way north so I wouldn't be deprived."

She was making a great fool of herself. He'd done this on purpose. He'd quite made her lose her good sense. Quite simply, he'd done her in.

She tried to take a deep, calming breath. It was very difficult. She still tried, saying finally, knowing she didn't have but a few moments to salvage her pride and the situation, "Hello, Celeste," in surely a voice that was too shrill and too loud. "So you are here to take this lout out of my bed. I'm delighted, truly. I was angry at him for quite something else. Please understand, I'm ecstatic you're here. I'm quite tired of pleading endless headaches and endless toe aches. Do you know that I have even tried to make myself become ill to keep him away from me? Ah, yes, now that you're here, I shall be able to smile again. I am so very hungry, but to eat would have made him think that my sickness was all an act. I won't have to pretend to illness any more. Now I can eat. Thank you, Celeste. Shall I show you to your room or would you prefer to sleep with his lordship in his bedchamber?"

She was well aware that his hands were tightening on her upper arms. She looked up at him, giving him a lot of white teeth. "Do forgive me for acting the shrew, Marcus. It is just that you took me off guard. Now that I see the magnificent benefits Miss Crenshaw offers to both of us, I realize quite clearly what a wonderful, thoughtful husband I have. Oh, my dearest Marcus, you are far too kind to me."

"I will kill you," he said between his teeth. He began to shake her, then stopped abruptly. "No, if I continue to shake you, you just might vomit in the rosebushes again. Mr. Biggs, the head gardener, was near to tears about it. You quite ruined his new bush. No, I shan't do that again. Now, madam—"

He paused, then he began to lightly caress her upper arms. His eyes were very blue. "If I'm a wonderful, kind husband, why you, Duchess, you are an equally magnificent wife. Now, if you don't mind, Celeste is doubtless fatigued—from thirst, you understand. Don't fret, my dear. I will see her to a chamber and take care of her needs." He patted her cheek, kissed her forehead as chastely as would an uncle, and turned to the young woman who hadn't said anything.

"See how lovely she is, Celeste? And here you were worried that she might not find you as charming as I do. Now, let me take you to your bedchamber and assist you out of that traveling gown. It is wrinkled and you do look heated—well, not really wrinkled and in truth it's I who am heated. Yes, a nice cool bath—ah, I'll wash your back for you—and then we will enjoy the remainder of the afternoon."

"Marcus."

"Yes, Duchess?" he said, turning.

"If you do not take your hands off her, I will do something that you will surely regret."

He dropped his hands immediately. "Now what, Duchess?"

"If you laugh at me again, I will also do something that you will surely regret."

"Not a stitch of laughter in this body, Duchess."

"Good. Now, Miss Crenshaw, you will follow Sampson and he will take you to your bedchamber."

Miss Crenshaw shook her head and giggled. "I think, my Lord Chase, my lady, that this is a stalemate. Both of you have done remarkable things to the other. You two have entertained me more in the past ten minutes than I have been for the past year at Drury Lane. And to think that his lordship even paid me ten guineas for my presence here. Thank you so much for allowing me to remain. Ah, may I remain, my lord, for just tonight? Oh, yes, my name is Hannah Crenshaw. Not this Celeste, a name that is obviously made up for it sounds quite silly really."

"Tonight is fine," the Duchess said. "You are too beautiful, however, to remain longer. I will see that his lordship is locked in his bedchamber. Badger is a fine cook. You just might want to stay, along with our American relatives, but you can't."

Miss Crenshaw giggled again and walked away from them, her bearing more sedate and elegant than the Duchess's.

The Duchess turned back to her husband, saw that he was nearly fit to burst with laughter, and slammed her fist in his belly. He grunted for her, then brought her against him, hugging her hard.

"I had you for a full five minutes. You're more ferocious than even Spears and Badger believed you'd be. Maggie wanted to wager that you'd return to being a silent stick, and fade away in quiet misery, but Badger said no, you'd wallop the daylights out of my poor body. Spears just sniffed and told me that the entire charade wasn't worthy of the earl of Chase."

She simply stared at him now for a very long time. Finally, she began to rub at his chest and arms where she'd struck him. "I didn't hurt you, did I?"

"Yes, I'm in frightful pain."

She switched from rubbing vigorously to caressing. He said in a sigh, "We have quite an audience, Duchess. There is Mr. Biggs, over there, hiding behind the rosebushes you nearly killed, doubtless there to protect his new blooms."

"I know," she said, stood on her tiptoes and kissed his mouth. She stared at him, lightly kissing his chin, his jaw, his ear. "You will never bore me, Marcus."

"You think you bore me? You just pulled off your left boot and beat me with it. Never would I have expected such a unique attack."

"A lady must make do with what she has available."

24

SHE LAY THERE staring into the darkness, waiting for him. She'd heard him come up just minutes ago. He'd been playing whist with Trevor, and his hired Celeste, who was really Hannah. The evening had been delightful, Marcus introducing Miss Crenshaw as a distant cousin, more distant even than his cousins from America, more distant perhaps than even China, and all had laughed and enjoyed themselves and Badger's cooking except Aunt Wilhelmina, who was in top form, even going so far at one point over gooseberry fool, one of Marcus's favorite desserts, to observe, "This is all quite inappropriate, this jollity. It is her fault. She was a bastard and thus doesn't know how one is to behave properly."

Marcus had choked on his gooseberry fool, managed to get himself back in control, and said, "I quite agree, Aunt Wilhelmina. Consider Miss Crenshaw a hopeful for my hand once I have gotten rid of the Duchess here. Do you approve of Miss Crenshaw?"

"She has breeding, that is obvious. I shall consider her for marriage with Trevor or James. Miss Crenshaw, have you a dowry that is worthy of my consideration?"

The laughter had burst forth, but Aunt Wilhelmina had seemed oblivious. Thank goodness the Twins and Ursula weren't at the dinner table.

But that was then and now it was dark, and she was still carrying a child he didn't want.

When the adjoining door finally opened, she felt empty and dull, all the evening's laughter sucked out of her.

"Well," he said after a moment as he sat on the edge of her bed, "I was hoping for a carolling hello and winsome smile. I get neither?"

She swallowed the silly tears. "I have a winsome smile. You just can't see it."

He lit a candle.

She turned her head away, but he was fast. He gently cupped her chin in his fingers and turned her to face him. He gave her a look more brooding than a hero in a Gothic novel. "Don't cry, Duchess. I would rather you shoot me than see you cry."

"I would rather shoot you too. It's nothing, Marcus, nothing at all." He snorted at that and she knew, of course, that because he was Marcus, he would dig and dig, and thus, she sat up and threw herself in his arms. "Please, Marcus, please forget that you never wanted me. Forget I made you marry me. Please forget I carry a child you don't want. Kiss me and love me."

He went very still, but not for long. When he was deep inside her and she was trembling from the aftershocks of the pleasure he'd given her, he dipped his head down and kissed her. His breath was warm and sweet in her mouth. "You were made just for me, do you know that, Duchess? Just for me. Feel, just feel how we are together. I never would have believed such a joining possible, but it's true. Feel us, Duchess."

She did. She'd believed herself beyond sated, so exhausted with pleasure that she surely couldn't want more, but his words and the touch of his fingers on her flesh, made her suck in her breath. It was she who brought his head down again and kissed him with all her heart, all the feeling that was within her, feeling that was older than the Duchess was surely, deep and full, all that feeling, and it was all for him and it always had been and it would be until she died.

He fell asleep with her gathered against him, her face in the crook of his neck. She wanted to sleep, but it eluded her. She wondered, for perhaps the hundredth time since she'd found out she was carrying his child, what she was going to do. Her arm was over his chest. Slowly, she caressed his warm flesh, feeling the strength of him, the power. She rested her hand finally on his hip, aware that her belly was pressed against his side and she was hot from the touch of his flesh.

Would she still be here at Chase Park when her belly would be rounded? If she was, would he still want to hold her like this, the child he didn't want between them?

He felt the wet of her tears against his neck. "No," he whispered against her ear, "no, Duchess, don't cry. Scream for me instead." He came over her, coming into her, and when she did find her release, she didn't scream, just moaned softly into his mouth.

The day, Marcus thought, was one of those few days in high summer when the sky was so clear, the air so fresh, it nearly sent one into tears, that or poetic raptures, that or a good fast gallop. He decided on the gallop. He and the Duchess had seen Hannah Crenshaw off early that morning. She'd had the impertinence to say to him quietly as he'd handed her into the carriage he'd hired to return her to London, "She's very special, my lord. I hope you see that. She's also unhappy. She shouldn't be. I trust you will see to it, and not become like so many husbands I have seen and known and none of them worth a pig's snout."

He'd said nothing to that, but he had wanted to box her ears for her damned effrontery. Instead, he'd just closed the carriage door and waved to the coachman. He had stood back, watching the carriage bowl down the wide drive.

The Duchess had said, "She was an experience, Marcus. You are a bounder, a perverse bounder, but your sense of humor pleases me. I suppose it is up to me now to outdo you."

He'd recoiled in immediate alarm. "No, don't even think it. Promise me, Duchess, not until you're well again."

"I am well again, Marcus. I'm pregnant and quite healthy."

"Yes," he said, his voice clipped, looking for just an instant at her belly, flat beneath her morning gown of pale blue muslin. He'd massaged her belly the night before, caressing her pelvic bones, oh yes, he'd felt with his hands how flat she was. It didn't seem possible his child could be there in her womb. He didn't look up when she sighed and left him.

He'd stood there, cursed quietly, then took himself to the stables.

As Lambkin saddled Stanley, he looked up again at that sky that deserved a poet's praises. The clouds were whiter than a saint's soul.

"Mr. Trevor took out Clancy," Lambkin said as he picked up Stanley's left front leg, crooning to the stallion as he examined the hoof carefully.

"Riding my horse without a by-your-leave," Marcus said, picking up his own saddle and hefting it over Stanley's broad back. "Damned encroacher."

"Aye, an excellent rider Mr. Trevor is, just excellent. Like one of them 'orse men, you know, my lord, 'alf of 'im a 'orse and the other 'alf a man?"

"A centaur, curse his damned eyes. A centaur was never named Trevor."

"Aye, that's it, and Mr. James was with him. He enjoys riding Alfie, a fine fellow old Alfie is, all spit and growl, but ever such a sweet goer. Mr. James is different from Mr. Trevor. He treats his 'orse like a man would a pretty lady. 'E's got magic in 'is 'ands, 'e does."

"Ha," Marcus said, gave Lambkin a sour look, and clicked Stanley from the stable yard.

On his ride he didn't see Trevor or James, even though he rode to the ruins of St. Swale's Abbey. Not a hair of him to be seen. Where was the damned bounder? Where was James? He found that he began searching for the dell and the oak tree and a well and something that could resemble a nine. A bloody nine. A Janus-faced nine. What the devil was that? Two nines back-to-back? Why did folk insist on leaving clues that were so obfuscated that even a brainy fellow like himself didn't stand a chance of figuring them out?

He saw a lone female on the narrow country road close to the drive leading into the Park, saw that it was Ursula, and pulled up Stanley beside her. "Good morning, cousin. Why aren't you riding?"

"The day is too magnificent. When I ride I'm too afraid I'll fall off and I wanted to see everything today. Even the leaves on the trees look greener today, don't you think? This is a day to treasure. It rains a lot here, my lord, a lot more than back home, although Baltimore is nature's blight. That's what my papa used to say."

He grinned at that. "You miss your home, Ursula?"

"Yes, but England is also my home since my papa was born here. Chase Park is the most incredible place. There are no houses like it in America. Oh, there are mansions, but they're new and shiny, not centuries-old with hidden passages and hidey-holes and clues for the Wyndham legacy if we could just find them."

He dismounted, looped Stanley's reins over his hand, and walked beside his cousin.

"Legacy? Why do you call it that?"

"Mother says it isn't just a treasure but rather a legacy meant for the younger son since the elder son becomes the earl and gets the Park, the properties, and all the money. Thus, it's a legacy for her husband and since Papa died, it's now hers."

"I see," he said, wanting to applaud Aunt Wilhelmina's circuitous logic. "Well, I fear that if there is a treasure or a legacy, it must belong to me, the earl. Sorry, my dear, but I shan't hand it over to your mama. Now, James and Trevor are out somewhere but I haven't seen either of them."

"No, nor have I. Trevor is getting impatient to leave. He keeps giving Mother harassed looks. As for James, he wants to find our legacy, but I don't think he wants to steal it from you, not like my mother does, if it truly is stealing, and as of yet, I'm not certain who it should belong to. I think I should like to have it though."

"Your mother," he said carefully, "is a very unusual person. Has she always been so very unusual?"

Ursula cocked her head to one side. "I think she has but she's become more unusual as I've gotten older, or as she's gotten older. It's difficult to know which when one is young. Do you think the Duchess is upset at what she says? She doesn't seem to be, though perhaps she should be, for mother is many times quite unaccountable. She does odd things, then forgets them. Or perhaps she doesn't forget, just pretends to."

"The Duchess is far too intelligent to be cast down by insults, no matter how smoothly couched. As for your mother forgetting things, that's interesting."

"It wasn't, until she mistakenly served some spoiled food to a neighbor and he nearly died."

"Did she, ah, dislike this neighbor?"

"However did you know that?"

"Wild guess. Look over at that oak tree. By heaven, it's older than you are, surely."

"Older than me, Marcus? More likely your age or my mother's age, but surely that's too old, even for a tree. Come now, it would be a mere sapling were it my age. Oh yes, Mr. Sampson said that a Major Lord Chilton was coming today."

"Oh good lord, I clean forgot, what with all the excitement."

"What excitement?"

"Er, Miss Crenshaw's brief visit."

"I heard Trevor and James laughing about that. James said the Duchess pinned your ears back on that one. Trevor said you did try, which was a good thing for a man to do occasionally, and that you did have her going wild for just a little while. Then he said something about her beating you with her boot, but that doesn't sound at all likely. What did he mean, Marcus?"

"I haven't a notion, the damned impertinent bastard. Excuse me, Ursula, for speaking so improperly within your hearing."

"It's all right. My brothers always do. Who is this Major Lord Chilton?"

"Actually, his name is Frederic North Nightingale, Viscount Chilton, and one of my best friends, though I didn't know him well until two years ago when our small party was ambushed by the French. You want to know what he said when I shot the soldier whose sword was barely an inch from going through his back? He said, 'Well, by God, saved by the man who has more sense than to touch Portuguese vodka.' I left him in Paris over a month ago in the care and keeping of Lord Brooks."

"What's Portuguese vodka?"

"Well, er, you don't want to know. I suppose I shouldn't have told you that." Oh Lord, thank God it was such an ambiguous idiom, for Portuguese vodka referred to the whores from southern Portugal.

"Oh no, how am I to learn if people don't tell things in front of me? Is he as nice as you are, Marcus?"

"Of course not. He's dour and brooding and surely he would hate this glorious day we're enjoying. He prefers menacing heaths liberally strewn with rocks and gullies. He's a man of moods and silences. He's dangerous and looks it. I quite like him."

She laughed and took his hand. He said easily, "Just don't let the Duchess see you holding my hand. She's very possessive, you know, quite jealous really. I would expect her to slit my throat if she saw this. I'm by far too young to croak it yet, don't you think?"

"Oh! You're dreadful, Marcus. The Duchess is more a lady than the queen."

"Given that our dear queen is the farthest thing from a lady I've ever seen, I'll give you that one. About the

Duchess, Ursula, she's already tried to do me in with a bridle, a riding crop, and her left boot. Yes, that sod brother of yours was right, she did get in several good wallops with her riding boot. She sat down on the drive, pulled off her boot, and ran at me like a banshee. I think a pistol is next on her list of weapons. Thank God she never carries one with her, else I might be underground with a tombstone over my head."

She laughed and laughed, then skipped away, calling over her shoulder, "You probably deserved all of it. I'm going to the small brook just yon. Please don't tell my mother you've seen me."

Had he ever been so young? Laughter bubbling out freely, without restraint? Yes, he had, but then Mark and Charlie had drowned that summer, and he'd lost his youth.

He remounted Stanley and rode back to the stables. He was met in the entrance hall with pandemonium.

His friend, North Nightingale, stood on the bottom of the wide staircase inside the house. In his arms he held the Duchess. She was unconscious or dead. Marcus yelled like a wild man.

Marcus, frantic with worry, knew she was in pain, knew she was weak and afraid, and thus said in a voice as soft as a lone raindrop pattering against a window, "Tell me all you can remember, Duchess. Try to remember what you were doing before you reached the stairs."

"I was going to have breakfast, nothing more, Marcus. I was at the top of the stairs. I remember thinking I saw something from the corner of my eye and I turned. That's all I remember. When I woke up this strange man was holding me and his face was whiter than the paint on the wall."

"That white-faced gentleman was Lord Chilton. I forgot to tell you he just might pay me a visit. You didn't meet him in Paris, but he was there. I will tell him you described him as strange, it serves him right. That should elicit at least a noncommittal grunt from him."

He'd spoken lightly, but inside, his belly was cramping with the fear he'd felt when he saw her. He remembered yelling, beyond himself in those few moments before he knew that she wasn't dead. He didn't realize he was squeezing her hand so very hard until she groaned.

"Damnation," he said, and began to massage her fingers. "I've had Trevor fetch the physician from Darlington. This one isn't a butcher like that wretched Tivit. He's young and he knows all the newest things." He frowned. "Perhaps he's too young. I don't want a young man looking at you or touching you. He might simply pretend to be objective, but I can't imagine such a thing, not with a young man and you being so damned beautiful and vulnerable.

"What a bloody coil, and it's all your fault. I don't want to worry about you either. I have it, I'll simply stay and watch every move he makes. If he succumbs to you, I'll thump him into the floor."

"Thank you, Marcus, for wanting to protect me from a young man's possible lustful advances, but I'm all right, truly. I wish you hadn't sent for him. Now he'll poke and prod about and make me drink vile potions. It's only my head that aches so abominably."

"You fell down the stairs. You hit other parts of yourself than just your head, which is so hard I really don't have too much worry about that. Do you forget you're pregnant? You could have harmed yourself. You could have done some sort of damage to yourself. You will obey me in this."

"Why would you care?"

"You ask me a question like that again, and I'll strangle you. I'll take my own riding boot to you. I don't want you hurt, is that so difficult for you to comprehend?"

She sighed and closed her eyes. "Yes, it is," she said, then turned her face away. He wanted to blister her ears, but held himself silent. He wanted to see what the physician— the young, quite good physician—had to say before he said anything more on the subject. He began to gently rub her temples the way Badger had shown him a while before.

She concentrated on ignoring the searing pain in her head. She concentrated on Marcus's fingers, gentle and strong, easing the pain more each moment. She remembered Lord Chilton's name from their days in Paris. He was a man both Badger and Spears very much wanted to avoid during all their machinations. He was, they said, very much Marcus's friend since they'd heard that Marcus had saved his life and he wouldn't take kindly to anyone coercing Marcus into doing anything. He was also dangerous, they'd said, and silent and very threatening.

She'd certainly given him a diverting welcome.

25

DOCTOR RAVEN, SURELY an overly romantic name for a man who was as short as the Duchess had been at twelve, was thin as one of the stair railings, and had the most beautiful head of blond hair. He didn't appear to be unduly influenced by the Duchess's overwhelming beauty. His voice was soft, his manner matter-of-fact. He even gave Maggie only a cursory look upon entering the Duchess's bedchamber, and that brought a grunt of surprise from her and a rude gesture. Marcus dismissed her, then immediately closed the door after her.

Marcus watched Doctor Raven closely, ready to smash him into rubble if he offended.

Doctor Raven said calmly, as he lightly touched his fingertips to her head, "Your husband tells me that you struck your head before, my lady. Yes, I can still feel a slight rising there just behind your ear. There is no swelling from this fall. I think you will have headaches for perhaps several more days, but nothing more. You will take some laudanum. It will help."

"She's pregnant," Marcus said. "She fell down the stairs and she's pregnant. There's more here than just her head."

Doctor Raven merely nodded and smiled easily at her. "Just lie still then and let me feel your belly."

Marcus moved closer to the bed. Doctor Raven merely eased his hands beneath the covers and felt her stomach without pulling up her nightgown.

"Do you have any pain or cramping?"

"No, nothing."

"Any bleeding?"

"No."

"That's good." His hands were light as the petals of a rose, yet she felt his knowledge in the way he touched her. She looked at him to see that his eyes were closed. She was, she supposed, a collection of familiar landmarks to him, and he was checking for something unfamiliar.

"Have you been ill, my lady?"

"She's been very ill, vomiting up her breakfast, her lunch, her dinner, and everything in between. She's skinny as a stick, but now she's felt well for at least a week and a half."

She grinned at her husband, who was hovering like a preacher over his collection plate in a room full of thieves. "I do feel quite all right now, Doctor Raven. I tire more easily than I used to, but Badger assures me that's normal."

"Badger?"

"He's our chef."

"And my valet."

"Interesting," Doctor Raven said. He didn't say anything more, merely continued pressing here and there, his eyes still closed. Then he pulled his hands away and straightened, bumping into Marcus.

"Well?"

"She appears to be fine, my lord. However, I would like her to remain in bed for two more days. She isn't very far along in her pregnancy and there might be aftereffects from that fall. The first three months in a pregnancy are the most critical. I simply don't know, no one does. Just keep her in bed and keep her calm. If she has any cramping or bleeding, have me fetched immediately."

The Duchess said gently, "Doctor Raven, you really can speak to me, you know. I hear quite well and I have a modicum of intelligence."

"I know, my lady, I know. But your husband appears to be very protective of you. I fear if I spoke to you he would accuse me of attempting to make an assignation. I'm young and just beginning my profession. I'm doing quite well. I don't wish to be cut down before I've even reached the prime of my craft."

"You're quite right. At times my husband is most unaccountable. I will remain in bed."

"Excellent. I will come to see you on Wednesday, if you have no more symptoms."

Marcus ushered Doctor Raven from her bedchamber. She closed her eyes, wishing the headache would just stop, but she knew it wouldn't. Badger would appear any minute now with laudanum. She didn't want it, but she knew she had no choice. She had too many hovering friends and a husband who appeared suddenly as possessive of her as Aunt Wilhelmina was of the wretched Wyndham treasure or legacy, whatever.

She dutifully drank down the lemonade Badger silently handed her, knowing it was laced liberally with laudanum. As she fell into a deep sleep, she remembered again seeing that shadow, that slight movement before she tripped and fell down the stairs. And she knew in that final instant before sleep claimed her that she hadn't tripped, that a hand had struck her hard between her shoulder blades, shoving her forward, and then she'd tripped. She heard again her own scream of terror, felt the blinding helplessness as she rolled and tumbled, trying desperately to grasp the railing to stop her fall, but she couldn't, and then, suddenly, there were hands to stop her, hands drawing her up, and she fell into welcome blackness.

"I don't like it, any of it."

"Nor do I. I've never been so scared in my life, Marcus. I was standing there in the entrance hall, being intimidated by all those ancestors of yours glaring down on me when I heard this horrible scream and looked up to see your wife tumbling down the stairs. I got to her as quickly as I could."

"If you hadn't moved so quickly, she would have hit the bottom of the stairs and been thrown hard onto the marble and probably been killed. God, it curdles my blood to think about it. Thank you, North. Now we're even. No more looking over my shoulder to see you behind me with you, in turn, looking over your shoulder for ruffians out to snatch my purse."

"Oh no, not yet, Marcus."

Marcus just shook his head. He'd never met a more stubborn, more loyal friend. "Have it your way, but I'm now in your debt, at least in my poor view. Like I said, when I came through that front door and saw you holding her and she was all limp, Jesus, I don't want to be that afraid again in my life. No, I don't like it, not a bit."

"Would you care to be more specific, Marcus?"

Marcus told him about the Wyndham treasure or legacy, told him of the Duchess finding the old book in the library and being struck down, told him about the American relatives, Aunt Wilhelmina in particular, who was eccentric in the extreme, and who had probably poisoned a neighbor. "When James Wyndham found her unconscious on the floor before dawn in the library, I wanted to believe that she was struck down because of that damned book, but now I don't believe it for an instant. Someone pushed her down those stairs, just as someone struck her down in the library and left her for dead."

"Good God, man, you become an earl, you get stripped of your wealth, you get yourself married, regain your wealth, and now someone is trying to murder your wife?"

"That's about the size of it. You want a brandy, North? My bastard uncle, God rot his soul, the former earl, has only the best French brandy."

As he poured North Nightingale a snifter of his uncle's prized smuggled French brandy, he heard him say, "A gentleman, your butler, I believe, was wringing his hands, nearly in tears, saying something about the Duchess being pregnant. Is she, Marcus?"

"Yes."

"Well? Is the babe all right?"

"I assume so. The doctor examined her. She's just to stay in bed for two days."

"Congratulations. On your marriage and on the coming birth of your son or daughter."

Marcus grunted.

North raised an eyebrow. "There's more here than just someone trying to murder your wife, find a buried treasure, and steal it from you, I gather."

"Damnation, it's none of your bloody business, North."

"Fine. I believe I'll go wash up before luncheon. I'm tired, my blood's thinned out from being scared out of my skin, and I want to recover my strength to meet this Aunt Wilhelmina of yours. Do you think she'll poison my soup because I saved the Duchess?"

Marcus laughed. "One never knows with Aunt Wilhelmina. It's true she has not a whit of liking for my wife."

"Your pregnant wife."

"Damn you, North, go away."

North just grinned, then looked thoughtful as he tossed the empty snifter to Marcus and strode from the room.

"Marcus said you were silent and brooding and ever so mysterious. He said you were dangerous."

"I did not, Ursula. At least not mysterious. He's about as mysterious as a toad on a lily pad."

"Well, you said other things very romantic like that. Are you, my lord?"

"Yes, I am. I'm a melancholy fellow with little wit, a gloomy sense of humor, and a shadow on my soul."

Aunt Wilhelmina announced to the table at large, "Gentlemen, particularly noblemen, Ursula, can be as surly as it pleases them to be. They believe it becomes them. The ruder they are the more romantic to ladies they think it makes them."

"Oh no, surely not, Mama. Surely rude and surly aren't at all like silent and dangerous and brooding."

"It's boring behavior, quite uncomfortable for those having to suffer it, and thus it is even more than surly. It is petulance and it is choleric. It is, as I remarked, a very manly thing to be."

So saying, Aunt Wilhelmina went back to her ham slices, covering each one carefully and thoroughly with Badger's special apricot jam.

Trevor was laughing. "Taken down by a lady from the Colonies, my lord."

"Do call me North. If I allow Marcus to be so familiar I might as well allow the same courtesy to his cousin."

Trevor nodded and raised his glass of wine. "Marcus, I have decided as the head of the American branch of the Wyndham family to remove all of us from Chase Park on Friday. Yes, old fellow, that's only four days away. Then you will have only North here to get rid of so that you may enjoy the company of the Duchess alone."

"Oh no," Aunt Gweneth said. "Willie, you didn't tell me you were going to leave so soon."

"If she would but die I could stay."

"Oh no! What did you say, Mama?"

"My dear girl, I said only that if she would but be willing to share dear Marcus with us, we could remain."

North stared at her, mouth agape. This was far more promising than mere poisoning. "That was astounding, truly marvelous," he said to Aunt Wilhelmina.

She stared at him. "You are supposed to be silent. You are supposed to brood. See to it."

"Yes, ma'am," North said and fell to his spiced pears, tangy with cinnamon.

"Willie, surely you don't wish to leave now. Why, it's really too unpleasant in London in the summer."

"Dear Aunt Gweneth," Marcus said, smiling at her, "you've never traveled beyond York. There are always amusements aplenty in London, no matter the month."

"Marcus, it's unclean in London in the summer. The heat makes everything smell abominable. I don't want them to leave. Trevor, is this your notion?"

"Yes, Aunt Gweneth. This game of the Wyndham legacy grows old. Besides, if there is indeed such a thing, it is yours, Marcus, not ours."

"Trevor!"

"Mama, take hope in the fact that we aren't paupers. Indeed, I even plan to improve our coffers by marrying James off to a proper English heiress. What do you think, brother?"

James looked frankly appalled. "Married! Me? Good God, Trevor, I'm only twenty years old. I need many more years of seasoning, many more years of—"

"Dissipation? Wild oats? Come now, James, I was thrown over the anvil when I was but twenty-two."

Marcus stared from one brother to the other. They seemed to be enjoying themselves vastly until James said, "Thrown! Good Lord, Trevor, you wanted Helen, you panted after her like a puppy, she was all you wanted."

Antonia said, "Ursula told us that Helen was the most beautiful girl in all Baltimore. She said it was a love match, like it was just out of Mrs. Radcliffe."

"She did, huh?" Trevor said, but he smiled. "She was very young at the time."

"But Trevor," Ursula said, confusion writ clear on her young face, "I thought you adored Helen. I thought she was the luckiest woman to have you until she died."

Fanny was silent. She was looking longingly at the spiced pears but took an apple instead.

Trevor merely shook his head at his sister, still smiling. He said now to North, "I understand that you, like Marcus, have wisely avoided the fighting on my shores and stuck instead to that very short fellow, Napoleon. I salute you both for your caution. I shouldn't have liked to stick my bayonet into either of your bellies had you attempted to come into Baltimore."

"Ho, Marcus, shall I take him outside and pound him into the ground?"

"You couldn't," James said. "Trevor is stronger than a horse and he's fast."

"I heard you say he was a dirty fighter, James," Ursula said.

"What's a dirty fighter mean?" Fanny wanted to know, the apple halfway to her mouth.

"That, my children," said Aunt Wilhelmina, "is quite enough. It is more than enough. You've quite overset my nerves. Sampson, please tell Badger to make me some lemon curd to settle my innards."

Antonia whispered to Fanny, "I think we should go tell the Duchess. She probably needs to have a fun laugh." The Twins slipped from their chairs after a nod from Aunt Gweneth, and out of the morning room.

"I still don't want you to leave, Willie," Aunt Gweneth said.

Marcus gave her a sympathetic smile. "We must allow such decisions to reside with Trevor, ma'am."

"Why? He's as young as you are, Marcus. Why should he have the final say? She's his mama; he's not her husband."

"He's still the man, Aunt Gweneth. He's the head of the family."

"Bosh," said Aunt Wilhelmina. "He's a mere twenty-two, twenty-three, at most. I told him that just the other day when he mistakenly claimed to be nearly twenty-five. I will speak to him, Gweneth. He will come to reason."

Trevor just shrugged, grinning down at his plate. Marcus and North exchanged expressions that none of the females at the table comprehended.

They faced each other in the Duchess's bedchamber.

"No. I forbid it. That's it."

"Marcus, I'm fine, I promise. I'll go quite mad if I stay in this bedchamber for another instant. Please, I want to go riding. I'll be most careful."

He had his steward, Mr. Franks, to suffer for a good two hours. Crittaker was hanging about, with a hopeful expression with fistfuls of accounts to review and a score of letters to answer. Two of his tenants wanted to see him. He said, "I'll ride with you. You can't go alone."

She threw her arms around him. "Oh, thank you."

He eased his own arms around her back and gently hugged her to him. "You're so skinny, Duchess."

"I won't be for much longer. By fall, I'll be as round as the pumpkins over in Mr. Popplewell's farm."

He said nothing. His arms loosened around her.

"Marcus."

She'd raised her face and he looked at her a moment, into those deep-blue eyes of hers, so very deep her eyes, filled with uncertainty, too much uncertainty, and oddly enough, caring. Caring for him? He supposed so. Otherwise, why should she have gone through with the marriage? A man's honor would carry him so far, but surely there were limits. A woman's honor? He didn't know, but he did know her. Her honor went deep. He kissed her then, his tongue lightly stroking her lower lip. She came up on her tiptoes, fitting herself to him more tightly.

"I can't make love with you yet, else that damned too young Doctor Raven would have apoplexy. No, Duchess, no. Ah, you taste marvelous, you know that? And you're so bloody soft and giving. You enjoy me, don't you?"

"There can't be another man like you in the world, Marcus. Even that poacher Trevor or the silent and brooding Lord Chilton can't come close to you."

He grinned even as he continued kissing her, nipping lightly at her lower lip, slipping his tongue into her mouth, his breath warm. "Is that a compliment or a condemnation?"

"You want me, Marcus. I can feel you."

"If you couldn't feel me then I should go slit my wrists. I want you every time I even think about you, anytime I smell that perfume of yours, whenever I hear your skirts swishing."

But he didn't want the child she carried because he hated her father so very much.

She wondered in that moment if he'd wanted her to miscarry the child. No, he wouldn't ever have wished for it consciously, not Marcus. She shook her head even as she moaned into his mouth, even as she accepted that child or no child, it was Marcus who was at the center of her life, at the center of her heart.

"By all that's holy, I want you." His hands swept down her back, cupping her hips, and pulling her hard against him.

"Yes," she said against his mouth. "I'm perfectly fine."

In the next moment, he pressed her against the wall, lifting her. "Put your legs around my waist." She did, not understanding, but that confusion lasted just a moment, just until he'd freed himself from his trousers, pulled up her gown and widened her for himself. He came up high into her and she was ready for him, warm and soft, so very eager, and she moaned even as he filled her, even as his fingers stroked her flesh, and his tongue was deep in her mouth. He climaxed, his big body shaking, clenching as his muscles released and tightened, pushing for he knew she hadn't yet reached her release and she knew even as she grew closer and closer that he wouldn't ever stop until she'd gained such pleasure she'd yell with it.

She gasped when the urgent feelings began to roil through her, tensing her legs, making her want to scream, but she didn't because she was gasping into his mouth, and he took her cries when they built and kissed her, pushing her and pushing her more until she was limp and exhausted against him. Slowly, her legs slid off his flanks. He held her close, still kissing her, stroking her, and he said, "I missed kissing your beautiful breasts."

"And I missed kissing your belly, Marcus, though I've yet to do it. You always distract me. Perhaps I could kiss you even lower, do you think?"

He groaned at that, lightly slapped her buttocks, then caressed them.

"Bathe yourself, sweetheart, and then, if you've still the energy for it, I'll take you riding." He paused a moment in the adjoining doorway. "If you'd like to try that, I shouldn't say nay."

She gave him a very inquisitive, very absorbed look that made his belly clench in lust. Perhaps, just perhaps, this was the *beyond* Badger had spoken about. She couldn't wait.

26

THE COLONIAL WYNDHAMS took their leave on Friday morning, mountains of luggage piled high atop the traveling chaise Trevor had procured for his family.

Aunt Wilhelmina said to the Duchess, "You look quite well again, more's the pity."

"What did you say, Mama?"

"My dear James, I only told the Duchess that she looked well and surely she could join us in the city."

"Just so, ma'am," the Duchess said. "Just so and I hope that you may fall ill of a vile verbal plague."

"And what did you say, Duchess?" James asked, grinning behind a gloved hand at her.

"Ah, I merely hoped your mother would call upon us again someday."

Aunt Wilhelmina stared hard at her, continuing in a lower voice, "It's remarkable how you are able to repair yourself time after time. Surely someday there will be an end to it."

"Doubtless you're right, ma'am. However, in the natural order of things, since you're many years my senior, you will quite probably reach your end before I do."

"One can only hope," Marcus said under his breath but still within hearing of his American aunt.

"You deserve to die too. Her insults you approve."

"Good heavens, Mama? *What did you say?*"

"Nothing at all, Ursula, merely that Marcus deserves a shy wife, one who doesn't insult her relatives, which is what the Duchess does, doubtless out of ignorance brought on by her lack of breeding."

307

The Duchess laughed.

"You are such a crone, ma'am. I hope you get clipped by a carriage wheel."

"Marcus," Aunt Gweneth nearly shrieked. "What did you say?"

"I just told Aunt Wilhelmina that she deserves a throne for her kindness and a new carriage."

"You have your nerve, young man."

"Yes, I finally appear to, don't I?" He gave her a slight bow, then turned away to Trevor. "Trevor, you mincing dandified sod, doubtless the Duchess and I will see you in London. How long do you intend to remain in England?"

"James wants to visit all the flesh pots, every gambling hall, every den of iniquity."

"Our capital is rich in sin," North said. "Thus it should take you a good ten years, then."

"James is very young. He's fast. I'll wager he has his fill in three months. Possibly less time were you to come to London and be, er, our guide. What do you say, North? Marcus?"

"Now, brother, don't rush me," James said, throwing up his hands. "A man must come of age knowing every vice in existence so that he may be a wise father to his sons."

"Goodness, you gentlemen are quite depraved," the Duchess said. "I don't know if I should allow Marcus to join you. Besides, my husband doesn't know anything at all of such places, do you, my lord?"

"Nary a thing," Marcus said cheerfully. "Not a blessed whit of a thing. Consider me a devout and pious Methodist when I enter the evil climes of London."

"You will write me often, Willie?"

"Certainly, Gweneth. Oh, how I dislike leaving the Wyndham legacy to *him* and to *her*. It's the *American* Wyndham legacy."

"Despite all the remarkable clues we found, ma'am," Marcus said easily, "I'm still not convinced there's anything to be discovered. This Janus-faced nine business with the lurking monster, surely it is a monk's ravings, nothing more. It's fancy, whimsy."

"I agree," Trevor said. He shook Marcus's hand, looked down at the Duchess, then lightly kissed her forehead, and stepped back. "Now, we're off. Marcus, take good care of your beautiful wife. North, I hope to see you again. If you come to London, Marcus has our direction. We'll all repair to those infamous flesh pots together. You're not a Methodist, I hope?" He kissed each of the Twins and Aunt Gweneth, then turned to wave good-bye to Sampson, Badger, Spears, and Maggie.

"You've got quite a collection of interesting specimens here at Chase Park," James said, waving now himself. "Maggie is quite the most unusual lady's maid I've ever encountered. She actually patted my rear end, Marcus."

"I trust you gave as good as you got," Marcus said, and assisted Aunt Wilhelmina into the carriage.

"I tried," James said, "but she just smiled at me and told me to come see her again when I'd ripened."

They watched the carriage roll down the long wide drive of Chase Park. They waved when Ursula stuck her head out the window and shouted another good-bye.

"How dispiriting it is when such loving guests take their leave," Aunt Gweneth said. "We'll be quite low now."

"It was Trevor's decision," Marcus said. "I swear, Aunt Gweneth, I didn't order dear Wilhelmina to leave, despite her strange proclivities and her quite malicious tongue."

"Still," Aunt Gweneth said, sighed, and walked with her shoulders drooped back into the house.

Maggie sniffed loudly when she was close enough for the Duchess to hear her. "That old besom is a horror. I don't trust her an inch, Duchess. I'm certain she was the one who pushed you down the stairs and struck your poor head in the library."

"How did you know about the stairs, Maggie?"

"Why, Mr. Sampson told me. And Mr. Badger. And Mr. Spears. We discussed it, naturally. That's why you were

never alone until that old crone finally took her leave. My
pity flies toward all the innocent folk in London."

"It does rather boggle the imagination," the Duchess
said.

"Amen, Duchess," Badger said at her elbow. "Now,
you're looking just a bit pale. Come into the Green Cube
Room and I'll bring you some nice tea."

The peace lasted until the afternoon. At one o'clock, just
when they were all settled down for luncheon, Sampson
appeared in the morning room and said in a voice of a
king bestowing a prize to his champion, "Your mother has
arrived, my lord."

"Good God," Marcus said, dropped the fork that held
a bite of rare roast beef, or as Badger called it—*rosbief
anglais à la sauce des fines herbes*—and rose. "She's early,
but why am I surprised? She was early in labor with me and
has never let me forget about the hideous pain I forced upon
her. I keep telling her that I have no recollection of it, nor
do I believe I planned to torture her. Also, since I arrived
early, did I not save her some pain?"

The Duchess rose to stand beside him.

He took her hand. "Everyone continue eating. The Duchess and I will sacrifice ourselves on the hearth of filial
duty."

The earl's mother, Patricia Elliott Wyndham, a lady of
fifty summers with only about forty of them apparent on
her face, was very elegant, small, with a lovely head of
thick black hair. Not a strand of gray in the entire lot, and
eyes as blue as her son's.

She eyed the Duchess up and down. "Marcus would
come home as a boy and speak of you. He said you were
quite the most unusual child he'd ever met, not at all like
the Twins who were little nodcocks, he'd say. He said you
were graceful and reserved and arrogant. He said if anyone
looked at you, your nose went directly into the air and didn't
come down. I didn't think he liked you very much. Why
then did he marry you? And without writing to tell me

of it until it was already done? And why in Paris, of all places?"

The Duchess smiled down at her new mama-in-law. "He fell in love with me, ma'am. He begged me to marry him, swore that he couldn't continue with life without me, that even his port and his food counted for nothing if he couldn't have me. He slavered. What could I do? I'm not a cruel woman. I didn't want him to starve, to thirst to death, to throw himself beneath passing carriage wheels, for he is a man of swiftly burning passion and when he becomes, er, passionate, he is capable of doing anything. I just happened to be visiting in Paris and he was there. There wasn't time for him to do his filial duty and consult with you. Isn't that true, Marcus?"

"Absolutely," the earl said. "Ah, which part of it, Duchess?"

"Also, ma'am, to be perfectly honest, I quite adore him myself. It was quite to my liking to marry him. I would have preferred if you had been there, but there wasn't time. I am so very sorry."

He stared at her, wondering, always wondering, for she had changed, his Duchess, and he couldn't be certain what she meant anymore. She adored him? She'd wanted to marry him? It wasn't just her damned honor, her sense of justice? Ah, there was thinking here aplenty for him to do.

"He always was a boy of intelligence and charm," Mrs. Wyndham said. "Yes, the girls in the neighborhood were always simpering at him, flirting endlessly with him. It made him quite conceited, I fear. He gave them all hope, my charming boy, teased them and gave each of them his special smile. I have always wondered, Marcus, did you take Melissa Billingstage into the Billingstage stable and up into the hay loft?"

"I have no recollection of such an event, Mama, or of this Melissa girl. She wasn't that quite delicious little flirt whose father was squire of Bassing Manor, was she? The girl with the huge pansy eyes and, er, quite substantial endowments?"

"You know very well—ah, there, Duchess, he's done it again, trapped me into my own accusations as quickly as a heron can snag pilchards from the sea."

"He is quite adept, isn't he, ma'am? And he's still quite conceited, but I must confess that it is part of his charm and thus part of him. His smile is probably the most special I've ever seen. It's to his credit that he practiced it to perfection when he was a boy since it gives me remarkable pleasure."

"She's just the girl I would have chosen for you, Marcus," his fond parent announced, taking the Duchess's hand. "I see you're wearing a strange wedding band. You must have mine for it has been in the Wyndham family for at least three generations. I will have it sent to you."

"Thank you, ma'am. Do you agree, Marcus?"

"Certainly. I forgot about it."

"She's your wife, Marcus. It must be on her finger."

"Er, just so, Mama. Welcome to Chase Park. How long do you intend to stay? Long or short?"

His mother gave him a frown that, if he'd had the Duchess's objective eye, he would have known he wore the same expression when he frowned. "Sampson said that the Colonials just left. Of course, I knew of it already. Dear Mrs. Emory, my very good friend, wrote me when Mr. Trevor Wyndham said they would be leaving today. But I didn't trust *that woman's* tactics. I've stayed in Darlington for the past two days and stationed a man here to tell me when their carriage finally rolled out of the drive and took a left turn. I always detested that Wilhelmina woman."

"But you've never met her, Mama."

"It doesn't matter. A mother knows everything. Isn't she a rude, utterly obnoxious old crone?"

"Yes," the Duchess said, "as a matter of fact she is. One never knows what will pop out of her mouth, and whatever does pop out, it's invariably an insult."

"I knew it. Well, my darlings, now I'm here, and every-thing will be so much brighter and happier. Where is Gweneth? Where are the Twins? What is this about the Wyndham legacy? And you, Josephina, you've been nearly murdered twice, according to Mrs. Emory. Do tell me all about it, my dear, I do so adore mysteries."

"Her name is Duchess, Mama. Josephina is the name of a goat or a mallard."

"Very well, I've no intention of abusing my daughter-in-law before she deserves it."

The morning was beautiful, the sky a radiant blue. It had stopped raining during the night, and the air was fresher and warmer than her husband's mouth when he'd kissed her with alarming thoroughness at the breakfast table before anyone else had arrived.

She looked over at him riding easily on Stanley, looking into the distance, and she knew he was looking for that oak tree perhaps or the dell with the Janus-faced nines, the well and the lurking monster. Come to think of it, it all did sound like complete and utter nonsense.

They hadn't spoken of the Wyndham legacy for a full three days now. It was a relief. She grinned suddenly, remembering the look on her mother-in-law's face when she'd walked into the morning room while Marcus was kissing her, his hand cupping her breast.

"Are there kippers this morning, my dear son?"

Marcus's mouth had gone utterly still on hers. His hand slithered away from her breast. "I don't know," he said, very slowly rising from where he'd had her pinned against her chair. "I didn't think you liked kippers, Mama. I thought you detested kippers."

"I do, my dear. I just thought it a good way to gain your attention without surprising you unduly. Good morning, my dear daughter. I see my son is providing you an example of his passion."

"Yes, ma'am."

"How odd that it would take such a carnal form. I believed you meant that he was passionate about causes, politics, world matters, that sort of thing."

Marcus snorted. "You thought no such thing, Mama. Now, come and sit down. I will serve you. Porridge?"

The Duchess said now to her husband beside her as she breathed in a deep breath of the wondrous fresh air, "I quite like your mama. Perhaps you gained your passion for causes, politics, and world matters from her? She certainly has deep fondness for Mary, Queen of Scots. Goodness, if she hadn't fallen asleep, I believe we would have heard every intrigue in the French court that revolved around the seven-year-old Mary. Oh goodness, Marcus, look at those black clouds. I fear we're in for a soaking."

In the next instant there was a sudden clap of thunder. Just as suddenly, the warmth of the day dissipated. Dark clouds billowed and roiled overhead, turning the afternoon into dusk. There was a streak of lightning.

Marcus cursed. "Damnation! Until three minutes ago there was no hint of a storm, no glimmer of a cloud, no—"

The Duchess giggled. "At least it's warm enough so that we won't take a chill. Shall we return to the Park?"

At that instant, there was a streak of lightning just beyond Birdie, cracking the branch from a maple tree, sending sizzling smoke upward. The branch fell in the center of the road. Birdie, terrified, reared onto her hind legs.

"Duchess!"

"It's all right. I've got her." She was leaning forward stroking the bit in Birdie's mouth as she'd been taught, no abrupt movements, when there was a sharp sound and Birdie flinched, then maddened, reared up again, tearing the reins from her hands.

Marcus wheeled Stanley against Birdie and grabbed the Duchess around her waist, ready to jerk her off Birdie's back. There was a soft pinging sound, then another. To his shock, he felt a sharp pain in his head. He raised his hand, realizing blankly that someone was shooting at them and that a bullet had just grazed his head above his left temple. For a split instant, he was in Toulouse again, bullets flying around him, hearing the screams of his men, urging them forward, then into a quick break around the center of the French line to sweep in behind them. So many bullets, and the blood, like a red weeping cloud covering everything.

She yelled his name, realizing what was happening.

There was another loud popping sound. The Duchess saw a huge chunk of bark go flying off a maple tree some ten feet beyond him. Without thought, she leapt toward him. There was another loud report.

She felt a sharp jab in her left side, even as she grabbed Marcus's shoulders, pressing herself against his chest, protecting him as best she could. Stanley reared, twisting madly beneath them. Birdie, terrified, galloped forward, leaving his rider dangling from her husband's arms.

"Duchess! Oh God—"

There came another shot and another. Marcus kicked his booted feet into Stanley's sides. "Quickly, you damned brute! Go!"

Stanley went as if shot from a cannon. Marcus held her tightly against him. She wasn't unconscious, but he knew she'd been hit, just as he had, but where, and how badly?

He wheeled Stanley about when the road curved and headed back to the Park through the fields. They would have made it if it hadn't been for the flock of starlings bursting from the protection of a huge thick-branched oak tree. The thunder cracked, the lightning sliced through the black sky, and the birds took mad flight. Stanley reared, twisting and snorting, tossing his great head. Marcus knew in that last instant that he'd lost his hold. He tried as best he could to protect her as they landed on a slight incline, rolling over and over until he landed on his back in a shallow mud puddle, the Duchess sprawled on his chest. He heard her moan softly, then she went utterly limp against him.

He managed to get them to the top of the incline, the Duchess unconscious over his shoulder, his hand beneath her hips, holding her steady even as the blood from the wound in his scalp bled over his eye, blurring his vision.

Stanley stood trembling, his eyes rolling, but he'd stayed, thank God, he'd not run back to the stables. It took some doing, but Marcus got them back into the saddle. She was unconscious, thus it didn't matter for Stanley ran like the wind. Marcus kept urging him forward, holding him loosely, allowing him to jump those fences he chose to. The last one was a high boundary fence and Stanley took it with a good foot to spare.

His arm was tight around her. His hand, he saw numbly, was wet with her blood and with his as well, for he'd also been shot in his left hand, something he'd just realized. Odd that he felt nothing, nothing at all except the deep corroding fear. It was the longest ride of his life. When he pulled Stanley up in front of the massive front steps of Chase Park, he was already yelling at the top of his lungs, "North! Spears! Badger! Get out here, quickly, quickly!"

He dismounted, pulling her easily up into his arms. Her head fell back over his forearm. Oh dear God.

North roared through the doors, Badger on his heels.

"She's been shot. Fetch Doctor Raven from Darlington, quickly, quickly."

Badger was at his side then even as North sprinted toward Stanley, caught his reins and was on his back and galloping away within seconds.

"Bring her upstairs now, my lord. Mr. Sampson! Oh there you are. Quickly fetch hot water and a lot of clean soft cloths. Lord Chilton has gone to fetch Doctor Raven."

Marcus wasn't aware that he was clutching her so tightly against him until Badger said gently, "Put her down, my lord. That's right, here on her bed. Good. Now, let's get her out of this gown."

Marcus was staring down at his hand. "I'm covered with her blood, Badger."

"Yes, my lord, but it's also yours. You've been shot too. My God, you were hit twice—your scalp and your poor hand. Jesus, this is unbelievable. There's too much pain here, too much misery. I don't want her to be hurt like this yet another time."

"God, I know, I know."

"What the devil happened?" It was Maggie, nearly shrieking, Spears right behind her.

"She was shot," Badger said calmly. "Let's get her out of these wet clothes so we can get the bleeding stopped."

"Not again," said Maggie. "Good Lord, not again."

Within minutes, the Duchess was lying on her side, the covers pulled to her belly, Marcus pressing down against the wound just above her left hip.

"Ah, at last. Here's Mr. Sampson with the water and cloths," Spears said.

Marcus took a hot wet cloth from him, raised his bloody hands and looked down at the riddled flesh, still oozing blood. The bullet, thank God, had gone through the fleshy part of her flank. "Jesus," he said, and began cleaning the wound. The bullet's entry was just a small hole, insignificant looking really, so minor, but the white flesh around the small hole was purple with the impact of the bullet and with her blood. He eased her toward him to look at where the bullet had torn through her outwardly. The flesh was riddled, torn furiously, the bleeding thick and slow.

He swallowed. He'd seen too many men's wounds during his years in the army, but this, no, this was too much. This was the Duchess, his wife, and she was slight and surely not strong enough to bear such pain. His hand clenched into a fist. He shook his head.

"That's right, my lord," Spears said quietly. "She needs help now, not rage. That can come later. We'll figure out what to do, don't worry. The bullet went through her, so she'll be spared that pain. I don't think it hit any organ nor did it go near her belly and the babe."

Jesus, the babe. He hadn't given a single thought to the babe, nestled there in her still flat belly.

He raised his head, gazing around the bed. Badger, Spears, Maggie, and Sampson were all there. He drew a deep breath, carefully folded a new wet cloth that Spears handed him, and pressed down again on both wounds. He felt Spears wipe the blood away from his face and dab it against the raw streak against his scalp. He didn't feel a thing.

Suddenly, Maggie stepped forward. "She's still got on her riding hat," she said, and began taking pins out to remove it. Marcus almost laughed. There she was, lying there on her side, quite naked, a pert blue riding hat on her head, the feather broken and bedraggled, but the hat was still there atop her tousled hair. He watched Maggie smooth out her hair. He pressed down harder against the wound where the bullet had exited.

"Now, my lord," Spears said in the firmest voice Marcus had ever heard, "it's time for you to get out of your wet clothing and let me bandage your head and hand. No, my lord, Mr. Badger will continue the pressure on the wound. Come along now. That's right."

It seemed a day but indeed, it was only two hours before North returned with Doctor Raven.

Doctor Raven said even before he reached the bed, "Has she regained consciousness yet?"

"Yes, but not really," Marcus said. "She's drifted in and out. I don't think she's been conscious enough yet to feel the pain."

"Good," Doctor Raven said, rolled up his sleeves, and gently shoved Marcus out of the way. "Excellent, my lord," he said after he'd lifted the pad and examined the wound. "The bullet went through her, thank God. You got the bleeding stopped. Yes, quite good. Now, while she's unconscious, let's clean this exit wound with brandy and then I've got to stitch her up."

"Will it leave an ugly scar?" Maggie said.

"Yes, but hopefully she'll be alive. What's a scar compared to being alive?"

"She won't die," Marcus said blankly. "My God, she won't die, will she? I saw so much poisoning, so much fever, so much delirium and then death, too much death. No, not the Duchess, there's so much I have to tell her. There's so much we have to do together. No, not her, she's my wife, you see."

Doctor Raven straightened, turned, and looked up at the earl. "Yes, she could die, my lord. However, I'm very good at my profession. Let's hurry. I want her unconscious, it will spare her pain."

If Doctor Raven thought that five men and one woman peering closely at everything he did was in any way unusual, he didn't say anything. Their fear was palpable, as were their worry and their caring. He hadn't the heart to order them out. The earl was holding her steady, one of his large brown hands over her ribs, the other on her upper leg.

"All right," Doctor Raven said. He sent the needle into her flesh and pulled through the thread. Marcus watched the blood seep through his fingers, soak the black thread, and he wanted to cry. "Just another moment," Doctor Raven said. "There's no need to stitch where the bullet entered," he added.

Then the Duchess moaned and all of them froze.

=27=

"OH NO," MARCUS said. "No, please, no."

"Hold her, my lord!"

Marcus rose then to give himself more leverage. She was conscious enough to feel the awful pain of the needle as it went through her ripped flesh, and she was gasping with it, heaving with it, trying to escape it, trying to jerk away from him, soft cries erupting from her throat, then cries, tears running down her face. Badger tried to get brandy and laudanum down her throat but it was difficult. By the time it took effect, Doctor Raven would be through.

"Steady, Duchess, I know it hurts. Dear God, I know. Hold steady, love, just a moment longer."

He kept talking. He had no idea if anything he said reached her, but it didn't matter. It was as much for him as for her. It seemed an eternity, but then Doctor Raven said softly, "There, that's the last stitch, now let me knot it off. All done now, my lord."

Doctor Raven looked up. "Mr. Badger, I'm going to turn her head just a bit. Give her some more brandy laced with laudanum. Quickly now. Mr. Spears, the bascilicum powder, please. Miss Maggie, dampen that white cotton cloth and have it ready. Mr. Sampson, just stand there and make certain everyone does what I told him to do."

Not many more minutes passed before her head fell back to the pillow. She was in a stupor, the pain, for the moment at least, far away from her. When he raised his hands from her body, he saw that he'd bruised her. He cursed.

"No, Marcus, stop it." North clasped his arm and gently drew him away. "Let Maggie put her in a nightgown after Doctor Raven's finished bandaging her. She'll be all right, Marcus. She will, I know it. Now, you've been shot yourself. Doctor Raven, it's now his lordship's turn. No, Marcus, come away, she'll be fine now."

"How the bloody hell can you know anything?" Marcus, his rage now bubbling over, turned on his friend, shook his hand off, and yelled, "Damnation, she could die! Do you hear me, all of you? She could bloody well die because she tried to protect me. She saw a bullet crease my damned skull and what does she do? She throws herself hard against me, trying to cover me. Me! Curse her hide, why couldn't she just yell at me to duck down? Why?"

"For the moment, my lord," Doctor Raven said, "it is a question that is moot. Now, let me see that hand of yours. Ah, good, the bullet went through the fleshy part of your thumb. Now, your head, my lord."

It was dim and shadowed in the bedchamber, only one candle lit beside the bed. She lay on her side, a pillow against her back to keep her steady and a pillow against her stomach and chest to keep her from rolling onto her belly. There was a light coverlet to her waist, nothing more. Her nightgown was soft white batiste, a school girl's nightgown, a virgin's nightgown, high-necked, small pearl buttons down the front, selected by him so they could get her out of it easily.

He rose and stretched, never looking away from her. She'd thrown herself at him, covering him as best she could. She hadn't thought, hadn't hesitated. Damn. If he'd had time, if only he'd had time, he could have thrown her facedown over his thighs, at least protected her that much, but everything had happened so quickly. Marcus thought back. There had been at least six shots. The bastard had used several pistols. There was no other way he'd have managed to fire in such rapid succession. Changing quickly from one gun to the next must have helped ruin his aim, thank God.

He leaned down and laid his right palm on her forehead. His left hand was bandaged. They'd both been lucky. The bullets that had struck them had gone clean through both of them. He cursed long and fluently. She was hot to the touch. She had the fever. He didn't pause, pulled his dressing gown closed, and went swiftly from her bedchamber down the hall to where Doctor Raven was sleeping.

"It's the fever," he said only when the young man shook his blond head and looked up at him.

"I'll be right there. Have Maggie fetch cold water and towels, my lord. Do you have ice?"

"I'll get Badger."

They were all gathered around her again at two o'clock in the morning. She was moaning softly, her head thrashing back and forth on the pillow, tangling her hair around her face.

Marcus wanted to cry. He leaned down and began wiping her face with the cold cloth, almost too cold to the touch, what with the ice floating in the basin of water.

"Strip her down, my lord. If the fever gets too high, we'll put her in a tub filled with cold water." It was then he seemed to realize that there were five men in the room. He cleared his throat. "Please, gentlemen, leave us now. His lordship and I will see to her. Please, go."

"No," Badger said.

"No," Spears said.

"Yes, do go, Badger, Spears," Marcus said. He clapped his hand on his shoulder. "I'll take care of her, you may be certain of that. No, don't argue, Spears, I feel fine, just a bit clumsy with this bandaged hand, but I'll manage."

When they were alone, even Maggie gone from the bedchamber, Marcus unbuttoned the small pearls and stripped off her nightgown. The bandage was still white and dry.

"Good, the bleeding hasn't started again," said Doctor Raven.

"What's your first name?"

"George."

"All right, George, show me what to do."

They wiped her down for more than an hour, taking turns, until just after three o'clock in the morning, George felt her forehead, her chest, and her hip near the bandage. "It's down. Let's pray it stays down."

"She's so weak," Marcus said as he fetched a clean night-gown and put her in it. "It's like she isn't really here."

"She's here, my lord, and here she'll stay, we'll see to it. She won't die, I swear it. I expected the fever. Now, you get some rest and I will stay with her and call you in the morning. The last thing I want to have to do is rub you down with ice water. You're too big."

She was dreaming: a lovely dream really, filled with flowers, all sorts of flowers, brilliant in both scent and color. She was sitting there in the midst of all the flowers, singing one of the ditties she'd written, the one about the sailors, which was a bit more than racy, actually, but it had sold the best of the lot so far. Mr. Dardallion at Hookhams had told her that it was so popular amongst the naval men he didn't think it would ever be forgotten. She thought of being immortal through a song, and it made her smile. Then she was back firmly in the meadow, amid all the daisies and the lilies. She turned to stroke her fingers over a velvet red rose petal when suddenly from behind the rosebush came a strange creature that looked for all the world like a tonsured, robed monk, but he was shriveled and shrunken, and he looked older than the barrowed hills behind him, and he said to her, "I was near the well, keeping a close watch, but you never found me. I waited and I waited, for hundreds of years I've waited but you never came. You're stupid, no imagination, not like me or my brothers when we decided what we'd do.

"He was Baron Dandridge then, just a simple baron was Lockridge Wyndham, but he helped us, tried to save us, but he couldn't, no one could, and we decided then that we would take care of him as best we could in case he lost everything. Aye, and that miserable king did strip us and our abbey to the bones, he and that miserable Cromwell and his bully boys. Then the baron did die, too soon, poor man, before his son knew what was what, but all the clues were there and several more generations spoke of the treasure and then even that stopped. All the Wyndhams have been ignorant and stupid. Even now you've given it up. So I had to come to you. Now, what do you see?"

And she said slowly, "I see a nine. I see another nine, but it's backwards."

"Do you now, Countess? Well, maybe yes and maybe no. You write those little songs, aye, they're clever, so why aren't you clever about this? Don't be so blind, or the next time I come to you, you'll regret it. Monsters never die, they live on and on. Don't you forget that."

And the shriveled old monk was gone and she was left in the midst of the flowers, but then they were wilting, turning brown, shriveling just as the monk had been shriveled, and the clean, clear air darkened and it became cold and colder still. Then she cried out, wanting now only to get away from all the rot and the devastation.

"Hush, love, it's all right."

His voice jerked her awake. She opened her eyes to see him standing over her, a white bandage around his head.

"You look like a pirate, dashing as the devil, ever so rakish. I wish you could capture me and carry me away with you. I'd fight you, but I wouldn't mean it."

"All right, I'll carry you away, but first, you've got to get completely well again. I'll tell you, Duchess, I'm damned tired of your being hurt."

"No more so than I am. You must have a black patch, Marcus. And your shirtsleeves need to billow out more. But you're so beautiful, yes, take me with you, to a pirate's island far away, perhaps beyond China but south where it's warm and we could just lie about and—"

She stared up at him then blinked and blinked again. "Perhaps I've gone mad."

"No, that's a fantasy I would gladly give to you if I could. Now, how do you feel?"

She fell silent for a moment, querying her body. "My side hurts, but I can stand it. I feel heavy and dull otherwise, it's strange, as if everything were going more slowly than it usually would. How does your poor head feel, Marcus?"

"My poor head is harder than a walnut, you know that. Now, about this heaviness you're feeling."

"And your hand. What happened to your hand?"

"The bastard who shot us hit me in the head, then you, madam, like Saint George, jumped all over me and then he shot you in your side and my hand when I pulled you against me. All in all we were both very lucky."

"Who did it, Marcus?"

"I don't know, but Badger left this morning for London, to see if our precious Colonial Wyndhams are there."

"Surely Aunt Wilhelmina couldn't have shot us."

"No, but she could have hired someone. Badger will discover the truth. If he needs help, he'll hire a Bow Street Runner. I don't want you to worry, all right?"

She nodded. "You called me *love.*"

"Yes, I did."

"This was the second time you called me 'love.' "

"Many more times than that, Duchess, you were just too far under the hatches to hear me."

"I like it, Marcus. If you'd wish to say it again, I won't be disagreeable about it." She paused just a moment, saw that he was frowning, and was afraid that he hadn't meant it, had just said it because he thought she was going to die. She said quickly, "You woke me up from the strangest dream. I was sitting in this field of flowers . . ." She told him the scents and the incredible colors of the flowers, of all the beauty that surrounded her, then about the ancient monk and what he'd said and how he'd been angry with her.

"So it could be Janus-faced nines or not. The monk said maybe yes, maybe no, the miserable lout. He said the monster lives on and on. All of it just more of a muddle. Now, Duchess, how did you know the name of that Wyndham ancestor?"

"Lockridge Wyndham," she said. "I don't know. The monk said he was the Baron Dandridge, then he said his name. It wasn't scary until the end, when all the beautiful flowers wilted and browned and rotted, all in the space of a few moments. But the monk and what he said to me, Marcus, I don't understand that."

"I don't either, but I refuse to accept it as some sort of visitation."

"Then what?"

"God knows. You must have read about Lockridge Wyndham in the family Bible, yes, that's it."

Suddenly there was stark terror in her eyes.

"What? What, damn you, what's the matter?"

"Oh no, Marcus, oh no." Then her back bowed up and she grabbed her belly, all the while crying out, "No! No! Marcus, please, no, no!"

Not even an hour later, just as the clock struck noon, she miscarried, blood gushing out of her, her body twisting and arching with the vicious cramps. Then, just as suddenly as it had started, it was over. She lay now in an exhausted sleep, her face shiny with sweat, her hair in a lank, dull braid. Her lips were so pale they were nearly blue. The wound in her flank had bled more, running together with the blood from her womb, and he'd known she would die, but she hadn't. At least not yet she hadn't.

Marcus said nothing. He simply looked down at her.

"I'm sorry, my lord," Doctor Raven said as he wiped his hands. "I thought it might happen, but I didn't want to worry you more. These things happen all the time, but I'm sorry it had to be this way."

Maggie and Mrs. Emory had cleaned away all signs of the miscarriage. The Duchess at least was clean, all the blood gone and she was just lying there, bloodless, swathed in white, the bandage around her belly white, the cloths between her thighs white, her nightgown white.

"She'll be all right."

But Marcus doubted that very much.

Doctor Raven was pleased he was alone with her. It was the first time her husband had left her, and now she was awake.

He merely smiled at her, waited a moment until recognition came into her very lovely blue eyes, then he leaned over her and gently laid his hand to her chest.

"Your heart is steady and slow. Is there any pain in your belly?"

She shook her head.

"I'm sorry about the babe, but there will be others, my lady. There is nothing wrong with you. It was the fall, the trauma to your body. I told his lordship that you're young and healthy. Yes, there will be an army of babes if you want them, once you've mended."

She shook her head again. "No, there won't be more babes. This was the only one and he wasn't meant to be alive."

Doctor Raven didn't understand her. He gently lifted her hand and closed his eyes as he felt the flutter of her pulse. "Please, try to relax." She lay quietly then, her pulse slow, and he saw the tears seeping beneath her closed lashes. She didn't make a single sound.

He heard the firm footsteps and automatically stepped away. Marcus gently dabbed the tears from her cheeks. "Shush, love. It's all right now."

"No, nothing's all right. Well, for you I guess it is. Everything is now the way you wanted it."

"Duchess—"

"I want to kill the man who shot us."

He drew back in surprise, then felt intense relief flow through him. "But I want to kill him too. How will we resolve this?"

She didn't answer him. She was asleep again.

"My lord."

"Yes," Marcus said as he turned to see Spears in the open doorway.

"I have a message from Badger."

Marcus faced his mother from across the morning-room table. "I didn't know she was pregnant, Marcus. Dear God, this is all incredible and here I was jesting about it and loving mysteries. I'm a fool. I'm very sorry."

He said nothing, merely played with the doubtless delicious casserole of whitefish made with white wine and tomatoes that Badger had prepared before he'd left for London.

"You impregnated her very quickly."

"Yes, probably on our wedding night."

"I don't like this violence, my dear, this wretched continued violence, all directed toward the Duchess, except for this last time. Who was that horrible man trying to kill? You or the Duchess?"

"With so many shots, I've come to the conclusion that he was shooting at both of us. Of course, the Duchess has been attacked twice already. God knows."

"Spears told me you'd gotten a message from Badger."

Marcus nodded. "He's on his way back soon. There's nothing more he can do there. All the Wyndhams are in London. Ursula was ill with a bad cold and so was that bloody dandified Trevor who looks like a centaur riding my stallion, so Lambkin tells me with a dollop of awe in his voice. As for Aunt Wilhelmina, evidently the old bat never went near her sick children for fear of catching something herself. As for James, he was staying with a young man he met their first day in London. He was out in Richmond. Badger rode there to make certain, spoke to one of the grooms and was told that Mr. Wyndham had indeed been there, though the young men had been ripping themselves up with brandy and card playing. So you see, all of them appear to have been there, but Badger couldn't really swear to it. Even if he'd seen each and every one of them and had witnesses swear to have been with them, it still doesn't mean they're innocent."

"It's that miserable old hag."

"That would be nice. As I said, any of them could have hired someone to do it, even that miserable old hag."

Aunt Gweneth came into the breakfast room, kissed her sister-in-law's offered cheek, smiled at Marcus, and said, "That Doctor Raven seems a pleasant young man."

Marcus grunted. "He's young all right."

"What does that mean, son?"

"It means I'm a fool. George is good, no matter his bloody young age."

"He's older than you are, Marcus. I asked him. He's twenty-eight."

"Yes, but I'm her husband and he isn't."

His mother grinned at him. "So, you're a dog in the manger. How very odd, my dear, to see a jealous side to you. I always thought you so above such petty emotions. How refreshing to find you delightfully human."

Marcus forked down a piece of bacon. "I know. I find it odd myself." He gave his mother a lopsided grin to which she remarked, "That smile of yours always melted any female heart in the vicinity, even your mother's. Now, tell Gweneth then about what Badger discovered in London."

As he spoke, Aunt Gweneth frowned, the muffin in her left hand still untouched. "It must be something to do with the Wyndham legacy."

"I believed that when the Duchess was struck down in the library and that old book stolen, but now? With so many shots, Auntie, he must have been after both of us. The treasure? Neither the Duchess nor I have the foggiest notion where that wretched treasure is or if it even exists."

"Actually," Patricia Wyndham said, rising from her chair, "I believe I just might have an idea. I've been thinking about it a good deal, Marcus. Would you please fetch the

Duchess's drawings for me? I'd like to study them, then we'll see." She beamed at her son and her sister-in-law, and left them motionless and speechless in the breakfast room.

Marcus stared at the pages stacked neatly in her small desk. He'd lifted out the drawings she'd made of the well and found other pages were beneath them. Sheet after sheet of music and the words written beneath the notes. The words on one sheet caught his eye and he read:

"'E ain't the man to shout 'Please, my dear!'
'E's only a lout who shouts 'Bring me a beer!'
'E's a bonny man wit' a bonny lass
Who troves 'im a tippler right on 'is ass.
And to hove and to trove we go, me boys,
We'll shout as we please till ship's ahoy!'"

Then he softly began to sing it, a melody very familiar to him, one every lad in the navy sang over and over again, laughing and toasting one another. Still, he couldn't believe it. The Duchess was R. L. Coots? She'd written all these ditties? He leafed more slowly through them, recognizing nearly all of them. There were at least twenty of them. Beneath the sheets of music were correspondence and legal documents. He smiled. Lord, she'd made a hefty sum on the more recent ones.

She'd supported herself and Badger. She'd done it alone. She had guts, this wife of his. He felt a spurt of pride that made him go soft inside. Pride and something else, something that was already there, deep and endless, this something that was surely love and he had it bad, no, no escape for him nor did he want to. Perhaps he'd loved her from the time she was nine years old and he'd called her the Duchess for the first time. God, he didn't know, but it was there now, this well of love for her with its unplumbed depths he knew would always be there for him.

Very carefully he returned all the sheets of paper back

into the original order. He shut the desk drawer.

She was sleeping soundly, on her side, her hair tumbled around her face and down her back. He saw the even rise of her breasts. He remembered his accusations when he'd gone to Pipwell Cottage. A man had to be keeping her, surely, for she was just a girl, naught more than that, and naturally helpless, as all females were, all of them needing a man to protect them, to support them, to care for them. She'd probably wanted to cosh him, ah, but then she'd been the Duchess, the original Duchess who, to protect herself, had simply drawn away into herself and said nothing, just became still and aloof, and terribly and completely alone. That Duchess would never have thrown a saddle at him, struck him with a riding crop, or hit him with her riding boot. Ah, but she'd written all these songs, that Duchess who was now his, and different too, because if he riled her sufficiently now, she'd likely shoot him.

She'd done it all by herself.

She'd never told him.

As he walked back downstairs, he heard Spears singing in his mind, ditty after ditty in his rich melodious baritone. The sod knew. Badger had told him. Probably even Maggie and Sampson knew. Everyone knew except him.

Why hadn't she told him?

He handed his mother the two drawings then left the Green Cube Room, whistling a ditty that was surely too risqué for a lady to have penned.

He prayed both of them lived a very long time. He wanted every minute of it with her.

=28=

BADGER WAS NEARLY frothing at the mouth as he said to Spears, Sampson, and Maggie, "Any of the bleeding bastards could have done it, any of them. Damnation, if they didn't have the guts for it themselves then they hired someone, aye, the miserable scoundrels. That old besom's behind it, you know she is."

"Mr. Badger, calm yourself. Anger won't help us find the truth here. You said it appeared that they all had alibis. Perplexing, most upsetting actually that you couldn't find out anything definitive. It is unsettling for all of us."

Maggie, who'd been studying her thumbnail, said, "Maybe we're looking in the wrong direction. Maybe it's someone right here. What was that man's name in the village? The man who owns that bookstore and is another Wyndham bastard?"

"I don't remember," Badger said, looking at her thoughtfully. "But that's a good idea, Maggie. I'll ride over there this morning and have a very nice little chat with the man."

"You be careful now, Mr. Badger. He might be a villain. We're abounding with villains."

He didn't take her words at all lightly. "I will, my dear. Incidentally, that gown you're wearing is most becoming. That shade of pomona green complements your brilliant hair to perfection."

"Thank you, Mr. Badger," she said, giving him a teasing grin.

"I," Spears said judiciously, "would prefer a soft yellow

on you. The green is too overbearing, too certain of itself, it overwhelms. Yes, softer colors would be more the thing on you, Miss Maggie."

Sampson looked at her only briefly and said, "Who cares what color she's wearing?"

Maggie laughed, patted both her glorious hair and her beautiful gown, and took her leave. She said over her shoulder, "Sampson is right, you know. Now isn't the time for undue vanity. I'm going to the Duchess now. The poor lady's feeling restless and bored. Perhaps the earl will let me wash her hair this morning. He's been hovering over her, treating her like a half-wit, she complains to me, but he's worried and I like to see a man so smitten. It's about time, I say."

"The earl," Spears said, "has at last realized how very lucky he is. I too am heartened he has finally succumbed. However, he has also been acting strangely for the past three days. I don't understand it."

Badger said, "You're looking for a mystery that isn't there, Mr. Spears. He's just very worried about the Duchess. Damn, why did she have to miscarry the babe?"

"Another score to settle with the person who shot them, Mr. Badger," Spears said. "It deepens her depression. She blames herself, which is ridiculous, but true nonetheless."

"She's also told his lordship that he now has his way. He'll never have to have a child by her body."

"What has he said to that, Mr. Badger?"

"I don't know. Both of them have closed down tighter than castles under siege."

Spears said, "True, Mr. Badger, but I think there's even more to it than that, although the miscarriage is more than enough."

"I would say," Sampson observed, "that the entire staff is dreadfully worried. The countess is very popular with them. As for the earl, his concern for her has brought them to viewing him as a just master and a husband who is on the mend, so to say. Indeed, I feel they're quite coming to respect him in full-measure, no mean feat that."

"He's still a bullheaded young man," Maggie said. "If I'd had my way, the Duchess would have taken a horse whip to him, not just her boot or a bridle. I have told her I much approve the change in her. Yelling cleanses a woman's innards wonderfully. It readjusts her view of things. A man, as all women know, can't properly listen until his attention is fully engaged. A whip, I say, would do the trick."

Wisely, none of the three gentlemen had a word to say to that.

Spears said finally, "I think I'll have a chat with Mrs. Wyndham. She's a dreadfully smart lady, that one."

Spears found Patricia Wyndham lying on her back on the pale blue Aubusson carpet in the middle of the Green Cube Room, staring at the ceiling. She was utterly immobile, and for one horrible moment, Spears was certain she was dead.

"Madam!"

She slowly turned her head and smiled. "Hello, Spears. Come help me up. I do hope the carpet is clean, but certainly it is. Mrs. Emory is a household tyrant. There, thank you, Spears." She dusted off her skirts, shook them out, then beamed up at him again.

"May I inquire what you were doing lying supine on the floor, madam?"

"You may, but I shan't tell you, at least not yet, Spears. Where is my son?"

"His lordship is probably giving orders to the Duchess, or to Maggie regarding the Duchess."

"He's such a sweet lad," she said.

That brought a choking sound from Spears's throat. " 'Sweet' isn't exactly an epithet I'd attach to his lordship. I, er, wished to ask you, madam, if you had any notion of who is responsible for all this misery we're having."

"I can't know everything, Spears."

"Do you know anything, madam?"

"Oh yes, I know quite a bit more than just anything. Indeed, perhaps soon now, I'll be able to clear at least some of this mystery up."

"I see, madam. Perhaps you'd like to have a judicious ear to pour some of your opinions into?"

"Yours, to be exact?"

"Exactly so, madam."

"Not yet, Spears. Forgive me, I'm not being coy, I'm just not quite ready. Untidy strings that don't weave themselves into the fabric, you understand? Now, I believe I'll see how my darling boy is doing with the Duchess. Poor girl, losing the babe has really pulled her down."

Not to mention being shot, Spears thought, but didn't say anything.

Her darling boy was yelling at the top of his lungs, his fond mother realized while she was still twenty feet from the Duchess's bedchamber. She opened the door to see the Duchess standing beside the bed, holding on to the cherub-carved bedpost and looking quite limp.

"Marcus," the Duchess said, a goodly dollop of temper in her voice that pleased her mother-in-law, "stop your shouting. For heaven's sake, I'm all right."

"You swore to me you'd stay in bed, damn you. Just look at you, white around the gills, sweating like a stoat, and out of breath and bed."

"My dears," Patricia Wyndham said, sweeping into the bedchamber, "this is surely not good for the Duchess's nerves. He's right, however, my dear, whatever made you get out of that very comfortable bed?"

"I knew you'd side with him."

"True, but what's a mother to do?"

"She was relieving herself, Mother. She actually thought to get out of bed, walk all of fifteen feet to the screen, and use the chamber pot. I won't have it, do you hear me, Duchess? Now, you're getting back into that bed this minute."

"Yes, Marcus, I know. I was on my way back to the

bed when you burst in here and started screeching like a crazed owl."

"Crazed owl? Good God, even your mental works aren't functioning properly. You mean you've already used the chamber pot?"

"Yes, Marcus, and I even managed to walk back to the bed all by myself."

Patricia Wyndham cleared her throat. "This is doubtless fascinating, children, but all this talk of the chamber pot can surely wait. Come, Duchess, I'll help you."

"You just stay put, Mother." He very carefully angled the Duchess so he wouldn't touch her side, lifted her some two inches off the floor, and carried her the remaining three feet to the bed.

Once he'd gotten her into bed again, on her back now for the pain in her side had lessened quite a bit during the past four days, he said, "There, now don't move or it will go badly for you."

"That sounds quite intriguing. Just what will you do, Marcus?"

"Sounding a bit testy, are we? As to what I'll do, I don't know, but whatever it is, you will like it immensely, and so will I."

"I hardly think that's a threat to convince me to obey you."

"My dears, surely you don't wish to contemplate marital themes just now? No, certainly not. Such subjects aren't best fashioned for a mother's tender ears. You, my darling son, are still my little boy, thus, you are bathed in sunlight and purity. Yes, at last you're both quiet. Badger told me to inform you that he's sending up luncheon. Shall we all dine together and enjoy a comfortable prose?"

"Good God, Mama, a comfortable what?"

"Prose, my dear. Ladies of more advanced years speak in that fashion, you know. It's soothing."

"Bosh," Marcus said, and pulled out a delicate French chair from the last century for his mother. "You're about as advanced as that hussy maid of the Duchess's."

"Ah, Maggie. Isn't she an interesting sort?"

Spears said from the doorway, "Perhaps Madam will be so kind as to tell her son why she was lying on her back in the middle of the Aubusson carpet in the Green Cube Room?"

"I would have expected a minimal degree of discretion from you, Spears. You have gravely disappointed me. No, Marcus, my body positions don't concern any of you at the moment."

"Bosh," Marcus said again, looking harassed. "What the hell were you doing on your back? Some new meditation?"

"My dear boy, it's none of your business."

The Duchess laughed. "Ah, thank you, ma'am. You've diverted his fire away from me."

His blue eyes came again to rest on her pale face. He leaned down and kissed her mouth. "If you eat your luncheon, nap awhile, then I'll allow Maggie to wash your hair."

"What about the rest of me?"

"I'll wash the rest of you."

"No, Marcus, no, you can't, I—"

"Be quiet, Duchess."

Patricia Wyndham rolled her eyes. "So much for my sunlight-pure boy."

She knew he would be thorough. Marcus never did anything in half measures. As for the wound in her side, she knew he wouldn't hurt her, that he'd be gentle as a sliver of sunlight through the summer maple branches. But she couldn't help but be embarrassed because she was still bleeding and there were cloths between her thighs. Perhaps he would leave that part of her alone. He did begin well enough, treating her as he'd treat a stick of wood or a doorknob, but when he'd uncovered her breasts, all his good intentions began to unravel. His fists clenched, his mouth tightened, and his beautiful blue eyes darkened.

"I'd forgotten how utterly acceptable you are. That is, I've dressed and undressed you, looked at you and held you, wiped you down with icy water, but it's different now. You're better and you're looking at me while I'm looking at you. It's unnerving. Now, don't move, I'll try to keep my hands on the straight and narrow, wherever that could possibly be since your body is nothing but delight for me."

He didn't manage to find any sort of straight and narrow, of course, but he did try, and when he was lightly washing her belly, carefully avoiding her bandaged side, he drew in his breath, closed his eyes, and went lower with the soapy washcloth.

"Please don't, Marcus. It's very embarrassing for me and I don't—"

He ignored her. "It doesn't bother me at all that you're bleeding. Thank God it's normal bleeding, and I don't have to worry that you'll die on me. No, just be quiet, Duchess, and trust me."

He looked at her face as he spoke, saw the shifting expressions even as his fingers found her. He'd meant to wash her, nothing more, truly, he'd not thought about anything remotely sexual, surely, well, all things sexual he'd thought about were spiritual, or perhaps they were just sexual themes in the abstract, theories, nothing more, but his fingers were on her and his eyes were looking at her and his hand was shaking.

It had been a long time, too long a time. He became aware that her breathing had changed, had quickened. Her eyes were wide and questioning on his face, her cheeks flushed. He smiled at her and thought, *Why not?* His fingers gently molded themselves to her flesh, but still, at first, her soft flesh was unwilling, but he was patient and he loved her and wanted to give her pleasure. There'd been so much pain for her, too much damned pain, why not pleasure, just for this once?

Finally, when she tensed, her back arching, he came up

beside her and kissed her until she cried out her release into his mouth.

"Oh dear."

"Hold still, Duchess. I still have your lovely legs and feet to wash."

Once done with a bath the likes of which she'd never imagined in her life, he folded clean cloths and pressed them against her, then dressed her in a clean nightgown.

"Stop looking at me as if I were a brute. I'm your husband. Your body is mine and I'll thank you not to forget it. I wouldn't ever allow George Raven to touch you like this, to look at you with lust as I do. Just me and always just me. So don't be embarrassed. I forbid it."

"It's difficult, Marcus. I trust you, I surely do. You're my husband, but I've always been so private and surely things that are only female should be kept private."

"No, that's silly. Obviously you don't trust me enough. I know what I'm talking about. Now, you've got some color in your cheeks, no doubt from the pleasure I just gave you." He paused, tossed the towels and other clothes on the floor, then turned back to her, suddenly serious, his expression very intent.

He looked down at his hands as he said, "Actually, Duchess, as my wife, you should tell me everything you feel, everything you think. You don't have to keep anything from me, be it physical or something you've done. Not any more. Not ever again. You can even continue to yell at me, to hit me, whenever I unwittingly chance to say something you dislike."

To his horrified surprise, she began to cry. She didn't make a sound, just let the tears gather, pool in her eyes, and slip down her cheeks.

"Ah, sweetheart, don't cry, please don't."

She turned her face away from him. He saw her hands had fisted on the covers at her chest. He reached out his hand to touch her, then drew it back.

"You know," he said finally, his voice deep and calm,

"I've been a great fool, perhaps so great a fool that even you won't be able to forgive me this time. And I know you've forgiven me more times than I can begin to count since we were both children."

He had her attention, he saw it in the lines of her body, tensing now, alert, waiting, but she didn't turn back to face him, just waited, and he knew she was afraid, and he understood that well enough.

"In Paris I was ready to strangle you I was so furious at you for taking matters into your own hands, for taking away my choices, and here I was the brave man, the man who was enjoying his rage, his bitterness, wallowing in self-pity. There's just something about being a man and having a woman take away control, it makes all of us a bit crazed, unreasonable, perhaps even irrational, though a man hesitates to believe such a thing about himself.

"You've always known, Duchess, that I'm quick to anger and say things that curdle even my own blood when I remember them later. I know I've said things to you that have hurt you unbearably. I've spoken like a fool and then proceeded to believe what I'd said to you.

"I wounded you deliberately because you were your father's daughter and God knows I still detest that old bastard for what he did, not only to me but to you as well. And so I punished you because he was dead and beyond anything I could do to him.

"Try to forgive me just once more . . . well, it's bound to be dozens more times in our future together if you'll have compassion for your fool of a husband. Have babies with me. Let's fill Chase Park's nursery with babes, and you remember how large that nursery is. Our children, just yours and mine, and your father be damned for his own bitterness, for his own despair, for he has nothing to do with us now, nothing to do with our children, with our future."

She turned slowly to face him. She raised her hand to lightly touch her fingertips to his cheek. "Do you really want to have an heir? A boy child who will be the future earl of Chase, a boy child who will carry my blood and your blood and thus my father's blood?"

"Yes. And he must have brothers and sisters."

"But why, Marcus? Is it because you feel pity for me since I lost my babe? You feel somehow guilty?"

"Yes, but that's not the reason."

"What is the reason?"

"I love you more than I ever imagined a man could love a woman. I want no more distrust between us, no more wariness because you'll never know what I'll do next. In the future when I berate you or send curses flying about your head, feel free to cosh me with a fireplace poker. On the other hand, if you pull one of your boots off to hurl at me, I'll be laughing so hard just perhaps you'll forget you want to kill me and laugh with me. I love you. Now, does that satisfy you? Do you believe me? Will you forgive me?"

For a moment, she was the old Duchess, silent, aloof, looking at him intently, assessing him, apart from him, and he hated it. He realized how much he wanted her to scream at him if she wanted to, that or kiss him and tell him he was wonderful, but at least now, at this moment, she was utterly silent, just like she used to be.

"I'll even let that damned young George Raven bring our children into the world, though I distrust him and his motives when he's with you. Now, stop being the old Duchess. Hit me. Yell at me."

"All right." She raised her hand, palm flat.

He eyed her, took her hand in his and drew it back down. He leaned down and kissed her very lightly on her mouth. "All right what?" he asked, his breath warm on her mouth.

"I'll hit you next Wednesday, yell at you on Friday, but right now, Marcus, tell me again."

"I love you and I still distrust George Raven. We will have to find him a wife. It will divert his lust from you."

She laughed and he felt intense heady warmth spread like brandy to his belly, or was it his heart?

"And I you, Marcus. I've probably loved you since I was too young to even know what it was. I deceived you into marriage not just because I knew I had to put things right after what my father had done, but because I wanted you for myself. You were so angry, I didn't think you'd ever change. I had to do something, Marcus, so that the Colonial Wyndhams didn't get what was rightfully yours."

"Rightfully ours. Rightfully our son's and his son's son and on it goes far into the future."

"Yes. Oh yes. Please understand. I couldn't let you not have what was yours."

"And when you came to me on our wedding night? Was it just to keep me from going off like a maniac and annulling our marriage out of misguided spite?"

"Yes, but perhaps not all. I didn't know what happened between men and women so I had no idea how wonderful it could be with you. It was probably more that than any other motive, but it's true. I was so dreadfully afraid you'd do something stupid that I came to you."

"And now why would you come to me and seduce me?"

"To drive you mad with lust, even madder with lust than George Raven, poor man. There is still a lot that I have to learn, Marcus."

"When you're healed, when you're laughing and dancing about again, I'll be the most attentive teacher in all of Yorkshire, hell, in all of England."

She smiled at him, a smile free of pain, a smile free of heartbreak, a smile filled with delight.

"Do you remember, I told you before that I want you to tell me everything now, all right?" He gave her a sideways look. "Really, Duchess, no matter what it is, you can tell me. There should be no secrets between us, not ever, as of this moment, all right?"

She cocked her head at him. She didn't say anything, just stroked her fingers over his face again, and he wondered if she would ever tell him about her songs and her outrageous pseudonym. R. L. Coots—wherever did she get that absurd name?

Ah, but Mr. R. L. Coots wasn't important, just she was, and Mr. Coots would come out sometime in the future, Marcus didn't care when. But he would have liked to tell her how very proud he was of her. He quickly dismissed it as he kissed her not just once, but again and again, showing her how much he loved her, trying to give more of himself to her, and she smiled with relish when he whispered what he was going to do to her when she was well again.

=29=

IT WAS THE Duchess who next saw her mother-in-law lying flat on her back on the floor in the middle of the Green Cube Room, just staring upward. She didn't say anything for a long time, just watched her look upward as if entranced with the ceiling. Then she too looked upward. The Green Cube Room was the only room in the entire house with a painted ceiling, actually groupings of paintings, all done it seemed by the same artist, all the scenes stretched out between the thick painted ceiling beams. She'd looked at these paintings since she was nine years old, particularly the Medieval ones. She'd thought them interesting, but she'd paid them little attention for they were just there, just a part of the house, a part of this odd chamber.

Patricia Wyndham was staring up at a small grouping or series of paintings, most of them scenes from village life in Medieval times. The paints had faded over the centuries but they were still vibrant enough to admire and study. She was even staring up at the Duchess's favorite series of Medieval scenes, the first one depicting a beautiful young maiden surrounded by her servants, all gowned in flowing white, a white wimple, high and conical with a pointed top balanced on her head, her pale angel's hair cascading down her back. She was seated atop what appeared to be a stone fence, leaning forward slightly, listening to a young gallant who sat at her feet playing a lute. The Duchess had always fancied she could almost hear the sounds coming from that lute, so spellbound did the maiden appear. She looked at the next scene, this one similar, but the young gallant was standing in this one and reaching upward to pluck something that seemed to be hidden in the thick branches of an oak tree. What was he reaching for?

She looked down and saw that her mother-in-law was still in rapt contemplation of the ceiling and continued her own perusal. In the third scene, a servant was handing the maiden a cup of water and the Duchess saw now that the maiden hadn't been seated on a stone fence, no, it was the ledge of the top of a well. The young man had pulled a lute from the branches of the oak tree. A lute in an oak tree?

Suddenly she froze. Her heart began to pound. Oh no, was it possible? She shook her head, then stared upward again. In the next scene, the young man was holding both lutes, one in each hand, and he was still smiling at the maiden, as if he were offering her one of the lutes, his attention still firmly fixed on her. In the next scene, he was still holding the lutes, but now he was looking over his shoulder. Someone was evidently there and the young man looked frightened. He'd taken the slender necks of both lutes and pressed the instruments together, back-to-back, holding them in one hand. A lute was perfectly flat on one side and bulged out on the other. Why, then, didn't he press the two flat sides together? Why the pregnant sides? It was awkward and difficult to hold them that way.

"Hello, my dear. I trust you're feeling up to snuff now? Of a certainty you are, else my sweet son wouldn't have allowed you to wander about alone. I'm looking at the ceiling. When I first visited Chase Park so many years ago, I was drawn to this room because of the paintings. So many of them, beginning with scenes from the Conqueror's time and moving up into the early years of the sixteenth century. In truth it was those last scenes that particularly fascinated me, for in some of them are my brave Mary, Queen of Scots, so stouthearted, so noble in the face of so much betrayal. You see there are no paintings of her beyond a child, so the artist must have stopped around 1550. But then I realized, just three days ago, that there was more to the paintings than just the artist's renderings of historical times. Have you seen it yet, Duchess? Ah, yes, I see that you do. Amazing, isn't it?"

The Duchess jumped, then looked down at her mother-in-law, who was still flat on her back. "It's easier to see everything from here. Come down, Duchess, and I'll show you."

The Duchess stretched out on her back next to her mother-in-law. "Now, my dear, tell me what you see."

"The maiden is sitting on the rim of the well and the oak tree is overhead. Just like the clues. Now, what about the Janus-faced nines and the monster?"

"The nine business has bothered me no end. It was just yesterday that I realized the truth of the matter. Look at the lutes, Duchess."

"Yes, the lutes. I was just wondering why he was holding them back-to-back, surely difficult since they're so fat."

"Think about music, my dear, think about what you would have if the young man were holding them facing each other."

"Oh goodness, it's not about nines, it's about music! Those are the nines, the Janus-faced nines."

"I believe so. I've played the pianoforte all my life and I swear to you this is the first time I am truly thankful that my mama forced me to read more music than to dance in the moonlight, which I was finally able to do with Marcus's father, that wonderful man. Do you know music, Duchess?"

"Yes," she said, so excited she could barely speak, "holding the lutes that way doesn't refer to nines, but to bass clefs, back-to-back bass clefs. Oh goodness, they look like nines. I've looked at these paintings since I was a child, yet I've never really looked, if you know what I mean. Even after knowing the clues, it simply never occurred to me that these paintings—oh goodness."

"Yes, indeed. The paintings are so familiar to everyone, but they were painted for a reason, at least these Medieval scenes were. Now, look at the next scene. The young man is looking at someone, someone who frightens him—"

"The monster."

"Yes, the monster," Patricia Wyndham said with a good deal of satisfaction. "The young man is now pointing to the lute. At what, I wonder?"

"The bass clef, that's what he's trying to tell us. See, he's pointing into the lower tree branches, then at the second lute. Ah, ma'am, we've been so very blind. The clues were here all the time, here for centuries, yet no one has ever thought, ever dreamed, except you, ma'am. I believe you're quite the smartest person I know."

"Thank you, dear child, but we don't have that wretched treasure yet."

"May I inquire what you, Duchess, and you, Mrs. Wyndham, are doing on your backs on the newly swept Aubusson carpet?"

"Yes, Spears, you certainly may. Come here and lie beside me and look up. You, my dear man, are in for a revelation. You asked me if I knew anything and yes, I most definitely know something now, as does the Duchess."

Some ten minutes later Badger looked into The Green Cube Room, looking for Mr. Spears. He blinked. Mr. Spears, the Duchess, and Mrs. Wyndham were stretched out on their backs, all staring up at the ceiling. Esmee, the earl's cat, was sprawled atop Spears's chest, quite at her ease.

"What in the name of the devil and all his minions is going on here?"

"Mr. Badger, just excellent. Mrs. Wyndham doesn't know everything, but she's very close. Come here and lie beside me, and we'll tell you."

When Marcus strolled by a few moments later, looking for his wife, he heard Spears saying, "But who is the monster?"

He looked into the Green Cube Room and stared. The Duchess said without moving, "Marcus, do come here.

We've nearly got the Wyndham treasure solved. Come and lie here beside me."

He obliged her and stared up at the paintings. "Good God. I've looked at all those scenes over the years, admired them and the brilliance of the paint, the skill of the artist or artists, but I never really *looked* at them, never even thought to—"

"I know," the Duchess said. "Me neither. Even if we'd known about the Wyndham treasure, I doubt we'd have connected it up with these paintings. But your mama did. That's why she was lying here three days ago. She realized there just might be a connection between the treasure clues and these paintings. Do you know how old this room is, Marcus?"

"We're in the oldest part of the house. I believe the Green Cube Room was one of just a handful left standing after the fire early in the last century."

"Actually, my dear son, I just read all the journals left by Arthur Wyndham, who was then the third Viscount Barresford. The most god-awful boring accounts of his life you can imagine, but he was informative in the third diary. The fire was in 1723 and most of the Elizabethan manor was destroyed, all except for the Green Cube Room and the library, where you found the tome. They were literally the only rooms in this entire wing that held together. Arthur Wyndham said that distinctly. He wrote in his diary: 'I have only the Green Cube Room and my library left and even they are so blackened with smoke I wonder if they will ever be as they were again. Although they have never been to my liking, they did survive and thus I'll return them to what they were.'

"Arthur Wyndham also wrote that his father and his grandfather had both admired the paintings on the ceilings and so he had them restored. Thank God he was a sensitive man, else all would have been lost."

Marcus said thoughtfully, "Why is it called the Green Cube Room? I remember wondering as a child and even asking, but no one knew, not even my uncle."

"I asked too," the Duchess said, coming up onto her elbow, felt the pulling in her side and quickly lay back down again. "No one knew. Sampson suggested it might refer to the old panes of glass in the windows. He believed it likely the windows were mullioned and perhaps set with green squares of glass."

"Yes, green glass, that would be it." This was from Maggie, who was sitting with her hands wrapped around her knees behind Spears. "There's something else. The room itself—don't you see? It's perfectly square."

"Ah," said Badger. "When the sun shines through the green glass into a perfectly square room then—"

"Yes, you'd have an illusion of a green cube, Mr. Badger," Spears said. "Colored glass was quite popular years ago."

"That could be it," Patricia Wyndham said. "All old houses have rooms named the oddest things, like the Presence Chamber at Hardwick Hall, a grand room that's so cold you shiver the whole time you're in it."

"Yes," Badger said. "That's from a ghost, no doubt."

"Then there's the Dial Room at Old Place Lindfield—I haven't the foggiest notion where they got that name—then there's the Punch Room at Cotehele House, where, I suppose, gentlemen imbibed liberally."

"Yes," Marcus said. "I think Maggie's right. She's solved the key to the name of this room."

"Ah, look, Mr. Spears," Badger said, pointing straight upward, "I see the well clearly now, and if I'm not mistaken there's your bucket, Duchess, wood and bound in leather. But where's that damnable monster?"

"Offstage, to the left, or nowhere at all," Marcus said. "I've studied the rest of the scenes and there's no horn-headed beast, no vile green gargoyle, nothing at all."

"Oh there's a monster, all right," the Duchess said. "He's there, even though we can't see him. I can feel him, can't you? Just look at the young man's face in that final scene.

He knows something awful is about to happen. It has to be the monster."

"So," Patricia Wyndham said, "in the first scene, our maiden is sitting on the edge of the well. The young man is playing his lute for her. He fetches another lute from the oak branches overhead. He then presses the lutes together and we've got our Janus-faced nines or Janus-faced bass clefs, and as the Duchess says, the monster's there, just not seen by us. That takes care of all the clues."

"Does it cover everything in your dream, Duchess?" Marcus lightly stroked his fingertips over her arm.

"I believe so," she said, giving him a smile that made her mother-in-law momentarily forget the clues and the treasure and stare at them with delight and relief.

"That treacherous monk in my dream, or whatever it was, even hinted that the Janus-faced nines weren't necessarily nines."

"So much roundabout flummery," Patricia Wyndham said. "Why didn't they just give the treasure over to Lockridge Wyndham? So much nonsense and convolution and confusion. No wonder none of the succeeding generations of Wyndhams found a thing, and even forgot about it."

"I daresay, madam," Spears said, "that the monks weren't alone in determining the disposal of the treasure. The Wyndham ancestor was certainly involved in hiding it, in providing clues to its whereabouts. Obviously he couldn't show himself with sudden boundless wealth or the king and Cromwell would have heard of it. Given the uncertainty of the times, they would have most certainly removed the treasure, and quite probably his head along with it."

"I'll wager," Badger said, "that old Lockridge Wyndham died before he could tell his children where the treasure was. Surely they must have known about it. It just got lost in succeeding generations."

"And the monks wrote two separate books about it," Marcus said. "One of them doubtless given to Lockridge

Wyndham and the other given to whom? We'll never know. At least it did end up with Burgess."

"Others read it probably but didn't realize what it was meant to say," Maggie said. "Now, this is all well and good and a bloody wonderful history lesson, Mr. Spears, but where's the Wyndham treasure?"

"There must be a small hidden space," Marcus said. "That small space, my friends, must somehow be attached to this room. Of course, we haven't a single clue what the treasure actually is."

"Or the treasure could be above the room," Badger said. He pointed upward. "The clue was to reach overhead for the nines, which the young man did. Then there's the well, and that's where the monster is, and perhaps the treasure."

"But a well goes down, not up," Patricia Wyndham said.

"Then," the Duchess said, rising to her feet, unconsciously holding her side, "the hidden room or space is directly below the oak tree and the well, under the floor."

"Not quite," Patricia Wyndham said. "To be precise, and I believe that precision is quite the key here, we must look right beneath those Janus-faced nines."

"Good God," Marcus said. "Sampson, fetch Horatio."

"Oh yes, Mr. Sampson, do hurry," Maggie said. "I'm so keen to find the bloody treasure."

The Aubusson carpet was rolled neatly against the far side of the room. All the furniture was moved away from a large area right below the Medieval paintings. Horatio, a carpenter with magic in his hands, was on his knees, his ear close to the wooden floor, lightly tapping his hammer. Suddenly, he raised his head and grinned, showing a wide space between his two front teeth. "M'lord, there's no support beam running all along here. I think I've found the empty space." He carefully began prying up the thick wooden strips of oak. Maggie was fidgeting, wanting him to hurry, cursing him and his persnickety ways. Who cared about the damned floor, who cared if it got scratched, wasn't it covered with that huge old carpet anyway? But Spears shushed her, saying, "Perhaps you could accelerate your hammer's momentum just a bit more, Horatio. It isn't a sacred burial mound you're digging up, after all."

It broke the tension, but just for a moment.

"Now, now, I've got to go easy. I don't want to splinter this old wood. Ah, yes, there it comes up, all clean and tidy."

"Quickly," Patricia Wyndham said. "Bring candles, Sampson!"

The space was made large enough for a man to ease down through the opening, which Marcus did, since he was the earl, though there was much grumbling, particularly from the women. "It's filthy and black down here, Mother, you'd hate it. There are more spiders than you can imagine. And you, Maggie, you would have ripped your gown for certain and gotten nasty spiderwebs in your hair. As for you, Duchess, you just keep your mouth shut. You're not well enough yet to fight with all the myriad gloom and bugs down here. Maggie, hand me down a branch of candles. I can't see a bloody thing with just one."

Then there was silence.

"Do you see anything, Marcus?" He looked up briefly to see his wife's face peering down into the dark space.

"Son, speak up, or do you want your old mother to expire from unrequited silence?"

The space was long and narrow, but very confined, not more than four feet high. He had to bend over almost double. The space seemed to stretch on endlessly, perhaps the entire length of the Green Cube Room. He held up the candles and clearly saw the floor beams. There didn't seem to be anything else, just blackness, choking dust, spiders, and enough cobwebs to smother a battalion. He continued searching, hunched over like an old man. Then the space ended after about twenty feet, obviously at the end of the Green Cube Room above. There was something leaning against a wall. The something wasn't a treasure chest. He drew closer, holding the branch of candles out in front of him. He drew to a startled stop before it. He called out even as he choked on the airless dust, "Oh my God, what the hell is this? A skeleton, yes, so it appears, but how's that possible?"

Marcus held the candle closer and drew a deep breath. It wasn't a skeleton, but rather a dummy, a figure probably stuffed with moldy old straw, a man to be hung in effigy, for there was a rope around his neck and the rope was drawn up tight and nailed over the dummy's head to the beam above it. The figure was dressed in fancy clothes from Elizabethan times. Marcus lightly touched the lace on a sleeve and it fell into dust. He held the branch of candles closer. The cloth face had been carefully painted: there was greed and avarice and cruelty on that stingy, heavy face, and dissipation and utter arrogance in those glass eyes staring sightlessly up at him.

He realized with a jolt that it was the king himself, Henry VIIIth, his face very much like the portrait painted of him by Holbein, only a bit younger. Marcus thought idly that it had taken a lot of straw stuffed in the frame to fill up the king's stout body. But why here? Hidden away?

He heard voices above him, all of them demanding, yelling, calling out, even the Duchess's voice, and she sounded very testy. He grinned, saying, "The skeleton is really a man probably stuffed with straw, Henry the Eighth to be exact, all ready to hang in effigy with a rope around its neck. Just a moment, there's more. Hold on."

It was at that moment he realized the fat figure, all outfitted in purple velvet and ermine and a ruff that was wider than a wagon wheel around the fat neck, was too fat. It wasn't stuffed with straw. No, it was stuffed with something else. He gently reached inside an opening above the ruff at the neck and pulled out a long string of the most exquisite pearls he'd ever seen. He pressed his hands against the rotting material and felt the shape of more jewels, coins, even several outlines of rosaries, a scepter. His fingers made out the curve of a gold-coin plate and a chalice. There was also the heavy outline of a book, probably the Bible, its cover no doubt embedded with jewels. There were most likely other precious Church relics as well stuffed in that body. It wasn't moldy straw, it was the treasure from St. Swale's Abbey and it had been here stuffed in that fat figure of King Henry VIIIth for well over three hundred years.

"I think, Spears," he called up, "that you need to send down some sort of long flat stretcher with ropes attached so we can pull it up. It's very heavy, so make the ropes and board stout. Our dummy here is stuffed with treasure, a veritable king's ransom in treasure."

"DO YOU HAVE any idea how deliciously decadent you look?"

She just grinned up at him, the luminous loop of pearls around her neck, dipping down past her navel to rest on her white belly. She wasn't wearing anything else, her husband having insisted that with the pearls lying on her flesh—ah, nothing more was necessary. She was, he told her now, to consider it his birthday present to her, perhaps for the next three years, so grand were the pearls.

"Yes, I know you think me wonderful, and I am. I found out from Aunt Gweneth that your birthday's in September, just around the corner."

"And I found out from Fanny that your birthday is in early October. Just perhaps I'll manage to find a fitting bit of jewelry for you to wear. Ah, about dear Fanny, I believe she's making you something very special for your birthday, Marcus."

"She'll get over this infatuation with me, or perhaps she'll go to her grave an old doddering woman still carrying a worn-out torch for me."

"She'll get over it," the Duchess said. "Just two more years and both the Twins go to London. She'll see you then as a drooling old man and dismiss you out of hand. Now, about my birthday. Three years, you say?"

"Yes, a good three years." He picked up the pearls over her stomach, looked at them closely and said, "They're more luminous now, just for these few minutes on that white belly of yours." He then bent down, and began kissing her stomach. She tugged at his hair and he raised his head, grinning at her. She said, "Very well, Marcus, I'll dress myself in the pearls again on the fourteenth. I will consider this my first birthday installment. And what shall I have you pose in, Marcus? I know, I want you to wear that incredible ring with the huge ruby."

"Nothing else?"

"No."

"When did you say your birthday was, Duchess?"

"I believe it begins in just about ten minutes. Actually, you've already begun it on my stomach."

He laughed, leaned down and kissed her, and began playing with the rope of pearls. "Damn," he said, between kisses, "we will wait until you are perfectly well again. You're still sore and I hate it, but there it is."

"I'm not at all sore. It's been well over three weeks. I'm perfectly well now, even my side."

He frowned at that, lightly tracing his fingertip over the still pink scar on her flank. He could still see the marks from the thread and remembered all too clearly how George Raven had stuck the needle in her white flesh then pulled it through, again and again. He gulped. The Duchess said, "Stop it, Marcus. It's over. I'm well. We both survived. Your hard head and your hand healed, albeit more quickly than I thought fair."

He shook his head. "You're right. It's in the past, thank God. You may be certain that I will take excellent care of you from now on. As to anything else, sweetheart, we'll wait until you're beyond perfectly well. No, don't argue with me, Duchess, though I want you to, just about more than anything, even more than Badger's splendid Carbonnade of Beef or his very splendid *medaillons de veau poches à la sauce au Porto.*"

"However do you know that French name with the poached veal?"

"My dear wife, Badger and I did the menus together during your illness."

She gave him a disbelieving look, but could only giggle.

He said, "By all the gods, to hear you laugh again. Do you know I want you to want me so much in return that you'll burst into tears, swear you'll poison me unless I take you right this moment?" When she started to speak, her eyes sparkling, he put his fingers over her mouth and sighed a martyr's sigh. "No, don't do it." He quickly rose from the bed again and put a good ten feet between them. "No, I'll just gaze upon you wearing those pearls, and sweat. Perhaps kiss your belly some more, but it hurts, Duchess."

"I hate to see a man sweat, Marcus. Hurting is quite another matter."

"Be quiet, Duchess. No, don't move, just lie there like a courtesan in a sultan's bordello, but I will migrate my mind to other things. I've a strong mind, I can do it. I've been thinking that the two chalices, that Bible, and the other Church pieces—including that relic which is some saint's finger bone, I suppose—should go to Rome. As for the rest of it, it stays here."

"Yes," she said. "I was thinking the same thing. I like what you gave to Maggie too."

"I wonder if she's lying quite without a stitch on in her room at this moment, wearing only that emerald necklace."

"No, she's sitting in front of her mirror brushing her glorious red hair, admiring the emeralds with her coloring. Your mother told me she was wearing her diamond tiara tonight to the dinner table. Ah, and the Twins are in alt over those bracelets you gave them."

"As for Spears and Badger, I told them they could both retire with the coins that were their share, but they were both quite put out with my suggestion. Spears looked down his nose at me, quite like your father would do to both Mark and Charlie when he'd caught them in a bit of mischief, and told me that he feared for my well-being were he not to be here to see to things.

"As for Badger, I fear for our dinner, given his black looks at my well-meant suggestion. He gave me this pursed look, his mouth all puckered like this, and said that such a worthless suggestion wouldn't go unpunished in Heaven. When I asked him what that meant, he said he would think about it."

"That's quite interesting to be sure; however, enough. Husband, I would like you to put on that ruby ring."

He shook as he looked quickly at her. "I've been amusing you," he said slowly, so hungry for her that he shook even more, "and all you've done is think lascivious thoughts about my tender self. Just look at you, all draped with those pearls around your breasts, and now you're lying on your side, and let me tell you, Duchess, that pose is more than wanton, thank the good Lord."

She took his hand and laid it over her breast and said very softly, "Marcus."

He gaped and swallowed with some difficulty and gaped some more. He stared at his hand, hard and large and brown against her smooth white flesh.

"Listen to me and cease trying to amuse me. I'm very well now. George said so just this afternoon."

"I wouldn't let him really examine you. He doesn't know, how could he? He's not a woman."

"Neither do you know and neither are you a woman. However, I'm a woman and I do know. You'll be gentle; even when you're not gentle, it's gentle enough for me, because all I can think about is what you're doing to me and how it makes me feel, and that's all that matters. Please, Marcus, put on that ring."

He muttered, gave her dark looks, and put on the ring. But she kept after him until he was quite as unclothed as she was, that large ruby sparkling in the late-afternoon sunlight pouring through the window. After that, he played with her pearls, each one of them, and the white flesh beneath each one, and when he came into her he was gentle, perhaps more than he'd ever been, and the sweetness of it filled her until it changed, becoming more, as it always did, until she couldn't bear it, and then she was in a frenzied place, filled with light and excitement that was unbearable yet she didn't want it to end. He was with her and she knew as she kissed his throat, his shoulder, her hands caressing his back, that he always would be with her.

When the Duchess entered the library the following Friday morning, looking for Marcus, she paused on the threshold, listening to him sing. His voice was a mellow base, not as beautiful as Spears's, but very nice nonetheless. He was singing the bawdy sailors' song.

He turned as he finished the last line, and grinned at her. "Isn't that a wonderful ditty?"

"It's certainly graphic. The tune is nice, don't you think?"

"Actually," he said looking down at his thumbnail, and worrying at it a bit, "I don't much like the tune at all. I was just thinking that I could have done much better. I have a talent, you know, for music, for tunes specifically, especially tunes for bawdy words and verses. I wish I knew the man who writes these songs. We could form a partnership. It's a pity. These wonderful words and rhymes, and they must be sung with these miserable tunes."

"Miserable! That's ridiculous, they're superb, well, not all of them, but most are quite acceptable, even occasionally exceptional. As for the "Sailor's Shore Song," I've heard that it's already sung everywhere, that it's popular, nearly beyond popular, and it won't be forgotten. It will live forever in the King's Navy. There, so much for your criticisms, Marcus. Miserable indeed."

"It's not bad, as I said, but I doubt it will be remembered beyond next month, beyond October at the very latest, surely not after my birthday. Why I've very nearly forgotten it already, particularly the tune."

She picked up a thick tome of *Tom Jones* that was laid atop a marquetry table, and hurled it at him. He caught it handily, remarking, "Goodness, I hadn't realized that *Tom*

Jones was so heavy. Such a light tale for so many pages. Just like those silly ditties, so very light they are, meaningless really, just brief stupid diversions. And without sharp and bright tunes to make them memorable. Such a pity I don't know the fellow who writes them. Poor thing, trying to survive without the valuable assistance of such a talent as mine."

She turned red, looked about for another thick book, didn't see one, and began running at him, hopping actually, because she was trying to pull off her left slipper.

She forgot the ribbons. When she looked down and tried to pull the bow free, she succeeded only in knotting the ribbon all the more. She cursed and he laughed. She shrieked at him even as she sat on the floor and began furiously pulling at the bloody knot, "You wretched sod! Those ditties are wonderful! How many do you know, anyway?"

He looked down at her there on the floor—utterly enraged, not at all the old Duchess, but his precious new Duchess, and she would surely kill him if she ever got that slipper unknotted—and he looked back to his thumbnail, saying in a drawling voice and enraging her all the more, "Oh, I suspect I know all of them, more's the pity, since they aren't really all that well done, just sort of well done, barely on the edge of being well done. Yes, I do know all of them."

"That's impossible, you sod. I know Spears is always singing them, but certainly you can't know more than just a few, not more than five at the very most."

The thumbnail received more concentrated study. He said, "I've been thinking I should go to Hookhams and see if they can't give me this Coots fellow's direction. Being a man, he's probably reasonable and would look at my offer of partnership as a gift from God. What do you think, Duchess? Ah, that knot is stubborn, isn't it? Do you want me to help you? No? I see, you're going to try the other one. It's about time. Anger is just fine, but the outlet for it is more important. Without the outlet, what is anger anyway?"

She'd switched to the right foot and the bow melted apart in her fingers. She jerked off the slipper, leapt to her feet, and ran right at him.

He was laughing when she began hitting his chest with the slipper, then he gathered her against him, pinning her arms at her sides. He nuzzled the side of her neck, whispering in her ear, "Do you think I should write to this fellow Coots? Inform him that I'll make him a success? Surely he's barely surviving now. What do you think, Duchess?"

"Damn you, what if Coots isn't a man at all? I don't suppose you ever considered that, did you? Not everything that's creative or original, or, or, clever and imaginative is done by men, you witless sod."

He rubbed his hands up and down her arms, but was careful not to let her free. "But of course it is, sweetheart. Face it, you're a woman, an above-average woman, a beautiful gracious woman whom I love, but still, just a woman and surely you must recognize that this Coots is a man with a man's talents, woeful though they be with regard to the tunes themselves. But only a man could produce songs that actually were worth something."

She growled, red-faced, utterly furious at him, and he began to laugh. He threw back his head and roared with laughter. Suddenly she became utterly still.

"You know."

"Know what?" He laughed harder.

"You know all about Coots."

"Of course I do, goose." He stopped laughing, hugged her so tightly against him that her ribs creaked. "Lord, I'm very, very proud of you."

"I could have hurt you throwing *Tom Jones* at you."

"Yes, you could have knocked my head off, but you didn't."

"I wish you'd stop laughing at me, Marcus."

"I did, just a moment ago. But you deserved it. You should have told me about R. L. Coots and the wonderful success you've gained. You should have told me when I first visited you at Pipwell Cottage and accused you of being kept by a man. Your pride, madam, makes me want to strangle you, that is, if I didn't have the same pride myself. Tell me, is there another song in the works?"

"Yes," she said, studying her own thumbnail, "but I seem to be having trouble with the tune. The words are clever, truly, but the tune is floundering."

He looked down at her, cupped her chin in his palm and kissed her, then just looked some more. He was thinking about those pearls and which was more luminous, the pearls or her breasts.

"All right, Marcus, either we go to the music room right now and you prove your mettle else I'll never let you forget it, never."

"Let's go," he said, then lifted her, set her on his desk and put her slipper back on her foot and deftly tied the ribbon. "Shall I knot the ribbon on that brutal slipper, or have you regained your control?"

"You'd best knot it."

It was very late, a late-summer rain pounding against the windowpanes. They were sitting in front of the fireplace even though the fire had quite died down to glowing embers, but they didn't care, for they were writing another ditty, this one about Napoleon and all his mistresses, a song the Duchess swore would never leave the bed-chamber. Marcus told her the rumor of the emperor's lack of majesty in his male part. She stared at him and said quite seriously, "How odd. I thought that all men were the same in that area. I mean, couldn't that song apply to all of you? There are differences, really?"

He turned red with outrage, yanked her against him, and kissed her until she was panting and laughing at the same time.

A knock came at the door, and Marcus cursed, then sighed. He called out, "Enter!"

It was Antonia and she was carrying a silver tray on her arms.

"Goodness," the Duchess said, leaping off Marcus's lap. "What do you have there?"

"A present from Badger. He said you were both to drink it down. He called it a por-ency drug, not to me, but to Spears, who was with him. I just overheard it and Badger looked very uncomfortable and he cursed."

"A potency drug?" Marcus said, trying to keep the smile off his face.

"That's right. When I asked him what that was, he said it was an aphrodisiac. What's that, I asked him, but he just wagged his finger at me and told me to make myself useful, so here I am. Spears looked as if he would cry he was so embarrassed. I think he was mad at Badger for telling me words I want to know but probably shouldn't. It was very curious. Fanny wanted to bring it so she could look at you and get all moon-eyed, Marcus, but I wouldn't let her."

"Thank you, Antonia." He said to the Duchess, "Just two more years."

The Duchess took the tray from Antonia and set it on a tabletop. She sniffed. "It smells like hot chocolate to me, with something in it I can't identify. Perhaps it's chopped snail toenails."

"Badger said you were to drink it and then do what you normally do. He said you'd know what he meant."

"The bugger. Yes, Antonia, we know. Thank you, muffin. Go to bed now."

When Antonia was gone, Marcus raised a cup and gave the Duchess the other. "To us, to snail's toenails, and Badger's attempt at heir-making."

"Hear, hear," she said and drank deep. "An heir. I surely like the sound of that."

They were asleep soon, snuggled together, her head tucked against his neck.

═══ 31 ═══

THE BRIGHT MORNING light shone in her eyes. Odd, but she didn't want to open her eyes, the light was too bright, it hurt, but finally, she did slit her eyes open.

"Hello, Duchess, it's about time you joined us. As you can see, your dear husband is already awake, unhappy with me and with his headache, and naturally he'd kill me if it weren't for the tight ropes around his hands and feet. Your bonds aren't quite as tight. I don't intend for you to suffer, not you, never you."

She stared in blank astonishment at Trevor. "I don't understand. Where are we? What are you doing here?"

"To begin with," Marcus said, his voice so calm it frightened her, "he somehow drugged that hot chocolate Antonia brought to us last night."

"Yes, certainly. She said Badger made it. I don't believe it. It's not possible, not Badger."

"Of course Badger made it and added the laudanum to it as well, just as we'd planned," Trevor said. "But believe what you will, whatever romantic, honorable swill enters your minds. But didn't you wonder at all when Badger came back here and told you that all the Colonial Wyndhams were accounted for in London? No, I can see you didn't. Pity, but too bad.

"Odd that you survived the bullets that day. Three bullets in your wretched bodies, but you still managed to live through it."

"You're a miserable shot," Marcus said.

Trevor very slowly turned to him, rose to tower over him,

364

raised the butt of his pistol and brought it down hard on his shoulder.

"Stop it, damn you!" She was struggling, yanking hard at the ropes around her wrists, ignoring the pain that ripped through her, yanking and pulling until Marcus said, "No, Duchess, I'm all right. Just hold still, love."

Trevor returned to his place, an overturned crate he was using as a chair. "What a brave hero he is, don't you agree, Duchess? Yes, my cousin Marcus needs to learn who is in charge now. Even now that he's in exquisite pain he won't accept that he's finally lost. No, Marcus isn't a man used to losing at anything. Ah, Duchess, don't look at me like that, with blood—my blood—in your eyes. Obey your husband, just hold still. I am sorry about you, my dear, but I have no choice about this, none at all.

"Ah, Marcus won't even moan from the pain and he does hurt, Duchess, he does indeed. Isn't that odd? He knows he's going to die, yet he holds to that myth, to that absurd men's code, whatever the hell it is, that dictates that he won't yield and he won't plead with me. Well, no matter.

"Duchess, if only you hadn't forced Marcus to marry you before that magical date of June sixteenth, I could have let you both live, or at least I would have considered it. All that lovely money, but then, Duchess, I learned you got fifty thousand pounds from your father and I wanted that too. I wanted all of it and the Wyndham legacy—which I never believed was real—and the title of earl of Chase, and now that's what I'll get. Everything. Now I'll have everything. I must remember to compliment your dear mother, Marcus, on solving the mystery. I'll do it whilst we're all in mourning for your double tragic deaths."

"But you're rich," she said, trying desperately to clear her head, which was aching abominably, trying to understand, trying to *talk* to him. "You said you were very rich."

"Would you expect me to admit to poverty, Duchess? I jested about it to allay any suspicions either of you might have had. I was so open with both of you. No, there's very little money left, though my family doesn't know of it for I've kept it to myself, for I am the head of the American Wyndham family and very soon now I'll be the head of the entire Wyndham family. My father—your uncle—was a wastrel, no other way to say it. He left us with food in the pantry, a little maid he'd gotten pregnant, and naught else. I was pleased he finally fell in a duel for making love to another man's wife. I was left with no choice. I was the head of the Wyndham family. No one else. Why do you think I married Helen? And I was but twenty-two years old. She was the richest girl in Baltimore and her father was a miserable old miller when all is said and done. No more, no less."

"But a very *rich* miserable old miller."

"Yes, my dear, beyond rich, at least that's what I believed at the time. I killed him then wooed Helen. She was so soft, so vulnerable in her grief, so tedious in her innocence, but I did enjoy her delicious little body until she grew large with child. Then it was easy, a fall from her mare from a spur I planted beneath the mare's saddle, left alone in the rain to catch a chill, and it happened as I planned it to. She went into labor and both she and the brat conveniently died, leaving me a broken man.

"But that money ran out. I was still the head of the Wyndham family. What to do? Then we heard from Mr. Wicks, bless his old man's kindly heart. He really believed the two of you would never reconcile your differences, whatever they were. The poor old bastard had forgotten about lust and youth. And you, Duchess, you lusted after Marcus since you were a child, didn't you? You wonder how I know that? Well, to give credit where credit is due, I must thank dear Aunt Gweneth and her lovely detailed correspondence with my mother all these years. She wrote of you, how she admired you—your serenity, your unpretentious modesty—how very well-bred you were despite your unfortunate antecedents, but how she suspected that you would set your hooks into Marcus since you couldn't have Mark or Charlie, for they were your half-brothers, and your dear earl father wouldn't allow that.

"Mr. Wicks didn't write all that much, but dear Aunt Gweneth did, every small piddling detail of her wearisome life, for she was a spinster, living off the charity of her brother and what else did she have to do? I learned about everything, about the earl's bitterness, his hatred of you, Marcus, because you didn't have the good taste to die with Mark and Charlie, and you, Duchess, the precious bastard whose mother he loved all his benighted adult life. Ah, how Aunt Gweneth despised your mother, Duchess, for she feared the woman's influence. She hated her sister-in-law, but she was a known evil, wasn't she? But your mother, what would the slut do once the countess was dead? We know, of course, he married your mother, the stupid fool, and we suppose he died a miserable man because she died first.

"Wrenching isn't it, all of it? Pitiful, really. But here we are and it's all very real now and nearly to the end. Did I tell you that I wanted to leave James in America for the boy has such a kind heart, as unsuspecting of evil as Helen was, but he wanted to come, insisted, so I made the best of it, insisted he was sullen and hadn't wanted to be here, and you believed it, even about the young lady he'd left behind in Baltimore. He had a fancy to meet you, Marcus, and you, Duchess. He doesn't know what life can be and how it can change men and make them what they don't really want to be.

"James won't learn, for I will protect him as I will Ursula. It will be only the best for both of them and they will die as innocent as they live in their innocence now."

Marcus thought, let him talk and talk and talk, even as he worked the knots that bound his wrists together. He'd believed Trevor would be a dandy, a fop, but he was none of those benign things. But he'd seen him as a man, a man to admire, a man to spar with, to share stories with, but he wasn't any of those things, he was evil and somehow twisted. Marcus realized then the truth of the rhymes and said blankly, "My God, you're the bloody monster in the clues. Always there, always waiting to do evil, to harm and to lie and to kill. That's what the monk meant in the Duchess's dream and that's what the poem meant. Where there's life there's evil and one must always be on guard against it. You're the evil here and you always were."

"Am I the monster? I don't really like the sound of that, Marcus, dear cousin. I suppose you're right, but still, it bothers me. I only do what I have to do. My mother is very expensive, you know. I told you, I want James and Ursula to have the very best and I couldn't provide it except this way. If Helen had been richer . . . ah, but she wasn't, the silly little slut. My mother adores French fashions. What was I to do? And Ursula will be beautiful very soon now, not more than two years now and she will be glorious, a woman men will want. She must have her chance, and I am the head of the Wyndham family. It is my responsibility to see that she has it."

"You're not the head of the Wyndham family, I am."

"Not for very much longer, cousin, not for more than a few more minutes."

"I don't suppose you would consider releasing us and returning to America," Marcus said.

Trevor laughed, threw back his head and laughed deeply, his strong throat working. "Your only release will be with your death, cousin."

Time, the Duchess knew, they had to have more time. The bonds about her wrists were loosening even more. He had been considerate, if such a thing could be said of him. He hadn't tied her all that tightly. He believed her a woman, thus not a threat to him. He hadn't bothered to tie her ankles. She had to keep him talking. She had to think, dammit. So much had happened, so much pain, and he'd been responsible for all of it.

She looked at him until he met her gaze. His eyes softened. It scared her to death, but she said calmly enough,

"So you have been planning this? For how long? And you said that Badger was your partner. How did you get together with him?"

Trevor leaned toward her. She jerked back, unable to help it. He just grinned at her. "I find I'm fatigued, Duchess, and quite tired of talking. I believe the two of you now understand why I'm doing this. I really don't want to kill you, Duchess, I'd much rather plow your belly until you became ugly to me, your belly all swelled out with child. Women with child should stay hidden. They're hideous. You should have seen Helen, all white and thin save for her huge belly. It was quite repellent. I wanted to call her a spider, but I couldn't, not until she was lying there, thrown from her mare, and then I told her what she was, what she truly was, and she screamed, not with terror from me but because the child was coming and it was ripping her apart."

Her bonds were free. He was seated on that overturned crate some six feet from her, a pistol dangling lazily in his right hand. What could she do?

"Well, Marcus, tell me, dear cousin. Who is the stronger? Who is the smarter? Who fooled you completely and utterly? Ah, yes, I am the head of the Wyndham family. I am fit to be the head of the Wyndham family, more fit than you. You and your asinine honor, your Englishman's code. It makes you blind, makes you gullible."

She leapt to her feet and jumped at him, clawing at his right hand, madly tearing and screaming at him.

Marcus jumped to his feet and threw himself at Trevor. But his hands were tied, his feet were hobbled, no more than a couple of inches between the ropes that bound his ankles. Trevor knocked him off easily enough, then whirled about and threw the Duchess to the straw-covered floor. He fell on top of her.

But he was looking at Marcus, who was standing, just barely, and he was ready to charge again. "Don't move, cousin, or I'll put a bullet right in her lovely mouth."

She felt the hard metal against her lips. He pressed harder until her mouth was open and she tasted the cold metal, felt it press against her teeth.

Marcus took several clumsy steps back.

"Sit down."

Marcus sat.

Trevor looked down into her white face. "I enjoyed dressing you last night. You have a very lovely body, a woman's body, but lithe and slender, curved so very nicely. Odd, but Marcus looks like me. But we're cousins, aren't we, so it makes sense. Large men, dark, well-made men, fashioned to impress other males and seduce women. Did I tell you that little Helen couldn't get enough of me? She loved to touch me, to kiss me all over. Of course, I taught her how to kiss a man. I let her have her way and pleased her in return, until she bored me, then that was all I let her do, kiss me and caress me.

"Shall I strip you before I have to kill you? No, you don't like that thought at all, do you, Duchess? I repel you. I didn't before but now I do. You love him, don't you? I always believed you did, even though he was too stupid to realize his good fortune. And now it's too late."

He got off her, rising slowly to his feet. "Well, you tried to take me down, Duchess. I like that. It proves you're of my blood, not cowards, either of you. But the time has come to finish this. I will make it quick, I promise you. I'm not cruel. All you have to do is drink a bit more, and you'll fall asleep just as you did last night. Only this time you won't wake up. I'm going to tie each of you to your horses. Unfortunately they will both go off the rather dramatic cliff just to the east of Trellisian Valley. I don't want to have to kill Stanley, he's a good mount, and as the earl of Chase, I would like to ride him now and again, but I must make it believable. I'll untie you once you're dead at the bottom of the cliff and drive back to London. I'll be there in the bosom of my family when we receive word of your tragic deaths."

"Why did you wake us up?" Marcus asked. "You could have given us enough and killed us without this charming scene you've played out. Ah, that's it, isn't it, Trevor? You wanted us to know it was you all along. You wanted to bray and brag and gloat."

Trevor rose, the gun raised, his face flushed, then it seemed he got control of himself again. Slowly, he sat down again on the crate. "Think what you will," he said, then shrugged. "It doesn't matter. The outcome will be the same. You'll be dead and I'll be the earl of Chase."

He looked from one to the other of them. "Life is so terribly uncertain, isn't it?"

Suddenly the Duchess began to laugh. It bubbled out of her, tears pooled in her eyes and she was nearly losing her breath she was laughing so hard.

He jumped to his feet, waving his pistol toward her. "Damn you, shut up!"

"Ah, but it's so very funny," she said and went into gales of laughter, full-bodied laughter that made Marcus so afraid he thought he'd choke on it. What the hell was she doing?

"What the hell is so funny? Shut up, I tell you!"

"You, Trevor." She hiccuped and laughed more. "You. You're so very funny. Actually, what you are is pathetic. You, the next earl of Chase? *You?* You're a bloody madman, that's what you are, insignificant, not really there as a man, just a shadow, yes, a madman, that's what you are. Yes, you're sad really, a loudmouthed preening cock, an ass braying like a man, a real man. You're nothing but a dismal excuse for a man, nothing more, just an excuse."

And she laughed and laughed until Trevor, his face blood-red now, fury roiling through him, roared to his feet, raised the pistol, and came over her. He had the pistol in his hand and he would strike her with it, hard and again and again, she saw it in his eyes, eyes she'd believed once so warm and filled with intelligence and humor. Now they just held death and his loss of control.

Just as he was coming down over her, she drew her legs back to her chest to give her leverage and power and she kicked him in the groin. She kicked him so hard that for an endlessly long moment, he just hung there over her, poised to strike her with that pistol butt, doing nothing at all now, not breathing, just staring down at her disbelieving, then he screamed and screamed, falling backward onto his back, clutching his groin, crying now, wailing really, the agony ripping him apart, and in those moments he was behind them, not even aware that they were there and that they were his enemies.

"Well done, Duchess." She saw Marcus roll over on top of Trevor, grab the pistol, and toss it to her, for his hands were tied behind his back and hers were tied in front. She caught it and held it in front of her.

"Get off him, Marcus. Let him suffer, then we'll see."

He rolled off Trevor and came up onto his feet. Slowly, he hobbled to her and sat down beside her. "Untie me if you can," he said.

She'd released his wrists when Trevor, finally enduring the worst of the nausea and the tearing pain, managed to sit up. He looked into the barrel of the pistol that Marcus now pointed at him.

He cursed very softly.

The Duchess wasn't laughing now, but her voice was calm, not the detached, dispassionate calm of the old Duchess, but a determined calm, a nearly ferocious calm. "My wrists are nearly free, Marcus. Don't bother with me, just keep that gun pointed at him. Just another moment. Yes, now I'm all right. Hold still and I'll untie your ankles."

When they were both free, Marcus stood slowly, the pistol never wavering from Trevor's face. He stomped his feet up and down to get the feeling back.

"Where are we?" he asked.

Trevor, still struggling with the grinding pain in his groin, was silent for a few more moments, then he shrugged. "I hadn't expected you to ask me that just yet."

"Why the hell not? There's nothing else to ask you. You've carried on about how brilliant you are, you the head of the Wyndham family, you the one who believes it his right to kill with impunity all in the cause of your damned duty, your responsibility to your mother and brother and sister. All right, tell me, cousin. Do they truly have no idea what you've done?"

"Perhaps. My mother hates both of you, naturally. Does she know? And Ursula, so sweet, at least she seems so, doesn't she? You've gotten to know James, an honorable boy, don't you think? He worships me. You'll never know for sure now, Marcus, will you?"

"You're quite mad, cousin. More important, you're sane in your madness and that is surely worse. Now you can tell me. Where are we?"

"I'll see you in hell before I tell you."

"You know something, cousin? It doesn't really matter, because you'll be in hell a long time before I will."

He raised the pistol, looked in that strong face that held too much resemblance to his own, and for that brief moment, he thought, *dear God, he's my cousin, he's of my flesh,* and he faltered. It was all Trevor needed. He kicked out at Marcus, sending grinding pain through his thigh, then lunged for the gun. Marcus wasn't quite fast enough. He felt Trevor's hands close around his wrist, squeezing it tightly, shaking his hand to free the gun, but he held tight.

Their struggle was a silent one, save for the grunts and heavy, ugly breathing. The Duchess was now on her feet, her hands free of the ropes, looking for a weapon, anything. She felt no fear for herself, just this nearly deadening fear for Marcus, and knew, knew somewhere deep down, that she had to tamp down on that fear. She managed it, flooding herself with savage frenzy and urgency.

They were on the hay-strewn floor now, still struggling for the gun, rolling over and over, panting more deeply now, sweating with exertion. She saw it then, a pitchfork, rusted with age, leaning crookedly against the far wall of the barn, looking none too sturdy, but no matter. She grabbed it—damn but it was heavy—and ran to stand over them.

But they were rolling over and over, first Marcus with the advantage, then Trevor, evenly matched. She saw that Marcus still held the gun, but Trevor was keeping well clear of it. She was terrified of striking Marcus. She circled them, waiting, waiting, wanting to scream each time it looked like Trevor would win.

Then, quite suddenly, the barn doors were flung open and brilliant sunlight streamed in.

Trevor, on top of Marcus at that instant, was blinded, and jerked back. It was all Marcus needed. He kicked him off and rolled away, coming up on his knees, raising the gun.

But the Duchess was faster. She raised the pitchfork over her head and brought it down with all her strength, striking Trevor squarely on the back of his head with the wooden handle, sending him sprawling on his face. He twitched once, then lay utterly still. She didn't know whether or not she'd killed him and she didn't care.

"Marcus!" She was beside him in an instant, not really aware that North, Badger, and Spears were standing over them.

=32=

BADGER PATTED HER back and clucked like a mother hen, feeling at once foolish at his display of emotion and so scared in his relief he wanted to yell with it.

"Chocolate!" he said against her hair, furious with himself. "Dear God, somehow that mangy bastard Trevor got laudanum into the chocolate I sent to you and his lordship. And like a fool I let Antonia carry it to you, never thinking—"

"But how did he manage it?" Marcus asked as Spears was examining his bloody knuckles and the bruises on his face. He looked over at his unconscious cousin, North beside him, feeling for his heart, as he spoke.

"I spoke to Antonia, just by chance really. Jesus, you can't imagine how that fear was curdling my toes when I didn't find either of you in bed where you should have been, all tight and cozy and tangled up together, like two ears of corn in a husk. The bed was empty and I don't mind telling you, and Mr. Spears will agree, I was nearly frothing at the mouth with fear. It turns out that Antonia paused only a moment to speak to Fanny and the Twins went into the bedchamber for a moment."

He didn't tell them that Antonia had been plenty mad because Fanny, the wretched flirt who wanted Marcus for herself, had demanded that she, not Antonia, take the chocolate to the Duchess and Marcus. They'd argued until finally they'd both fetched a sovereign from Fanny's bedchamber, then they'd tossed it to see who would carry the chocolate to the Duchess and the earl.

"The Twins evidently were arguing about something. And while they were carrying on, even going to one of their bedchambers, Trevor quite easily poured laudanum into the chocolate they'd conveniently left in the corridor."

"Damnation," Marcus said. "What if they hadn't argued? What if Antonia alone had been carrying that chocolate unbothered by her twin? I think that Trevor would have hurt her, both of them if necessary, perhaps even killed them as swiftly and remorselessly as he would a fly. What are two twins, fifteen-year-old cousins to him, after all? How the bloody devil did he get into the house?"

It wasn't all that hard, so no one said anything. It was all so frightening, it still made Badger's tongue thick and dry, sticking to the roof of his mouth.

It had been close, too close, so close that even now his heart was pounding faster than when that sod of a nag *Midnight Fleet* had beaten all odds and won at Ascot just last week.

He stroked his hand over the Duchess's back, crooning like a damned turkey all the while. She got a grip on herself and drew back to look up at him. "He wanted us to believe that you were in this with him."

"I beg your pardon, Duchess?"

She grinned at the outrage in Spears's voice. "Marcus and I knew Badger couldn't be involved with him, Spears. Never for a moment did we doubt you, Badger, never. But it pleased Trevor to taunt us with it."

"See that you never doubt me in the future either."

"I agree. A most unworthy thought of a duchess and an earl," Spears said. "Most unbefitting either of you. Mr. Badger is a man beyond men."

"Amen," said Marcus. He looked over again at North, who'd returned just two days before after visiting a military friend in Castleford, leaving only after he'd been certain that Marcus and the Duchess would be all right after they'd been shot. "Will he live, North?"

"Yes, I think so. The Duchess gave him a solid hit but

his pulse is strong as is his heartbeat. If you like, Marcus, I'll take him to Darlington and see that he's put safely in the gaol. I'll even hire guards to keep an eye on him around the clock."

"I'll go with you. I don't want to let him out of my sight again until I know he's safely locked behind some very sturdy bars. Yes, the guards are an excellent idea."

"What happened, my lord?" Spears asked. "I mean, why is Mr. Trevor still alive?"

"I had the gun and I was ready to kill him. Then I realized who he was—my cousin, a Wyndham, my flesh—and I couldn't do it. It was the chance he needed. He jumped on me."

"That's right, Marcus," North said. "Don't flail at yourself. I'm glad you won't have his blood on your hands—either of your hands, for that matter. Have him deported to Botany Bay, a wonderful place I understand, savage as hell itself. Let him finish out his life there. I daresay he'll make his way amongst all the other criminals. At least you'll be safe from him then."

"Yes," Marcus said slowly, "Botany Bay. I do believe I could arrange that without too much difficulty. There's no reason to have an ugly scandal if we can avoid it. Even though Aunt Wilhelmina deserves any and everything, Ursula and James don't. I don't want them hurt more than they have to be."

"I agree," Badger said. He saw that the Duchess was nodding also, then turned to Lord Chilton. At North's nod, he added, "There, that's all of us, my lord. Ah, I should add that Maggie was beside herself, let me tell you, screamed at Mr. Spears and me, even at poor Lord Chilton, who surely wasn't to blame, cursing us that we wouldn't bring her with us."

"The picture painted with your words, Badger, quite boggles the mind," Marcus said.

The Duchess managed to find a remnant of a smile, then said, "We won't have to worry about him ever again. Thank

God, Marcus, you're safe. You're what's most important to any of us, and even if that's not quite true, then you're what's most important to me, at the very least. Oh dear, I was so scared he would kill you, so very scared. Don't you ever do something like that again."

She pulled herself out of Badger's comforting hold and walked straight to her husband. He pulled her close and just held her, silent for several moments. He raised his head finally, saying, "How did you find us?"

Badger said, "We went to the stables after I found Mr. Spears and told him you and his lordship were gone and what I suspected. Not that it was necessarily Mr. Trevor, you understand, just that there'd been *foul play,* as Mr. Kemble of Drury Lane calls it, and sure enough, both Stanley and Birdie were gone. Lambkin was fit to eat the horseshoe nails, my lord, utterly stammering he was with confusion and mental turmoil. Ah, yes, I tracked you here," he added simply, as if it were the most common ability on earth.

Marcus looked from one of them to the other. "You tracked us here, Badger? This is beyond what you are supposed to be able to do. You are the Duchess's valet. You are our cook. You know a lot about medicines. Now I hear that you tracked Stanley and Birdie here?"

"Well, my lord, it wasn't all that difficult, truth be told. You see, Stanley has a strange shoe, put on by the Duchess's father, some three years ago, a shoe in the shape of a star. Why, you might ask? I haven't the foggiest notion. It wasn't difficult, as I said, to follow you and find you here in old MacGuildy's barn. Poor old man, dead now and no one cares that this barn is falling apart and that's why Trevor Wyndham brought you here. He rode Clancy around the estate many, many hours as I recall."

North shook his head. "All I had to do was follow orders, Marcus. These two had everything well in hand. I'm sorry I left, Marcus. Damnation, I knew that the danger wasn't over by a long shot."

"You, North, are just angry because you missed finding the treasure with us," Marcus said, and punched his friend in the arm.

"Alas, that's part of it, I fear."

Spears said, "However, my lord, having you at our side gave us additional confidence. In your anger, you wore a dark, quite menacing look that would challenge the devil himself."

There suddenly came a loud shriek from the barn door.

"Ho! I knew we'd find you! Damn you, Mr. Spears, and damn you even more, Mr. Badger, I knew we'd find you! Ah, and Lord Chilton, well damn you as well, you sneaking lordship! Oh, hell and the devil, all the fun's over! It isn't fair, I've missed all of it."

The Duchess looked at Maggie, dragging a red-faced Sampson behind her, then looked up at her husband's astonished face. "How," she asked, giggling, her breath warm against his throat, "how could you ever imagine that Maggie would willingly miss any of the fun?"

"Ho! What's this? Good God, it's Mr. Trevor, and he's sprawled in a very ungentlemanly fashion on the ground. Whatever has happened?"

Epilogue

IT WAS LATE that night, a night of warmth and closeness and lingering fear and the weight of staggering loss, that Marcus, the Duchess, and all their friends, who just happened to be their servants, were seated in the dining room, the earl having insisted that all of them dine together, at least this evening, despite Spears's vehement and quite vocal disapproval.

Marcus's mother, bless her heart, had hauled Aunt Gweneth and the Twins off to her own sitting room and told them that it was their own private banquet, that the earl was a man with odd notions that must be respected since he was the head of the Wyndham family, and thus they would conduct their own private party and leave the earl and the Duchess to theirs. She frowned at Fanny, who had the temerity to point out that Lord Chilton wasn't a servant and he was allowed at their party.

When Badger's smiling kitchen minions brought out the bottle of chilled champagne, Sampson, the Wyndham butler for fifteen years, a man of astute judgment, reserved demeanor and sober of mien, rose, cleared his throat and announced, "My lords, my lady, Mr. Badger and Mr. Spears, I should very much like to make an announcement. Miss Maggie will be remaining here with the Duchess as her personal maid. I will also be remaining at Chase Park as butler."

He paused and Marcus frowned. "I should hope so, unless, naturally, you feel that there's been too much impropriety, too much disorder and untidiness in a nobleman's house."

Sampson cleared his throat again. "That isn't quite what I meant, my lord. Actually, what I meant to say and what I shall say now is that Miss Maggie has agreed to become Mrs. Glenroyale Sampson. That, my lord, er, is my given name."

"Oh my," the Duchess said. She rose from her chair and walked to Maggie, leaned down and hugged her. "Congratulations, my dear. It's wonderful. Sampson is a very fine man. And that emerald necklace looks marvelous on you."

Maggie, laughing, looking like a coquette while she batted her long eyelashes at the earl, said to the Duchess, "Well, he's a man of great stability, you know, not given to haring off to mills to see those poor men pound each other to death with their fists, or drinking too much ale at that horried inn in Bramberly, or gambling away all his coin at the nest of vipers in Eglington. Yes, I've decided it's better to permanently settle down with a stable man, one who also thinks with his head and not just with his— well, never mind that. In any case, I've decided not to return to the stage in London."

"He is stable," Badger said. "He does think with his head. He will be faithful. He will take good care of Maggie. He will be tolerant of her occasional flirtatious lapses. Mr. Spears assures me that Mr. Sampson is just what all of us will admire."

"I, for one," North said, "certainly admire his *sang froid*. I was witness to his dealings with an impertinent tradesman just yesterday, Marcus. The man was apologizing, ready to kiss Sampson's highly polished boots before he left."

"Good God," Marcus said. "Duchess, what do you think of this?"

"I think," she said, grinning around the earl's huge table, "that Sampson is quite the luckiest man in the world."

"That is most kind of you to say so, Duchess," Sampson said, clearing his throat yet one more time, "but I beg you to consider that Maggie here is also a very lucky lady. She saved Mr. Badger's life and look what wonderful things have transpired for her in reward for her outstanding good deed. She will have me as her husband and Mr. Spears and Mr. Badger as cohorts. Everyone needs cohorts in life, Duchess, everyone."

"A husband isn't a bad thing to have either," the Duchess said.

"Hear, hear," said Maggie, winking at the earl, "and his lordship here is shaping up quite nicely, don't you think so, Mr. Spears?"

"Indeed, Maggie, indeed."

The earl flung up his hands and yelled for another bottle of champagne. He turned to Lord Chilton, who was chewing on Badger's fruit meringue on a sponge biscuit. "Well, North, does all this marital bliss warm your sinner's heart? Make you want to consider some leg shackles yourself?"

North took his time swallowing. He looked around the table. He smiled at the Duchess. "Actually, Marcus, all this overflowing of mating euphoria quite makes me want to hare off to that mill Maggie spoke about. Tomorrow, I think. I want to put a good five miles between me and the rest of you by noon. I've done my visiting now and gotten my fill of excitement, jollity, and familial closeness. Now I want to go home to Cornwall and brood in solitude, hug my gloom close to my breast and no one else's. In short, I will remain as I am, alone and quite happy with my own black cloud and seclusion. Yes, I'll walk the moors with my dogs and be quite as somber in my thoughts as any good man should be."

"We will see, North, we will see," Marcus said, and raised his champagne for another toast. "To his lordship's seclusion," he said. "May it end in the not-too-distant future."

"To his lordship's imminent demise as a black-hearted, quite handsome bachelor," Maggie said. "He's not a man to be wasted on dogs or moors."

"Hear, hear," the Duchess said.

"Your mother was very concerned, my lord. Begging your pardon, Duchess, but I must move on now to other matters. Thus, I read everything I could find on this Botany Bay, and found that we were right. It's a thoroughly nasty place, primitive as that area around the Ganges River. No one manages to escape this Botany Bay. I told this to your mother, my lord. She then stopped fretting about Mr. Trevor. I told her it was at the end of the earth and filled with venomous serpents. She was quite relieved. I don't believe she'll speak of it again, my lord."

"Well," Maggie said, tapping her fork against her champagne glass, "I wouldn't be content to send him there, all whole-hided, no indeed. Poor Duchess—she just smacks him on his head. Men don't get hurt when smacked on their heads. No, she should have taken that pitchfork and done him in then and there. I would have known what to do."

"Botany Bay isn't an easy place," Badger said. "I agree with Mr. Spears. Master Trevor won't be taking any trips away from there."

"Still, you were all too kind, too easy on that devil. What matter if he was kin? He lost all his rights when he was so very wicked. Trying to kill the Duchess, trying to do away with both of you and he would have, that one. He wouldn't have stopped and felt all kinds of guilt, no, he would have done away with both of you."

"That is quite enough, my dear," Sampson said kindly but with a certain sort of firmness that made the Duchess stare at him. "Surely the topic has been abused sufficiently. Mr. Trevor won't escape that place. Everyone is safe. You have more than enough to think about now without the inclusion of that man who will shortly be gone from England."

The Duchess grinned at the look of utter astonishment on Maggie's face. "Is that you, Mr. Sampson? You said that to *me?*"

"Yes, indeed, dearest."

"Well, well, the man is capable of surprising me. *Me!* I quite like that, Mr. Sampson, perhaps. Once in a while. Mayhap twice a week."

"Hear, hear," the Duchess called out, looking toward her husband as she spoke. She was fingering the beautiful pearls that were looped about her neck, and she was smiling, a very soft smile.

"Twice a week?" Marcus said. "No, surely more than twice a week."

"His lordship isn't adhering to a gentleman's code if you asked me," Maggie said. "Not like Mr. Samp—, er, my dearest Glenroyale here."

"Surprises are quite nice, aren't they?" the Duchess said, still looking at her husband, still fingering those pearls.

Photo © Charles William Bush

Catherine Coulter is the #1 *New York Times* bestselling author of more than eighty novels, including the FBI Thriller series and A Brit in the FBI international thriller series, cowritten with J. T. Ellison. She lives in Sausalito, California, with her Übermensch husband and their two noble cats, Peyton and Eli.

Ready to find
your next great read?

Let us help.

Visit prh.com/nextread

Penguin
Random
House